THE DERRING-DO CLUB

Volume Four

Also by David Wake

NOVELS
I, Phone
The Derring-Do Club and the Empire of the Dead
Hashtag
The Derring-Do Club and the Year of the Chrononauts
The Derring-Do Club and the Invasion of the Grey
Crossing the Bridge
Atcode

NOVELLAS
The Other Christmas Carol

ONE-ACT PLAYS
Hen and Fox
Down the Hole
Flowers
Stockholm
Groom

NON-FICTION
Punk Publishing (*with Andy Conway*)

THE DERRING-DO CLUB

in

Death on the Suez

DAVID WAKE

WATLEDGE BOOKS

First published in Great Britain by
Watledge Books
Copyright © 2019 David Wake

This paperback edition 2019
1

ISBN-13: 978-1-78996-016-7

Cover art by Smuzz
www.smuzz.org.uk

For
Ytterbium

This adventure of the Deering-Dolittle sisters takes place after the sky battle of 'The Invasion of the Grey'.

CHAPTER I

Miss Deering-Dolittle

It was enough to make one want to commit murder.

Earnestine Deering-Dolittle plonked her medium kit bag on the bed. She'd packed her penknife, lock picks, compass, flashlight, opera glasses, goggles, matches, handkerchief, whistle, pencil and notebook, just one pack of Kendal mint cake, Tabasco sauce and a clothes peg. These items had come from her small adventure kit...

No, not '*adventure*', obviously. Not that.

Before she had gone 'up the river', Mother had strictly forbidden adventures. *Keep them safe,* mother had said, meaning her two sisters; *no exploring, no trouble, no adventures.*

But this was more... *sightseeing.*

Sightseeing was good. Yes, sightseeing was perfectly acceptable. Sightseeing broadened the mind. And one needed a Sense of Sightseeing. It added a certain zest to life.

A sudden gust of wind attracted her attention; the curtains moved as if touched by an invisible hand. Outside, the light changed, the setting sun losing its grip upon the day. Soon the blistering heat would subside. The breeze had shifted from the Egyptian interior to conjure cooler air from the Mediterranean. From her hotel window, the city of Tanis lay before her like an unfolded map. The ancient ruins lay just there, a mere two miles away and easily reachable with a brisk walk.

Why not?

She was twenty-one, after all, cursed with a sightseeing-erous nature and destined to be an old maid. No man would be interested in her. She was a spinster older than a married sister and she had a disfigurement down her left cheek that looked like a duelling scar. So sightseeing was all she could look forward to.

Just a few more items needed.

She checked her revolver: she knew she shouldn't have one, but it had come in useful when facing the undead, not that she expected reanimated corpses in Egypt. However, one had to be ready for anything when going on a little sightseeing.

She popped the gun into the outside pocket of her Medium Sightseeing Kit and considered how to stow the ice axe. It was still wrapped in brown paper and string from the shop.

Or should she take her umbrella?

It was more likely to rain in Egypt than it was to snow, but it was protection from the sun that was needed and she had just the thing.

Earnestine picked up her pith helmet, checking inside where she'd written *'E. J. Deering-Dolittle'*. It had only ever been worn in the shop and when she'd shown it off to her younger sisters, Georgina and Charlotte, as if it were a new bonnet. She put it on now and tucked those errant loose strands of her red hair under the brim. It did make her look like a brave sightseer.

A sharp rap came upon the door.

Quickly, Earnestine stood between the entrance and the bed with all its incriminating evidence.

"Who is it?"

"Ness, get a move on, the carriage will be here."

"Gina, I... er..."

But her sister came straight in. "What are you doing?"

"Nothing," Earnestine said, sidling sideways as Georgina walked to the window.

"You're planning an expedition."

"One is not."

Georgina turned and raised an eyebrow.

"What?" said Earnestine.

The smile on her sister's beautiful, but smug, face made Earnestine's jaw clench. Georgina pointed to the elegant bonnet and black veil that sat perfectly upon her neatly styled, dark hair.

Earnestine snatched her pith helmet off her own head. "One... er..."

"Is coming to the Consulate dinner and that's that."

"But Gina," Earnestine said, patiently through gritted teeth. "The ancient city of Tanis is just there. And the Map Room–"

"Don't you need the staff and the headpiece?"

"Yes, yes, but..." – oh, it was like trying to keep a stiff upper lip while chopping onions – "you can use string pulled across to show the rays of the sun, and then it's just the Chamber of the Serpents and–"

"Which sounds awful."

"It's just a name, there won't be real serpents... and then the Well of Souls containing the Ark of the Covenant. The actual Ark of the Covenant."

"Well, it'll have to wait."

"But this is my last chance. We're going on the ship in the morning!"

"There'll be plenty of things to see on the cruise."

"Cruise! It's not the Nile, Gina, it's the Suez."

"Which will have sights to see."

"It's a canal. There won't be any advent... sightseeing."

"Well, never mind," Georgina said. "Now, put that down and come along. We don't want to keep the men waiting."

Earnestine held on to her pristine and unused, as fresh as when she'd taken it out of its box, pith helmet. If she let go now, the chance would slip through her fingers.

But Georgina came over, gently took the hat off Earnestine and discarded it with a flick of her wrist. It landed on the still-wrapped ice axe.

"You might meet an eligible man," Georgina said. "That would be an adventure."

"I beg your pardon?"

"At the Consulate dinner, there will be eligible men."

"So?"

"You could catch one."

"And, pray, how does one go about catching one?"

"With subtle hints."

"Georgina," Earnestine replied, "I sometimes wonder if you've actually met any men."

"I was married," Georgina asserted.

And Earnestine had to bite her tongue to avoid pointing out that her sister hadn't been married that long. She'd have to go through with this farce, she knew, because she could not hurt her sister's feelings. But it vexed.

"How does one do these subtle hints?" Earnestine asked. "Men don't just drop into one's lap, do they?"

There was a knock on the door.

"Who is it?" Georgina shouted.

"Caruthers," came the reply. "The carriage awaits."

And so, they were whisked away to the Consulate... but only after Earnestine had to wait and wait for Georgina to check on the nurse, who was looking after her daughter, Philippa, and then mount a search party to find Charlotte yet again.

All this time, Earnestine waited with singular patience, and checked her watch for the umpteenth time. All these wasted minutes! As the second hand ticked around the dial, she calculated that she could have been half-way to the ancient ruins, three-quarters maybe, seven-eighths even, possibly actually in the Map Room...

"You're looking quite handsome," Caruthers said.

...and perhaps already digging towards–

"Miss Deering-Dolittle?"

"Yes?"

Captain Caruthers stood there, dependable as always, waiting with her patiently. He smoothed his chevron moustache and then straightened his scarlet, dress uniform jacket.

"Lovely night," Earnestine said. "The Colonel not joining us?"

"War wound playing up."

"Shame."

"It's been a long journey and we're only halfway to India."

"Indeed."

It had been a long journey.

They'd been past Glastonbury without looking for the Holy Grail, they'd changed trains in Paris without checking for the resting place of Mary Magdalene, they'd sailed straight past the ruins of Troy without even stopping, and now they were going to a five-course meal in some stuffy Consulate, without sneaking a mere two miles to the hiding place of the most extraordinary archaeological find of the new century.

Vexed did not begin to cover it.

And where were Georgina and Charlotte?

Earnestine could be reading the tablets with the Ten Commandments by now.

Ah! Finally! There they were.

Hotel staff came out to move the beggars and street traders back, so they could board their four-wheeler.

No-one spoke on the carriage journey. It wasn't far to the Consulate; about the same distance as the ancient city, but in the wrong direction.

And the first person Earnestine saw, when stepping down from the footplate, was the President of the Royal Expeditionary Society, her arch-nemesis: Sir Archibald Reevers.

That fat, beetroot-faced man, along with his lanky secretary, Mister Rake just had to be in Tanis to steal what she could have excavated and rightfully claimed for herself. It was bad enough that they kept turning down her applications, but now they were following her to her archaeological sites to prevent her explorations.

No, she wasn't going to discover anything and write it down for posterity. It was as if she didn't exist.

So, yes, it was all more than enough to make one want to commit murder.

Mrs Merryweather

Oh good, Georgina thought, there was Sir Archibald. He came from a good background with a good standing and a good fortune, with a rotund shape that spoke of a healthy appetite and a merry complexion that suggested a jovial countenance, and he was the President of that exploring club. She knew that Earnestine had a passing interest in archaeology, so Sir Archibald would make a jolly suitable match.

And they'd met before.

Captain Caruthers led them from the carriage, through the ornate gates and into the formal gardens that surrounded the British Consulate. Shade was provided by the impressively tall palm trees that dotted the gardens. They were a genus Georgina would have to look up when she got back to the hotel. She hoped Pippa was all right without her. Much as she enjoyed this respite, she did worry.

It was a short walk to the building itself, an imposing white edifice constructed in the classical style that fitted well with the Roman period of Egypt's history, complete with Corinthian columns and a marble portico.

A tall, thin man dressed in a sombre frock coat stepped forward to greet them.

"Captain Caruthers," he said.

The Captain did not take the offered hand. "Rake."

"And?"

Captain Caruthers walked on to talk to Sir Archibald.

Mister Rake seemed to take the slight in his stride.

"Miss," he said, formally, "allow me to introduce myself. I am Rake, personal secretary to Sir Archibald."

"It's Mrs Merryweather," Georgina replied.

"Delighted."

He took her hand.

"Mister Rake," she said.

His hand was cold.

Georgina turned with her other hand extended. "May I introduce..." – where was Earnestine? – "...my other sister, Miss Charlotte."

"Delighted."

Charlotte leaned to look around Mister Rake, quite rudely.

"Lottie!"

Charlotte snapped to attention. "Mister..."

"Rake," he said.

Charlotte smiled. "As in thin as a–"

"I have heard that before."

There was an awkward second or two.

"Shall we?" Georgina said gesturing to the inviting warmth emanating from the Consulate. The Union Flag fluttered in the breeze, cooler now in contrast to the day's dry heat.

Mister Rake accompanied them up the steps and inside.

"Ooh, look," said Charlotte, and she skipped away.

"Lottie..." but she'd disappeared into the throng. Georgina so hoped she wouldn't embarrass them.

"She's young," Georgina explained.

But of course, Mister Rake was dressed in a sombre frock coat and didn't sport any medals. Charlotte was drawn to the shiny medallions, all the crosses and stars, and, unfortunately, to the tales of blood and thunder that went with them.

"Mister Rake, are you very important?"

"It's not good form to boast," Mister Rake replied, "but I deal with Sir Archibald's business for the Royal

Expeditionary Society. I arrange events like this Consulate dinner, I plan expeditions and... well, expeditions. Back in London, I run the Society on a day-to-day basis, all the tours and lectures, and I keep foolish funding applications, like your sister's, away from Sir Archibald."

"Earnestine can be jolly determined."

"Yes, but, I mean, a woman running an expedition."

"I quite understand. Do you have a good salary?"

"Passable."

"What's your background? Eton? Harrow?"

"Eton, obviously."

"Good, good, good," Georgina replied, mostly to herself.

"Farouk! Farouk!" exclaimed Mister Rake, suddenly.

An Egyptian ran forward, dressed in a long blue and white robe with a grey, European waistcoat that would not button up around his girth. He held a red fez in his hands.

"Mister Rake."

"Would you take Mrs Merryweather and Miss Charlotte's shawls."

"Of course, of course," he said, plonking his fez upon his head and hesitating to take Georgina's shawl.

"Farouk is joining us on the SS *Karnak*," Mister Rake said.

Georgina nodded and handed over her shawl, and then realised that Charlotte, who was no longer with them, had 'forgotten' hers anyway – again.

"This way, this way," Farouk said.

"He's our guide," Mister Rake explained.

Farouk led the way to a reception room full of invited guests. It was bright and wonderful, full of scarlet uniforms, dazzling gowns and foreigners in exotic fancy dress.

"You're booked on the SS *Karnak* too?" Mister Rake said.

"We are."

"Then I shall see you aboard, no doubt."

"No doubt."

"I just need to... if you'll excuse me."

"Of course."

Mister Rake bowed and left her standing alone.

Georgina seized her chance and opened her handbag. She took out her notebook and her S. Mordan & Co mechanical pencil. In her neat, cursive script, she wrote: 'Sir Archibald' and 'Mister Rake', giving each a line to themselves. The two men were talking, Sir Archibald appearing jolly short and portly next to his tall and thin secretary.

The pencil needed a twist to bring forth more lead.

Lead?

Perhaps she needed three choices for Earnestine – a gold casket, a silver casket and a lead casket, as it were.

Glancing around the room, she saw the British Ambassador, various dignitaries, a couple of captains and a lot of foreign men. In the corner, she spied Earnestine, talking to an Eastern gentleman, bald, but handsome, and dressed in a European smoking jacket, who wouldn't do at all.

Another tall, thin man dressed in the customary black frock coat, a civilian uniform more uniform than the military, stepped forward. He seemed attractive and well-to-do, if rather forward, with a sharp pencil moustache. Her own pencil hovered in readiness.

"I am Monsieur Jacques," he said. "Mademoiselle?"

And French. That would never do either.

"Mademoiselle?" he repeated. Now she looked, she saw his louche manner and ostentatious clothes.

"It's Madame."

"Would you care for champagne? Kir? Cognac?" he said, indicating the servants standing to one side with trays of aperitifs.

"A small sherry perhaps."

The man, Monsieur Jacques, went over to fetch one.

Georgina smiled. It was so useful to have a man to take care of matters. She was quite right to be researching suitable matches for Earnestine. Although, it was a shame that there wasn't a male Deering-Dolittle available in the family, someone to take the eldest sister to one side and tell her not to be so silly. He could introduce a fine gentleman with prospects and explain that Earnestine's life was now blissfully sorted: it would be Earnestine's duty to make this man happy.

"I saw you talking to Sir Archibald's secretary," Monsieur Jacques said. "Do you happen to know what Sir Archibald is doing?"

"An expedition, I imagine."

"I imagine not. He's booked on the *Karnak* and there is nothing of archaeological interest along the Suez, so he must be up to something else."

"Must be," Georgina said. "How do you know he's booked on the SS *Karnak*?"

"Me also."

Georgina took a moment to sip her sherry.

"I examined the passenger list," Monsieur Jacques continued. "Sir Archibald and his secretary, a Colonel Fitzwilliam and his Captain, an American heiress, a Doctor and even a Pandit."

"Pandit?"

"An Indian priest."

"I see."

"Quite the menagerie," Jacques said. "There's even le Club Derring-Do."

"That would be my sisters and me."

"You are le Derring-Do?"

"Deering-Dolittle was my maiden name."

"Your sister," Monsieur Jacques looked across the room, "très admirable."

Georgina looked across at Earnestine, just as she laughed and put her hand over her mouth in a coy fashion. She was admirable, spirited, with the quick temper of the redhead, but sensible, tall and strong for a young lady. Perhaps someone like Monsieur Jacques might be acceptable.

"She has the hair blonde," Monsieur Jacques said.

"Oh, you mean Charlotte."

"Charlotte... si jolie. Is she une Mademoiselle?"

"Miss Charlotte, yes."

"Bon."

Georgina finished her sherry. "I must find my sister... my other sister."

"I take my leave then," Monsieur Jacques said. He bent to kiss her hand.

Once she had her limb back and he'd mingled away, Georgina turned to find somewhere to put her empty glass and was shocked to find herself face-to-face with the ugliest countenance she'd ever seen. The man positively leered at her, his features crisscrossed with vivid scars and his teeth jagged and foul. His breath was... Georgina had to turn away.

The man chuckled.

"Mister, I... er..."

He licked his lips and stared up and down her body without any shame.

Mister Rake came to her rescue. "Al Rachid, there you are, man."

"Al Rachid is here." The foreigner gestured with his hands, charmlessly, a parody of the floating, waving salutation of these parts.

"Outside, I said," Mister Rake insisted.

"Now inside."

"Well?"

"He does not have it."

"Does not have it on him or does not have it here?"

"I swear," this al Rachid said, bowing, but not taking his eyes off Georgina, "he does not have the book on his person."

"In that case, perhaps he didn't bring it."

"They swore he would have it on him."

"It must be in his hotel then," Mister Rake said. "That will be all."

Al Rachid grinned.

"You'll be paid. Just make sure everything's ready."

"I serve." The Egyptian backed away.

"I must find my sister," Georgina said.

"Mrs Merryweather. I take my leave again."

"Mister Rake."

Georgina moved away through the throng towards Earnestine. She was still talking to some Egyptian. As she went she nodded to various people: Captain Caruthers was with some army chums, Sir Archibald was deep in conversation with a woman festooned with jewellery. Finally, she intercepted Charlotte before Monsieur Jacques pestered her.

"Can I have a lemonade?" Charlotte asked.

"No, you'll ruin your appetite."

"Lemonade is a drink!"

Finally, she reached Earnestine, but now she had Charlotte in tow, so it was not the best time to bring up such an important conversation.

"Lemonade, of course," Georgina said.

"Thanks," Charlotte replied, and she weaved away instantly.

"You spoil her," Earnestine said. "She needs taking in hand."

So do you, Georgina thought, but you need your hand taken.

"Why are you smiling?"

"Oh, nothing. I'm enjoying the fine company."

Perhaps, Georgina considered, she should pick an outsider, someone that Earnestine could reject and so be persuaded gently in a suitable direction. There were a few captains, for example, chatting to their family friend, Captain Caruthers. Captain Conway... and another she didn't know. She resolved to ask Captain Caruthers who the other one was and then toss a coin between Captain Conway and Captain whoever. Or ask Captain Caruthers who might be the most suitable match.

Yes, gold because Sir Archibald had money and status; silver... on account of the slight grey that distinguished Mister Rake's temples and lead for an army officer, because they used lead in their ammunition.

She felt jolly pleased with herself.

"Gina," said Earnestine, "what's the matter with you?"

"Oh, er... Ness. I have, sort of, a list of three."

"Three?"

"Yes, a kind of..." – Georgina laughed, but it sounded so forced even to herself – "gold casket, silver casket and lead casket."

"Iron."

"Sorry."

"It's an iron casket."

"It's lead," Georgina insisted, feeling that the real point of the conversation was slipping away. "In *The Merchant of Venice*, it's lead. It's about a choice of suitor."

"Lead, iron – what's the difference?"

"There's an incredible difference."

"Between iron and lead?"

"Yes. You'd soon realise so if you tried building your steam engine out of lead and put iron of your church roof."

The dinner gong sounded.

Miss Charlotte

Charlotte sat between two officers: Captain Caruthers – but she already knew all about his medals – and Captain Conway. It had been easy to arrange; she'd simply switched her place name with another's and then feigned ignorance.

Those on Charlotte's table also included an Egyptian, Mister 'Jetty' or something, Pan-singing-Mark, and Mister thin-as-a, the civilian secretary. They were quite boring. There were five other ladies, including her sister, Earnestine, but at least in polite company, she wouldn't be bossy.

An American voice cut across the throng from the far side of the Dining Room. "Why am I seated here? This is intolerable."

"Mrs Albright, Mrs Albright," said a pompous looking civilian... oh, Sir Archibald R-something. *Rivers?* "Please sit here."

"Mister Rake was supposed to organise matters," the woman, Mrs Albright, screeched.

During starters and the fish course, no-one talked about anything exciting as there were young ladies present, by which they meant Charlotte, Earnestine and some other women from the Consulate. All she got was comments about having to eat sheep's eyes – *yuck* – but they'd just been teasing; the main course was beef.

"No pork here," said Captain Caruthers.

Luckily, the conversation improved as the wine flowed.

"You served in India," said a man with a towel wrapped around his head. He'd only had the vegetables.

"That's right, Pandit, fine country," Captain Caruthers replied. He looked at Mister Rake. "*We did our duty there.*"

"You were there too?" asked the Indian.

"I was there in a civilian capacity," Mister Rake said. "In Supplies and Deployment. I made sure everyone had the right equipment and that the right people were in the right place."

"Or not," said Caruthers.

"So," said Captain Conway, quickly, "Miss Charlotte, do you know anything about the American Indian Wars?"

"Oh yes," said Charlotte. "Red Indians, cavalry, Custer's Last Stand."

"Well," he said. "The thing about General Custer..."

And then the meal went jolly quickly.

There was a speech by the vice-Consul, Lord Thingumme; apparently, they had important people amongst them like Sir Archibald Reevers, President of the Royal Expeditionary Society, Mrs Albright from America, the reverend Pandit Singh Maçon – *blah-blah-blah* – and even the Derring-Do Club.

"Ooh."

Charlotte accepted the applause with a beaming smile and even stood to bow.

Earnestine's jaw tightened such that the tendons on her neck stood out and the scar on her left cheek went white.

There was a choice of puddings and cake; she had to lean back in her chair every time the port was passed in front of her and the battles got bloodier and bloodier.

"If you'll excuse me," Pandit Singh Maçon said, retreating, so he missed the rest of the Anglo-Afghan war. Mister Rake went with him.

The ladies had to withdraw.

By this time, Captain Caruthers' anecdotes were trapped behind enemy lines – they were down to their last twenty rounds with Thuggees closing in on all sides – when Charlotte was ambushed.

"Charlotte," Georgina said. "Ladies retire."

"Yes," Charlotte said, "I'll see you later."

"Ladies!"

"Yes, I'll... oh. Do I have to?"

Of course she had to traipse off to some boring room and Mrs Albright, the American woman weighed down by necklaces and beads, droned on and on about spirits and how sensitive she was. She didn't sound sensitive.

Charlotte slipped out to 'go and see her aunt'.

It was cooler outside, the grass green and the trees far too straight and narrow to climb, with their branches high up. There were torches lit along the paths, bright patches pushing back the looming darkness.

She walked round, hardly off the path at all.

A raised voice, then a shout.

She edged forward to see what was going on and found Captain Caruthers and one of the Egyptians about to fight. The Captain balanced on the balls of his feet and his hands fisted in readiness.

She hid behind a tree to watch.

Yes, it was a face off. They stood two sword lengths apart and talked at each other.

If only they'd speak up.

And then Mister Rake came along the path.

"Shall I arbitrate for the arbitrator?" Mister Rake said, loudly interrupting the two combatants. Charlotte couldn't see their reaction, because the tall secretary was in the way.

And then he fell over.

She scooted around to try a better angle, but by the time she reached a new observation post, it was all over.

Captain Caruthers, who must have picked the secretary up and was now practically holding him up, met her on the path.

Charlotte went over helpfully.

"Lottie," the Captain said, "Mister Rake is unwell."

"Did you hit him?"

"Tempting as that might be, no. He... fell down."

"Isn't that code for–"

"Yes, Lottie," the Captain said, "can you get the gate?"

The Captain nodded towards the formal garden's fence. There was a small gate leading outside.

Charlotte lifted the latch and held it open.

The Egyptian, a strong man with a completely bald head despite his young age, joined them. He took Mister Rake's other arm and they struggled together to get the man through.

"Thank you, Lottie," Caruthers said. "You can go back inside now."

"I can't," Charlotte said sweetly. "There's no-one to escort me."

"When did that ever... never mind. But stay with us."

"It may be dangerous," the Egyptian said.

"Don't worry, Djehuti," said Caruthers. "Lottie's with us, we'll be quite safe."

"We'll take him to my hotel."

Even though it was night, beggars still lined the steps, but Mister Djehuti cleared the way with a command.

Luckily, it wasn't far.

Mister Djehuti had a jolly luxurious room, a suite, at the top of the European Hotel. He and Captain Caruthers plonked Mister Rake on a chaise. He looked dead to the world.

"I'll fetch a blanket," their host assured them, "and look after him until he's slept it off."

"We'll take our leave," Caruthers replied. "My thanks."

"Yes, thank you," Charlotte said, "Mister D... erm... jutty?"

"Djehuti," he replied. "And I'm delighted to have met you and your sister."

Caruthers cleared his throat.

Charlotte and the Captain marched down the stairs, across the lobby and out into the still night. Beggars, aroused by the noise they were making, approached but Caruthers tapped his leather holster. The shapes melted back into the darkness.

"Guns are always useful," Charlotte said.

"They can be."

She shivered; she didn't have her shawl.

"Here," said Caruthers, slipping off his jacket. She took it, and held it as he refastened his Sam Browne belt and cross strap. Once he'd adjusted the holster, he helped her into the scarlet uniform.

Charlotte was grateful. She'd have been more grateful if the British Army allowed her to form the Women's Auxiliary Fusiliers and she could wear a uniform of her own. Earnestine and Georgina would object: *Rampant Bloomerism!*

Who cared?

They paraded along the front towards the quay.

"I need to check on something," Caruthers said.

They reached a large vessel with paddles amidships, like a small floating hotel with three storeys. A large brass plate announced it as the SS *Karnak*.

A human chain along the gangway passed supplies up. Other men struggled aboard with larger items, including large blocks wrapped in cloth.

"Ice," said Caruthers.

"In Egypt?"

"You can't get it here," he explained. "Transported from some mountain, no doubt."

Charlotte shivered. "We don't need ice."

"You'll be glad of it in your lemonade tomorrow."

Five crates lined the dock ready for loading: two oblongs, short and long, one tall crate, one round drum and finally a square one.

Caruthers lit a cigarette, a clear sign that he wanted to stay and observe. Snug in his scarlet jacket, Charlotte was quite happy to do so. If they went back to their hotel, her sisters would only send her to bed.

A rope creaked.

The workmen swore in their foreign tongue.

Others supervised in desperate English.

A crate rose upwards suspended from a wooden crane, swayed from side to side as it was manoeuvred over the deck, and finally, descended to be swallowed by the hold.

The next crate, one of the oblongs, was roped up ready.

"Careful, careful, dammit man, be careful," Sir Archibald commanded, stepping forward. He'd been standing in the shadows. "Where's Rake? Farouk, tell them to be careful."

The Egyptian guide leapt forward, comically gesticulating to the dockhands.

"You don't like Mister Rake, do you?" Charlotte said.

"No," said Caruthers.

"Why not?"

"He let us down badly."

"Was that when you were surrounded by Thuggees?"

"Waiting for reinforcements. Never came. Rake... we lost good men. Sometimes there's no justice."

Captain Caruthers took out his silver case again. He took out a cigarette, tapped it against the metal and lit it. His face shone for a moment in the light of the match.

"Did a lot of men die?"

Caruthers paused as if counting. "Too many."

Charlotte nodded to herself. She stepped away, not far because she wasn't that foolish, but enough to give the Captain a little space.

Behind them, away from the quayside, a flash attracted her attention, just a glint, a reflection, but a vivid scarlet like an army uniform or blood. Light from the dock briefly illuminated the buildings except for the silhouette of a tall figure with a bulbous head. The red flashed again, a third eye in the centre of the forehead.

It was dark again.

When the swinging lights shone there once more, the figure was gone.

"Did you..." she said.

"What is it, Lottie?"

"Nothing."

"That's our ship, the SS *Karnak*," Caruthers said. "Do you know much about ships?"

"Oh yes," said Charlotte. "The uniforms and ranks are different."

Caruthers laughed.

"There'll be a Captain on board."

"Abdul is a Skipper," the Captain said, "not a Captain."

Finally, the square crate was lowered into the ship, this time by white Europeans shouting instructions to each other in English. When it was done, one of them saluted the Captain and they all made their way back to the Consulate.

Caruthers relaxed and dropped his cigarette onto the flagstones.

"Time to get back to the hotel."

"Oh, but..."

"Early start in the morning. It's not far to the mouth of the Suez Canal and we don't want to miss the southbound convoy. We have to be on board before seven bells."

"When's seven bells?"

"Seven thirty."

CHAPTER II

Miss Deering-Dolittle

They were late. It was practically seven by the time they, and all their luggage with Pippa in her perambulator, were waiting to walk up the ramp onto the SS *Karnak*. So many Europeans and Americans were moving from the hotel to the steamships that there had been a run on Egyptian porters. Most travellers were heading for the Nile cruise and only a motley few lined the quay to board the SS *Karnak*.

"It's nearly the Ancient Egyptian New Year," Earnestine said. She bit her lip.

"Is it?" Georgina replied.

"Yes," – keep it on the calendar, she thought – "this is the second day of the intercalary month. Their year was three hundred and sixty days long."

"Like the degrees in a circle?"

"It's Babylonian. To correct for the sun's year, they added five days at the end. This is the first day of those five."

Georgina was checking her notebook. "Mmm."

Earnestine breathed out slowly: she'd got away with it.

"Where did you hear that?" Georgina asked.

"Oh..." – bother – "...no-one. Just someone."

"Someone?"

"I can meet people... I mean, I can do things when you're not around."

"I didn't say you couldn't."

Another ship departed, steaming away from the dock, bound for the Nile and excitement.

"Who was it?" Georgina insisted.

"Oh... look! Our ship has to be next."

The other ships had made steam and departed towards the wonders of Ancient Egypt leaving just one solitary vessel behind. Eventually, the port stewards deigned to remember it and those unfortunates going the wrong way.

"That's Mrs Albright," Georgina was saying. "With Sir Archibald. He's jolly important, isn't he? Ness?"

"Yes, Gina. Lottie, don't wander off."

"Ness, I was just–"

"There's no ice cream stand."

"I wasn't. I'll just go over by... there?"

"There are men there," Georgina said. "You have to keep away from men. And put your sunhat on."

"I could buy a souvenir."

"The treasure maps are all fakes," Earnestine said.

"Monsieur Jacques," Georgina continued. "He's French, but quite dashing."

"Well, he shouldn't run," Earnestine said. "That ramp doesn't look safe."

"No, I meant he's handsome."

Earnestine looked: "Is he?"

"Yes. French. But... what do you think?"

"I think 'Deering-Dolittle' comes before 'Jacques'."

"That's true. And it's ladies before gentlemen," Georgina said. "That man with the turban is the Pandit."

"Bandit?" Charlotte giggled.

"A pandit is a sort of priest in India."

"He's Sikh," Charlotte replied. "They're the warrior caste."

"And that's Mister Rake coming ashore again," Georgina continued. "He's quite tall. Isn't he, Ness?"

"I suppose."

"He has a prestigious position with the Royal Expeditionary Society."

"I have met him."

"He's jolly important, organises tours, deals with correspondence, rejects funding applications and so forth. He was telling me."

"What?"

"And he organises events and lectures at the Royal Expeditionary Society. He has a regular income."

"And the rejecting of funding applications?"

"He makes sure only the sensible ones reach Sir Archibald's desk."

"Sensible?"

"Those organised by a man."

Earnestine couldn't reply, such was the pressure with which she ground her teeth.

That man.

That horrible man.

That tall, thin rake that stood next to that round tomato of a knight. That stick plotting in the background to thwart her.

"Are you all right?" Georgina asked.

"Quite," Earnestine managed.

It was their turn to show their tickets. Captain Caruthers helped Colonel Fitzwilliam – "I'm not an invalid, Caruthers!" – up the ramp. The poor Colonel, their family friend, was suffering from an old war wound to his foot.

"This way," the Colonel said, waving his stick forward.

Georgina pushed little Pippa along in the perambulator. Earnestine held her umbrella aloft to shade the child and Charlotte followed, collecting flung toys as she went.

A steward, who spoke good English, checked their tickets.

"This way, Colonel, Captain, madames and..." – he peered into the perambulator – "mademoiselle."

The ramp sprang as they walked up.

That was their party, all aboard: Colonel Fitzwilliam and Captain Caruthers, the three sisters and Earnestine's niece. No maid, no funding, no expeditions... Earnestine could... words failed her.

They were allocated cabins on the starboard side, which was good, and Georgina had the largest cabin for her and her daughter.

Earnestine had the second largest.

She unpacked her things; her clothes, undergarments, boots and then her various kits. One item lay in her palm for a few moments longer than the others.

Her Webley had a solid weight and smelt of oil. She opened the cylinder and checked – unloaded. The wooden case had twelve rounds and six slipped into the chambers easily.

It would take only one.

She put it away safely in her unmentionables drawer.

Once round the deck, she decided. Some fresh air would do her good.

Charlotte was already outside, probably because she hadn't unpacked properly, gazing out at the Mediterranean.

"My cabin's really small," said Charlotte.

"Don't lean over the railing," Earnestine replied. "It's dangerous."

Charlotte stood pouting.

Shouts came from the quay, ropes were untied and hauled aboard before the engine belched smoke from its funnel. The paddles heaved, almost lost the battle to push against the sea and then the ship eased away. No-one waved them off from the shore.

Soon the steamer was making progress furiously churning the water on both sides in a frenzy. The land gave way on the starboard and the Suez canal stretched away as if forever.

The SS *Karnak* joined the line of vessels making the long voyage from the Mediterranean to the Red Sea. The land on either side became increasingly flat and featureless.

"There's nothing to do," Charlotte said.

"Let's explore." *No exploring,* her mother had said.

"Yes, let's," said Charlotte running off.

"Don't..." but Earnestine thought she might as well have a look around.

The SS *Karnak* had four decks.

The windowless 'below' deck, the hold, was reserved for cargo and crew, while the next two decks had cabins that opened onto the walkway around the side, although the front of the ship had the kitchens and other sections for the running of the vessel. The lower deck of cabins was empty as no-one wanted to voyage along the Suez. If the ship had been assigned to the Nile, it would have been fully occupied.

She wondered why they weren't assigned to the lower deck. It was easier to reach, particularly with a perambulator, but then she realised that the higher you were, the better the breeze.

The top deck was the Dining Room, Smoking Room and Library, all amidships, and an open Sun Deck aft. There was a corridor in the middle between the Smoking Room and the Library, with store rooms as well, so passengers could pass easily from port to starboard.

Earnestine strode briskly around the walkway that encircled the cabins and then, having gone up the staircase, she went around the top deck. Like all the decks, the walkway was sometimes open with a rail and sometimes enclosed with windows.

The Egyptian heat was stifling. The blades of the paddles sliced the water outside, driving the ship forward as the steam engine chugged away, but there was no cooling influence from any breeze or moisture. The horizon surrounded them, unbroken, shimmering in the heat haze. They might have well been in the middle of the desert. They *were* in the middle of the desert. The Suez Canal went straight through it.

She finished her circuit: this was the limit of what she could explore. It wasn't going to be a sightseeing-*ous* voyage.

Eventually, she reached the Smoking Room where other passengers had gathered.

There was an Arab gentleman with beady eyes leaning over to pester the Colonel.

"I'm fine," Colonel Fitzwilliam insisted. "It's my war wound."

"Then let me examine it," said the foreigner.

"Who are you anyway?"

"What's going on?" Earnestine asked.

"Madam, I am Doctor Timon, a physician, and I have studied at Cairo and Edinburgh. I merely wish to examine this patient."

"Is the Colonel your patient?"

"Not as such, but I thought I'd be of service."

"Perhaps not," said Earnestine. "Thank you, kindly."

"You are his nurse?"

Colonel Fitzwilliam interrupted, "I am here, you know."

"I'm family... I mean, the Colonel is part of my sister's family, not exactly related, more a family friend."

"I see."

"I'm Miss Deering-Dolittle."

The Arab looked about him through his round glasses, unsure what to do next, but then Monsieur Jacques came in and so Doctor Timon found a seat.

"Thank you, my dear," said the Colonel. "Would you mind fetching me a brandy?"

"This early in the morning?"

"It's for my leg," he replied, and then he leant forward. "Better than anything any quack would prescribe."

Earnestine nodded and fetched a brandy from the drinks table.

While she was pouring a measure, the turban-wearing Pandit came in, bowed to everyone, and then sat at a table. He took out a chess board and carefully set out the pieces, ready for a game.

Earnestine returned to the Colonel with his glass of restorative.

"Thank you, my dear."

She sat and appraised the assortment of passengers.

"The pieces are assembled," Pandit Singh Maçon said. "Anyone want to play?"

Earnestine did not.

She stood.

The men stood too, although the Colonel didn't manage to get to his feet fully.

She went to the Sun Deck at the stern of the ship. There was no-one about, so she stood so very alone. The wide expanse of the Mediterranean narrowed to a tiny outlet. Tanis and its extraordinary secret drifted away back into the past. They were on the canal going down the straight and narrow path, her journey constrained and dictated by men's engineering works.

How could she live a life of high sightseeing if people like Rake thwarted her at every turn?

"I could kill him."

Mrs Merryweather

Pippa would not settle.

It was cool in the morning, so she wanted to play, crawl away and shout. Later in the day, she would be hot, bothered and troublesome and finally, at night, she'd be restless and noisy.

Georgina carried her on her hip, bouncing her, distracting her.

"Look, the water," she said. "Look, sand... more water... and sand here."

She passed Sir Archibald and Mister Rake.

"It went perfectly," Mister Rake said. "Amenemope knows... Mrs Merryweather."

"Mister Rake. Sir Archibald."

"Madam," said Sir Archibald.

"Would you mind getting the door for me, please," Georgina asked.

"Of course," said Mister Rake, pulling open the door to the corridor that led inside to the Library and the Smoking Room.

"And the next one, please?"

"I'll come with you."

"We'll talk later about what Amenemope knows," Sir Archibald said.

"Very well, Sir Archibald," Mister Rake said. "This way, Mrs Merryweather."

Mister Rake was as good as his word and opened the next door into the Smoking Room. It was full of passengers with raised voices, so Georgina considered simply turning around and leaving. However, it turned out to be only one person shouting; Charlotte was being berated by an American woman.

"This! What is this, but filth and blasphemy."

"It's just a book," Charlotte whined.

"Excuse me, what is going on?"

"Lot-lot," said Pippa, holding out her hands with such force that she nearly pitched out of Georgina's grip.

"It's just my steamport novel," Charlotte explained.

"Novel, pah," said the American throwing the book back. A card fell from it to the deck.

"Now I've lost my place," said Charlotte.

"Excuse me, Missus..."

"May I introduce Mrs Albright," said Mister Rake, coming to the rescue. Men could be so thoughtful. "This is Mrs Merryweather."

"At least you aren't one of these dreadful Deering-Dolittles."

"Actually, before I was married, I was–"

"What's this?"

"Excuse me."

Mrs Albright bent down and picked up Charlotte's fallen bookmark.

"It's Death!"

"Surely–"

"See! Death!"

The card was a tarot card depicting a skeleton on horseback brandishing a scythe.

Georgina too was shocked: "Charlotte!"

"It's alright," Charlotte said. "A gypsy gave it to me."

"A gypsy!" – Mrs Albright staggered back as if struck – "You have brought death onto the ship."

Pippa started to cry.

"See how the innocent understand!" Mrs Albright screeched. She grasped the necklaces of beads dangling down her front. "I have one of my heads."

"Charlotte, perhaps you should go to your room," Georgina suggested.

"What for?" said Charlotte, incensed.

"For Satanism!" Mrs Albright informed them.

"Lottie, please," Georgina begged. "Go and write your letters."

"I'm being sent to my room?"

"Lottie, promise."

"I promise," Charlotte snapped and then she stormed out.

"Lot-lot," Pippa wailed as her aunt left, and then the child was inconsolable.

"Perhaps the Dining Room, Mrs Merryweather," Doctor Timon suggested to Georgina. "Mrs Albright, would you like a powder, a little cocaine, or a mixture of laudanum."

"Please, that would be such a comfort," Mrs Albright said. "I'll take it in my cabin."

The American found she still had Charlotte's tarot card and, after dithering, she handed it to Mister Rake.

"Thank you," said Mister Rake, confused.

Then Mrs Albright put the back of her hand against her forehead and swept out of the room.

This left only the Colonel, the Pandit, Mister Rake, who pocketed the bookmark, and Monsieur Jacques.

"I'm so sorry," Georgina tried to say above her daughter's racket.

She escaped.

On deck, she saw Earnestine standing at the stern, gazing at the scenery. The other way, someone skulked in the shadow of a doorway... oh, it was Captain Caruthers.

Georgina found the Dining Room. It was already being prepared for elevenses by the exotically dressed Egyptian waiters. Dodging them, she tried walking up and down to settle Pippa. The child squalled, fighting her mother's grip to be allowed to fling herself to the floor.

"Please. Please."

The Egyptian waiters looked upon her with sympathy, but scooted away whenever her perambulations took her towards them.

So, Mrs Albright had a head because of the noise.

What about Georgina? Her head had been pummelled into a state of unthinking exhaustion.

Bringing her child had been madness. But then, Philippa was her husband's daughter and they were going to India to–

What was that?

There was a sudden quiet.

Had she heard a bang?

Pippa looked about; perplexed.

Was Georgina going to have to buy a firearm and shoot off a round every time she wanted some peace and quiet?

"There, there," she said.

Pippa was falling asleep, resting to gain strength for the afternoon and the night's bout of screaming no doubt.

Georgina placed her gently onto the comfortable seat by the door. Pippa was so peaceful, her hand moving as she breathed. The heat would build, so a blanket would be a mistake.

Georgina stood bolt upright.

Another noise.

That noise she knew.

That really had been a gunshot.

Miss Charlotte

Charlotte dropped quickly and unnoticed from the upper to the lower deck. She landed easily and nipped through the passage adjoining the starboard to the port side, then it was an easy climb up the railings back to the upper deck.

Everyone was looking inside the ship, a queue forming to enter the corridor by the Smoking Room.

"Wha'sss..." – she took a deep breath – "what's going on?"

"There's been an accident," said the Egyptian gentleman... Doctor Timon, that was it.

"Has there?" she said innocently.

"This is no place for a young lady."

"No," Charlotte agreed. "Can I see?"

She pushed around him, but Doctor Timon grabbed her and yanked her back.

"Please, wait in the Smoking Room, Child."

She'd seen, though. "But–"

"Please. Pandit, if you'd be so kind."

The Pandit bowed. "This way, Miss."

"But–" but it was no use.

The Pandit led her to the Smoking Room, which was just a few yards straight down the central corridor. The other passengers had assembled there too.

Charlotte paused to stare through the frosted glass that made up the top half of the Smoking Room's door. Between the fancy letters, the reversed 'g' and 'R', she tried to see into the Library. Doctor Timon was struggling to close the door, so she saw the far wall again.

Doctor Timon spotted her though with his small, sharp eyes, magnified by his round glasses, and waved her away.

Charlotte smiled back innocently.

"Lottie!" – it was Earnestine – "Get out of the way, I'm trying to watch."

Her sister was sitting on a comfortable armchair like an agitated giraffe, her neck craning around trying to see.

"I was looking," said Charlotte.

"Come and sit down," Earnestine insisted.

Charlotte did so; she never had any fun. Ooh, there was a plate of Turkish delight.

Everyone else was seated; no one spoke.

"You're jolly red-faced," Earnestine whispered.

"No."

"You haven't been running?"

"No, not running."

"Well, be quiet. And don't touch those, you'll ruin your appetite."

"But–"

"They broke the door. See?"

Charlotte couldn't until she leant against Earnestine. Doctor Timon was still trying to close the Library door.

"Doctor Timon kept me away," Earnestine said. "He thought I was going to faint."

"Did you?"

"No. But that didn't stop him pushing smelling salts in my face. What did you see?"

"A man shot." Charlotte lowered her voice, "Blood everywhere."

"Yes, I saw that. Anything I didn't see?"

"What did you see?"

"Not who it was."

"Whoever he was, he's been murdered."

"He?"

"A tall man."

Monsieur Jacques appeared in front of the Library door, talked briefly to Doctor Timon and then came in.

"Sacré Bleu."

Earnestine glanced around the room, frowning.

Captain Caruthers arrived too.

Monsieur Jacques poured everyone drinks. "Sherry, mademoiselle?"

"She can't," said Earnestine, "and not for me... oh, thank you, Sir Archibald."

"Are you all right, my dear?" Sir Archibald asked.

"Yes, thank you."

"You aren't feeling faint?"

"No, one's quite fine."

"You could have a lie-down."

"I'm fine, Sir Archibald."

"I saw Doctor Timon trying to revive you."

"There was no need."

Her sister even got sherry, disgusting Charlotte thought, but what about lemonade? Sir Archibald and Monsieur Jacques finished serving the ladies (except Charlotte, of course) and poured whiskey or brandy for themselves and the other men.

"When's someone going to take charge?" Earnestine whispered. "It's Mister Rake."

"I didn't see," Charlotte replied, "but it could have been."

"Everyone else is here."

Charlotte looked round. "Except Gina."

CHAPTER III

Miss Deering-Dolittle

"One of you is a murderer."

Earnestine fixed her attention on each in turn, hoping her gaze would alight upon a guilty expression.

Nine faces stared back at her.

It was a good job Georgina wasn't present as she'd have insisted that she leave it to the men. All they had done was sit or stand around, drinking and smoking.

Captain Caruthers met her gaze.

It was typical of the Englishman to have a stiff upper lip when certain handsome foreigners had eyes that sparkled with passion and... it was jolly hot in here.

However, she did not need to sit down, lie down or calm down; she needed someone to get on with it. So, finally, she had taken the matter into her own, perfectly capable hands.

"Yes?" Sir Archibald demanded.

"Well, that's it... one of you is a murderer."

"That much is obvious, my dear, but which of us is it?"

"Ah."

"We thought you were going to explain."

"Sorry."

The slightest fleck of mud, the holding of a whisky glass in the left hand, a misspoken word or something, anything – anything at all – that might be a clue.

But she saw nothing or, perhaps, she observed nothing.

Georgina appeared, finally, and without Philippa. "What's happened?"

"A chair, my dear," said Colonel Fitzwilliam. "We don't want to upset you, but Mister Rake has had an accident."

"Oh dear, nothing serious, I hope."

"I'm afraid he passed away," the Colonel said.

"He was murdered," Charlotte added.

Georgina sat.

Of the dozen chairs in the Smoking Room of the SS *Karnak*, eight were now occupied. There were four empty places. Captain Caruthers and herself stood, no-one risked the wobbly spare and, finally, the chair favoured by Mister Rake, Secretary to the Royal Expeditionary Society, was empty. He would not be sitting or standing ever again.

"Madame, would you like a sherry or a gin?" Monsieur Jacques suggested, leaning over Georgina.

"No, thank you," Georgina replied.

"Do you need one of Doctor Timon's wonderful powders?" Mrs Albright suggested. "I have a spare fan in my cabin."

"I'm quite well, thank you."

This was all getting away from the point, so Earnestine raised her finger. "The crew were all in the forward part of the ship preparing dinner, or steering, or whatever."

"I can vouch for that," Georgina said.

"Can you?"

"Oh yes," Georgina said, "Pippa and I were in the Dining Room. We heard nothing–"

"Not surprised, with that tyke," Mrs Albright murmured under her breath.

"Except, perhaps, a shot."

"And Mister Rake was found in the Library towards the stern," Earnestine said, pointing. "He was shot."

Everyone glanced at the glass window in the top half of the door. The reversed lettering, 'Smoking Room', did not obscure the view down the short passageway to the Library. Mister Rake had bolted the Library door from the inside. There had been a shot. Doctor Timon had banged on the door; it had been forced open and... Earnestine could still smell the ammonia, perfume and vinegar.

"So that leaves nine suspects," Earnestine concluded.

"There are ten of us," Sir Archibald corrected.

Earnestine double-checked around the room, counting as she went...

1. **Mrs Merryweather**, who always looked serene and beautiful, even wearing her black mourning clothes, despite the oppressive heat
2. **Colonel Fitzwilliam**, their old family friend, sat by the drinks cabinet with a brandy.
3. **Captain Caruthers** leant against the door jamb, handsome in his light khaki uniform, holding a tumbler of whisky lightly in his strong grip.
4. **Doctor Timon**, olive-skinned and narrow features, with intelligent, darting eyes behind his round glasses.
5. **Sir Archibald Reevers**, President of the Royal Expeditionary Society was next, with the bottom two buttons of his waistcoat undone.
6. **Mrs Albright**, the American millionairess, fussed with her chain attaching her spectacles. She wore too much make-up and used a walking stick. Earnestine could easily imagine her doing the deed; she murdered the English language.
7. **Monsieur Jacques** lounged, his long legs stretched out, with a haughty expression and a crème de menthe balanced between his thumb and forefinger.
8. **Pandit Singh Maçon**, the educated Indian, sat upright, his dark eyes unfathomable beneath his purple turban. A scarlet jewel, hanging like a cap badge, caught the light.
9. **Miss Charlotte** sat with her legs up on the upholstery by the plate of Turkish delight – *the empty plate of Turkish delight* – fiddling with a lock of her blonde hair.

...that was everyone.

She'd gone from her right thumb to her left index finger – it was nine.

What was Sir Archibald on about? There were nine. Nine! She'd counted them all. He can't possibly have included Pippa as a suspect, so nine. Nine... oh, *bother*.

10. **Miss Deering-Dolittle**, the eldest, most responsible, dowdy and put-upon of the sisters – herself, who stood holding her left thumb feeling foolish.

"Ten," she agreed.

"Nine," said Captain Caruthers. He took a sip of his whisky. They'd all needed a stiff one after the shock. Earnestine could still taste sherry on her tongue; she'd have preferred a Scotch too, but she was a young lady.

"Can you not count, Captain?" Sir Archibald said.

Caruthers smoothed his chevron moustache. "If Mrs Merryweather can vouch for the staff, then I'm sure they can vouch for her."

"Oh, yes." Earnestine glanced at her sister. It couldn't have been Georgina and so they'd made progress already. "So, that leaves eight."

"Eight? You can eliminate someone else?"

"Well, I didn't do it."

"How do we know that?" Pandit Singh Maçon observed.

"Well, I'm... one doesn't do that kind of thing."

"I am a Knight of the Realm," interjected Sir Archibald. "President of the Royal Expeditionary Society. My reputation is above reproach."

"Of course, Sir Archibald."

"And, for heaven's sake," Sir Archibald continued, "Colonel Fitzwilliam here was a Colonel in the British Army. Fought in Uttar Pradesh, damn it."

"There's no need for the D-word in front of ladies, Sir Archibald," Caruthers said.

"And I can vouch for Captain Caruthers," Colonel Fitzwilliam said.

"Of course, Colonel," Earnestine agreed. "It couldn't possibly be the good Captain."

"One of the three musketeers, don't you know. Best men in my command," the Colonel continued. "Stood up against those Thuggee blighters."

Earnestine bit her lip: one of the three musketeers, indeed. There had been three of Major Dan's 'mountaineers', army officers sent to perform certain tasks abroad for the good of the Empire, but Captain Merryweather, her sister's late husband, had passed away and the other... well, the less said about him, the better; he'd hardly been beyond reproach. But that was the past.

"My sisters, obviously," Earnestine began.

"Why are your sisters excluded?" Sir Archibald asked.

"Well, Georgina couldn't and Charlotte wouldn't."

"Women are quite capable of murder."

"One supposes that certain lower classes might–"

"Quite capable."

"Yes, thank you, Sir Archibald."

"I can tell you many a tale of the ladies committing acts of unspeakable violence."

"Thank you, Sir Archibald."

"The fairer sex–"

"Sir Archibald!"

"It's the curse!" Mrs Albright exclaimed. She held her hands up, fingers splayed awkwardly as she turned her gaze upon each of them in turn. "The Curse of Ancient Egypt. The gods reached out from the afterlife to strike him down for his desecration."

"Poppycock," Sir Archibald said. "I've excavated numerous tombs and there's nothing to this 'curse' nonsense."

"The spirits will have their revenge."

"Mrs Albright," Earnestine said. "Mister Rake was shot. Hardly the action of a mummified Pharaoh."

"You mark my words. It'll be a curse."

"We should be looking at these foreign gentlemen," Sir Archibald continued, indicating the far side of the room with a gesture large enough to point over the English Channel had it been there. "No offence."

"None taken, Sir Archibald," said Monsieur Jacques.

"There you are then," Sir Archibald concluded. "A Frenchman, an Arab and an Indian – take your pick."

"I have taken the Hippocratic oath," said Doctor Timon. "Besides, I didn't know the man."

"Oui, why would we kill such a man as..." Jacques began, and he ended his sentence with an uncaring 'boof' of a shrug.

"Mister Rake was a fine gentleman," Sir Archibald said, "and a good secretary. The Royal Expeditionary Society will sorely miss his expertise."

"He was hardly that," said Colonel Fitzwilliam.

The Captain glanced quickly at his superior.

"And will you miss him, Monsieur?" the Frenchman enquired.

"It's 'Sir'," Sir Archibald replied, "and of course I shall miss him. The man was indispensable."

"Where was everyone when the shot was fired?" Captain Caruthers asked.

The answers came thick and fast.

"Here."

"Here."

"On deck."

"In my cabin."

"Here."

"In the Dining Room."

"The Dining Room?" Caruthers asked.

"Yes, that's correct," said Georgina. "I didn't hear anything. I was... Philippa was upset and I thought it best to avoid the rest of you. Mrs Albright was quite clear on the matter of her noise."

Mrs Albright backed her up. "That's quite correct. Her noise brought on one of my heads. Doctor Timon here kindly helped in that regard."

Doctor Timon smiled and nodded.

"I suffer most terribly on account of my spiritual nature," Mrs Albright explained.

"Mrs Merryweather," Caruthers said, ignoring the American. "Just to confirm this, did the servants see you?"

"You can't suspect Gina," Earnestine said.

"I don't. Mrs Merryweather, did anyone see you?"

"Yes..." Georgina said, thinking. "The waiters were preparing the Dining Room."

"All the time?"

"Indeed, they were in and out all the time."

"Then it's clear," Captain Caruthers announced.

"What's clear?" Sir Archibald demanded.

"Any one of us could have shot Mister Rake, anyone, with the sole exception of Mrs Merryweather."

"We've established that, man," Sir Archibald said. He shuffled around in his bucket chair, looking from Captain Caruthers to Colonel Fitzwilliam. "We've established it."

"So," Caruthers continued. "One of us."

"That's what I said."

"But, Sir Archibald, you could have done it."

"Nonsense."

"But you could."

"I know where I was and what I was doing," Sir Archibald announced.

"Precisely," Caruthers continued, "but so do I, so do we all, but none of us can prove it, except for Mrs Merryweather."

"Oh yes," Georgina said, "I was with Philippa in the Dining Room."

"Witnessed by the crew."

"They don't mind Philippa's noise."

"We don't mind her either," Mrs Albright said. "We simply needed a rest from it."

"So, it seems obvious," Captain Caruthers said, "that Mrs Merryweather must become our Investigating Officer, as it were."

Sir Archibald's cheeks flushed. "I beg your pardon!"

"She's the only one eliminated as a suspect."

"Poppycock! We can't have a woman in charge, no disrespect, Mrs Merryweather, but honestly."

"I quite understand," Georgina said.

How could Georgina understand, Earnestine thought, knowing that she herself could be... whatever the good Captain had said? What was the point of talking to her sisters about suffrage, if they took no notice? The British Empire was ruled by a woman, for goodness sake. Earnestine was not Queen Victoria, but why couldn't she be in charge? Women had every right to be treated equally with the vote, land ownership and free expression. She was sorely tempted to give them all a free expression.

Earnestine didn't voice this opinion aloud, obviously.

"To my mind," Captain Caruthers continued, "it's either we appoint our own Investigating Officer or we hand the investigation over to the local authorities."

"Local authorities!" Sir Archibald exclaimed. "You can't mean the Egyptian wallahs?"

Captain Caruthers shrugged.

"Oh, really!" Sir Archibald. "This is intolerable. First, I lose a perfectly good secretary and now this indignity."

"The local authorities will be most thorough," Monsieur Jacques said.

"But they take bribes," Sir Archibald insisted. "Damn it, man, but—"

Captain Caruthers interrupted, "Mrs Merryweather has done the Empire stalwart service, and she was married to a fine, upstanding officer of my own regiment. I think she can be relied upon to be discreet and thorough."

"If you say so."

"Indeed, I do," Captain Caruthers confirmed. "Mrs Merryweather, will you step forward?"

Georgina hesitated.

Oh, this so vexed Earnestine. Why hadn't she been looking after her little niece, she thought, and then she would be the Investigating Officer. She was the eldest, and at twenty-one, the only one of the sisters who were of age.

Eventually, Georgina nodded. "I will do my duty."

"Excellent," said Caruthers, settling the matter.

"However," Georgina said, "I must warn you. I will fulfil the obligation diligently and uncover the truth, wherever that takes me."

Captain Caruthers held Georgina's gaze for a long moment: "Understood."

Mrs Merryweather

Georgina decided to base her investigation in the Dining Room where she could keep an eye on Philippa. There were plenty of tables from which to choose and it was cooler than elsewhere on the SS *Karnak*. Pippa could play on the rug.

She picked a suitable spot with her back to the bow and a good view of the door.

Yes, she thought, time to deduce who did it.

She set out her notebook, inkbottle and pen, carefully aligning them to the table.

Pippa sat on the floor, heedlessly flinging cutlery about. She'd tried getting the child to play with something safer, but it hadn't worked. At least she wasn't screaming. Could she be teething? If only she could nip down the road to the pharmacy for Mrs Winslow's Soothing Syrup. Morphine was such a blessing: '*A mother's friend*', as the advertisement put it.

The foolscap notebook had thin lines and a margin in faint red, with a card cover.

'*Murder*', she wrote.

Now what?

She must write down what was true and proceed from that firm foundation.

So, carefully, she enumerated a list.

1. Sir Archibald Reevers.
2. Colonel Fitzwilliam.
3. Captain Caruthers.
4. Pandit Singh Maçon.
5. Doctor Timon.
6. Monsieur Jacques.
7. Mrs Albright.
8. Miss Deering-Dolittle.
9. Miss Charlotte.

The gentlemen seemed to come in pairs. Both Sir Archibald and Colonel Fitzwilliam were on the large side, though Sir Archibald's overbearing demeanour contrasted the Colonel's friendly nature. Captain Caruthers and Pandit Singh Maçon were quiet men ready for action, though the Captain tended to lean against things, whereas the Indian sat stiffly upright. This scheme fell apart with Doctor Timon, who was a short, nervous man hiding behind glasses, and Monsieur Jacques, who was tall, thin, louche and self-assured. Mister Rake had been tall and wiry too, a dour version of the rakish Frenchman.

As for the ladies, Mrs Albright was an American, Earnestine was a handsome, confident young woman and Charlotte was pretty – pretty exasperating!

There were three legs to the stool: motive, opportunity and method.

Motive – no-one really liked Mister Rake.

Opportunity – everyone, except for herself.

Method – apparently it was a locked door mystery.

It had happened in the Library; this was all she had discovered. As soon as she'd walked into the Smoking Room, they all started helping. Would she like to sit here?

A gin? Doctor Timon could find a powder. Mrs Albright had a spare fan in her cabin.

It was galling that she had not witnessed it herself, although that would mean she would be a suspect and therefore disqualified as the investigator. That might have been a blessing as she would have avoided this chore.

Ah, but wait!

She did witness events. Perhaps not the actual murder, but the frame within which it occurred. The first task, then, was to fix this in her mind and write it down.

"Could I trouble you for a glass of iced lemonade, please?" Georgina asked a passing waiter.

The Egyptian bowed and went away. She was never sure if they understood. He came back briefly with the fruit bowl he'd forgotten to put down on the table.

So, she'd left the Smoking Room with Pippa at about 10:30am, just after Doctor Timon had taken Mrs Albright to her cabin for some powders.

That left Colonel Fitzwilliam, Monsieur Jacques, Pandit Singh Maçon and Mister Rake (the victim) in the Smoking Room.

As she'd made her way, Georgina had seen Earnestine at the far end of the boat, leaning on the aft railing and looking out back along the Suez Canal.

This left – she checked her list – Sir Archibald Reevers, Captain Caruthers and Charlotte's whereabouts, unaccounted for. They had all probably (but not definitely) been in their cabins. Charlotte should have been in her cabin writing her letters. Charlotte had said she would. She'd promised. So, she had been in her cabin.

But Georgina couldn't be sure of that. Definitely couldn't be sure. The fact that Charlotte still hadn't written any letters was a testament to the young girl never doing what she was told.

And, of course, everyone could easily have moved almost anywhere after she'd gone to the Dining Room – it was a large boat. However, this was the opening position, the pieces laid out on the board, as it were.

So, after each name on her list, she added a location.

1. Sir Archibald Reevers.
2. Colonel Fitzwilliam, Smoking Room.
3. Captain Caruthers.
4. Pandit Singh Maçon, Smoking Room.
5. Doctor Timon.
6. Monsieur Jacques, Smoking Room.
7. Mrs Albright, cabin.
8. Miss Deering-Dolittle, on deck.
9. Miss Charlotte.

That seemed a good start.

When she had returned, they had all been in the Smoking Room in something of a quandary, and it had taken quite a few requests for them to tell her, a weak and fragile woman – 'we don't want to upset you, my dear' – that Mister Rake had been found 'passed away' in the Library.

The locked Library!

Oh, wait! Georgina remembered that when she'd taken Pippa to the Dining Room at 10:30am, she'd seen Captain Caruthers. He'd been smoking while standing in the shadow of a doorway. With a quiver, she recalled his furtive glance – he'd been lurking.

Did this make him the prime suspect?

Of course not (it was far too early to jump to conclusions), but she added 'on deck' after the Captain's entry in her list.

Georgina had taken the starboard side, out of habit. It was the morning, so it was in the shade. That would explain the shadows that hid the Captain from view.

Most of the passengers would wish to warm up in the early mornings. The nights could be bitter, so they'd favour the port side before breakfast. Soon, the sun's heat would reign supreme and everyone would move to the cooler side, then swap back to port after noon.

The advice was always to book a cabin '*port out, starboard home*' on Nile cruises, for this reason. And what applied on the ancient river, also held true on the modern canal. The journey from Tanis, on the Mediterranean, to Suez at the point of the Gulf of Suez and thence the Red Sea was almost directly south.

Did this mean that anyone moving along the boat on the sunny side would be unobserved in the brightness?

Perhaps.

What was the best advice for an Investigating Officer?

I keep six honest serving-men, Georgina thought, quoting Kipling, *they taught me all I knew; their names are What and Why and When. And How and Where and Who.* They'd been sent this wonderful advice a few years ago and she imagined that Kipling would publish it in a collection soon enough.

She had a list for 'who' already.

'When' was clearly after 10:30am and before she was called back to the Smoking Room, say 11:30am. People heard a shot. She had heard a shot.

Just four more honest serving-men to employ, and what she needed were the facts... evidence. So, the best course of action would be a systematic approach. And, now she considered the matter, the solution would surely present itself easily enough. All she had to do was interview each suspect and whoever lied would be the murderer.

"The game's afoot," she said.

Philippa looked up from chewing a fork.

"Pippa, who shall we question first?"

Her baby gurgled in reply and flung the fork across the carpet.

"Yes, I don't think it matters either."

Georgina picked up the bell and rang it.

Philippa glanced about looking for the source of the enchantment, so Georgina rang the bell again and the baby laughed.

"Madam, I am here, abject apologies," said Farouk entering. "Farouk did hear the first time, but, alas, I was too far away. Humble apologies."

"Sorry, Farouk. My fault. I was ringing the bell for Pippa."

"Of course, Madam."

Farouk was a friendly, if portly, Egyptian gentleman hired as a Guide (although for what perplexed Georgina as they weren't stopping to visit anywhere). He dressed in a long robe, striped white and blue, with a grey waistcoat of a European style.

"But I did want something, Mister Farouk."

He whipped the battered fez off his bald pate. "Just Farouk, Madam."

Georgina smiled. It was difficult to object, because he just didn't understand that they couldn't possibly be on first name terms.

"Farouk, would you be so kind as to ask everyone to come in, one at a time that is, for questioning?"

"Terrible business, terrible shame, terrible luck."

"Yes, if you'd be so kind."

"Any particular guest first, Madam?"

Georgina considered this. She'd like them to come in alphabetically, but trying to explain that to a native of Egypt, with its three writing systems and thousands of strange hieroglyphs might take forever.

"I don't think so," she said.

"As they come then, Madam."

"Indeed," said Georgina. "Please send in the first suspect."

Miss Charlotte

When Farouk, with his funny hat, arrived in the Smoking Room... well, Charlotte was first because she had been waiting. She didn't want to sit in the Smoking Room with a lot of adults looking glum, so she jumped up, shouted "Me!" and then skipped down the passageway to the Dining Room.

Georgina was sitting, jolly formally behind the dining table. She had her notebook out and turned the page as Charlotte sat in front of her.

"Now Lottie," Georgina began. "This is a serious matter."

"I know that."

"Good. You must answer properly and fully."

"Yes, I know that."

"And truthfully."

"Gina!"

Like everyone Charlotte knew, Georgina had a tendency to go on and on about obvious things that Charlotte knew already. It was as if they thought she wasn't paying attention.

"Charlotte?"

"Yes... what?"

"I beg your pardon."

"I beg your pardon?"

"Were you listening?"

"Yes."

"When Mister Rake... when... that is... when..."

"He was murdered."

"Yes."

"Shot," said Charlotte, before adding helpfully, "blood everywhere."

"Yes, yes, Charlotte, perhaps not quite so fully."

"Sorry, Gina."

"Now, where were you when you heard the gunshot?"

"I didn't hear a gunshot."

"Why not?"

"I wasn't doing anything."

"I didn't say that you were."

"But you suspect me."

"It's my task to suspect everyone, even you and Ness."

"That's not really fair."

"I am the Investigating Officer."

"I don't even know where the pantry is."

"Oh, Lottie."

"I was playing levels."

"What's levels? You don't mean there are more rules for that High Tea, Noughts and Crosses on the three-tier cake stand game, do you?"

"No."

"Biscuit Battles?"

"It's not called that, it's Tea–"

"Not that Russian Craig's Game?"

"Kriegsspiel. It's Prussian. And no, you wouldn't let me bring my dice and metal pieces."

"Then what is it?"

"It's like Scrumping."

"Scrumping? There are no gardens with apple trees here."

"It was the climbing part of scrumping."

"Climbing?"

"I was bored."

"How can you be bored?"

"There's nothing to do."

"You could write a journal. We're in Egypt, which is jolly educational, and worthy of record."

"Gina..." – (for all her academic study, her sister could be so dense) – "...we're on the Suez Canal, there's nothing to see."

"If you think that's true, then write it down."

"It's still true whether you write it down or not."

"You could read. Homework and..." – Georgina saw Charlotte's expression – "You could read for pleasure."

"Pleasure?"

"You were given a shilling to buy a steamport novel."

"I bought one."

"Was that the book Mrs Albright objected to?" Georgina said. "What is it?"

"It's not a military book!" Charlotte replied. "It's not."

"So, what is it?"

"It's a steamport book."

"Yes, but what is it?"

"It's a... quite good."

"Charlotte?"

"It's a Marie Corelli."

"Oh, that melodramatic nonsense."

"It's not," Charlotte said. "It's about a penniless writer, who becomes a millionaire."

"That is nonsense. Writers don't make money."

"He inherits money. That's believable."

"What's it called?"

"Oh... it has a subtitle. The Strange Experience of One Geoffrey Tempest, Millionaire."

"And the title?"

"Oh, I forget."

"Charlotte, it'll be on the front."

"*The Sorrows of...* you know."

"Charlotte?"

"*The Sorrows of Satan.*"

"Oh, really! Honestly! It's occult hokum. No wonder Mrs Albright objected."

"Theosophy is–"

"Nonsense Charlotte, utter nonsense."

"But–"

"If you'd only come to the Natural History Museum."

"It's full of dead animals."

"It is not!"

"It is."

"Charlotte!"

"I don't want to be called Charlotte," Charlotte said. Both her sisters used it when they were being disapproving, which was all the time. "Charlotte's such an old-fashioned name."

"It is not. Your grandmother was called Charlotte."

"I'd rather be called... Marie Corelli–"

"Marie's an old-fashioned name."

"No, Marie Corelli in her novel, *The Sorrows of Satan*, has a lady writer character with a new and exciting modern name."

"What's she called?"

"Mavis."

"Mavis?"

"Yes."

"There's no such name."

"Marie Corelli invented it for the character."

"It's made up then."

"All names are made up."

"Don't be silly," Georgina said. "However, you have a book to read, so how could you be bored?"

"I lost my place when Mrs Albright took my bookmark. And I can't read it all the time, so I was bored."

"Well, there's been a murder now."

"I know. It's jolly exciting."

"Lottie, please, this is serious," Georgina said, spoiling the fun. "A man has died."

Charlotte put on her serious expression.

"So, 'levels'?"

"You go from the top deck to the lower deck by swinging on the railing," Charlotte explained.

"The railing of the staircase? That's dangerous, Charlotte, and worse, it's unladylike."

"Not the staircase, the railing around the deck." Why did no-one ever understand her?

"The deck? Lottie, that makes no sense. You can't mean that you swing, outside the ship, like a monkey?"

"That's it."

"Charlotte Deering-Dolittle!"

"No-one saw."

"That's hardly the point. Where was this?"

"Outside the ship. I did say."

"Which side?"

"On the left," Charlotte explained.

"The port side."

"That's what I said."

"Then people will have seen you, because in the morning before breakfast, people warm up on that side."

"I don't get up that early."

"I know."

"So, I don't need to warm up."

"Don't you get too hot?"

"Yes," Charlotte admitted. "Please, could I have a lemonade?"

"No."

Charlotte glanced at the table and saw, obviously, that the glass, with mint and a slice of lime, had contained lemonade or tonic or something jolly nice. "I'm parched."

"We're in the desert."

"Can I have trifle then?"

"Desert, not dessert."

"You've had—"

"Were you wearing your sun hat?"

"Yes."

"Like now?"

"I always wear it."

Georgina arched an eyebrow.

"Apart from this one, single time when I left it in the Smoking Room."

"So, it's in the Smoking Room?"

"Or my cabin."

"Charlotte, when you were misbehaving, who saw you?"

"No-one."

"Captain Caruthers was standing on the deck watching."

"He was not," Charlotte said, but she shifted uncomfortably. "He won't tell on me, will he?"

"Won't tell? Charlotte, I'm the Investigating Officer. He doesn't need to tell on you, because I already know."

"That's all right then."

"No, it's not."

A fork clattered to the floor. "Lot-lot," said Pippa.

"Ahh, Pippa," said Charlotte. She leant down and whisked the little one up onto her knee.

Pippa's hand went straight out to pull at Charlotte's blonde hair.

"Oi, Pippa."

"Lot-lot."

Charlotte bounced Pippa up and down to make her giggle. At least one member of the family was always pleased to see her and didn't tell her off. "Auntie Lottie will teach you how to shoot."

"No, Auntie Lottie won't," said Georgina.

"And we'll join the army."

"No, you won't."

"The Women's Auxiliary Fusiliers."

"There's no such thing."

"Spoilsport."

"When did you last see Mister Rake?"

"Breakfast."

"Did you talk to him?"

"No, he was at the other end."

"When did you last talk to him?"

"At Tanis, before we boarded, when he... sort of... you know... fell down."

Charlotte giggled and Georgina found herself smirking. "Charlotte, don't make fun of the deceased."

"I'm not, but he was... like a Lord."

"He had been drinking with Mrs Albright, I remember."

"Yes, and he interrupted when Captain Caruthers and that Arab were about to fight."

"Haroun al Rachid? That horrible man with the scarred face? I'm not surprised. I had the impression that he was mentally disrobing all the young ladies."

"Do you think he was clever enough to cope with all the stupid buttons, stays, catches, fastenings and clips?" Charlotte said. "Anyway, I didn't mean him. I meant Mister Jutty."

"Mister *Djehuti* and the Captain were going to fight? I'm sure not. What would they have to fight over?"

"I don't know, I couldn't hear."

"Were you spying on them?"

"No, just taking a walk."

"What did you think of Mister Djehuti?"

"He wasn't an officer."

"Don't tell me what he wasn't. What did you think of him?"

"But he wasn't... I don't know."

"Go on. What happened?"

"Well, Mister Rake slipped on the grass. It was wet. They'd been watering it. That's the only way that the British Residence there looks so green amongst all the sand."

"It did look like an oasis."

"Yes, so he arrived, said something like he was there to arbitrate for the arbitrator, and then fell over. The Captain and the Egyptian took him to an hotel."

"There, see. Captain Caruthers and Mister Djehuti couldn't have been about to fight if they helped one another with poor Mister Rake."

"They were, then they weren't."

"So, Mister Rake stayed in Mister Djehuti's room?"

"He had a suite."

"And then what happened?"

"Captain Caruthers wanted to see the cargo loaded on the SS *Karnak*, so we watched that and then we went back to our hotel. Then someone insisted I go to bed."

"It was for your own good. It was jolly late."

Charlotte made a face.

"So, summing up," said Georgina checking her notes, "when Mister Rake was killed, you were on the port side clambering about?"

"Yes."

"Did you see anyone else?"

"...no."

"What do you mean '...no'?"

"I didn't *see* anyone else."

"But?"

"I heard them."

"Who?"

"Guess."

"Lottie!"

"Lot-lot," said Pippa.

"Yes," Charlotte said, teasing Pippa. "Auntie Lot-lot."

"Don't teach her baby language."

"She taught me."

"Lottie, who did you hear?"

"Apart from Ness lecturing me about wearing my sunhat and keeping away from men, and not to buy any treasure maps, and–"

"Lottie!"

"I heard Sir Archibald and Monsieur Jacques talking. And then Mister Rake and Monsieur Jacques."

"What were they talking about?"

"A book. Monsieur Jacques wanted to buy it."

"What was it?"

"I don't know, but they were talking guineas."

Charlotte made faces at Pippa, while Georgina scratched an entry in her notebook.

Her niece laughed.

Charlotte made noises.

Pippa giggled.

Georgina tutted.

There had been a murder, an exciting murder, and somehow Georgina had made the whole thing nothing more than a tedious test.

"Can I go now?"

"Yes, please send... whoever's next."

"Can I stay and listen?"

"No."

"Why not? I can't cheat. I've given my answers."

"Lottie."

CHAPTER IV

Miss Deering-Dolittle

"Left or right," Sir Archibald said, "which do you think?"

There were always choices.

The waiter was hovering to take her order, for example.

"Lemonade, thank you," Earnestine said.

The Egyptian waiter bowed and then continued around the room.

"Gin and Tonic," Mrs Albright said.

"Good for malaria," Colonel Fitzwilliam said. "I'll have another brandy."

Once Charlotte had gone to be interviewed, the men decided that it was acceptable to talk if they didn't mention the actual murder. Whoever was the culprit – she glanced around the room again – they shouldn't be allowed to cheat and modify their story. No-one had confirmed this thought out loud; it was merely a tacit agreement.

Monsieur Jacques and Pandit Singh Maçon started a game of chess.

"Once round the deck, I think," said Captain Caruthers. "Anyone... Colonel?"

"I'll sit this one out," the Colonel replied.

"Miss Deering-Dolittle?"

"C'est dangerous," said Monsieur Jacques, "we should stay together."

"Or in twos," Mrs Albright said.

"Not if you are with the murderer," the Colonel said.

"Oh my!"

"In threes perhaps."

Earnestine checked the room; eight, so they couldn't manage threes until Charlotte came back.

"I'll risk it," said Caruthers. "Miss?"

She edged her seat back in readiness to rise. "Captain... I'll–"

Her lemonade arrived on a silver tray.

"Thank you," she said. "Captain, is it something important?"

"No, nothing," Caruthers replied.

It chafed, just sitting here doing nothing. Opportunities for young ladies never just presented themselves.

Georgina would be diligent, but she was clearly going to need help in her capacity as the Investigating Officer. Obviously, Earnestine couldn't assist openly, but if, say, one was to, for example, discover something of use and report that fact, then Georgina would only be too pleased to have the benefit of her elder sister's wisdom.

There were basically three groups.

Charlotte returned, bright and cheerful, and interrupted Earnestine's train of thought as she plonked herself down on the chair.

"May I have a lemonade too?" she said. "Thirsty work answering questions."

Four groups, Earnestine realised: Expeditionary, Military, Foreign and the Derring-Do Club. (Earnestine chided herself – she mustn't let the foolish name Charlotte had coined become common currency.)

And she must be careful not to tar each member of each group with the same brush. For example, Monsieur Jacques was a very different sort of foreigner to Doctor Timon and Pandit Singh Maçon.

Monsieur Jacques (white) lost another pawn to Pandit Singh Maçon (black).

Logically, Georgina would concentrate her investigations on the foreigners. They had some strange ideas, after all. So, to take up the slack, Earnestine thought she could investigate the expeditionary contingent.

Sir Archibald Reevers was still droning on about royal tombs in Egypt.

"At the end," Sir Archibald repeated, "is it to the left or the right?"

Earnestine sipped her lemonade.

Charlotte took a glass from the waiter and just guzzled it down – please, don't let her burp. The child should mind her P's and Q's.

There were rules after all. Etiquette. One drove a carriage on the left-hand side of the road. One passed the port to the left. One always stood on the man's left. As was right and proper. She knew that.

"To the right," she answered.

She knew it because that was how she had been brought up. It was how society worked. How the British Empire had civilised the world, even this desolate land, and how mankind made progress.

"Ah, my dear, there you are wrong. Upon entering and going down the passage, you turn to the left to enter the tomb itself."

"If one is a man," Earnestine said. "I am a woman."

"Ah, I stand corrected," Sir Archibald admitted. "Left, if it is a Pharaoh, but right for a Pharaoh's wife."

As if she didn't know this already! There were books for goodness sake. There were libraries everywhere in England solidly built with cornerstones, declaring which entrepreneur-turned-philanthropist was responsible for the education of the populace of a particular parish.

"You see, my dear," Sir Archibald said.

"Yes," Earnestine replied, "a woman is always right."

Charlotte giggled.

Earnestine allowed herself a thin smile.

"Exactly, my dear."

"Isn't that the wrong way round," Mrs Albright said. "A lady is always upon the gentleman's left."

"One imagines," Earnestine explained, "that the arrangement is such that when they leave in the afterlife, they meet again in the main passageway in the proper arrangement."

"Why yes, of course," Mrs Albright said. "To save time. You wouldn't want to waste a single second of eternity."

"Quite."

Just then, Farouk entered, taking off his fez. "Ladies, Gentlemen. Mrs Merryweather is ready for the next person."

"Damned waste of time," said Sir Archibald.

"Perhaps, ladies first," said Captain Caruthers. "Mrs Albright?"

"Why thank you kindly," said Mrs Albright. "But I feel a head coming on. I shall pass."

"You will have to answer questions eventually."

Mrs Albright struggled out of her chair, straightened her pearls and untangled her glasses, collected her walking stick and then headed for the door. "Later, later," she said.

Earnestine realised that she was the last of the 'ladies first', so she'd be next.

"While the ladies gather their strength after such a shock, perhaps I should be next," said Doctor Timon.

"Why you?" Caruthers asked.

"I have nothing to hide," said Doctor Timon. "And I did examine the body."

"In that case, be my guest," said Caruthers, standing aside from the door.

"If you'll excuse me, ladies," Doctor Timon said bowing to Earnestine and Charlotte before he made his way out.

"Odd that he goes before a woman," said Caruthers.

"Foreign," said Colonel Fitzwilliam and then, seeing others in the room, he added, "No offence. Should know the proper form, women first and on the left and all that."

"But why can't a woman stand on the right?" Charlotte asked. "I know that the shield protects the man on the left, and so on down the line, and that the strongest warrior must hold the right. But why can't a woman hold the right?"

Sir Archibald smiled benevolently. "When you grow up, little one, you'll understand."

"I am gro... the man on the right has more fun," Charlotte said. "He gets to wield the sword or the gladius or the xiphos."

"You are knowledgeable, child."

"And so stab straight into the enemy's abdomen spilling his guts all over–"

"Charlotte!" Earnestine followed this up by tightening her jaw and giving Charlotte a stare.

"Come on, Lottie," said Captain Caruthers, holding the door open, "once around the deck before I help the Colonel back to his cabin."

"But–"

"Have I told you about Uttar Pradesh?"

"Yes," said Charlotte, "but I wouldn't mind hearing about the medals again."

Captain Caruthers laughed at this. "There's more to it than medals."

"I know," said Charlotte, ducking under the Captain's arm. "There's the fighting first."

Earnestine's hand went to the left side of her face to touch the wretched scar Charlotte had given her. For a moment, she remembered al Rachid, the unpleasant Egyptian she'd met in Tanis with a face covered in scars. And there had been that jolly nice Mister Djehuti – she smiled – he'd been handsome and knowledgeable, and quite the conversationalist.

The Captain was looking at her strangely, still holding the door even though Charlotte had gone through. Past them, Earnestine could see down the tiny passageway to the T-junction. It went left and right, port or starboard, like an Egyptian tomb. Straight ahead was the door of the Library. It was closed, padlocked with a new clasp. She'd sat here and kept watch on the door after Mister Rake's murder. Doctor Timon had guarded it, handing the task to Monsieur Jacques when he had arrived. She'd had a clear view. No-one had gone in. Mister Rake, given the obvious injury, had not come out, of course.

The Captain and Charlotte left, stepping out into the sunshine.

The door slammed shut.

Their shadows moved past the windows of the Smoking Room.

Charlotte had forgotten her sun hat again.

Colonel Fitzwilliam settled in his chair. From experience, Earnestine knew he'd soon be asleep.

"I resign," Monsieur Jacques said. "Bien joué."

Pandit Singh Maçon began to tidy the chess pieces away. "Thank you for the game."

Monsieur Jacques picked up a copy of *Le Figaro*, which was weeks old now, and leafed through the pages.

Now or never, Earnestine thought.

"Sir Archibald," she said. "I'm very sorry for your loss."

"Quite, my dear."

"One was wondering... idly..." Oh, this was terrible, absolutely no way to broach the subject.

"Yes, my dear?"

"What precisely you were searching for here, or near, or perhaps slightly further afield, of the Suez Canal?"

"I'm not searching for anything."

"Sir Archibald?"

"Nothing at all."

Monsieur Jacques smirked.

Obviously, the Frenchmen knew all about whatever it was that the President of the Royal Expeditionary Society was secretly doing. Whereas, someone who subscribed to the Society's monthly pamphlet, and attended those public meetings which tolerated the presence of women, was being kept in the dark.

It was vexing.

She wanted to spit, and stamp her feet, and generally act like Charlotte.

"Of course, a holiday then?"

"Yes, my dear."

Stuff and nonsense!

The President of the Royal Expeditionary Society had travelled nearly 4,000 miles by hansom, ferry, three trains, steamship, litter and paddle steamer in order to cruise along a modern *canal*, a mere fifty miles from the Nile river.

All that history; all those pharaohs, tombs, embalming, mummification, rituals and curses – ignored.

All those myths; all the way back through the Age of the Gods to the creation of the world in 28,000 BC (if one believed Eusebius in his Chronicle and did the arithmetic); Isis resurrecting Osiris, Horus defeating Set, Thoth gambling with the moon for five more days in the year – all ignored.

Gosh, Earnestine realised, today was the second of those five extra days, the intercalary 'month' that kept the ancient calendar synchronised to the motion of the sun just like the Georgian calendar's leap year. The Egyptian New Year would be next week, Tuesday, 11th September. She should probably do something special to celebrate given that she was actually in Egypt. When in Rome and all that.

It was all so fascinating.

And so disregarded, just as they'd ignored Alexandria, the Valley of the Kings, Thebes, Cairo, Luxor, the Pyramids, Karnak... and... and everything in order to travel along the endless dribble of water surrounded by absolutely nothing!

She wanted to explore, to visit far-off lands, have exciting sightseeings, and make a name for herself, but she knew that she had no control of her destiny. Her family, the Deering-Dolittles, were famous, or perhaps infamous, for going up the wrong river. Her father and uncle, then her mother, and how she yearned to rescue them.

Now, here she was going up the wrong river.

No! Not even a river, but a canal.

She needed a man in this world, a man to take charge and do what she wanted him to do.

"Are you all right, my dear?"

"Of course, Sir Archibald."

Earnestine was being dragged along the canal because they were going to India on account of Georgina. Her late husband, Captain Merryweather, had financial affairs that required sorting out and, by chance, Colonel Fitzwilliam and Captain Caruthers could do with visiting the Raj. The Captain's 'just popping over' sounded decidedly unlikely; however, the matter at hand was Sir Archibald.

Sir Archibald had had the choice.

One didn't take a canal holiday in Birmingham when one could go boating through Stratford-upon-Avon.

One didn't punt around Manchester's canal if one could take a gondola around Venice.

One didn't go to Suez in preference to taking a voyage past all the sites of Ancient Egypt. They could easily have gone as far as, say, the first cataract at Aswan and explored all those extraordinary places that she'd read and read about, but never seen.

The Suez canal, perhaps, if one was a member of the Canal & Waterways Hobbyists Club, but not if one was the President of the Royal Expeditionary Society.

One didn't. One just didn't.

"My dear, do you need some air? Another lemonade?"

"One's fine, thank you."

Pandit Singh Maçon interrupted, "If you'll excuse me, I shall retire to my cabin."

Monsieur Jacques agreed, "Oui, this heat."

The two men made their way out, leaving only three of them in the Smoking Room.

The Colonel snored.

"Knowledge, Sir Archibald, is all I want," Earnestine said, and she leant forward to generate an air of conspiratorial confidence. "What is it that you are looking for?"

"I can rely upon your discretion?"

"Of course."

He glanced left and right as if checking the passages of a Royal tomb before he leant forward too.

This was it. Finally, she was being taken seriously. She'd be a proper explorer, rather than some inferior-gendered dreamer.

"My dear," Sir Archibald confided. "I am searching for the Garden of Eden."

Mrs Merryweather

"Doctor, please," Georgina said, indicating the chair opposite. "Could you explain in your own words what happened?"

"Certainly," Doctor Timon said. He took his round glasses off, polished them carefully before he replaced them in front of his hypnotic eyes. "I was in the Smoking Room, reading. I heard a shot and rushed to see what had happened. The door to the Library was locked. Pandit Singh Maçon and Monsieur Jacques broke it down. It was not strong. Once it was fully open, I saw at once that Mister Rake was dead. Shot. I am sorry, but that was the case."

"That's all right, please continue."

"I kept everyone away. There were ladies present."

"That was most commendable. And Mister Rake?"

"Quite dead. I took his pulse. It was not necessary, but I did so out of habit, you understand. I am a Doctor. I have taken the oath to save lives. The others saw me do this."

"Others?"

"The Deering-Dolittle sisters, Monsieur Jacques, the Albright woman... everyone."

"And then?"

"Colonel Fitzwilliam and his Captain, Caruthers, took charge. The ship's skipper was informed. We sent for Farouk. When everyone was gathered, yourself included, Miss Deering-Dolittle accused us all of being murderers and Captain Caruthers suggested you as the Officer of Investigation."

"Everyone was there?"

"Eventually."

"I meant when the body was found."

"My concern was for Mister Rake, and the passageway was cramped, but I remember Monsieur Jacques, Sir Archibald, Mrs Albright, Miss Deering-Dolittle, Miss Charlotte... the others were probably behind them."

"And Captain Caruthers?"

"No... I think he came in later."

Georgina consulted her notes: "Pandit Singh Maçon?"

"The same."

"And Colonel Fitzwilliam?"

"He was in the Smoking Room."

Georgina tapped her notes with her pen making a tiny spidery shape.

"I'm sorry I can't be of more help."

"You have been most helpful," Georgina said. "What did you think of Mister Rake?"

"I hardly knew the man."

"But we all attended the formal dinner in Tanis, so you must have gained some impression."

"He was fastidious, obviously loyal to his employer, Sir Archibald Reevers. He was his secretary."

"Did you have any conversations?"

"Nothing beyond pass the salt, milk, honey and so forth at breakfast."

"And in Tanis?"

"We discussed the journey and the weather, he was English so that goes without saying, and he asked about my patients – confidential I'm afraid, so I couldn't talk about that – and he talked about Sir Archibald's research."

"Anything specific?"

"Digs in Central America."

"Do you have a gun?"

"Absolutely not. I am a man of medicine. I am here to save lives."

"I meant no offence."

"Will that be all?"

"For the time being."

"Very well, good day, Mrs Merryweather," the Doctor said before he bowed formally and left.

Farouk, who had been lingering outside, reappeared.

"Madam?"

"What did you think of Mister Rake, Farouk?"

"Wonderful man, quite important, not as much as Sir Archibald of the Royal Expeditionary Society."

"Did you play chess against him?"

"Shah Mat? He did not ask me."

"Shah Mat?"

"It is the Persian name for chess," said Farouk explained. "It means 'the King is helpless'."

"Were you involved in any of Sir Archibald's previous expeditions?"

"Oh no, no, alas, my cousin, Fadil, he went. Valley of the Kings, Karnak, Abydos. He showed the Sir plenty of pyramids, tombs and temples – very good Guide. They found many mummies."

"Strange that Mister Rake did not mention that to Doctor Timon," Georgina mused. "Sir Archibald is famous for his Egyptian research and yet Mister Rake only talked about Central America. He has, I think, looked into the Incas and the Aztec pyramids."

"Ah yes," said Farouk, "but those are only stepped pyramids. Egypt has the proper pyramids."

"So I've heard."

"Madam, if I might ask, why are you here?"

"My late husband had business in India and the Colonel and the Captain kindly came along to keep us company. There were matters for them too, they said."

"My apologies."

"That's fine, Mister... Farouk. Could you bring in the next witness please?"

"With pleasure, Madam."

Farouk nodded, desperate to please, and then hurried off.

Why, thought Georgina, did her explanation to Farouk sound so hollow? Did she really need to go to India? She had felt somewhat persuaded, believing that the Derring-Do Club should be prudent after that business in Plymouth. But, she wondered, if there had been more to it.

And now there had been a murder.

Were they connected?

She checked on Pippa. She was lying amongst some blankets flat on her back, her tiny arms quivering ever so slightly as she breathed. She had Arthur's hair colour, brown or blonde, she was never sure, rather than her own dark locks.

"Mrs Merryweather."

It was Sir Archibald Reevers, President of the Royal Expeditionary Society.

"Sir Archibald, if you'd be so kind."

They sat opposite one another.

"Could you tell me where you were when the shot was fired?"

"You can't suspect me."

"No... I mean, I must ask the question."

"Perhaps I can save you the trouble," Sir Archibald said with a wonderful veneer of patience. "It wasn't me, so you can cross me off your list and get on."

"Sir Archibald, for form's sake if nothing else."

"Oh, very well," Sir Archibald said. "I was on deck looking for that wretched man Rake... I mean, looking for Mister Rake."

"Which side?"

"Side?"

"Of the boat."

"Port. I heard the shot and ran to the Library. Not exactly ran, as there were others in the way, and not exactly the Library, just in the general direction."

"I understand."

"When I got there, Doctor Timon and Pandit Singh Maçon had opened the door. Doctor Timon held everyone back, but I saw into the room, the dead body, the blood splattered on the wall and all that. Dreadful. Quite appalling. Sorry, I shouldn't have said."

"It's quite all right telling me the details," Georgina said. "Please continue."

"Timon sent everyone back to the Smoking Room. I poured a glass of sherry for Miss Deering-Dolittle, who is a fine woman, fine woman – does she do shorthand?"

"Yes, I think so. Sir Isaac Pitman's system."

"Fine woman... and then a whisky for myself."

"Was everyone there?"

"Captain Caruthers joined us later, along with that Frenchman, Monsieur Jacques."

"And then?"

"Farouk fetched the Egyptian wallahs, you arrived, Miss Deering-Dolittle generally got things on track. We weren't sure of the hierarchy. I'm a Knight of the Realm, but perhaps this comes under military jurisdiction, and so that would be the Colonel, but he has a war wound, you understand, and so the Captain might have stood in."

"Yes."

"And there were medical considerations, so Doctor Timon was in charge of that. Eileen... I mean Mrs Albright took quite a turn. Shock. It affects those afflicted by the spirits, or so she tells me."

"Why are you here?"

"Farouk came to fetch me."

"In Egypt?"

"Oh, fine country, lots of history, and it was about time I ventured forth. It's been a long time since my last expedition."

"Where was that to?"

"Egypt."

"Valley of the Kings, Abydos, Karnak?"

"And so forth, my dear."

"Do you remember Fadil?"

"Fadil... Fadil... not a mummy I'm aware of. I've tended to specialise in royalty and high priests."

"He was your Guide on your previous Egyptian expeditions."

"Oh, Fadil, yes."

"He's Farouk's cousin."

Sir Archibald swivelled round in his chair to look at the door as if to see the Guide standing there. "Is he, now? Is he? How coincidental."

"Are you here on an expedition?"

Sir Archibald turned back to face her. "Absolutely not, whatever gave you that idea? No, no."

"Why aren't you exploring the Valley of the Kings?"

"There was nothing to discover there. Salt's man, Belzoni, declared as much eighty years ago. There might be one or two trifles left. My research uncovered a route to a possible gateway to King Solomon's mines. This is fascinating because many believe that–"

"Thank you, Sir Archibald, but perhaps we could stick to the matter in hand."

"Of course, Mrs Merryweather."

"Do you own a gun?"

"Yes."

"Where is it?"

"In a box amongst my things."

"Whereabouts?"

"I don't know, you'll have to ask Rake... ah, in his room somewhere."

"What can you tell me about Mister Rake?"

"Sebastian... Merchant Taylors, not Oxbridge. Gleneagles, I think. I've known him... oh, seven or eight years. He's been my personal secretary for five. Excellent chap. He's risen as far as he can without the right connections. Except..."

"Except?"

"Recently he asked for a raise. Imagine. I'm not made of money. The allocation of funds from the Society has to go through a committee. It isn't the behaviour of a gentleman to ask."

"Quite."

"Hardly a motive for murder," Sir Archibald insisted.

"More a motive for him to murder you."

"Nonsense, he'd have to seek a situation elsewhere."

"Yes, of course. That will be all. Thank you."

Once Sir Archibald had left, Georgina checked her notes and made one or two additions. It was confusing. She could imagine them all coming to the narrow corridor by the Library, no-one really sure of who was there and who wasn't, and then they discovered the body.

Pandit Singh Maçon was next in turn.

The Indian sat bolt upright, formal and attentive. The jewel in the front of his turban caught the light and twinkled, but his eyes were dark, giving nothing away.

"Pandit... that's like 'reverend', isn't it?"

"Indeed, you are well informed."

"Well, could you tell me what happened when Mister Rake was killed?"

"I was reading in the Smoking Room, along with the Colonel."

"He could verify this?"

"I'm afraid the Colonel was sleeping."

"Please continue."

"There were two shots, quite distinctive. One quiet, much earlier, which I didn't consider a shot until the second one, which was loud. I went to investigate and Doctor Timon was trying to get into the Library. The door was locked, so naturally, I tried to assist. Its construction was strong, so I went to collect a crowbar."

"Crowbar?"

"I returned with a fire axe."

"I didn't realise that the door was smashed down."

"It wasn't," Pandit Singh Maçon assured her. "We used it as a lever."

"Who was there?"

"By this time, there was the Doctor, Colonel Fitzwilliam... he took the American woman, Mrs Albright, into the Smoking Room."

"I see," said Georgina as she made notes. "And then?"

"Then we forced the door."

"Could someone have hidden behind it?"

"No, it opened fully and banged against the wall."

"Did you go inside?"

"No, Doctor Timon went in to check the man's pulse, but he was clearly dead. I could see this from the door. The blood was quite plain to observe."

"I see."

"There was nothing that could have been done. Doctor Timon suggested that we move to the Smoking Room. Farouk, the Egyptian Guide, was called for and he informed the Skipper."

"Was the room disturbed at all?"

"No, Doctor Timon was careful to ensure that the door remained closed until the Skipper and the First Mate arrived. He stayed on duty and was joined by the Englishman, Caruthers, and the Frenchman, Jacques."

"Did they arrive together?"

"I'm afraid I didn't see. I was by this time in the Smoking Room. Once the crew had taken control of the situation, Doctor Timon came into the Smoking Room too. You came in some time later."

"Yes."

"That is all I can say."

"Did you know Mister Rake?"

"Not particularly. I met him in Tanis. He seemed organised and a decent fellow."

"Didn't you play chess with him?"

"I played chess with most of the men in the hotel."

"Not the women?"

"I imagined you couldn't play chess."

"I can."

"But not well," Pandit Singh Maçon said. "A woman's mind tends to wander and I prefer a challenging game."

"Oh."

"Women's thought patterns have their uses."

"Thank you."

"You were saying?"

"Yes. Did you play chess against Mister Rake?"

"Three times, and then he suggested best of seven, but the dinner gong sounded."

"Then you did have a conversation."

"We concentrated on the game. Sicilian Defence, if you know what I mean, and he was devious, often trying to hide a wider strategy in apparently simple moves. He had a tendency for distraction tactics."

"Distraction tactics?"

"He'd call for a drink, or start a conversation with someone else, when I was trying to make a move."

"Yes, I know what you mean," Georgina replied. "Do you own a gun?"

"No."

"But Egypt can be dangerous."

"Anywhere can be dangerous, even London, I believe."

"But you don't carry a gun."

Pandit Singh Maçon flicked his walking stick up, touched the handle and slid out the first few inches of a long steel blade. "I carry my gupti."

"Do you know how to use a gun?"

"I'd look to those English officers, Fitzwilliam and Caruthers. They are trained to use guns and they're not afraid of killing. They've served in Africa and India, most likely massacred thousands."

"No doubt," Georgina said. "Why are you here in Egypt?"

"Would you like a drink, Mrs Merryweather?"

"I'm fine, thank you. Why are you in Egypt?"

"I am travelling to India."

"So are we."

"Then perhaps we will see one another again."

"I look forward to it. Thank you."

The Pandit stood, bowed and made his way out.

As Georgina checked her notes, it struck her that they were rather like describing a chess game. Perhaps she should devise a system of notation.

The Colonel was having difficulty with his war wound, so Georgina went to see him. The crew wanted to prepare the Dining Room for a delayed luncheon anyway. They laid out a buffet of cold meats and hummus with flatbread and a soup. There was already a queue outside of those she'd already interviewed.

Georgina was glad to stretch her legs, no matter how briefly, during the short walk from the Dining Room to the Smoking Room. She took Pippa.

"Ah, Mrs Merryweather... Pippa, Pippa," the Colonel said.

Pippa reached out to yank his whiskers.

Sir Archibald was also present.

"Excuse me," said Georgina, trying to control her child, "could we have some privacy, please, Sir Archibald?"

"Of course," Sir Archibald replied. "I need to have a word with Mrs Albright anyway."

Georgina waited until Sir Archibald had left.

"So, Colonel," she said, "when I left the Smoking Room this morning, before the murder, there was yourself, the Pandit, Monsieur Jacques and poor Mister Rake."

"Was there?"

"Yes, and after I'd left, what happened?"

"Dashed if I know, my dear."

"Well, did you leave the Smoking Room at all?"

"No," Colonel Fitzwilliam explained. "I stayed here. My foot, you understand, jolly painful in this heat."

"I'm so sorry."

"Can't be helped. I had a spot of brandy to numb the pain."

"And what did you all talk about?"

"No idea, I'm afraid."

"Did you fall asleep?"

"Heavens no... might have dozed a bit."

"And... when you stopped dozing."

"Everyone had gone."

"So – Pippa, please – no-one can vouch for your presence?"

"And I can't vouch for theirs."

"So... er..."

"There was a bang! Quite woke me up."

"A bang? The gunshot."

"No, don't think so. That came later."

"So, a bang, then a gunshot."

"That's the ticket. Perhaps five minutes later. People came running. Doctor Timon. Others. All gathered around the corner in the passageway, but I couldn't see, I'm afraid. When I got there, I helped Mrs Albright back here. Then they all came in here, quite shocked, and apparently, Mister Rake had been sort of shot."

"And then?"

"We all had a conversation and Caruthers put you in charge," concluded the Colonel. "My dear, how are you finding it?"

"Perplexing."

"It's that locked door business."

"Yes."

"That Indian, Singh Maçon is a Pandit – that's a priest. You know what these eastern mystics are like. They have special powers. I've seen men float, move things with their minds, climbs ropes and simply disappear. They can walk through walls. Kill a man with a single touch of their index finger. Appear before you even though they are a hundred miles away."

"You think he killed Mister Rake?"

"A locked door, or a solid wall, means nothing to his kind. He probably went to the hold directly below the Library, brought a rope up out of a wicker basket and climbed up it like a monkey straight through the ceiling."

"If he can kill people with a single touch, then why would he use a gun?"

"That's Indians for you, perverse bunch."

"Still, he says he doesn't have a gun, just a sword," Georgina said.

"Doctors know how to kill people."

"Yes, Doctor Timon would know about drugs and potions, but not guns."

"What about that American? They shoot anything that moves. Always killing each other. The Wild West was just one long shootout."

"But Mrs Albright is a woman."

"Just like Annie Oakley, Calamity Jane, Lillian Smith and all the others."

Georgina remembered what Pandit Singh Maçon had said. "Colonel, do you have a revolver?"

"Of course. What are you suggesting?"

"Colonel, please."

The Colonel sighed and handed over his sidearm. Georgina examined it and then put it to her nose. It smelt of mothballs and brandy, but there was no ghastly explosive odour.

"You're checking for cordite?"

"Yes, 'cordite', is that what it is?"

"It hasn't been fired recently."

Georgina nodded.

"You should check the ammunition too," the Colonel said. "Here. Here."

He reached over and showed Georgina how to open the top break.

"All the cartridges," the Colonel explained. "And each has a bullet on the end."

"Unless you reloaded."

"It would still smell of cordite."

Satisfied, Georgina returned the weapon to its owner and wiped her hands on a napkin.

"What did you think of Mister Rake?" she asked.

"Didn't drink. Queer chap."

"Did you talk to him much?"

"'Fraid not."

"At Tanis?"

"Not at my table and then he didn't come to the bar. Not that I ever wanted to see him again."

"Again?"

"He was a civil servant in India," Colonel Fitzwilliam said. "We knew him. Pen-pusher. Dreadful business. We were in the Punjab, the regiment, tricky situation. The blighters had us cornered. We sent for help to the local garrison, but... it was Rake and he prevaricated. Said afterwards it was out of concern for the soldiers there and he needed to protect the civilians. But it was to save money. Or cowardice. We'd all have liked to have found him in a dark alley."

"We?"

"Dan, Caruthers, Merry, McKendry, Williams and Stocky, even Tregellian and pretty much everyone in the Officers' Mess."

"Really?"

"Then. Not now. Water under the bridge and all that."

"You didn't bear him any ill will?"

"Oh, ill will, yes, but nothing more."

"And the others?"

"Shouldn't think so."

"Captain Caruthers?"

Colonel Fitzwilliam paused... "Long time ago."

"Thank you."

"All jolly awkward. No hard feelings. How are you finding it, my dear?"

"Still perplexing."

"I'm sure you'll figure it out."

Miss Charlotte

"So, erm..." Charlotte began.

"Charlotte."

She smiled and kicked her feet out as she walked. Captain Caruthers was a good chap, although somewhat reticent to tell her about his battles.

They reached the end of the port deck and turned into the sunshine. Charlotte squinted and held her hand up to shield her eyes.

"Where's your parasol?" Caruthers asked.

"Oh, it's..."

"In your cabin?"

Charlotte nodded.

So, the Captain turned again to go forward along the port side. The paddles at the side of the boat churned away, propelling them forwards. The desert passed gently on either side, surreal because it appeared unchanging and so they seemed stuck like some ship in a bottle.

"Why are you here?" she asked.

"To keep you company."

"No... going to India?"

"A few things to sort out."

"Can I help?"

"Of course."

"Can I have a gun then?"

"Lottie, it's not that sort of thing."

But what sort of thing was it? Charlotte wondered.

After the dinner at Tanis, when they'd walked to the docks, she'd seen all the cargo being loaded onto the SS *Karnak*. Boring luggage and archaeology stuff mostly, but Captain Caruthers had supervised something that hadn't been trusted to the locals. He'd preferred staff from the Consulate. She'd heard of the diplomatic bag, but never the diplomatic crate. What on Earth could it be?

"And what did you load onto the ship?"

"Nothing."

"Nothing?"

"Nothing at all."

"Except a crate."

"It's nothing, Lottie, nothing."

They passed over the paddles. It was hotter on the other side without the cooling moisture flicked up from the wheels.

"I think we've walked enough, Lottie," Caruthers said.

"But I'm fine."

"The sunlight can kill the unwary, particularly someone of your complexion. I've seen men, strong men, driven mad by the heat."

"Was that in India?"

"Yes."

"During a battle?"

"Lottie."

They came back into the Smoking Room; there was only the Colonel there.

"You just missed Mrs Merryweather," the Colonel said. "She's gone to put Philippa to bed."

"Come on, Fitz," Caruthers said. "Once round the deck."

"Already?"

Caruthers made a show of checking his pocket watch. "Already."

"Well, help me up and find my blasted stick."

Caruthers bent over to assist the poor Colonel out of his chair. His wound bothered him greatly, his foot all bandaged, and he winced, bearing it well. Charlotte found his stick leaning against the back of his chair. It was a good stout length topped with a silver handle. She passed it to the Colonel, who smiled, and then limped as he put weight on his foot.

"I can manage," Colonel Fitzwilliam said, swatting the Captain's hand aside before hobbling to the door. "It's this wretched heat."

The Captain shook his head.

"So," Charlotte said, knowing it was her last chance, "what's this crate?"

"It's just a tank, a water tank."

"And in the tank?"

"Just something that will make a difference."

"Ha, difference!" Colonel Fitzwilliam guffawed. "Very droll."

"You stay here, Lottie."

Charlotte stayed put, found her sunhat (stupid thing) and her steamport novel. Her bookmark was missing, so she had to flick back and forth to find her place – the foreign Aristocrat Lucio was about to give Mister Tempest advice about his inheritance.

The hairs on the back of her neck seemed to prickle. She looked up and saw Sir Archibald and Mrs Albright staring at her as if she had done something wrong. She'd not noticed them come in.

"The Captain said to stay here," Charlotte said.

"Then sit and don't make any noise," Mrs Albright commanded.

Charlotte made a face after she'd carefully turned away from Mrs Albright.

There was silence for a while.

A murder, imagine, just there in the Library – exciting.

And this crate – mysterious.

And–

"Are you still reading that vile book?" asked Mrs Albright as she snatched the book away. *The Sorrows of Satan* by Marie Corelli dropped to the floor and fell shut. And she'd only just found her place again.

"It's mine."

"And the 'Death'."

"It was a tarot card and I lost–"

"I know what it is," Mrs Albright said. "You are a foolish girl to tempt fate like that. A man has died because of it."

"It wasn't my fault."

"Child, go and fetch my shawl."

"But–"

"At once."

It simply was not fair. Just because Charlotte was shorter than her sisters and younger and looked stupidly girlish with long blonde hair and was forced to wear 'pretty' dresses, everyone thought they could boss her around. She wasn't some child crawling under machines in a satanic mill 'up north' who had to be quick about it; she lived in Kensington and knew all about the military. In the Women's Auxiliary Fusiliers, when she finally persuaded everyone that it was a good idea to have such a fine body of women, she would dispense with all this authoritarian nonsense and live like a proper important officer, then she would be the one giving orders.

"I gave you an instruction, child," Mrs Albright commanded. "I can't go, I need to use a stick."

"Yes, Ma'am, shawl, ma'am."

"And less of your insolence."

Charlotte curtseyed and gave Mrs Albright her best, knowing smile. "Ma'am, yes, Ma'am."

Like everyone's, Mrs Albright's cabin was on the next deck down, so Charlotte skipped over to the railing and vaulted it. Easy as the trees in Professor Chadlock's orchard. She hadn't been scrumping for simply ages.

"Lottie?"

It was Captain Caruthers and the Colonel on the lower deck. Her sudden appearance had taken him by surprise.

"Captain, can't stop, Field Marshal Albright is waiting."

"You be careful."

"I'm always—"

"Lottie."

She found the shawl easily enough.

Why did Mrs Albright want her shawl?

Once the sun was down, then maybe, as it got jolly cold at night, but in the afternoon, it was positively baking.

Oh, what did Charlotte care?

She scampered back up on the outside of the ship – no-one saw – except that the stupid shawl caught on a hook or something, and she had to tug it free.

Captain Caruthers and the Colonel just rounded the bend at the stern as Charlotte reached the window of the Smoking Room.

"...she'll be back in five minutes," Mrs Albright said.

Charlotte smirked; not if you avoid the staircase, she thought.

"I'm not sure, that's all," said the deep voice of Sir Archibald Reevers in reply.

"The High Priest Amenemope will have the answers," Mrs Albright insisted. "We of the Hermetic Order are certain of this."

"But it's not needed. Rake got the book."

Rake? Charlotte leaned closer. Georgina would be pleased she was listening.

"Yes," Mrs Albright said, "but where is it now?"

"He hid it, wretched man."

"And it's only useful if the answers are there."

"There's some translation required, I imagine, but I assure you that the instructions are quite clear. The ancient shrines are like milestones. Rake checked it."

"Well, what was the use of bringing Amenemope all this way, if you aren't going to perform the ritual."

"It was a Plan B."

"Amenemope was Plan A, the book is Plan B."

'A' for 'Am-something-moppy', Charlotte thought, 'B' for 'Book'.

"Please, Mrs Albright... fellow illuminated Adeptus Exemptus."

"We will reach the Third Order," Mrs Albright said. "We will commune with the Secret Chiefs."

"Let me translate the book, when we find it, and then we'll see. Can we raise Amenemope?"

"Of that, I have no doubt," Mrs Albright said. "Where is that dratted girl?"

Charlotte almost shouted that she was on her way, but she bit the words back and scampered around to come in through the door.

"Mrs – *ah* – Al – *ha* – bright," she said, pretending to pant, "your shawl."

"I've decided that I don't need it," Mrs Albright said, rather proving Charlotte's opinion that it had been a fool's errand to get her out of the way. "Please return– What's this? This is frayed!"

"It was like that when I found it," Charlotte said instantly.

"Child, you are quite wicked."

Charlotte felt aggrieved; she hadn't done anything to the stupid thing.

"I shall have words with your guardian. Who is it?"

"Earn... I mean, Miss Deering-Dolittle."

"Your sister?"

"Yes."

"No wonder you are such a wayward child."

CHAPTER V

Miss Deering-Dolittle

Earnestine seethed back to her cabin, angered the door open and infuriated with the furniture. When she had done with that, she smouldered in the centre of the room.

And it was so hot!

Sir Archibald had treated her like a child. *There-there*, let me tell you a fairy story, indeed.

She mangled her fingers together and raged until her teeth hurt. She should really calm down.

"I am not going to calm down!"

She leant over her dressing table and took as deep a series of breaths as her corset allowed.

Her journal was open on the page about Tanis. She still hadn't written down those lovely things Mister Djehuti had said and she was beginning to forget them, but she was too vexed to do it now.

Sir Archibald had murdered Mister Rake; it was obvious. Mister Rake had finally broken, unable to stand being kept from all the wonders of the Ancient World, so Sir Archibald, because he was cruel and had employed Mister Rake just to turn down all her applications, had killed his long-suffering secretary. Even if women won the vote, suffrage would never extend to the Royal Expeditionary Society funding a mere young lady like herself.

And now... she had completely lost her thread.

Yes, Sir Archibald had murdered Mister Rake because he was up to something.

The Garden of Eden: *give one strength!*

A youngster still sucking their thumb in Sunday School, having been read the first two chapters of the Bible, knew perfectly well that the Garden of Eden, buried as it probably was under layers and layers of history that required the diligent use of dynamite, trowel and brush to remove, was nowhere near Egypt.

She found her King James' Bible and flicked through *The Book of Genesis* to chapter II, beginning at verse 8.

8 And the LORD God planted a garden eastward in Eden; and there he put the man whom he had formed.

9 And out of the ground made the LORD God to grow every tree that is pleasant to the sight, and good for food; the tree of life also in the midst of the garden, and the tree of knowledge of good and evil.

10 And a river went out of Eden to water the garden; and from thence it was parted, and became into four heads.

11 The name of the first is Pison: that is it which compasseth the whole land of Havilah, where there is gold;

12 And the gold of that land is good: there is bdellium and the onyx stone.

13 And the name of the second river is Gihon: the same is it that compasseth the whole land of Ethiopia.

14 And the name of the third river is Hiddekel: that is it which goeth toward the east of Assyria. And the fourth river is Euphrates.

15 And the LORD God took the man, and put him into the garden of Eden to dress it and to keep it.

16 And the LORD God commanded the man, saying, Of every tree of the garden thou mayest freely eat:

17 But of the tree of the knowledge of good and evil, thou shalt not eat of it: for in the day that thou eatest thereof thou shalt surely die.

There! See! The man couldn't be looking for the Garden of Eden. Anyone was quite capable of reading six verses and working it out. If she only had her proper atlas she could put her finger on exactly where Eden, and its garden to the East, was likely to be, and near the Timsah Lake on the Suez Canal, it was not. This voyage led to the Red Sea, whereas the Tigris and Euphrates flowed into the Persian Gulf. That was the other side of Arabia, for heaven's sake – a good 500 miles away!

So what else could it be?

Troy had been found a few decades ago by consulting the ancient texts.

Atlantis... well, she had her own theory about that.

The Lost Ark of the Covenant... oh, it grated so. They had been in Tanis for that formal dinner – actually in Tanis at the northern end of the Suez Canal – and no-one had gone to the ancient site to look for the Well of Souls.

King Solomon's mines were in the Timna Valley in the Holy Land... probably.

The Holy Grail was hidden in southern France, or possibly Scotland.

The Spear of Destiny?

Confederate gold – she knew where that had gone.

Crystal Skulls?

Excalibur?

She knew that Sir Archibald had loaded two crates onto the SS *Karnak*. They had to be full of trowels and brushes, spades, theodolites and survey poles, labels, boxes with straw padding, dynamite and all the other items that a carefully organised dig needed. If she had just the merest glance, she'd know what Sir Archibald expected to find.

So, a short walk around the deck and then, perhaps, a jaunt to the hold. She grabbed her small kit bag.

As she came out of her cabin, she saw Mrs Albright opening her door further along. She had her back to Earnestine... just go around the other way and–

"Miss Deering-Dolittle?"

She'd been seen.

Mrs Albright waved her stick aloft in greeting.

Earnestine grimaced, "Mrs Albright."

"I'm just returning my shawl. That dratted girl has damaged it."

Earnestine did not need to ask which dratted girl. "I'm so sorry."

"She stormed off – quite rudely – when I was giving her a piece of my mind."

"Oh dear."

"She should be taken in hand."

"We try."

Earnestine had to wait while Mrs Albright threw her shawl into her cabin.

"You are a woman of some standing."

"Hardly."

"An independent spirit, though," Mrs Albright said. "Unmarried at what, twenty-five?"

"I'm twenty-one."

"Not quite the spinster I'd imagined."

"Quite."

"Have you ever been asked?"

Earnestine touched the side of her face, her hand betraying her. There was that dreadful scar down the side of her cheek that no amount of hair straightening ever quite veiled properly. "I have," she replied.

"I see," said Mrs Albright, "but they never came up to the mark?"

"Quite the contrary," Earnestine said, remembering the fine, young and handsome, regal bearing of her first burning desire. "He was a Prince."

"They always seem like a prince at first and then come the disappointments," said Mrs Albright. "Take it from me, I've been married six times."

"Six?"

"Not at the same time."

"Quite."

"I am going upstairs to be interviewed by your sister."

"Georgina, yes."

"I hope she won't be too long."

"I'm sure she'll be direct and to the point."

"I've been quite affected by this whole business."

"It's upsetting."

"The spirits are a great comfort."

"I'm sure."

"My Spirit Guide is Atis, the High Priest of Atlantis."

"Oh."

"And I hope to converse with Amenemope quite soon."

"Well, I won't keep you," Earnestine said, "one must get on."

"Of course," said Mrs Albright and she waved her stick ahead before climbing the central staircase to the top deck.

Earnestine dallied and then descended as quickly as she could. If anyone was around, say a member of the crew, she could always claim to be lost.

No!

She was from the Deering-Dolittle family, famous for their explorers, so she couldn't possibly say she was lost. She'd have to say–

"Madam, can I assist you?"

"Ah, Farouk... it's... that is to say, one is simply... and it's 'Miss'."

"Miss?"

"Yes. I'm not married."

Farouk raised a quizzical eyebrow. His fez almost touched the pipes that crossed this passageway.

"I've not met the right gentleman," she explained. Oh, this was terrible. 'I came down to the lower deck looking for a man' – what sort of excuse was that? 'Lost' would have been better. It almost made Earnestine admire Charlotte's ability to spin a yarn when caught.

"The gentlemen are all in the Smoking Room or on the sun lounge, Miss."

"Are they?"

"Or in their cabins."

"One couldn't possibly go into a gentleman's cabin."

"No, Miss."

"One has a reputation."

Farouk smiled. "The Derring-Do Club I have heard so much about."

Earnestine tightened her jaw. "Yes. That."

"And is it true that you–"

"Most likely."

"And–"

"Unfortunately."

"A–"

"Farouk, our Mother forbade us to go on adventures. 'No adventures,' she said, and she was most explicit."

"And this?"

"One's just popping down to check upon one's travelling trunk."

Farouk moved his head away from her. "Miss?"

"This way, I believe."

Earnestine led the way along the passageway. The décor was industrial iron and basic wood; there were no fine wallpapers or carpets down below.

The door to the aft hold was metal and it was locked.

"Miss, only those with items in the hold have a key."

"And the Skipper."

"Yes, Captain Abdul has one."

"And the Guide?"

"Alas," Farouk said, his hands gesturing apology.

"I see."

"So I will escort you to the gentlemen, yes? And..."

The small kit pack had her lock picks.

"Miss? Alas, Farouk believes you are not allowed..."

The twizzle end wouldn't quite engage.

"...or capable, so–"

The lock clicked and Earnestine opened the door wide as she stood upright.

"You cannot go in, Miss."

"I can."

"You cannot."

"The word you are looking for is 'shouldn't'."

"That's what I said."

She gave him a thin smile. "Hardly."

Inside, the mechanical heartbeat of the ship was appreciably louder. The metal walls must be thin and close to the Engine Room. The great paddle wheels sounded like a hundred mangles.

"You see," she said, brandishing the half-diamond, "lock picks are a sort of permission."

"Miss, that is not true."

"My sister is the Investigating Officer," she said as she nipped inside. "Please fetch an oil lamp."

Farouk hesitated, his fez in his hands now as he was drawn into Earnestine's underhand activity.

"If we are caught, Miss?"

"Then keep watch."

Farouk lingered at the entrance, keeping a step on the side of honesty as he struggled with the moral dilemma.

"Lamp?"

"Miss."

She had to go to him to take the lamp, but at least he lit it for her. He slipped his box of matches back into the watch pocket of his grey waistcoat.

Inside, it was damp underfoot; pools of water had collected and stained the floor with rust. She looked up to the large cargo hatch in the ceiling through which the crane had lowered the crates, trunks and freight. This was the stern of the boat, the only section without upper decks.

There were barrels to her left, chaotically arranged, but the passengers' large items were–

"*Arrgh! Gak!*"

"Miss, Miss?" Farouk crossed the threshold.

A wretched droplet of water had fallen down the back of her neck.

"I'm fine... one's fine. Thank you, keep watch."

Farouk did so, his head hung low, incriminated now he was inside the hold.

Earnestine made her way over to the right-hand side with as much dignity as she could muster.

This part of the hold was used for passengers' storage. There wasn't much; mostly the hold was empty. If they'd been on the Nile, then this section would have been packed with the antiquities of ancient Egypt, all carefully wrapped and boxed ready for the voyage back to the safety of a European museum.

Five crates of various sizes stood in a row. They reminded Earnestine of little Philippa's toy blocks: cube, tall, long, cylindrical and misshapen.

The cube belonged to Caruthers. She held up the lamp to check the manifest pinned to the wall – it was a 'tank'. It had started its journey in ~~London~~, ~~Calais~~ to ~~Paris~~, the Orient Express through ~~Strasbourg~~, ~~Munich~~, ~~Vienna~~, ~~Budapest~~ and ~~Bucarest~~ to ~~Istanbul~~, then the voyage to ~~Cairo~~, before ~~Tanis~~ and along the canal to Suez before Bombay and a list of exotic names in India. Those places already visited had been crossed out. And 'tank' – 'water tank?', 'fuel tank?', 'fish tank?' Hardly likely to be important.

The tall one belonged to that ghastly Mrs Albright woman. Easily opened, it contained a variety of paraphernalia as if she was planning a stage show: a folding table, a box containing a crystal ball and so on.

The round drum belonged to Pandit Singh Maçon and this opened easily too... and it was empty!

Ah ha!

A long crate and a short crate, both marked for Sir Archibald Reevers and counter-signed by Mister Emrys Rake, and they even had the Royal Expeditionary Society Coat of Arms stencilled on the top.

She checked the manifest of the short one: expeditionary equipment. She squinted through the gaps in the wooden boards and saw trowels, buckets, archaeology poles and lumps of canvas that were probably folded tents.

So, he *was* on an expedition – she knew it!

The long one was marked 'crate'. Really! Honestly? Its journey list went ~~London~~, ~~Calais~~, ~~Paris~~, ~~Strasbourg~~, ~~Munich~~, ~~Vienna~~, ~~Budapest~~, ~~Bucharest~~, ~~Istanbul~~, ~~Cairo~~, ~~Tanis~~, Suez and then return.

Return?

Why was he taking this crate for a holiday?

It galled her to feel so ignorant.

What was the President of the Royal Expeditionary Society up to, so far from the usual haunts of Egyptologists?

"Garden of Eden," she murmured under her breath.

"Miss?"

"Keep watch, Farouk."

The crate itself was long, much like a large coffin.

She hung the lamp from a hook jutting down from a beam and searched around for a crowbar.

The nailed-down top *eeekked* open.

"Miss? Shhh..."

She fished out her Misell Electric torch to flash into the murky depths.

It contained a coffin.

Or, more accurately, a wooden sarcophagus of the Middle Kingdom period, possibly early Second Intermediate Period, certainly upper class, probably one of the adept scribes or a high priest – someone important, but not a Pharaoh – constructed in Thebes.

She got the crate's lid off and the hanging lamp lit the contents.

Yes, late Middle Kingdom, if she wasn't mistaken, and the hieroglyphics suggested a wealthy high priest, but she couldn't be completely sure without consulting her textbooks. She considered going back to her cabin for them, but even her large kit would be too cumbersome with various leather-bound volumes crammed inside. There was a limit to what she could carry around.

Farouk's indulgence would have a limit too.

"Miss, what's in it?"

She glanced up at Farouk by the door. "Nothing."

"This is a mummy," he said, coming closer.

"Possibly."

"It is sacrilege to desecrate the dead."

"If there is a body in here."

"We will be cursed."

"Well, you could carry on guarding the door and then it would only be myself opening it."

"Miss, you are foolish."

"Best foot forward."

"Most foolish," Farouk said. "I can understand what they are saying about your Derring-Do Club."

"That's Charlotte's silly name for us," Earnestine insisted. "We're simply on an... sightseeing."

"You bring it upon yourself," said Farouk as he backed away to the door. "There is a curse!"

Superstitious mummery, Earnestine thought.

But the wind rattled the oil lamp.

And the shadows leapt as though they were alive.

Earnestine shivered – poppycock.

Carefully, she lifted the carved top.

An inhalation sighed like lungs filling, and then the top slammed down again.

"Miss?"

"Farouk, it just slipped."

She lifted the top again.

This time it did not appear to breathe, but simply came away to reveal a gaunt, wizened corpse wrapped in the bandages of a mummy. Tall for a mummy, perhaps 5' 6", although it was hard to tell. Intact in comparison to others she had seen, but still showing the signs of the decay she'd expected. Strange to see one without a surrounding glass case and a neat card of explanation.

If the bandages had been painted, the dyes had long ago faded. Checking the body, Earnestine found a clean rectangle upon the wrappings at the man's thigh, about the size of a cloakroom ticket. She recognized it as the mark left by the removal of a British Museum label.

There were no Canopic jars or burial goods, either long ago looted from the tomb or left behind in Great Russell Street.

It was just an old body wrapped in old material.

But the empty eye sockets of the corpse seemed to stare back at her, the swinging light created dark pupils, animated as if the High Priest's attention moved. Its mouth lay open in a silent scream or in the act of casting a curse.

Creepy, she thought, and she let the lid drop.

"Have you finished?" Farouk said.

"Yes."

Farouk closed the door behind him: "You must say a prayer to protect yourself from the curse."

"Must I?"

"You have desecrated a pharaoh."

"He was a High Priest and I think his tomb was desecrated quite some time ago."

"Even so, I will pray for you."

"Much obliged."

She checked the manifest again.

From London to Suez and then return.

It made no sense.

She shook her head at the wonder of it. Sir Archibald Reevers was smuggling mummies into Egypt.

"Miss," Farouk hissed, "someone's coming."

A faint footfall.

Someone was coming.

Someone on tiptoe.

The heavy metal door squeaked.

There was nowhere to hide.

Mrs Merryweather

Georgina took her dozing child to her room and placed her carefully in the cot. Thankfully, Pippa lay still, and stayed quiet, as Georgina moved her hands away like someone who had just perfected a fragile flower arrangement.

She had four suspects left to interview: Captain Caruthers, Monsieur Jacques, Mrs Albright and Earnestine, so she set out to find them.

There was no-one in the Smoking Room and then, like horse-drawn trams, Captain Caruthers arrived (with the Colonel) followed by Mrs Albright and Monsieur Jacques.

"Oh good," Georgina said. "I need to ask you all questions."

The Captain settled the Colonel into his chair.

"I'm all right, man, damn it."

"Sorry, Colonel."

"We cannot be questioned together," Mrs Albright said.

"Absolutely," Georgina agreed. "Mrs Albright, would you mind waiting in the Dining Room for me."

"Oh, very well."

Monsieur Jacques held the door for her.

"Good afternoon," said Mrs Albright.

"Bon débarras," Monsieur Jacques replied with a nod.

"Thank you," and Mrs Albright was gone.

"Captain, I... er..." Georgina glanced at Monsieur Jacques.

"I'll wait on the Sun Deck," Caruthers replied.

"There's also Earnestine, if you can find her."

"I'll see what I can do," the Captain added, before he left too.

Colonel Fitzwilliam was asleep. If only Pippa would nod off that quickly. Perhaps she should try a drop of brandy at bedtime.

"Would you answer a few questions, Monsieur Jacques?" Georgina said, going over to a table away from the old man.

"For l'investigatrice, anything," he said, leaning nonchalantly against the bar and towards Georgina. His tall, lean frame allowed him to loom over her. He'd used some wax or cream to make his pencil moustache sharp and pointed.

"Lovely and... where were you when the crime was committed?"

"I was in my cabin."

"Alone?"

"Sadly."

"So, you've no alibi. What happened?"

"I heard a... how you say, 'Phut'."

"Phut?"

"Oui, 'phut', 'poof', noise."

"Gunshot?"

"Who can say? It was a noise. My cabin, it is the furthest from the Library."

"Is it?"

"And the loneliest."

"I'm sure... I mean, that's a shame."

The man shrugged as if it was nothing to him and everything to the world.

"Did you see the body?"

"Non, I was too late. I arrived with the Captain."

"The ship's captain?"

"Non, that Caruthers."

"You arrived together?"

"Non, I came from le port, he from le tribord."

Georgina made a note and wondered how she could get all the movements, the comings and goings, properly fixed in her mind.

"Is that all, Mademoiselle?"

"It's Madame."

"Oh, oui."

"I have a child."

Jacques shrugged expressively: "I have known many mesdemoiselles with child."

"Monsieur Jacques!" she exclaimed.

The Colonel woke, spluttering.

"Perhaps upon the continent and in exotic lands," Georgina continued, "but I am English."

"Pardon."

The Colonel flustered and then added: "Yes, dash it, man, I knew her husband."

"Pardon, Colonel."

"He was a fine man, was Merry."

"Thank you, Colonel," Georgina said.

"The very idea, Jacques. Mrs Merryweather is a fine, upstanding and moral woman."

"Yes, thank you, Colonel."

"We could go somewhere else for your questions," Monsieur Jacques proposed.

"Yes, where do you suggest?"

"My cabin... your cabin."

"Monsieur Jacques!"

"It would be private."

"I think not. Perhaps we should just continue here and Colonel Fitzwilliam can act as chaperone."

"As you wish, Madame."

"So, Monsieur Jacques, why are you here in Egypt?"

"Business."

"What business?"

"And a little pleasure."

"I don't believe you are travelling on?"

"Non, I turn back at Suez and return to Tanis."

"Why travel down, just to travel up again?"

"To see the canal. My ancestors built it."

"Do you have a revolver?"

"Non, I have un Browning de Belgique."

"What's that?"

The Colonel coughed: "He means an automatic."

"What's the difference?" Georgina asked.

"Here, hand it over," the Colonel said, struggling in his chair.

Monsieur Jacques pulled a stubby piece of black metal from an inside pocket.

The Colonel took it, expertly removed its magazine and checked it. He nodded, smelt it and then handed it to Georgina.

It was a nasty, sneaky, underhand little weapon and reeked of cologne. When Georgina handed it back, Monsieur Jacques snapped the magazine into the handle and secreted it back into his jacket.

"Did you know Mister Rake?" Georgina asked.

"I never met him before this trip."

"Did you talk to him much?"

"Non, perhaps at déjeuner, dîner, drinks."

"What did you talk about?"

"With you English, it is always the weather. How hot, how warm, how dry... how you miss the rain et le brouillard et la soupe aux pois."

"And Egypt?"

"Oui."

"Did you talk about Egypt?"

"Oui."

"What exactly?"

"How hot, how scorching, how unpleasant..."

"Did you talk about business?"

"I have no business here."

Miss Charlotte

Child! Honestly. She was sixteen. Just.

Charlotte had skipped along, then idly twizzled around on one foot like a little girl, so she could scan up and down the deck without drawing attention to herself.

There was no-one about.

All clear.

She'd vaulted up and over, dropped down on the far side, but holding on.

The almost still water lapped below as she climbed down. It was easy, no more difficult than scrumping in Professor Chadlock's orchard tree back in London, although the narrow wooden walkway on the lower deck was slippery.

She'd made it inside.

The guttural noises of the crew's chatter carried in the echoing interior of the hold.

She snuck inside, keeping low and taking the twists and turns between the crates and barrels as they came. It was like a labyrinth.

The door to the hold was unlocked.

Strange, she thought, but it was practically an invitation.

It was wet underfoot, and pokey, but luckily a lit oil lamp swung from a fixture.

She'd have to check them all, but... *jackpot!*

The first along was labelled as Captain Caruthers, Tank, London, Calais, blah-blah, blah-blah, Calcutta.

She wrinkled her nose. Surely India could make its own water tank. Or was it an expensive fish tank to keep exotic Indian fish?

It was nailed down.

She glanced about and clearly lit directly under the oil lamp was a crowbar. As she took it, she saw that the crate it had rested on had all its nails sticking out. Someone needed a hammer, not a crowbar. It had a big coat of arms on the top, so it belonged to Sir Archibald Reevers.

There were other boxes: another one of Sir Archibald's, a round drum for Pandit Singh Maçon and a tall thing belonging to Mrs Albright.

She went back to the Captain's and eased the lid off.

It was full of straw.

Charlotte felt down inside, much as she might at a fête playing lucky dip. The trick, she thought, was not to settle on the first package, but to pretend she'd not found anything and dig deeper for something big.

Ah ha!

It was cold, round and slightly larger than her hand.

She pulled it out.

It reflected the light with a golden glow, but it was just a brass gear.

How disappointing.

It looked complicated too with numbers around it from '0' to '9' that repeated a few times. It was probably for... something Georgina would find fascinating enough to lecture about, but it wasn't like it was a military uniform, a weapon or anything actually interesting.

She felt inside again, ferreting in the straw, but there seemed to be no end of these odd gears, according to her questing fingers.

There were plenty, so she thought she'd keep this one to show Georgina how clever she'd been.

Then she heard something.

The top from the other crate clattered down.

She hefted the crowbar like a mace and crept towards it. Inside, she saw a sarcophagus and with a creeping terror, she realised that the lid was rising, a hand appeared from below the lid as the ancient Egyptian mummy came back to life.

But it wasn't a Pharaoh reanimated as part of a terrible curse, just because she'd desecrated his crate by stealing his crowbar.

No.

In a moment of horror, like when a dunked biscuit falls asunder, Charlotte knew it was worse.

Far worse.

Far, far, worse...

CHAPTER VI

Miss Deering-Dolittle

"Charlotte Deering-Dolittle!"

"I was just putting it back." Charlotte jerked round in wild panic. "I haven't broken anything."

"You've pulled those nails out of that crate."

"By accident."

"With a crowbar?"

"I just..."

"What are you doing here?"

"I was lost."

"Lost?"

"Yes."

"That is simply the worst excuse I have ever heard," Earnestine said in a tone that brooked no argument. "Why are you here?"

"I was checking on my crate," Charlotte said.

"You don't have a crate."

"The heat... confused me, so I came down here where it is much cooler."

Oh, thought Earnestine, that's quite clever. "Don't be ridiculous, Charlotte."

"I was helping Georgina."

"A likely story."

"Why are you here?"

"I was... Farouk here is giving me a tour of the ship."

Charlotte looked around.

Earnestine was alone, except that a lump grew from the shadows from the round barrel and reluctantly clambered out into the feeble light. Farouk, with a dreadful, embarrassed expression, crumpled his fez before him, now that he was involved in two competing criminal endeavours.

"Farouk," said Charlotte.

"Miss Charlotte," said Farouk.

"And Ness, what are you doing here?"

Farouk spoke, "Miss, I really think–"

"Please, Farouk," Earnestine said, pointing at her sister, "one is chastising one's undisciplined sister."

"Yes, but perhaps Miss Deering-Dolittle, you could do it somewhere where we won't be caught. Farouk's constitution isn't built for adventures."

"Ooh," said Charlotte, "this is an adventure."

"No, it is not!" Earnestine insisted. She turned on Farouk. "Don't give her ideas. This is not an adventure. No adventures. Mother said–"

"Ness," Charlotte interrupted, "you're not supposed to be here either."

"Ah," Earnestine had her now, "so you admit you're not supposed to be here."

"All right, but neither are you."

"One is on a mission for the Investigating Officer."

"That's what I said."

"No, it isn't."

"It's completely the same."

"Helping Georgina might be finding a toy that Pippa has lost and therefore you have no business skulking around in the hold, whereas I am on official business – quite different."

"Official?"

"Perhaps pre-official."

"Pre-official?"

"In that Georgina doesn't technically know about it yet," Earnestine admitted. "Sadly, one has to accept that Georgina has little idea of how to proceed, so..."

"I thought she was quite thorough."

"Hmmm... so one thought to lend a helping hand."

Charlotte's face shone: "It is an adventure."

"Not at all," Earnestine insisted. "It's a helping hand, nothing more."

"Are you looking for treasure?"

"Certainly not."

"Did you use a map?"

"Charlotte, you know perfectly well that so-called treasure maps never lead to treasure."

"Yes, I know perfectly well, so where do we start?"

"Ladies," said Farouk, "perhaps upstairs?"

"We don't start anywhere," Earnestine said.

"And I'm not looking for a toy or treasure," Charlotte explained. "I was checking Captain Caruthers' crate. It's not a tank."

"I could fetch lemonade," Farouk suggested.

Earnestine glanced at the Captain's crate.

"And Sir Archibald's?" Charlotte asked.

Earnestine eyes narrowed.

"Fair's fair."

"It's not a game."

Charlotte smiled sweetly.

"Sir Archibald Reevers is smuggling mummies."

"Stealing antiquities!" Charlotte squealed. "That's a motive for murder."

"Not really," Earnestine replied. "Firstly, he's British, and, secondly, he's the President of the Royal Expeditionary Society, so he's quite entitled to rescue and preserve Egyptian relics. And thirdly, he's smuggling them *into Egypt.*"

Charlotte made a face: "Don't be silly."

"Seriously," Earnestine said. "The crate has travelled all the way from London and has not been opened in all that time."

"It's open now."

"One happened to... don't answer back."

"Miss, perhaps we should go upstairs," Farouk pleaded. "More comfortable."

"When we're ready, Farouk."

"But, Miss, they are calling for you."

"Don't be absurd."

But it was true, a faint cry wafted on the air: "Miss Deering-Dolittle... Miss Deering-Dolittle..."

"What now?" said Earnestine.

Mrs Merryweather

Mrs Albright had been waiting in the Dining Room by walking up and down, fiddling with her pearls and crashing her stick into the furniture.

"About time."

"I'm sorry, Mrs Albright," Georgina explained, "I was delayed by Monsieur Jacques."

"I wouldn't get too friendly with him, if I were you."

"I was asking him questions."

"My dear," said Mrs Albright as she settled into a chair, wriggling to get comfortable. Her stick fell off its perch at the back and clattered to the floor, as the woman fussed with the chain connected to the arms of her spectacles, before perching her glasses on her nose. Her large, mascaraed eyes peered forth. "Ask your questions."

Georgina sat opposite: "Where were you when you heard the shot?"

"I was in Atlantis."

"I beg your pardon."

"Atlantis."

"But... surely Atlantis cannot have sunk in the middle of the desert?"

"Atlantis... or was it ancient Thebes?"

"I'm sorry?"

"I was preparing myself to commune with the venerable High Priest, Amenemope, in readiness for his return to our realm."

"Realm... ah, where were you really?"

"Do you mean in the corporeal sense?"

Georgina thought about this: "Yes."

"I was in my cabin, meditating."

"Can anyone vouch for you?"

"Of course."

"Who?"

"Let me think," Mrs Albright said, pondering. "Atis, my Spirit Guide, the High Priest Amenemope and the Secret Chiefs."

"Chiefs?"

"Our agents in the spiritual plane."

"Our?"

"The Hermetic Order of the Golden Dawn."

"Oh."

"We conduct spiritual research, prophesy involving palms and animal entrails, high tea and formal dinners, that sort of thing."

"You sacrifice animals?"

"Chickens."

Georgina glanced at her notes, trying to fathom how to get back to normality.

"The shot?"

"I sensed something was amiss, dear, something appalling. My Spirit Guide informed me thus. A dreadful act, death, and only the beginning."

"I see."

"I am a sensitive, you see. Gifted with divine powers and able to see the past and future."

"And afterwards?"

"And in the hereafter too."

"I meant after you heard the shot?"

"I rushed to spiritually assist the passage of Mister Rake from this world..." – Mrs Albright leaned over, grasped Georgina's wrist and stared so wide-eyed that her foundation cracked visibly – "...*to the next!*"

"And physically?"

"I went to the Smoking Room for a drink," Mrs Albright said. "It was a most dreadful shock."

"I'm sure."

She let go of Georgina to thrust her hand out, her fingers heavy with various rings. "See. I'm all aquiver."

"Yes."

"Aquiver."

"Who else did you see?"

"I saw no-one and everyone. We all gathered in the Smoking Room and Doctor Timon gave me something to calm my nerves. I suffer terribly from nerves."

"Do you remember Mister Rake and what happened at Tanis before we boarded?"

"He kept me company at the dinner, if that's what you mean. Nothing sordid. He was a gentleman keeping me company and he was fascinated by what I had to tell him about the other world."

Georgina stifled a yawn; she was becoming far more sympathetic with Mister Rake, who had clearly suffered a lecturing and probably deserved all the drink he had imbibed.

"We are hoping to raise the High Priest Amenemope, if Sir Archibald would put aside his objections."

"Mister Rake drank that night, didn't he?"

"He didn't touch a drop," Mrs Albright said.

"Surely you are mistaken?"

"Not at all," she said. "He told me that he was pleased to be in a Muslim country because there was a better choice of temperance drinks."

"A better choice?"

"Oh yes, he was quite enthusiastic–"

"Mister Rake?"

"He said if you can develop a taste for the spices, then the Middle East is a garden of delights for someone who has taken the pledge."

"I see," Georgina said. She didn't. This Mister Rake seemed very at odds with the tall, thin, sour gentleman she remembered.

"I had a gin and tonic," Mrs Albright added. "I would have avoided it, but Mister Rake said it was acceptable because it was for my nerves and in case of malaria. I've been warned that Africa is rife with malaria. Anyway, I had a few for medicinal purposes and he had that herbal brown liquid that smelt quite vile, but he liked it."

"I see."

"And so, you see, we talked about the spirits and about a lack of spirits," Mrs Albright cackled. "Do you see?"

"Oh yes. Jolly amusing. And after that?"

"I went back to my hotel. Farouk took me."

"Did you talk to anyone else there…" Georgina checked her notes. "Al Rachid, Mister Djehuti, Captain Conway–"

"Jetty?"

"Djehuti."

"Yes. Swarthy. I didn't take to him at all. He seemed to find my explanations of Egyptian mythology funny for some reason."

"Did he now?"

Miss Charlotte

"Charlotte," Earnestine said. "I have to go. Tidy up."

"I've tidied my room," Charlotte said.

"Don't whine! Tidy this up," Earnestine said, waving her finger to include most of the hold. "And then write your letters."

"I didn't make this mess." Charlotte looked about her, aghast. "It's smelly and oily."

"Not the… close the crates and make it look like we weren't here."

"How?"

"Nail the tops down," Earnestine insisted. "Farouk, lead the way."

"I?"

"You're a Guide."

"Of course, Miss."

"Then guide."

Farouk led the way, perhaps doing so to extend the distance between himself and the hold, and so remove himself from any wrongdoing. Or perhaps he genuinely relished being a Guide.

A voice questioned the Egyptian as soon as he stepped out of the hold.

"Have you seen Miss Deering-Dolittle?" It was Captain Caruthers.

"Captain, I... have found her." Farouk stepped aside with a flourish to reveal Earnestine to the Captain.

"Captain," Earnestine said.

"Miss Deering-Dolittle," Caruthers replied. "We were searching, but you couldn't be found anywhere."

"I'm here now," she said. "Can I help?"

"Your sister wants to see you."

"Is that worth such a search party?"

"Something might have happened to you – there has been a murder – and... she's in the Dining Room."

"I'll go there directly."

"I can show you the way," Farouk said.

"One knows the way."

"I am the Guide."

"Of course."

Their footsteps receded, clattering up the steps distantly, and Charlotte was left alone in all the mess.

Nail the tops back on?

Earnestine had all the fun (not that Charlotte fancied lying in a sarcophagus with a mummy) and Charlotte had to tidy up. At least it wasn't Georgina telling her to write her letters home.

Charlotte struggled to get the wooden lid to fit properly, trying it this way and that until the British Museum symbol was facing the right way. She used the crowbar to bang the nails in.

Every other one bent horribly.

CHAPTER VII

Miss Deering-Dolittle

Georgina was waiting for her, looking jolly self-important behind a table set out as if she had an office.

"Ness," Georgina said, indicating a vacant chair.

"Gina."

Earnestine sat.

"So... er... what happened?"

Earnestine was taken aback: "Is this how you've been conducting your investigation?"

"Yes."

"Just 'what happened?'?"

"Yes."

"Couldn't you ask more specific questions?"

"Ness!"

"Ask a specific question," Earnestine said. "You could have interviewed me first and one could have helped you come up with a proper approach."

"You couldn't be found. Where were you?"

"About..." Earnestine said, forcing herself not to look down towards the hold. "Nowhere one wasn't allowed."

"And where were you when the shot was fired?"

"The shot, yes. On deck... taking in the sun."

"In that outfit?"

"I was on the deck–"

"Starboard or port?"

"I'm not sure."

"What could you see?"

"Desert. What else is there to see?"

"Was it sunny?"

"Yes, I was at the back."

"The aft?"

"Can one make one's statement or is one going to be constantly interrupted?"

"Do you have to say 'one' all the time?"

"One likes to speak properly."

"Sorry. Go on. Ness."

"One was on deck, aft, starboard, looking at the view and one heard a 'bang'."

"Go on."

"That's all."

"And then you did..."

"I went to see what was going on. I came inside via the starboard hatch and the others were trying to open the door to the Library. After some faffing – you know what men are like – they got it open. It was only bolted from the inside."

"You saw that."

"I heard the metal bracket break and the door bang against the wall."

"Go on."

"Well, there's not much more. Doctor Timon held me back, as it would be too much for a young lady. Apparently. Absolute arrant nonsense, of course, but he meant well. Doctor Timon then went in to examine the body and declared him dead – Mister Rake that is – but he really didn't need to as it was obvious. The man had been shot. One couldn't see his face, but the blood was all up the wall. I could see it clearly from the doorway. Doctor Timon asked if I was going to faint. Of all the foolish things. I went to examine the body too, but Doctor Timon used smelling salts on me."

"You'd fainted?"

"No!"

"Then why?"

"He said it was a 'precautionary measure'. Anyway, Doctor Timon sent everyone back to the Smoking Room and Farouk went to inform the Skipper."

"Why do you think he did that?"

"He's Egyptian and the Skipper is Egyptian and... have you tried talking to the Skipper? It's not like that guttural noise can possibly be English."

"And then?"

"The Skipper came with the First Mate to see the body."

"How do you know this?"

"I happened to sit with an excellent view down the passageway. The Smoking Room door is glass."

"Happened?"

"Yes, one sat... can I tell it?"

"Please."

"And they announced he was dead. The First Mate guarded the room until they'd fitted a new clasp for a padlock."

"So the room wasn't touched by anyone?"

"No."

"Who did go in?"

"The Skipper... the First Mate stood in the way. Doctor Timon originally, but he only went in to the feel the man's neck for a pulse."

"And you saw all this with your own eyes?"

"Yes."

"I see."

"Yes, I did see."

"Was everyone present in the Smoking Room?"

"Eventually."

"Eventually?"

"Let's see... I think Colonel Fitzwilliam was already there, Doctor Timon came in after he was relieved. Pandit Singh Maçon had helped open the door. I was with them. Monsieur Jacques and Captain Caruthers sometime after."

"From which direction."

"My left, and I was facing backwards... so the right side of the boat."

"Starboard."

"For Captain Caruthers. Monsieur Jacques came from the other side. And finally, Mrs Albright and yourself."

"I see... any theories?"

"You're the Investigating Officer."

"Yes, any theories?"

"It's Monsieur Jacques," Earnestine said. "I mean, what business does a Frenchman have here?"

"I think you are being prejudiced, and he's not here on business."

Earnestine leant over the tablecloth, glanced left and right. "Then he's a spy."

"A spy?"

"He's certainly not here as a tourist, is he?"

"Why would the French send a spy to Egypt?"

"Oh, Gina. Honestly. You spend too much time in the Natural History Museum looking at stuffed animals and rock creatures."

"Fossils are not rock creatures."

"Yes, we had a lovely day out at Lyme Regis walking along the beach and looking for rock creatures, but once you've seen one whirly shape, you've seen all the whirly shapes."

"Ammonites are fascinating–"

"But not as fascinating as *Amun*-ites. Egyptology is the future, not dead rock creatures."

"Ness, they are not–"

"I know."

"And you are always stuck in tombs, Ness. You should spend more time with the living. You're not going to meet a gentleman in a tomb."

"I am not always stuck in tombs."

"You're always reading about them."

"It's educational."

"So, to educate me, you were standing at the rear of the boat when the shot was fired."

Earnestine shuffled in her seat. "Yes."

"Any witnesses?"

"Probably... Mrs Albright."

"Did you see anyone else?"

"I was looking at the scenery."

"The scenery?"

Earnestine felt the muscles in her jaw tighten: "Yes."

"Did you see Captain Caruthers?"

"No, he wasn't on deck. He arrived later after everything had happened. I suspect he was in his cabin." Earnestine glanced across at Georgina's notes. Her handwriting was neat, of course, but it was upside down and consisted merely of significant words: 'Albright, Smoking Room, Caruthers, on deck...' "You've written that Captain Caruthers was on deck. He wasn't."

"He was."

"I'd have seen him."

Georgina snatched her notebook away and closed it to hide the contents between the hard, blue covers.

"Is that everything?" Earnestine said, satisfied she'd corrected Georgina's mistake.

"What did you think of Mister Rake?"

"He was an awkward stickler for paperwork," Earnestine replied. "I had to submit my application to the Royal Expeditionary Society three times before it was sent upstairs to be rejected. But, apparently, he rejected them himself. His ideas about women's suffrage were positively Regency."

"Not your applications for expeditions," Georgina said. "About the man in question and, in particular, since this voyage began."

"Voyage on a canal?"

"Ness, you can be very awkward."

"Me?"

"Mister Rake... start at the formal dinner in Tanis."

"That?"

"Yes, please."

"You think what happened there has any bearing?"

"It might."

"The man was drunk."

"Would you explain?"

Earnestine thought back to when they'd arrived at Tanis. It was only yesterday, but it seemed longer. They'd checked into the hotel and the guests were all invited to the Consulate for a formal dinner. Earnestine selected her burgundy dress (even though it didn't go with her pith helmet), Georgina wore mourning black and Charlotte had ignored their suggestions, so Earnestine had picked out a particular severe-looking outfit for their contrary sister. Before she'd managed to escape to go on a sightseeing, Captain Caruthers had presented himself in his dress uniform to escort them.

"We all arrived together," Earnestine said.

"We?"

"Those booked on the SS *Karnak*."

Sir Archibald Reevers had represented their group to the vice consul. He was a Knight of the Realm and the President of the Royal Expeditionary Society after all. Mrs Albright held onto his left arm and waved her stick about like a flyswatter.

Earnestine had avoided Sir Archibald and found herself near Captain Caruthers.

"Let's try and enjoy it," Caruthers had said. He'd offered his elbow and Earnestine hooked her hand through.

There was a buffet – frightfully European – and the first dishes were curried this, spiced that and peppered sheep's eyes.

"They're for the tourists," Caruthers said. He was far more experienced in matters of travel than Earnestine. True enough, sensible dishes existed further down the tables, though even these had been exotically presented.

There was sherry.

Spirits for the gentlemen.

Thankfully, the day's oppressive heat dissipated and the evening breeze blowing from the Mediterranean was pleasant.

It struck Earnestine that this was like a fancy-dress party: gentlemen in their black dinner suits and ladies in the fineries were expected, but there were men in turbans, fez hats and robes, women covered head-to-toe, garish clashing colours, strange headdresses... there was even a Scot wearing a kilt.

*"This is a meeting place for Europe, Africa and Asia,"
Caruthers explained.*

Earnestine knew this from studying maps.

The curry was jolly spicy.

"I've tasted stronger in the East End," the Captain had said. "Can't wait for Calcutta."

"We had a buffet," Earnestine told Georgina.

"I was there, Ness, but I sat at the other table."

"Oh, yes, you were with Mrs Albright and Pandit Singh Maçon."

"Yes, and you sat with Sir Archibald and Mister Rake."

"Oh yes."

"And who else?"

Farouk introduced everyone, Sir Archibald first, to those gathered on the big table clothed in white linen. Eventually, he worked his way along to Earnestine herself.

"Miss Deering-Dolittle," said the ever-present Farouk. "May I present Mister Djehuti."

Earnestine presented her hand to a tall gentleman of a golden complexion, young and completely bald, whose eyes sparkled with intelligence and humour. He was handsome like a brass statue of some Greek god. Earnestine felt quite weak at the knees and...

"...are you feeling all right, Ness?" Georgina was saying.

"Yes, perfectly, what's the matter with you?"

"There's nothing the matter with me."

"Then don't fuss."

"You were going to tell me about the dinner."

"Yes," said Earnestine. "Farouk introduced everyone."

"So..."

"Pandit Singh Maçon, Mrs Clemens, Captain Caruthers, Miss Jennifer, Captain Conway, Charlotte, Mister Rake, Mrs Bertram, Sir Archibald, Mrs... can't remember and... and... myself, of course."

"There was no man between you and Mrs whoever?"

"Oh, there was."

"Who?"

"A man."

...with this liquid voice, like honey, with clear and precise diction that oozed education and confidence. His name, Djehuti, sounded like a harmonious bell when he repeated it for her. Not that Earnestine was affected by such matters as strong hands, carefully manicured nails and the gushing water she'd spilt all over the table. He was so understanding, making out that it was really his fault, which it was, because he'd made her hand tremble.

"And?" said Georgina interrupting.

"And... some Egyptian man."

"Egyptian?" Georgina asked.

Djehuti chimed to her again: "I forget his name."

"Go on."

"Well..." said Earnestine, trying to gather her thoughts.

A person's name, their 'Ren', wasn't something one should even pretend to forget.

But she did feel weak talking to Georgina - the heat, it must be – and...

...and she was breathless. Even in the cool breeze, she'd needed her fan. The heat in this country beggared belief. Mister Djehuti smiled, an unforced generous expression.

"What brings you to Egypt, Miss?" he'd asked, his English impeccable with only the slightest accent.

"The study of the ancient civilisation."

"Our ruins."

"Not at all," Earnestine said. "We pride ourselves in our engineering and science, but the baton of progress, now so firmly held by the British Empire, was once Rome's, and before that Greek and Egyptian."

"Really?" He teased her; she knew it, yet she didn't mind.

"Of course. Reading and writing, astronomy, and a civilisation that lasted over three thousand years."

"I know, I was there," he joked. Others, listening in, laughed.

She did too, genuinely: "Oh, you can't be that old. You're in your prime, thirty, thirty..."

Earnestine blushed, and then startled at her own peculiar reaction.

Mister Djehuti was gentlemanly enough to pretend not to have noticed: "And you must be all of eighteen... nineteen."

"Twenty-one."

"Of age?"

"Yes."

"Young and yet knowledgeable."

"I've studied."

"Study is so important."

"Oh, I so agree," she said, putting her hand lightly upon his arm... and then snatching back the reckless thing.

He leaned closer...

"...are you all right, Ness?"

"Yes, fine, don't fuss."

"What did you talk about?"

"I didn't talk to anyone."

"At the dinner, there must have been conversation."

"The weather, travel arrangements, Sir Archibald talked about excavating the Valley of the Kings... nothing of import."

...and closer still.
"I believe Tanis to be the resting place of the Ark of the Covenant," she had been saying. This was usually the point when she was interrupted–

"Only you've gone jolly red."
"I'm fine, Gina, honestly."

–when talking about... what had she been talking about?
She'd completely lost her thread. Something about the Well of the Souls and a way of fabricating the Staff of Ra without the headpiece. The headpiece, she thought, rested in San el-Hagar and...
"...but, Mister Djehuti, one's going on."
"Please, continue." And Mister Djehuti had listened attentively, genuinely interested in her theories, nodding and asking sensible questions.

"Mister Rake?"
"What?"
"You're jolly distracted, Ness."
"One's fine."
"What did Mister Rake say?"
"Let me think."

Back at the dinner, she'd had something Mister Djehuti recommended: marinated apples that tasted divine and the juice dribbled down her chin.
"Will you trust me?" he'd asked.
She did, she would, yes...

"Mister Rake?"

"Who?   Oh, he sat the other side from me and talked about the weather, travel arrangements and excavating the Valley of the Kings."

"Just like Sir Archibald."

"Yes, that's all we talked about, Gina."

"And what did Mister Rake drink?"

"Wine, brandy, whisky, what men usually drink.   I didn't notice."

Because Mister Djehuti's eyes had been bewitching. She'd pulled her hair across the left side of her face, but he'd stopped her, gently – and shockingly – tucked it away.

"Your scar means you have lived," he said. "Admirable."

A chair scraped gratingly as it was pushed back.

"And afterwards, who left first and so forth?" Gina asked.

"I think Captain Caruthers excused himself first."

"And Mister Rake?"

"Probably went to the bar."

"And what did you do?"

His hand had touched her cheek, gently, in a caress that made her shiver.

"Are you cold?" he'd asked.

"No."

"Shall we take a stroll?"

They'd gone outside along a path lit by torches and sat beneath an arbour where a bench afforded a view out to sea. An awning hung above, its shade no longer needed now that the sun had set. The Mediterranean stretched out like a mirror reflecting the majestic sweep of the heavens. The moon looked clear and round in the sky.

"What do you think of Egypt?"

"I've not seen much," Earnestine admitted. "I've read. Do you read?"

He smiled at some joke: "I read and write."

"I didn't mean as a hobby."

He smiled again.

"I keep a journal," Earnestine added. "Do you?"

"It is good that you keep a journal."

"One should always have something sensational to read in the train."

"Oscar Wilde."

"You've heard of him?"

"I read and write," Mister Djehuti said. "It is my life."

"Ness?"

"Yes?"

"What did you do?"

"I went for a walk to clear my head."

"Were you with anyone?"

"Certainly not!"

They'd sat, practically touching, and they'd just talked as if they'd known each other for years.

"The stars are clear," Earnestine said. "And the moon. It's a full moon on the day after tomorrow, Saturday."

"In five days' time, it is also the start of the new year."

"Tuesday? September, the 11th?"

"It is the first day of the Ancient Egyptian year."

"Oh yes, the 1st of Thoth."

Mister Djehuti had smiled and she felt proud that she knew so much about his cultural heritage.

"So, it must be the month of Mesore," Earnestine continued, "the fourth month of low water."

"That ended yesterday," Mister Djehuti said. "Today was the first of five epagomenal days."

"Oh yes, the intercalary month to shift everything back to the right date. Like our February 29th."

"The extra days won from the Moon."

"By the god Thoth."

He smiled: "Your hair, it is red. Is it natural?"

"I beg your pardon."

"I have offended?"

"No, it's just that a man does not usually ask a young lady about such things."

"All the women I have known are dark haired like your sister, Mrs Merryweather, but you and..."

"Charlotte."

"Yes, Miss Charlotte, are different."

"Well, blondes are silly, flighty... girls."

"I see. And those with hair like smouldering fire?"

"You are teasing me."

"A little."

"Well, those of us with hair like 'smouldering fire' tend to fly off at the handle and throw things."

He laughed, a deep, unaffected carillon: "Now who is teasing."

"One's not teasing, one is warning."

"Then I will be careful."

He was quite the most beautiful man she had ever seen: "Exciting," she said. "Egypt, I mean. There could be whole cities buried beneath the sand."

"There are many relics buried in the sand."

"Yes, just waiting to be discovered."

"You'd like to discover something ancient in Egypt."

"Oh yes."

"I prefer living things, modern things. You are full of life and new ideas. And beautiful."

She fussed with her hair on the left side of her face. "I am not."

"Red hair, I think, means you love life."

"Poppycock."

"I should like to whisk you away on a magic carpet."

"Please."

"Did you talk to anyone?"

"Gina? Oh! Polite conversation, small talk, nothing that led anywhere, nothing that could possibly have led anywhere. The weather, travel arrangements, carpets."

"Carpets?"

"Interior decoration."

"And Mister Rake? There was an incident."

"That was later."

Servants had brought out torches and placed them into holders to light the way around the gardens outside. The fire made the scene primaeval, the stars wheeled above them in the sky, the same constellations that mankind had seen since God had first put Adam and Eve in the Garden of Eden.

Despite the breeze, Earnestine felt hot. The close proximity of Mister Djehuti comforted and almost burned.

"Earnestine," he said, carefully pronouncing each syllable and stressing the first to the extent that she heard her 'E' and the 'A'. "What does your name mean?"

"Earnest. Serious."

"Names are so important. We believe that one of our five souls is our 'Ren'."

"Ren?"

"Your name," Mister Djehuti said. "If it is written down, remembered, then it lasts forever."

"Oh, yes, er... Bâ, Jb, Ka, Ren and, er..."

"Sheut."

"Yes, your shadow."

"A life has a straight path from child to adult to wise," he said. "The souls are tests. You have choices, the right name, a time to be humble, to let your spirit run, to fly and go softly like a shadow. You will remember?"

"Oh yes. I'll write it down in my journal. Tests for my Bâ, Jb, Ka, Ren and Sheut."

"Why do you remember them in that order?"

"It's alphabetical."

"The Roman letters."

"That's it," Earnestine said. "English uses the Latin alphabet."

124

"You are as serious as your name implies."

"One tries."

"But I think there is a passion within you. It is like a Djinn–"

"Djinn?"

"Genie. If you let the genie free, its magic is powerful, intoxicating, and it can never be returned to the bottle," he said, fascinating her. *"But you bury yours within your bosom, just as there are many relics buried beneath the sand here."*

"Buried?"

"In your heart. As we say, your Jb."

"Things don't last, Mister Djehuti."

"If we remember them and write them down, some things last."

"But not forever."

"Yes, even forever."

"Ness, what was the incident?"

"Mister Rake turned up having had one too many."

She remembered that the light from the torches had seemingly burned across his features.

"Ness– Miss Deering-Dolittle," Captain Caruthers said when he came upon them by surprise. "And Mister Djehuti."

"Captain," said Mister Djehuti.

Caruthers nodded back, touching his forehead in a casual salute.

Earnestine smiled up at him. He was a good, stalwart friend, she knew, and... he wasn't leaving.

"Captain?" she asked.

"Is everything all right?"

"Of course, why wouldn't it be?"

"Simply asking. So long as you are sure."

"I'm sure."

"Certain?"

"He is worried for your safety," Mister Djehuti explained.

Earnestine was genuinely perplexed: "Safety?"

They were in the grounds of the British Consulate in Tanis in the middle of the British Protectorate. The hint was in the title: 'protectorate'. Not only were there waiters, but also dozens of British officers a mere two dozen yards away. What was she thinking? She was quite capable of looking after herself. She did not need a man.

"If this is what you want?" Caruthers said.

"Yes. Thank you, Captain."

Caruthers nodded again, turned smartly and marched stiffly away.

"One's sorry about that interruption."

"It is no matter," said Mister Djehuti. "He likes you."

"Who?"

"The Captain."

"Oh, Caruthers, yes. We go back a long way. I've known him years... months."

Had it really been only that long since they'd first met during that dreadful business with the Austro-Hungarians? It seemed longer. Little Pippa was nearly nine months old, so it was... gosh, eighteen months, less than two years certainly. Yet it seemed she'd known him forever.

She'd been a schoolgirl at the Eden College for Young Ladies. She'd changed – she tried then to tug her curls around to hide the vivid scar down the left side of her face – and grown. Perhaps she wasn't a young lady any more. She should, or at least society expected her to, find the right match and settle down.

"Shall we?" Mister Djehuti said.

And this fine, beautiful foreign man had courted her! He'd... with his arm... and she'd put her hand through, so... and then... and they were walking in the garden practically alone together... that is, without a chaperone and technically out of sight of the party.

And she'd laughed at his jokes.

She hadn't been able to help herself.
And then...

"And then... Ness?"

"Mister Rake ruined everything."

"Ruined what?"

"Nothing, nothing at all. He appeared drunk and then Captain Caruthers, who also turned up again."

"Again?"

"People were going back and forth through the gardens, it was like Piccadilly Circus. I said that at the time. Anyway, Captain Caruthers said to us something like, 'Mister Rake is drunk. We need to get him to his hotel. We don't want him making a scene in the Consulate.' And–"

"Us?"

"There was Captain Caruthers, Mister Rake and– like I said, we had no peace."

"We?"

"Me, everyone, anyone! Can one tell this?"

"Please."

"It was too far to his hotel, so a kind gentleman – who happened to be passing – suggested his rooms in an hotel, and he and Captain Caruthers took Mister Rake between them, after... well, after... and that was it."

"It's getting to be like Piccadilly Circus here," Earnestine had said.

"If the young lady will excuse me," Mister Djehuti said. "I shall take my leave."

"Of course."

"Come on, Rake," Caruthers said. He hoisted the Private Secretary up with the man's arm around his shoulder. They staggered away leaving Earnestine with Mister Djehuti.

"Goodnight Miss," Mister Djehuti had said, the firelight flickering in his eyes. "If I could gamble with the

moon for five more days, I would like to spend them with you."

Earnestine gazed up at the nearly full moon, briefly; its cold light nothing in comparison to the fire in Mister Djehuti's eyes.

"Miss Deering-Dolittle, you should follow your heart, not your head."

And then, for a moment, a brief, precious moment, it was as if the sunlight had caught the Statue of Eros and the horse-drawn carriages seemed to pause in their hectic rush, the street vendors ceased their hectoring and all was still. Piccadilly Circus and all its unnecessary haste no longer existed.

The Statue of Eros, the Greek God of Desire, seemed to stare downwards... no, she was wrong in her metaphor, the Statue of Christian Charity in the centre of Piccadilly Circus was often mistaken for a representation of Eros, but was actually Anteros, his brother, the Avenger of Unrequited Love.

Quite forwardly, Earnestine held out her hand to be kissed. She'd not hoped for anything else, of course, because that would have been unbecoming.

But Mister Djehuti turned her hand over and kissed her palm, which was jolly shocking, exciting and gave Earnestine a tingling all over.

It had been quite a step over her firm line in the sand.

And then he leant forward and kissed her on her lips.

Mrs Merryweather

In the Dining Room, Earnestine was gazing off into the distance again and sighing – what was the matter with her?

"Ness?"

"Yes?"

"You were saying?"

"Was I? Where was I?"

"Taking forever to explain what happened to Mister Rake."

"Mister Rake?"

"The man who was murdered."

"Oh, that Mister Rake, yes..."

Her sister's bizarre behaviour was causing Georgina a great deal of concern: "Do you need a cup of tea?"

"I'm fine. What's the matter with you, Gina?"

"Ness, please."

"Mister Rake, later on in the evening, outside by the... outside. He came upon Captain Caruthers."

"Was the Captain alone?"

"Quite alone."

"So, you were alone with the Captain?"

"No, one was not alone with the Captain. What are you suggesting? I was with... I was alone, walking in the cool – it was jolly hot, Gina – and I came across Captain Caruthers. He was arguing. With someone."

"With who?"

"I don't know. He... anyway, nothing happened, it was all a misunderstanding."

"But–"

"The point!" Earnestine said, raising her finger. "Mister Rake turned up out of nowhere, drunk. So, anyway, Captain Caruthers and... an Egyptian took Mister Rake to an hotel room."

"Farouk?"

"What?"

"The Egyptian who helped?"

"Farouk, yes. No. It was the other Egyptian."

"The other Egyptian? Al Rachid?"

"Him!"

"Yes?"

"The man with his face full of scars?"

"Yes, poor man."

"Poor man! No, it wasn't that ghastly al Rachid, it was... one of the other Egyptians. It is Egypt, Gina, there are a lot of them about."

"And then they went off and what did you do?"

"I went inside and had a stiff drink."

"Was that wise?"

"We're on holiday."

Georgina wrote 'other Egyptian' in her notes: "Do you remember his name?"

"Er... Reevers is smuggling mummies into Egypt."

"What?"

"Sir Archibald is smuggling a mummy *into Egypt.*"

"He's allowed, isn't he? He is the President of the Royal Expeditionary Society."

"*Into* Egypt."

Georgina had no idea what Earnestine was suddenly going on about: "Why?"

"One doesn't know," Earnestine said. "But he's up to something."

"I don't see the relevance."

"It's some secret expedition and Mister Rake was his personal secretary – motive, Gina, motive."

"So, stealing antiquities."

"Some raise handsome sums."

"There's nothing hereabouts by the Suez to excavate, is there?"

"No."

"So, what is he up to?"

"He's not looking for the Garden of Eden that's for sure."

"Of course not," Georgina said. "It's a myth."

"And it's not here!"

"Could it be something else? Didn't Moses wander the desert for years on the way from Egypt to the Holy Land? This is desert. You could probably cover a lot of ground in forty years. What about the Ten Commandments and the Ark of the Covenant?"

"Gina," said Earnestine, exasperation in her voice, "the Ten Commandments are in the Ark of the Covenant and the Ark of the Covenant is buried in Tanis."

"We were in Tanis."

"I know! And the President of the Royal Expeditionary Society boarded this foolish boat instead of digging for the Well of Souls."

"The what?"

"The Well of Souls in Tanis. Did you listen to anything Father said?"

"He said not to go chasing fame and fortune with a treasure map."

"Yes, that, and the Ark of the Covenant is in Tanis."

"So, Sir Archibald must be looking for something else."

"Yes! Finally! Write it down."

Georgina considered how best to record this long list of what Sir Archibald was not looking for. And was the business in Tanis important? And why had Mister Rake got drunk? Why was Earnestine so distracted? Was she hiding something?

"Gina, will that be all?"

"Yes, thank you."

"Can I go?"

"Thank you, yes, Ness. Off you go and have an adventure."

"No adventures."

Earnestine got up smartly, smoothed her burgundy dress down, and made her way to the door.

Captain Caruthers was just coming in.

They paused, their profiles aimed at each other.

"Captain," Earnestine said, formally.

"Miss Deering-Dolittle," Caruthers replied.

Earnestine was gone: the Captain paused and then came forward.

"Captain," Georgina said, waving to the chair opposite.

"Investigating Officer."

"Can you explain what happened?"

"Straight to the point," he said. "Can I smoke?"

"Of course."

Captain Caruthers lit a cigarette taken from a small silver case.

"Well," he began, "there was a shot, quite clear, and when I arrived at the connecting corridor by the Library there was quite a commotion. Doctor Timon had taken charge, keeping people away until the ship's crew arrived."

The Captain paused, a private smile appearing under his chevron moustache.

"What is it?"

"Doctor Timon was worried that Miss Deering-Dolittle was going to faint, so he accosted her with smelling salts. You can imagine how that went."

Georgina smiled too, before forcing her laughter away. She could well imagine that moment.

"Once the Skipper of the *Karnak* had looked into the room, it was sealed with a new lock. I think you saw that."

"I heard it."

"So, the scene was pretty much undisturbed."

"Who went into the room?"

"Doctor Timon, Captain Ahmed, I think, but that's from what I've heard. I wasn't there myself."

"Where were you?"

"I was in my cabin."

"But I saw you on the deck."

Caruthers shuffled uncomfortably in his chair. "I might have stepped out on deck briefly to enjoy the view and smoke a cigarette."

Why did the man say he was going on deck when there was no view, just desert, and there was a perfectly good Smoking Room on board? It wasn't like he couldn't smoke in his cabin. Here he was smoking in the Dining Room. The crew smoked in the Engine Room and the ghastly smell of their Turkish tobacco was barely hidden by the reek of oil and coal dust.

"Did you know Mister Rake?"

"No."

"From earlier?"

"No."

"Perhaps India?"

"No."

"But we've shared a journey."

"We exchanged pleasantries. I saw him about, running errands for Sir Archibald."

"Errands?"

"Collecting some crates at Tanis, organising things with the natives and so on."

"And at Tanis... during that dinner?"

Again, the Captain shuffled, tapped his ash out on a side plate and smoothed his moustache.

"It was nothing."

"With Mister Rake?"

"Oh, yes, he turned up drunk. Outside, afterwards. Argued with the Frog and that... Egyptian."

"Which Egyptian?"

"Djehuti."

"What was the argument between Monsieur Jacques and Mister Rake?"

Caruthers shrugged: "Hard to tell. It was between a man with a thick French accent and someone who was slurring his English. A book, I think, he wanted to borrow it. There aren't that many books in the Library here, so I suppose they both wanted to read the same one."

"This was before we boarded the SS *Karnak*," Georgina pointed out.

"Oh, that's right. Another book then."

"What are you doing on this voyage?"

"Helping you travel to India."

"So I can sort out some business to do with my late husband's estate?"

"That it. And to see the country again."

"Just that?"

"Perhaps a little something for Major Dan."

"What's that?"

"Nothing of relevance to your investigation."

"Surely that's for me to decide."

"Seriously, nothing of relevance."

Georgina could see that the Captain wasn't going to be moved on this one. What was Major Dan up to? He often sent Captain Caruthers on 'mountaineering expeditions' and maybe it wasn't any of her business. He had a crate on board, she knew, as well as his travelling trunk.

"Do you always carry your revolver?"

Captain Caruthers tapped his holster: "Foreign climes."

"May I?" Georgina asked holding out her hand.

"If you'll be careful. It is loaded."

"I've used one before."

The Captain unbuttoned the holster and handed over the firearm. It was heavy, an ugly thing in Georgina's delicate hands, and she struggled with the latch to open it.

"Shall I?"

"Thank you, but no. I have been shown how... *ah-ha*, there."

The thing hinged open revealing the shining ends of the bullets. Or cartridges. Georgina had long ago learnt not to say either word, because she always got them the wrong way round. She poured the 'things' out onto the table where they clattered and rolled. All six shells (or were they rounds?) had the pointy ends intact.

She smelt the gun, putting it right against her nose. It smelt of oil and leather from the holster.

"When did you last clean this?"

"Tuesday."

"Before Mister Rake's demise then."

"Yes."

There wasn't a hint of that cordite smell.

"Does it pass?" Caruthers asked.

"Thank you."

Caruthers took the revolver back, leant over and rescued his... ammunition, and reloaded carefully. His smile was impish.

"Will that be all?" Caruthers asked.

"Thank you," she said.

"I'll be off then," he said, and he stood and nodded.

Once the Captain had left, Georgina went down her notes carefully.

1. Sir Archibald Reevers, on deck, port.
2. Colonel Fitzwilliam, Smoking Room.
3. Captain Caruthers, on deck, starboard.
4. Pandit Singh Maçon, Smoking Room.
5. Doctor Timon, Smoking Room.
6. Monsieur Jacques, Smoking Room.
7. Mrs Albright, cabin.
8. Miss Deering-Dolittle, on deck, aft.
9. Miss Charlotte, levels.

Sir Archibald was known for his temper, so perhaps Mister Rake had failed him. He was here on an expedition, obviously, but he wouldn't admit it.

Colonel Fitzwilliam's war wound made him a near invalid, but he was quite capable of walking over to the drinks cabinet and he was just across the passageway from the Library when the shot was fired.

Captain Caruthers said he was in his cabin, but she had seen him skulking in the shadows. What had Major Dan asked him to do and would he have killed to achieve it? Yes, he would. And they had history back in India that the Captain didn't want to talk about.

Pandit Singh Maçon was travelling from India to India, via the Suez Canal, which was very sinister.

Doctor Timon swore he'd not talked to Mister Rake, yet they had argued about buying a book back in Tanis.

Monsieur Jacques said he helped force the door open, but he appeared to have arrived late. What had he been up to? Where had he gone? And he was French.

Mrs Albright was after esoteric knowledge; her whereabouts were unknown and she had known of the death before it was possible according to the Laws of Natural History. She'd said that Mister Rake was teetotal, and yet everyone else said he was drunk.

Earnestine's account of whatever happened in Tanis was riddled with holes. And sighs. And longing looks. What was all that about?

Charlotte had said she wasn't doing anything. Oh, where to start? She didn't know where the pantry was – honestly! It was as if she thought Georgina had been born yesterday. Or was it a double bluff?

And having been down the list, Georgina stabbed the page with her pen: *tap, tap, tap.*

So, that was it; everyone lied.

Even her sisters!

Even Captain Caruthers!

Therefore, indubitably, they all did it.

Miss Charlotte

"I can hear something," said a screeching voice. It was Mrs Albright with a voice that could always be heard.

"Oh lummy," Charlotte whispered aloud.

She jumped across to Captain Caruthers's crate, pulled some straw out, but there was no room. She glanced at the others, saw the round one was empty and leapt inside that. Once in, she had to lean out again to pull the lid over her. Just in time.

Three-legged footsteps came in: *thud, thud, tap.*

"It was here," Mrs Albright said.

"It was the engine," said Sir Archibald.

"I'm sure."

"You are imagining things."

"I am a sensitive."

"Here he is. Get the crowbar."

"Where is it?"

"By the hammer."

Hammer! There was a hammer somewhere, Charlotte realised – oh bother.

"There's just a hammer."

"It'll have to do," Sir Archibald said. "Hand it over."

"You won't open it with that."

"Nonsense... put the lantern in the middle so I can see what I'm doing. That's it. Hmm, this hasn't been nailed down properly."

"Never mind that."

Charlotte heard the top of Sir Archibald's crate being levered off and just when she'd managed to get it back on.

"This was a High Priest of Thoth," Sir Archibald said. "He knew a great many secrets."

"Secrets of the occult?"

"So they say."

"You can feel his power emanating from the other side. He looks almost alive, as if ready to rise again."

"Trick of the light."

"See, here, someone has come out of the crate recently."

"Nonsense. No, no, utter nonsense."

"High Priest Amenemope, you know."

"He can't hear you, my dear."

"There's no time to lose, we must consult the spirits."

"If you are sure?"

"Sir Archibald, remember what Mister Rake said."

"That Amenemope knows."

"We must ask Amenemope himself. He knows where the Book of Thoth is hidden."

"When?"

"Tonight."

"Where?"

"The Library?"

"But that's where... it's bad taste."

"It is close to the spirit world. Mister Rake will be our guide. He has gone on before us, crossed over to the other side. The dark veil will be tenuous there."

"Very well, but Amenemope... we can't bring him up on deck and into the Library."

"That isn't necessary, Sir Archibald, he just needs to be close."

"Then tonight," Sir Archibald whispered. He was useless at whispering; Charlotte could hear every word. Then he started to hammer the nails back in, causing Charlotte to jump.

"We shall prepare straight away," Mrs Albright said.

"I have a task to perform first," Sir Archibald said. "Since Mister Rake's unfortunate demise, I've found I have to do everything myself."

You and me both, Charlotte thought.

Charlotte counted twenty elephants, then thirty 'phants before she finally used the mantra 'fifty-one, etcetera, one hundred'.

They had gone.

She struggled out of her hiding place.

Why was the Pandit's crate empty?

And Sir Archibald had made a worse job of sealing his crate than Charlotte's attempt. He'd also hidden the hammer again. Or taken it with him.

She could smell burning.

There was a black mark on the top of the crate with the sarcophagus where the seal of the British Museum had been scorched away. Charlotte was sure it hadn't been like that before.

Some power had erased the symbol.

The sooner she got out of this creepy hold, the better, but first, she was determined to seal up the Captain's crate perfectly. They'd taken the hammer – typical. Even so, it went swimmingly until the fourth nail.

"Ow, *ow*, bally thing!"

CHAPTER VIII

Miss Deering-Dolittle

All Georgina had done, Earnestine realised, was ask a lot of questions that had interrupted her train of thought. It was quite absurd that Georgina was the Investigating Officer. There was no such position and surely Earnestine was eminently more suitable. She was barred just because she was a suspect. If only she hadn't been staring across the desert in the hope of seeing the Nile. She wanted to see the world, to explore, to light the fuse, explode the dynamite and uncover who knew what ancient treasures.

But she had to wait. Her sister was going to be all-important and self-righteous, while Earnestine had to kick her heels.

It chafed.

Earnestine's nature was, after all, one of action and high sightseeing.

And she was not going to think about that man in Tanis. Instead, she'd think about something else. For example, what was Sir Archibald Reevers really looking for?

Earnestine strode down the staircase and then along deck to the bow, passing the doors to various cabins as she went before she reached the narrowing point. She clambered up onto the prow and reached the end of her constitutional.

Ahead, the vast line of the Suez Canal stretched to the far horizon, its green water trapped by banks of earth on either side. She held her arms out as if trying to take flight, like a seagull hanging on the wind. With her eyes closed, she wished she could fly: the Nile, Karnak, the Temple at Luxor, Giza, a dig in the Valley of the Kings, everywhere... anywhere.

If she'd wanted to see a canal, she could have gone to Venice.

Or Birmingham.

A man had talked to her at the formal dinner in Tanis – less than a day ago – who had been bronzed and athletic-looking; foreign, but with eyes that twinkled with knowledge and humour. He seemed to have seen the world, despite his young age, and Earnestine yearned for such experience.

Mister Djehuti.

He'd smiled, warmly, and she'd explained that she was one of three sisters.

"Your parents?"

"Lost."

"I am sorry."

"Lost on an expedition. They'll be found," Earnestine had insisted. "In the meantime, I have to keep the peace."

"I too," he had said, "have had to arbitrate in family feuds and separate order from chaos."

"You must talk to my sisters," Earnestine had said. "Georgina is order and Charlotte – over there making a spectacle of herself – is assuredly chaos."

"Perhaps they are the embodiments of the goddesses Isis and Hathor?"

"And myself? Which ancient Egyptian goddess do you see in me?"

"Ma'at of Truth, Justice... divinely beautiful and strong, she holds a sceptre of power in one hand and an ankh to symbolize eternal life in the other."

"I have only my umbrella."

"And she has wings to fly."

To fly... imagine. To feel the wind in your wings and soar above the earth like a goddess.

It was a dream.

She could feel the breeze on her face, the wind rushing past, her hair streaming out behind as much as her hairstyle allowed.

But just a dream.

Best to keep the genie safe in his bottle.

Earnestine lowered her arms.

She'd flown a few times before and those occasions had been screamingly frightening experiences of plummeting awfulness – never again.

She opened her eyes once more.

The entire landscape had a constructed appearance, for indeed this was a man-made world. Modern day French Pharaohs had used forced labour to construct this horizontal monument, tens of thousands of workers digging, and many thousands had died over the ten years of brutal construction. The British Empire had opposed such barbarism and a stop had been put to it, eventually.

It had opened over thirty years ago, and Earnestine smiled when she remembered that the first vessel to use the canal was the Royal Navy's HMS *Newport*. The night before the grand opening, Captain Nares had navigated his Philomel-class gunvessel through the waiting ships under cover of darkness, and without lights, to be at the head of the queue. He'd been reprimanded by a well-pleased Admiralty. Even then, when the French administered the canal, Britain ruled the waves of this narrow strait.

Of course, it was all properly British now.

Ahead, other boats manoeuvred, their white sails flapping occasionally, but they seemed like models on a lake as they were so far away. It was single lane, all boats at this time moving south from Tanis and once they reached the Great Bitter Lake, other vessels could pass and the canal would become northbound.

The straight edges of the horizon and the canal met at a distant vanishing point.

It pulled!

The perspective was such that she leant out, a giddying falling sensation.

"Careful!"

Earnestine pulled herself back: "Sir Archibald."

"It's an intoxicating view, my dear."

"Yes, it is."

"Are you pleased to see it?"

"One would have preferred the Nile."

"The Nile?"

"The pyramids, temples, archaeological sites rather than this empty, desolate wasteland."

"I quite agree, my dear," Sir Archibald agreed. "I can't understand why Captain Caruthers brought you all this way to show you something so devoid of interest."

"Yes, quite, my thoughts entirely."

They stood in silence, the sun setting on the starboard side and appearing to ripple as the desert heat rose into the atmosphere. Soon, the temperature would drop to something bearable and then it would become surprisingly cold. Clear nights required winter outfits and she had packed woefully, thinking Egypt always hot.

Distantly, a ship called out like a whale.

What was the man up to? Only one way to find out.

"Sir Archibald," Earnestine said as nonchalantly as she could.

"Why, Miss Deering-Dolittle."

"One's condolences again about poor Mister Rake."

"Yes, yes, I am bereft."

"Yes, most upsetting."

"My dear, my paperwork, it's all over the place."

"Oh my, perhaps..." Earnestine paused. It wouldn't be seemly to appear in such a hurry and she shouldn't overplay her hand with any enthusiasm. It was like Charlotte's game when she'd moved the Battenberg to the sandwich plate. "That is... one might be of assistance."

"Could you?" He seemed both hopeful and doubtful.

"I have been of service in the Patents Pending Office with filing and such matters." Indeed, she had worked with a Mister Boothroyd in that office in a valiant attempt to impose order upon his documents.

"Indeed," he said. He narrowed his eyes. "I heard that was a front for... other concerns."

"It still involved filing, Sir."

"Filing and what else?"

"Filing and discretion."

"Excellent, my dear."

Here it was, the critical move, Earnestine realised. How to casually inquire as to what the h-word he was up to? Garden of Eden, honestly; he'd be telling her tales of Adam and Eve next.

"Miss Deering-Dolittle?"

"Sir Archibald?"

What did the man want from her?

She wanted to know what he was up to, but he had always blocked her attempts to organise an expedition. Or his secretary, Rake, had. Sir Archibald was probably going to suggest she went home, thinking that a woman travelling to India was foolhardy.

"It is not easy for a young lady such as yourself to make her way in the world. Particularly one as interested in exploration as yourself."

"This is true."

"And I find myself without a secretary."

"I'm genuinely sorry for your loss, Sir Archibald," Earnestine said. Then added through gritted teeth, "Mister Rake was a fine gentleman, I'm sure. It must grieve you greatly and the inconvenience must be considerable."

"Indeed," Sir Archibald agreed. "Who is going to organise my papers and catalogue my discoveries?"

"Quite."

"An important book has gone missing."

"That is vexing."

"And you are also a young lady of some common sense and decorum."

"Thank you."

"So, I propose an alliance. I am the chairman of the Royal Expeditionary Society, a prestigious appointment, and I can always secure the necessary funding. Together, we would make a formidable team – my leadership and your clerical thoroughness. The world, Miss Deering-Dolittle, I offer the world, the whole globe to explore."

Earnestine gasped aloud!

She was flabbergasted.

To be part of such a team, to be finally accepted upon expeditions was something she had dreamt of ever since she could remember. All those hours poring over maps and her father's big atlas, imagining the jungles, deserts and savannahs, the temples and tombs to discover. She'd be dressed in a long khaki dress, hacking her way through the jungle with a machete, smashing through glaciers with her ice axe with her trusty umbrella ready for any drizzle. Though native guides would fear local superstitions, she'd press on to uncover ancient edifices, historical wonders and fabulous treasures.

"Think of it," Sir Archibald continued. "I could take you under my wing and see that the vagaries of this man's world are not as onerous as they have been... Miss?"

"Sorry," Earnestine replied, startled. "One was miles away."

She had woefully misjudged the man. He understood her difficulties as a woman in this man's world, as he said, and to be taken under the auspices of the Society – literally under his wing with an office in the Royal Expeditionary Society's offices in the east wing of their fine building – was truly a good turn of luck. He offered her the world.

"One doesn't quite know what to say," she said. "It's all so sudden."

"So, Miss, do you accept my proposal?"

"Of course."

Sir Archibald beamed: "And you can get my papers in order, Miss Deering-Dolittle."

"As soon as possible."

"Then let's not stand on ceremony," Sir Archibald said. "We shall announce our engagement over dinner."

"Yes, of course, I do..." – What? Proposal? Ceremony? Engagement? – "I beg your pardon?"

Mrs Merryweather

Why would they all have done it?

Maybe they did it to taunt Georgina.

It was all a joke and Mister Rake was only pretending to be dead.

Mister Rake?

The only witness she hadn't interviewed and he had actually been there when the murder occurred.

A post-mortem would be out of the question with the facilities offered on the ship and Georgina could well imagine the howls of protest; she, a mere member of the weaker sex, couldn't possibly perform such a gruesome undertaking. But human beings were simply another form of animal. They were imbued, of course, with a soul raising them to a higher plane, but once they were dead, they were just so many bones, cartilage, blood vessels and intricate tubing.

If Doctor Timon prescribed smelling salts *before* fainting, then who knew what leeches the man might fall back upon if he thought she was about to suffer from the hysterics. Probably best to sneak along to wherever the body had been laid to rest. Farouk would know.

It was important to do this as soon as possible. For starters, any evidence might be destroyed, and furthermore, in this climate, things went off. Unless they were thoroughly dried out and mummified, but that process would hardly preserve any clues.

Pippa was still sound asleep.

That didn't bode well for the night-time; however, seize the day.

She went to the door: "Farouk."

"Madam."

"Where is Mister Rake?"

"Madam, Farouk is so sorry, my apologies," Farouk replied, his hands alternatively scrunching and smoothing the fez he held in front of him, "but Mister Rake met with an... unfortunate accident. Yes, accident."

"I know that. I'm the Investigating Officer."

"Of course, but he's quite dead. The dead don't come back to life."

Georgina shivered: she knew differently.

"Perhaps a lie-down, Madam, the heat does not agree with those of your fine complexion."

"No, Farouk, I must see Mister Rake."

"He is... passed on."

"His body, Farouk. I'm not simple!"

"Yes, apologies."

"Where is his body?"

"Doctor Timon insisted he was stored in the Cold Room."

"Ah ha."

"Will that be all?"

"Can you take me to the Cold Room?"

"Madam!"

"You're the Guide... guide."

"Yes, Madam."

Farouk, clearly unsure whether to put his fez back on, led the way. The Cold Room was in the depths of the ship, forward, and under the Dining Room. They passed the hold and–

"Charlotte, what are you doing in there?"

"Just looking."

"Looking at what?"

"I'm bored."

"Then write some letters."

Charlotte made a face.

"Or fill in your journal."

"Gina! That's like doing lines."

"Nonsense. In years to come, you'll be able to read it and it'll remind you of this trip. All this will be conjured up and you'll be able to live through it again."

"Live through all this nagging again, you mean?"

"Charlotte, go to your room and finish your letters," Georgina insisted. The girl was up to something, skulking around below decks, but Georgina didn't have time for any nonsense.

"I can't finish my letters."

"Why ever not?"

"I haven't started them."

"Charlotte Deering-Dolittle!"

"I'm sorry, I would have done, but there was a murder."

"That is no excuse."

"Gina... do I have to?"

"Yes, your cousins will be expecting news."

"The Surrey Deering-Dolittles! I have to write to them?"

"Yes, Charlotte."

"There's nothing to write about."

"Oh, for heaven's sake, there's been a... *no!* Absolutely not. You are not to mention the murder to the Surrey Deering-Dolittles."

"But..."

"Our side of the family has a bad enough reputation as it is."

"Then what?"

"I don't know. Think of something. The weather."

Charlotte made her well-practised face again.

"Now, Lottie."

"I'm going."

The child smirked at Farouk as she snuck by.

"And write your journal!" Georgina shouted after her.

"I will."

"And study some Natural History... chemicals."

"I will."

"And do your French homework!"

"I will."

"Letters, journal and French!"

Charlotte made a noise and was gone.

Further along the passage, Georgina startled suddenly.

Ahead, a rat stared back at them, its eyes reflecting the lamp's light so that it shone evilly.

"Madam, keep back, it's a... I don't know the word."

"Rat. Rattus norvegicus."

"Ratratusicus?"

"Yes, jolly unhygienic."

"Is that the Latin name, Ratratusicus Jolungenic?"

"No... just 'rat'. Please get rid of it."

"Yes, Madam."

Farouk stepped forward, hesitated, and then the brown creature scampered away by itself.

He turned and smiled, a friendly action that proved to her that he had teeth missing.

"Thank you."

Farouk took her further forward, almost to the far staircase that led up to the Galley, and to a door marked 'Chambre Froide'. Like all the other doors, it was raised from the floor with rounded corners and a large handle.

Farouk opened it for her.

"Are you sure, Madam?"

"Quite."

"Do you want me to come in with you or... I could watch the passageway for you?"

"That will be fine."

"Thank you, Madam."

"Farouk, where were you when the shot was fired?"

"I was with the crew smoking a hookah with the First Mate, Donkor. He is my second cousin's second cousin on my aunt's side."

Briefly, Georgina tried to create a mental family tree, but she gave up. "Where was this?"

"In the Map Room."

"Ha!" Georgina exclaimed. If Earnestine found out about that, they'd never see her again.

Inside the Cold Chamber, it was wonderfully cool on account of the ice blocks stacked at the sides. There was water underfoot as the Egyptian heat whittled away the supply.

The larder was well packed with hanging meat, butter and other perishables. There were numerous dead chickens, each with their throat cut and their blood drained. The culinary practices of foreign climes left a lot to be desired. That... or Mrs Albright had collected blood for some unholy ritual.

The food was packed to one end opposite a table that had been put aside for the body.

She grimaced. This was hardly satisfactory.

At least they'd wrapped him in several sheets.

Georgina carefully pulled back the layers, aware that this must be much like the archaeologists of the British Museum when they were examining an Egyptian mummy. They hoped, she supposed, to learn about their lives, whereas she hoped to uncover the truth about a death.

Mister Rake seemed much like he had in life: haughty, tall, dark-haired with a small, bushy moustache. His eyes were closed, so he was no longer looking down on everyone and everything with disapproval.

Part of his head was missing.

"Farouk," she called. "I need more light."

"Madam," said Farouk, coming in with the oil lamp. "Farouk feels sick."

"It's probably all that foreign Egyptian food."

"Farouk is Egyptian."

The corpse's face became strangely animate as if he was coming back to life. An image of her late husband came to her for a moment, a ghost from the past, but she shook it away.

"Farouk, hold the lamp steady. I can't examine this with the shadows moving like that."

"Madam," said Farouk. He tried harder, but it was a difficult task to perform with his eyes closed.

The entry wound was slight, an angry black hole showing signs of scorching. When she felt around his head, she realised that the exit hole was a complete mess.

It wasn't a joke and he wasn't pretending to be dead.

Scorching?

That meant he was shot at point-blank range.

He must have let his assailant get very close, so did that mean the murderer was someone Mister Rake knew?

But, of course.

Having shared the dinner in Tanis, everyone knew everyone.

She pulled back the sheet further to check his clothing.

His pockets: a silver cigarette case, matches, Egyptian phrase book, French phrase book, a wallet with sterling, francs and Egyptian geneih, with a collection of loose change consisting of piastre and 'oshr el-ersh. They'd all learnt to have this loose change easily to hand to scatter on the floor and so distract the endless hawkers and beggars that swarmed around Europeans.

Also tucked in the wallet were an opera ticket, a playing card and a piece of paper. She unfolded the latter and found it to be a printed page ripped from a reference book describing Tenenet, the ancient Egyptian goddess of childbirth and beer. What strange ideas these ancients had? Childbirth and beer, when everyone knew that a mother's drink was gin.

The playing card was from a tarot deck and depicted Death.

His shoes were well polished, indicative of a good upbringing, but the backs had been scuffed recently. She couldn't quite imagine how that wear and tear had occurred.

That was everything from top to bottom.

Georgina tucked the white sheet back around the body, somehow emulating the ancient Egyptian priests.

Poor man.

Irritating man.

She fiddled with the piece of paper and the tarot card, and tried to collect her thoughts.

Someone shot him and it was evidently deliberate. It wasn't like there'd been a shooting party bagging pheasant or that they cleaned firearms in the Library. Whoever did it, approached to within an inch, and... Georgina raised her hand, finger extended – *bang!*

So, that was 'how'.

They shouldn't leave him in the larder like another piece of meat. They shouldn't leave the pieces of meat with a body in this makeshift mortuary. Although surely, they were the same matter. There wasn't really any other choice in this land of the baking sun. Where else was there ice? You could hardly make it here.

Georgina put a gentle hand upon Farouk's arm: "Come on, Farouk, I think I've learnt everything I can here."

"No-one came, Madam," said Farouk, clearly relieved that this ordeal was over.

"Thank you, Farouk."

"Where now?"

"The Library."

"Is that wise, Madam? A man died there."

"I've just been examining his body."

"Yes, Madam," Farouk said. "I'm not used to European ladies being so... I don't know the words."

"Forthright and sensible?"

"Yes, those are better words than... other words."

"Farouk!"

"Madam?"

"The Library, please."

They closed the door tightly, sealing the tomb behind them, and they didn't see the rat on their return.

Miss Charlotte

Well, Charlotte was going to show Georgina by writing the stupid letters.

She sat at her writing desk in her cabin – the smallest cabin ever – and just because she was the smallest didn't mean she had to have the smallest cabin. Georgina had the largest, because of Pippa, which made sense.

"Monsieur Jacques! Monsieur Jacques!"

How could Charlotte concentrate on her letters home with that screeching accent?

Seriously?

Mrs Albright was haunting her: first in the Smoking Room, then in the hold and now by yelling outside her cabin door. They'd lost a book. It was jolly distracting. It made Charlotte imagine that perhaps she could lose her French books. Although to be fair, she had no idea where her French homework was. Perhaps there was a book stealer on board as well as a murderer.

Her sisters kept going on and on about her not paying attention and missing things, but this boring (apart from today) journey was just one interruption after another.

'*Dear*' – that was as far as she managed to write.

She pushed the letter away, but that only uncovered her French homework. There it was, the blue hardback notebook with its faint ruled lines, semi-conjugated verbs and apparently bad penmanship. The French wanted funny splodges above their letters, so it was hardly her fault. Maybe she should study some Natural History. Charlotte pulled her unfinished correspondence back again.

'*Dear*' – could she write to each cousin separately, copy the same letter out again and again, and claim she'd written lots of letters, which she would have done, and so escape this punishment?

"You must help us tonight."

There she goes again – just when Charlotte was getting somewhere – *screech-screech-screech*.

"In the Library."

Charlotte couldn't even remember what she was supposed to be doing. Something... was it verbs, chemicals or the correct terms of address for bishops? Your grace, your graceas, your graceamus, your graceatis chloride – *no!*

It was her letters.

But what could she write? Charlotte mused. Georgina had suggested the weather... the weather here was sunny. It had been sunny all week. They expected it to be sunny all month. Next year, no doubt, it would be sunny. When the ancient Egyptians lived in the country, it was sunny. It had never not been sunny.

"The veil between us and the spirit world will be tenuous there," Mrs Albright elaborated outside her cabin. If that were true, Charlotte pitied the spirits having to hear her high-pitched racket.

The Surrey Deering-Dolittles were horrible anyway. They pulled Charlotte's hair. They certainly didn't deserve letters about Charlotte's exciting adventures in Egypt and all the wonderful things she'd seen and done, did they?

"Yes, I do insist, Monsieur Jacques."

Might as well be locked in a cell, Charlotte thought.

The best thing to do would be her French homework, then her sister wouldn't nag her about that, and then she might let her off doing her letters home.

But her French book was still full of strange letters, weird lines, hats and demandezs to conjugate the verb.

"We will conjure him from the spirit world," Mrs Albright screeched.

Where was she? Conjure the verb... ah, she wished the ancient spirits, those ancient mummies, would come to life, steal her homework to learn all they could about the secrets of the living, the conjugating, the ghastly smells and the secret titles of the powerful and boring.

She needed some fresh air. She'd been working on her letters *and* her French homework for simply hours.

When she stepped onto the deck, Mrs Albright and Monsieur Jacques startled.

"Don't forget, tonight," Mrs Albright said before she gave a sharp look in Charlotte's direction. And Charlotte hadn't done anything.

"Mademoiselle," Monsieur Jacques said. At least he paid her some attention.

Perhaps she could persuade him to do her French homework and she, in turn, could do his English homework.

"Monsieur," she said. Ah, this was homework. Georgina couldn't possibly complain. She'd managed a whole word of French conversation. In for a centimes, in for a franc, she thought: "Le temps est clément."

"Tu parle français."

She carried on with, "Er... oui."

"Tu es une jolie femme."

"Oui, je suis jolly fam."

He looked at her strangely.

"Jolly famished... I could murder some cake."

He smiled, finally understanding. "Cigarette?"

Charlotte made a face.

"You know something of my country?"

"Oh yes," said Charlotte. "Alesia, Austerlitz, Crécy, Agincourt, Waterloo... oh, sorry."

"P'ah! What is it to me. I prefer the pastimes of peace. Faites l'amour pas la guerre."

"Oh... how... interesting." Clearly, this man was about to go on about the countryside or boules. Why couldn't he know some exciting anecdotes like the Colonel? Charlotte could never tire of hearing about the Thuggee uprising or the battles against the wicked Boer or–

"We French are a passionate people."

Just imagine, Charlotte thought, all those warriors falling before the steady onslaught on British Army fire. The Lee-Enfield .303, bolt action, 20 to 30 rounds a minute, which was a proper modern gun.

"If you understand my meaning."

"Oh yes," said Charlotte, wondering what he meant.

"Do you have wine in your cabin?"

"No, sorry."

"We could go to my cabin, a little wine, a little pleasure."

"Ooh, do you have cake?"

"Perhaps, little one, if you were good to me, I could be good to you."

"Lovely."

"Perhaps..."

"I'd like a lemonade."

"Lemonade?"

"Yes... I mean, oui."

"My cabin is along here."

They strolled through the connecting passage to the port side, and then along the deck passing various other cabin doors, keeping in the shade as they went.

"Ici, this is my cabin," he said, opening the door with his key. "Do you like it?"

"It's exactly the same as mine only the mirror image."

"Oui. Do you like the bed?"

"It's all exactly like mine."

Jacques closed the door. "You are on le tribord."

"Letribord?"

"Starboard side."

"Oh, yes, apparently on account of my youth. And in the afternoon, I can't go back to my cabin for a lie-down, because it's like an oven."

"You can lie down here."

So, Charlotte sat on the bed, bouncing up and down on the springs. It was so much cooler than in her cabin. What was that acronym, 'Lorb' – 'Left out, right back'?

Jacques dug out a bottle: "Wine? Brandy?"

"Lemonade?"

Jacques handed her a glass of red wine.

Charlotte sniffed at it.

He sat beside her.

In amongst the great long list: don't run in the corridor, don't climb trees, don't consort with cadets, don't eat before meals, don't put your elbows on the table, don't giggle, don't let your mind wander, don't... well, it just went on and on and on. But there was something about men and bedrooms, she was sure of it.

"Santé."

"Oh, santy."

They clinked glasses.

Charlotte was so grown up, she knew that. Earnestine and Georgina always treated her like a child. If only they could be like Colonel Fitzwilliam or Captain Caruthers, who understood.

Something tickled her ear: "What are you doing?"

Monsieur Jacques was twirling a lock of her blonde hair.

Charlotte tugged it away from him. The last thing she wanted was, say, Earnestine or Georgina to catch her like this and insist that she brush her hair a hundred times. Everything in her life was just endless punishment: lines a hundred times, brush a hundred times, I've told you a hundred times.

It wasn't like she ever did anything wrong.

Monsieur Jacques was stroking her shoulder now, leaning in closer, smelling of wine and not garlic. He finished her wine for her, put the glass down on his dressing table and turned towards her, putting his now free hand on her knee.

"What do you want?" Charlotte asked, being jolly direct and forward.

"Un petit bisou."

"I'm sorry."

"Oh, but you are too cruel."

"No, it's just that you keep speaking French and I left my dictionary in my cabin," Charlotte said, shifting away. "I could go and get it."

"I could translate for you."

"Or just speak English."

"As you wish."

"What does 'un petty be sue' mean?"

"A little kiss."

"Are there any accents, graves, hats or silly dillas on it?"

"Pardon?"

"Are there... you know, funny lines above the writing?"

"In what?"

"In 'un petty be sue'?"

"Non."

"That's good to know."

"I could do something for you."

"You'd help me?"

"Of course."

"Oh, thank you."

"You have no experience."

"Well, I've tried, but it's difficult."

"Your sisters, they watch you."

"Like hawks, I'm not allowed to do anything."

"You should be allowed to do whatever you want for pleasure."

"I think so too."

"I will show you."

"Thank you again... I mean, merci, merci."

"I will be gentle."

"Because it's so hard."

"You can tell already?"

"Can you do it right away?"

"Oui, let us not delay," said Monsieur Jacques, unbuttoning his shirt collar and pulling off his tie.

"Yes, let's not waste a minute, then we can have cake."

"In these matters of the heart, it is best if the man takes the lead."

"Is it?"

"As between a man and a woman."

"I'm sorry?"

"As if they are married."

"Come again?"

"The conjugal rights. You understand?"

"Conjugal, yes! I'd love that."

"I am so glad."

"Conjugating always confuses me. I do this, you do that..."

"I will do for you, and show you what to do for me."

"And could you help me with my reclining?"

"Of course, lie back."

"Sorry, I meant my declining."

"It is no decline, a loss of the innocence, ma chérie, it is more a blossoming of your femininity."

Charlotte jiggled up and down on the bed: "This is so good of you."

"It is an honour to help you grow to womanhood."

"Oh, I'm so glad. I'll fetch the book."

"I need no instruction guide, I know how to treat a woman."

"My exercise book."

Charlotte jumped up and skipped to the door.

It was wonderful, utterly enchanting. No wonder Georgina went on and on that men should be masterful. A French Master doing her French homework was clearly better than a girl having to do it herself.

In fact, as she opened the door, there was Georgina.

"Oh, Gina, I–"

"Charlotte Deering-Dolittle!!!"

"What?"

"I saw as I walked to the Library, but I didn't believe it."

"I know–"

"What do you think you are doing?"

Oh lummy, Charlotte thought. First, her sister saying her full name in that tone, and now being asked what she thought she was doing. It was wrong, wasn't it, in some strange mysterious way that was about to make no sense. But Georgina had told her to write her letters and do her French homework – actually told her – so Charlotte knew she was absolutely in the right.

"I was doing my French homework."

"Charlotte Deering-Dolittle, what codswallop!"

Charlotte flinched, but no smack landed.

Monsieur Jacques, his hastily replaced tie all askew, appeared behind her, ready to rescue her – thank goodness.

"Madame," Monsieur Jacques protested, "la Madamoiselle–"

"Silence!"

"Madame, je–"

"BE QUIET!"

Charlotte explained patiently. "He's French. He knows French. It was French."

Georgina grabbed Charlotte by the ear and yanked her along the deck to the passage. It twisted, so painfully, and it was all Charlotte could do to keep up with the angry tempest.

Halfway along the passage, Farouk appeared: "I have the key, Madam."

"I'm busy, Farouk," Georgina commanded. "I'll meet you by the Library."

Charlotte saw an opportunity. She could help her with whatever it was, and hopefully, Georgina would forget whatever it was that was bothering her. "I could–"

"In!"

Charlotte had no choice as Georgina hoicked her into her cabin.

"Gina, I–"

"What if you had to marry Monsieur Jacques?"

"Marry!"

"Because if you did, your children would all grow up speaking French and you wouldn't be able to talk to them."

"But–"

"Key?" said Georgina, holding out her hand.

Charlotte handed over her key.

"Gina, I was–"

"Write your letters. Do your French homework."

"What's the point of French homework, if I'm not allowed to talk to Frenchmen."

"Men, Charlotte. You're not allowed to talk to men."

And with that, Georgina slammed the door and locked her in.

Charlotte leant over to talk through the keyhole: "He's not a cadet."

But Georgina's stomping steps had already thwacked their fury into the distance.

What had she done wrong this time?

Neither sister ever explained.

It was so unfair.

CHAPTER IX

Miss Deering-Dolittle

Proposal? Ceremony. Engagement!

Earnestine felt all of a dither.

She should go back to Sir Archibald at once and explain that she was confused. Or did she want to be betrothed? He was a 'good catch', wasn't he? And being married didn't actually exclude gaining funding for expeditions? Did it? She just didn't know what to think.

She needed advice, so the last person she wanted to meet would be either of her sisters, so she bumped into Captain Caruthers, which was worse.

"Captain Caruthers."

"Miss Deering-Dolittle."

She could ask him, couldn't she, she thought, because he was a good, stolid friend of the family. Someone dependable and kind.

"Captain, you are a gentleman, are you not?"

"I hope so."

"It is simply that one has a question."

"I too have a question... but... well, you know you can ask me anything."

"I know."

Caruthers took a silver cigarette case from his pocket, took one and placed it between his lips ready to light. He had a box of matches.

The trick was how to phrase it.

"Would you?" he asked, once he'd inhaled and then let the smoke drift out lazily into the desert heat. "Would you ask your question?"

"Ah. What, pray, do you think a young lady should look for in a gentleman?"

"I think that rather depends on the families in question."

"Of course, jolly sensible."

Young boys ran along the shore trying to keep up with the steamship. There were always boys trying to keep up, Earnestine thought.

"However, what if the young lady does not have a family as such."

Caruthers regarded her for a moment: "You are talking about yourself."

"Young ladies in general and only hypothetically."

"But yourself as an example?"

"That would be sensible."

"In that case, what is it you want?"

"Well, that is... it is not what one wants oneself, but simply that one finds that one has no family and you... my sisters are hopeless on these matters. So many of our family are... gone or lost on an expedition. And you are someone I can trust."

"Thank you."

"So, what should I be looking for?"

"Someone to provide."

"Eminently."

"Wealth and position in society."

Earnestine thought of Sir Archibald Reevers, who most certainly did have money and class. She knew no-one else of that rank.

"Captain, what else?"

"For you though, there is more," Caruthers said, leaning on the railing and looking at the calm water flowing underneath. "You are special."

"Me?"

"You could have any man you wanted," said Caruthers.

Earnestine touched the side of her face. "Nonsense."

"You're handsome."

Handsome?

Georgina was beautiful. Gentlemen flocked to hold the door open or pull back a chair for Georgina.

Charlotte was pretty. Men of all types positively buzzed around her, which said a lot for men's predilections.

But handsome?

Not with this ugly scar down the side of her face.

"No man comes up to talk to me," she said.

"I'm talking to you."

"Yes, true, but you're someone safe," she said.

"Safe?"

Earnestine felt flummoxed: "One wants what every young lady wants."

"I think you rather want more."

"I don't wish to be rich, just secure, and I have no ambitions to be Lady this or Countess that."

"I rather referred to your character," Caruthers said. "You have a yearning spirit that wants to spread its wings and see the world."

"Poppycock."

"Miss Deering-Dolittle. Ness, if I may be so bold. This is the case."

"You'll be saying I want adventures next."

"You do."

"Nonsense. Anyway, Mother forbade it."

"Life is an adventure."

She couldn't think of any reply, so she leant on the railing a few feet from Caruthers' elbow. The Captain carried on smoking, lost in his thoughts. Ahead of her, there was nothing but desert, and there was nothing in that particular desert, not even relics, to warrant any attention.

"If only," she said, but mostly to herself.

They stayed for a while, standing apart.

Mrs Merryweather

Farouk was waiting patiently by the Library. He had the key to the padlock from the ship's Skipper.

Georgina wondered what the crew made of all this.

Possibly they found the activities of the Europeans as mysterious as the passengers found the crew's activities. She'd been on boats and ferries before, vessels as large as this one, and the actions of the crew had made some sense. Here, the Egyptians mumbled and then did things that seemed contrary. Rope was uncoiled and coiled, planks moved and put back, things hoisted and lowered, all seemingly without reason.

Yet the ship had steamed away on time and made steady, if slow, progress along the canal.

Georgina took several deep breaths to calm down. She must be logical and systematic here.

It wasn't much of a Library. The faded sign had originally announced 'Salle de Bibliothèque', but someone had painted that over with the word 'Library'.

Georgina opened the padlock that secured the temporary clasp. She was glad that the... what to call it? The 'Stage of the Transgression' perhaps? Whatever the terminology, it had been secured and thus conserved.

She swung the door open.

It banged against the wall causing her to jump.

Even though she'd been in the room before, pleased to find somewhere that might be a quiet bolthole for her and Pippa, it now seemed unfamiliar and alien.

She should check on Pippa. Her daughter had been asleep, but she might have woken.

"I'll stand guard," Farouk suggested.

"Jolly good."

Two armchairs and a chaise half surrounded a small table. Other chairs lined a wall, ready to be brought into play for bridge. A white sheet hid the chaise from view as if the room had been abandoned.

A set of shelves kept half a dozen novels covering everything from Dumas to Molière. Hardly a good selection. Georgina noted that there was no Natural History and only one Egyptology text.

It was more of a reading room, somewhere quiet, tucked into the middle of the ship with no external windows and so it would be decidedly hot towards the end of the day; however, upon stepping inside, she found it to be cool.

There were oil lamps aplenty. Without natural light, these were needed if reading was the order of the day.

The door was solid.

Suffocation would seem the greatest peril.

Georgina made a slow circuit.

The books were coated in dust, except for one. She fiddled it free and flicked through it. Something flashed to her attention. It took a while to backtrack and find it again.

A page had been ripped out. It was a chapter on the gods and goddesses of Ancient Egypt and, judging by the alphabetical arrangement, it must be a page on – she checked the contents – Tenenet, a female goddess of childbirth and beer.

Tenenet?

Mister Rake had this missing page about the goddess tucked in his wallet – why? She checked the contents: Tenenet was followed by Thoth.

She dug out the page from her pocket.

Overleaf was a description of the god Thoth. There was a woodcut depiction. He was the bird-headed one, and Georgina skimmed down the page: temple in Khmun... shrines in Abydos, maintains the universe, arbitration, writing, five extra days in the year, and... oh! The god of science. She liked that. Also, he oversaw the judgement of the dead. She liked that not one bit.

Was she judging the dead?

Should she pray to Thoth?

She returned the book to its place carefully, trying her best to observe, but not interfere with the scene.

The oil lamps were half-full.

There was nothing secreted down the back of the armchairs' upholstery except for a few piasters, one shilling, 3d and a centime, and a single black chess piece.

The carpet at the head of the chaise was a darker colour. Blood, Georgina realised with a shock. When she lifted the sheet, she saw that the chaise itself was similarly stained in a deep crimson.

She shivered.

Someone had cleaned the wall, but the bright, bleach marks clearly indicated a pattern of splatter. There seemed to have been an awful lot of blood.

The assailant had been at the foot of the chaise. By standing on tiptoe and then crouching, she tried to see what angle made sense, but she couldn't work it out.

Mister Rake had been tall.

He'd probably been sitting on the chaise.

So, this was the logical position; perhaps further back if it was Captain Caruthers or Monsieur Jacques, closer if it had been Charlotte and somewhere in between for the other seven suspects.

Georgina felt guilty.

How could she suspect Caruthers? Or her sisters? Charlotte was naughty, cake always went missing, but surely not cold-blooded murder. But she had been caught consorting with unsavoury Frenchmen.

And Charlotte was jolly accomplished in the use of firearms.

As was Caruthers.

And Colonel Fitzwilliam.

A revolver, Georgina thought, as a rifle would be inappropriately awkward in the small space.

Every gentleman on board had a revolver, except Jacques, who had an automatic, and the Pandit, who had a gupti. However, simply because he had shown her his sword, it didn't mean that he hadn't a gun somewhere else.

Opportunity: everyone had a gun and no-one could have got in (or rather out again) to fire the shot.

Ooh, that was a thought, she realised. A locked door mystery was easy, utterly straightforward and without any sort of complications leading up to, and including, the actual murder. Then you had to get out of the room.

No, that wasn't really a thought.

The ceiling was plain, the floor consisted of scuffed wooden boards and the walls were painted metal. There were photographs of the ship at various locations on the Nile hung on the port wall. She supposed they were there in case someone became so engrossed in a book that they forgot where they were.

She checked behind the door. The lock was broken, damaged when Doctor Timon and Monsieur Jacques put their shoulders to it. Or was it Pandit Singh Maçon levering it with an axe? Part of the bolt's clasp remained attached, the thick screw bent but still holding firm.

She looked under the armchairs and chaise, where she found another piaster's worth of loose change and a knight to go with the castle.

How had this been done?

She should be systematic and write down every possibility and then, one by one, eliminate them. Whatever was left, no matter how improbable, would be the truth. Or so that consulting detective story in *The Strand Magazine* would have her believe. Indeed, it made perfect sense.

So... suicide.

He can't have committed suicide, because–

But no.

Systematic.

She must write down the possibilities and then examine each in turn.

She locked up, thanked Farouk and kept the key.

Back at her cabin – Pippa looked so peaceful asleep – she gathered her notebook and set about her task with gusto, later with determination and finally with a hot chocolate and a biscuit.

She carefully worked through the options starting with the victim.

Was 'suicide' and 'accidental' really both 'the victim did it'?

Could someone hide behind a secret door?

Finally, after much consideration and another Garibaldi, she felt that her list was complete. There were no other possibilities to include, no item that needed splitting into alternatives and nothing to usefully combine.

She took a brisk walk around the deck, seeing the familiar sights of the great canal and the desert. It was jolly hot on the port side.

Back at her cabin, she checked her list, re-crossed a 't' and felt satisfied.

1. Suicide.
2. Accident.
3. Automatic device.
4. Shot through window/door/hole.
5. Door locked from the outside.
6. Secret door.
7. Perpetrator hid in the room.
8. The first person to enter fired the shot.

There was also the matter of more than one person being involved, a murderer and an accomplice. She must take this into account with each possibility.

The first three would have left the gun, or the gun and mechanism, within the room.

She checked her notes from interviewing the witnesses: no gun or anything suspicious had been found. Someone could have taken the evidence away, but three at least had

had a good look just as the door had been opened, Earnestine included, so that seemed unlikely.

She crossed them out.

The next three involved the room itself. She realised that she hadn't examined that so thoroughly upon her first attempt, so, armed with her notes, she went back.

The Library was as she had first seen it.

Killed there, she thought, and fell back... no, he was lying upon the chaise.

Georgina got down and, on her hands, and knees, she went over every inch of the floor, then the walls, finally the door itself. She probed, pulled and prodded.

There was no hatch or hole present anywhere.

No hollow sounds to reward her bruised knuckles.

She found a dining chair and clambered up to examine the ceiling. Again, her tapping and testing revealed nothing, except a well-made construction.

Very well, she thought, and she continued her examination of the walls from the other side, which involved moving boxes in the storerooms, clambering atop the flat roof on top of the boat and causing some consternation in the kitchen below.

One of the storerooms next to the Library had a recent scorch mark on the floor, the charcoal blackened her fingertips, and room smelt of cleaning fluid.

There was no secret door through.

There was no hole through which a shot could be fired.

The door itself was a ship's hatch, the metal fitting perfectly to create a watertight seal. No string could be wrapped around the bolt that could be taken outside the room, no magnet could work its apparent magic through the stout construction, and no... she had no other ideas.

She stepped out into the passageway and looked all around the edge again.

This was impossible.

However, there was one more possibility.

Back at the door to Charlotte's cabin, Georgina fumbled three keys: Library, her cabin and Charlotte's.

Charlotte was standing in the middle of her room looking contrite, a picture of absolute innocence, as if butter wouldn't melt in her mouth. (Although, it often did and she'd then wipe her fingers on her dress.)

Georgina was not fooled; she knew Charlotte could change her expression at will.

"I'm sorry," Charlotte said. "It won't happen again."

Georgina had no time for this clearly rehearsed nonsense. "Charlotte, I have a little game for you."

"Oh, yes, it's afternoon tea, so—"

"That will ruin your appetite for dinner," Georgina said. "I was thinking of Hide and Seek."

"Aren't we a bit old for that?"

"Lottie, you are not forgiven, but I find I am in need your assistance."

Georgina held the door open and Charlotte followed dutifully. They marched to the Library door.

"Charlotte, go inside and hide."

"Give me a hundred at least," said Charlotte as she stepped inside.

"Ten."

"Jolly good."

The door closed.

Why did the door have a bolt on the inside, Georgina wondered... *nine, eight... hmm...*

Georgina opened the door and ignored the angry looking Charlotte to study the bolt.

It was a standard door, so the extraneous bolt was simply an accident of construction, easier to include than to exclude.

It was broken, the remaining screw almost torn free, and bent from the force exerted to break in. It had taken some effort, hence the need – as she remembered from the witness statements – for three strong men to open it and the use of an axe. They'd described it banging all the way to the wall, so no one had hidden behind it.

"Gina," Charlotte said, "this isn't fair. There's nowhere to hide."

That much was completely obvious. The chaise was the only piece of furniture of any size, pushed into the corner and it afforded a mere two inches underneath.

"Yes," Georgina agreed. She went to leave.

"Is that it?"

"Yes, Lottie, thank you."

"But..."

"Investigating."

"I never get any fun."

"No."

"I have a deerstalker hat and a magnifying glass."

"In Kensington, yes."

"But I have them."

"Go and... have afternoon tea, I'll join you when I'm finished."

"Right ho."

"But don't ruin your appetite for dinner..." but Charlotte had already rushed off.

Back at her writing desk, Georgina carefully crossed out numbers 4 to 7 on the list of possibilities.

So, she considered, the first person to enter fired the shot.

There were three gentlemen who broke down the door, but it was the Doctor who kept them back and examined the corpse. However, he did so in full view of the others in the corridor. Perhaps only two of them had a good view due to the size of the doorframe.

The Doctor could not have fired a shot.

He'd have been seen.

It would have been heard.

There were three or four men at the door, all trustworthy (although clearly, someone in their party was not) and they had all witnessed each other.

Earnestine too.

So, Georgina crossed out the last entry on her list. She sat back and contemplated the results.

1. ~~Suicide.~~
2. ~~Accident.~~
3. ~~Automatic device.~~
4. ~~Shot through window/door/hole.~~
5. ~~Door locked from the outside.~~
6. ~~Secret door.~~
7. ~~Perpetrator hid in the room.~~
8. ~~The first person to enter fired the shot.~~

That was it.

That was 'where'.

So, she concluded, it was impossible, completely impossible, and therefore no-one did it.

Miss Charlotte

It was Afternoon Tea – finally.

Charlotte had thought she'd be locked in her room all afternoon, but she'd escaped, strangely by having to test a locked room.

Captain Caruthers joined her in the Dining Room. "Lottie."

"Captain. Fancy a game?"

"You'll have to remind me of the rules."

"Oh, it's simple," said Charlotte indicating the three tiers of plates containing cakes, scones and sandwiches. "This is like noughts and crosses, but Battenberg counts two—"

"Two?"

"Yes."

"You've changed the rules."

"It's an expansion... they have different cakes today."

"I'll pick it up."

"I'll be Mother," said Charlotte and she poured a full cup for Caruthers and a half-cup for herself.

"Half-cup opening, eh? When can I say, 'More tea Vicar'?"

"Not when I'm Mother. One lump or two?"

"When you're half a cup ahead... one."

Charlotte selected a cube and plopped it in his cup.

"Lottie," Caruthers said, stirring, "what do you remember of Tanis?"

Charlotte pondered for a moment: "I don't think there's ever been a battle there."

"I mean the dinner we had at Tanis."

"Oh! Egypt medal, Khedive's Star, of course. They were all 1882, 1884 and 1885, although there was a Toski, which was 1889. Then some of the younger officers had the India Medals and–"

"Not the medals. About what happened?"

"What do you mean 'what happened'? We had a meal, I wasn't allowed wine, there was port, I wasn't allowed that either, there was a lot of tedious talk about trade through the canal, tea prices, import duties, the fact that you can't get a good curry this side of Bombay."

"Oh, Bombay curry... yes, that's very true."

"Will we have curry tonight?"

"Vegetarian, I believe."

"Why vegetarian?"

"The Pandit won't eat meat as he's Sikh, Farouk and the others won't eat pork as they are Muslim and Mrs Albright won't eat fish when Mars is in Pisces."

"What about chicken?"

"Depends on its star sign, no doubt," Caruthers added. "What I mean about Tanis was–"

"May I join you?" It was Georgina, probably just to spoil Charlotte's fun.

"Certainly Mrs Merryweather," the Captain said, standing.

"Shall I be Mother?" said Georgina, sitting.

"We've done that. I'm Mother."

"What's the tea?"

"Oolong."

"I'll have a cup then and..." Georgina pondered the options with her finger.

"You've not had any tea," Charlotte said.

"I was... you're not playing that silly game, are you?"

"We might be."

"You shouldn't play with your food."

"It's not playing, there are rules!"

"It passes the time and it's been a long journey by train and boat," Caruthers pointed out.

"Tea then, half-cup, and a sandwich... this mustn't spoil your appetite for dinner," said Georgina.

"Battenberg counts two."

"Don't talk nonsense," Georgina said. "Why did you put the Battenberg on the second level?"

"I made a bad move."

"You invented these rules."

"I know."

"I'll give you a ham sandwich then."

Charlotte showed Georgina her plate.

"You've eaten something already!"

"It wasn't ham," Charlotte said.

"Good, because they don't allow it in these parts."

"Don't allow sandwiches!"

"They don't allow meat of the cloven hoof, like ham."

"Why not?"

"It's in Leviticus, Numbers and Deuteronomy. It's the same for the Jews and Muslims."

"But..."

"What were you talking about?"

"The dinner at Tanis."

"Oh."

"Charlotte sat with Captain Conway and myself," Caruthers said. "And that Egyptian chap."

"Oh, yes," said Georgina. "What did you talk about?"

"The Battle of the Little Bighorn," Charlotte answered. "Did you?"

"Oh yes, loads of Indians – not Indian Indians, but American Indians – riding horses and firing guns and going round and round."

"Really?"

"The 7th Cavalry was surrounded by Indians, all around, firing in every direction," Charlotte said, her eyes lighting up. She pointed her finger out and fired off a few imaginary rounds at the circling Cheyenne and Sioux. "Killing them, loads of them, six shooters, bang, bang, bang, and then heroically in a last stand–"

"Charlotte!"

"They were all killed–"

"Charlotte!"

"But think of it–"

"I'd rather not," Georgina said. "I'm sure it wasn't really like that. Where did you hear of all this?"

"Captain Conway told me."

"And what does he know of it? Was he there? No, of course not."

"He might have talked to a survivor."

"Lottie, he was pulling your leg. How can there be a survivor if they were all killed?"

"Sitting Bull, Red Shirt and all those Indians in Buffalo Bill's Wild West show. They were all in the battle. They performed in front of the Queen, toured all Europe, London, Birmingham and–"

"Lottie, what's that to do with Mister Rake?"

"Nothing."

Georgina's mouth moved, but she didn't say anything.

"Mister Rake was on my right and Captain Conway on my left."

"Did he drink?"

"Wine, port..."

"So he had far too much?"

"Oh yes, Captain Conway drank a triple Islay and that was after the wine and port."

"Not the Captain, Mister Rake."

"Oh him. He kept passing the port really quickly, he hardly had any, and I wasn't allowed, so Captain Conway... he knew loads about the Battle of–"

"But Mister Rake didn't drink?"

"He had tonic water."

"With gin?"

"Just tonic water and lemon – good for the digestion, he said, and for malaria – and he had that Cara... carrot... carrotdee..."

"Karakadey?"

"That's it."

"Tea made from the Hibiscus flower."

"Yes. Cold. Horrible."

"So, Mister Rake didn't drink?"

"Not at the meal," said Charlotte, "but he must have later, because he... fell down. Perhaps it was something he ate. It was jolly strange food."

"And that's all you can tell me about Mister Rake," Georgina said, "despite spending the whole evening sitting next to him."

"He was quite dull."

Georgina sighed.

"I've finished my tea, so I can choose a scone."

"Did..." said Caruthers, choosing his words carefully, "...Mister Djehuti say anything about anyone else in our group?"

"I don't think so."

"But he was at our table."

"Mister Djehuti? He begged our forgiveness and joined that boring conversation."

"Boring conversation?" Georgina asked.

"You know... Sir Archibald, Ness and those consulate women interested in archaeologists. Thirty minutes waiting to go in, while they talked about the later middle intermediate period versus the middle-middle intermediate period. Mister Djehuti said that there were really three intermediate periods and Earnestine went all red."

"Archaeology is not boring," Georgina explained. "It's a modern, cutting-edge discipline and... Charlotte, you're eating a scone."

"I finished my tea."

"But you've not had a sandwich."

"I'm not allowed, otherwise it will spoil my appetite for dinner."

"Yes, but in the game, you can't have a scone until you've had a sandwich. You can't keep changing the rules."

"I didn't change the rules, you did."

"Mister Rake was definitely drunk," said Caruthers.

"Was he?"

"I was... talking to that Djehuti fellow and Rake arrived intoxicated."

"Didn't you help Mister Rake home?"

"Oh... well, it was nothing."

"Please, I am the Investigating Officer."

"I don't wish to speak ill of the dead, but Mister Rake had had one too many, if you know what I mean."

"I do."

"Although he didn't smell much of alcohol, I must say. The strange food probably didn't help. Although he's been to Egypt before, so he ought to have known."

"And you took him to your hotel?"

"Not exactly. He stayed the night with Mister Djehuti. We plonked him on a sofa."

"Djehuti? In his room?"

"He had a suite."

"When was this," Georgina asked. "I thought Mister Djehuti went outside for some air like Earnestine."

The Captain's cup clattered in its saucer.

"I saw her leaving with him," Georgina insisted.

"You must be mistaken."

"I don't think so."

"Lottie," Caruthers said. "Whose move is it?"

"I've been Mother... do you want to be Mother?" Charlotte said.

"I'll pass, but I'll take a sandwich," said Caruthers, easing a neat triangle from the lowest tier of the three plates.

"And what did you do after that?" Georgina asked.

"I went to the docks."

"For what reason?"

"Clear my head, check on the cargo, not for any reason, you understand, and then I went to the club on the front."

"But if Mister Rake didn't drink–"

"He didn't," said Charlotte.

"...then he must have been pretending to get to this Mister Djehuti's room and... I overheard Mister Rake talking to that al Rachid man. It's... oh, 'I swear, he does not have the book on his person... it must be in his hotel'."

"Sir Archibald and Mrs Albright were talking about a book," Charlotte said. "Amen-moppy knew where it was hidden."

"What book?"

"They didn't say... no, wait! It was something like the Book of Thoughts."

"I do wish you'd pay attention... that's another scone."

"Valid move."

"How can that be a valid move?"

"If you missed it, then you missed it."

"Are you suggesting that Rake was up to something?" Caruthers said, swirling the pot to take over as Mother.

Georgina looked him in the eye: "A lot of people were up to something, Captain."

Caruthers shifted in his chair to get comfortable.

"Charlotte, put it back."

"But..."

"You need your appetite for dinner."

Charlotte realised she was caught and so carefully returned the scone, but to the top plate.

Georgina raised an eyebrow at her.

She was never allowed to get away with anything, Charlotte thought, as she moved it down one to the middle plate.

"I think we need to count points," Charlotte said.

"You're the only one who's had a treat," Georgina complained.

Charlotte smiled, sweetly: "Am I? Oh, well, that's another game to me."

"Not if it's ruined your appetite for dinner."

"That's not a rule."

"It's a house rule."

The gong rang for dinner.

CHAPTER X

Miss Deering-Dolittle

No-one was sure whether they wanted to be all crammed together in the Dining Room or not. Whereas breakfast had been a noisy, almost jovial occasion, dinner was positively frosty. Even in the heat, which was only just beginning to ease off as the evening progressed, there was a chill in the air.

Fear.

And no-one knew where to sit.

Any one of them could be the murderer.

Usually, each day's seating plan would have gradually rotated them around the room, directing them to a different table each evening while maintaining an alternation of gender. That way, over the course of the journey, no gentleman monopolised the company of any particular lady.

This evening, however, Earnestine sat with her sisters.

"I don't want any more surprises," Georgina said to Charlotte. "Especially with regard to men."

"What's been going on?" Earnestine asked.

"I dealt with it," Georgina said, "and it's hardly a conversation for the dinner table."

Earnestine eyed Charlotte.

"And no surprises from you either, Ness," Georgina added.

"Of course not."

"Tell me things *before* they happen."

"Always," Earnestine said.

The opening course was soup, something safe, but there were already dangers in the conversation.

"Countries always suffer under imperialism," Pandit Singh Maçon explained to the Colonel.

"Nonsense," said Colonel Fitzwilliam. "We bring civilisation."

"India had a thriving civilisation before the British arrived."

"I think you'll find the French arrived first."

"And Egypt... Mister Farouk, how do you feel under British rule?" said the Pandit, turning to the Guide.

Farouk startled: "I... oh... Farouk is more used to answering questions on our antiquities."

"But rule by the British?"

"Well." He glanced around the company. The British far outnumbered everyone else present by six to five, including himself. "They are very kind and civilising. We are used to being conquered. Libya, Nubia, Assyria, Persia, Macedonia, Rome, Islam – Allah be praised – the Turk, France and now the beneficent British. We have enjoyed their protection for a glorious eighteen years."

Earnestine realised that the British had been in Egypt since Georgina had been born.

"We French gave you this canal," Monsieur Jacques said.

"For which, Farouk and all Egypt is most grateful, Monsieur."

"The French didn't manage to complete the Panama Canal," Mrs Albright said. "The United States will see that fine link completed, trust me."

"But to be ruled thus, Farouk," Pandit Singh Maçon continued, "is a burden."

"Perhaps it is Egypt that is a burden to the great Queen Victoria?"

"I'm sure President Loubet will gladly take the burden back off you," said Monsieur Jacques in a comment aimed across the table at Fitzwilliam and Caruthers.

"I'm sure we'll manage," Captain Caruthers said.

"But do you really feel protected by the British?" the Pandit insisted.

"Oh, for heaven's sake," Earnestine said. "It's the 'British Protectorate of Egypt' – the hint is in the title."

"Just words."

"He's happy, man," said the Colonel to the Pandit, but indicating Farouk, "just leave it be."

"One is simply making conversation."

"Trouble, more like," the Colonel replied. "In India, everything was going well, trade increasing, crime down, and then these Thuggee blighters turn up spreading rumours, lies, fakery and got all the natives in such a hullaballoo with their blither. We had to get the garrison across from the Punjab before we could put a stop to it."

Pandit Singh Maçon flinched.

"And I am sure they were all grateful, Colonel," Farouk said.

"There!" said the Colonel, thankfully settling the matter. "Pass the port please."

"Was it jolly exciting?" Charlotte asked.

"Lottie," Georgina warned.

"Oh, but..."

"I'll tell you later," the Colonel said.

"Forgive me," Pandit Singh Maçon said, placating, "the British have given India many wonders. The railways, the civil service, industry, irrigation, the gold reserve fund–"

"There! See!"

"And I am sure that at this very moment, other wonders are due to be introduced."

"What do you mean by that?" Captain Caruthers asked.

"Merely that I'm sure your Prime Minister, the Lord Marquess of Salisbury, who served as your Secretary of State for India, has great plans for the Crown Rule in India."

"The Raj is a good thing for the Indian," the Colonel said.

Pandit Singh Maçon smiled thinly.

The Colonel poured himself a generous measure of port and then passed the decanter onwards.

The soup finished, it was fish next.

"We're about to leave part of the canal and enter the Great Bitter Lake," Earnestine said.

"Not before time," Georgina said.

"How is your investigation going?"

"It's proceeding."

It was exactly as Earnestine had feared: "You aren't getting anywhere."

"I have eliminated…"

"Who?"

"Everyone," Georgina said. "I think it hinges on what happened in Tanis."

Earnestine felt her face burning. She couldn't let Georgina know about the fleeting moment she'd stepped into the garden alone with that handsome Egyptian gentleman, who meant nothing to her, obviously, with his intelligent, disarming eyes.

"Charlotte discovered something," Earnestine said, her tone low to prevent anyone else overhearing.

Georgina looked at Charlotte: "French verbs?"

The main course was slices of beef, or a vegetarian option, with sautéed potatoes or rice, asparagus, cucumber sauce, and beans in a savoury jelly.

"Look," said Charlotte, showing Georgina the metal cog hidden beneath the table, in a napkin. "Captain Caruthers and Colonel Fitzwilliam aren't bringing a tank to India. It's… this."

"A gear?"

"Yes."

"How do you know this?"

"I went down to the hold and looked."

"In the hold? On your own? You shouldn't have looked."

"It was all right," Charlotte replied. "Ness was with me."

Georgina shot an angry look at the eldest sister. "I'm trying to keep her on the straight and narrow, and away from Frenchmen, and you are encouraging her."

"One was not," Earnestine insisted. "One was down in the hold and–"

"You?"

"Sir Archibald is organising an expedition and he's also sneaking mummies into Egypt."

"Mummies into Egypt," Georgina said. "Give me strength."

"Don't get cross with me. I told you this."

"Don't... honestly."

"One went down to the hold to help you."

"'One went down...' Ness, honestly," Georgina whispered angrily. "I'm the Investigating Officer. You should have asked my permission."

"One should ask your permission?"

"Yes, you should."

"One thought one could–"

"You're always being such a madam, Ness. Always speaking like you are better than everyone else. You are so stuck-up."

"One is not."

"'One is not'... *you* are!"

As the waiters cleared the plates away, everyone kept a respectful silence.

"I thought it would help."

"No more surprises, Ness."

"Of course not."

"No more."

"One will tell..." Earnestine bit her lip and started again: "I will tell you everything."

"Beforehand."

"Yes, beforehand."

At that moment, Sir Archibald Reevers stood and tapped his wine glass with his fork.

Ting-ting-ting.

He had everyone's rapt attention.

Oh lummy, Earnestine thought.

"Ladies and gentlemen," he said, looking about to ensure everyone could hear him. "We have all heard the terrible news about my Personal Secretary, Mister Rake, so I thought it best to lighten the evening with some good news."

"Hear, hear," said the Colonel. "We could do with some good news."

Earnestine thought so too: if nothing else to mollify Georgina.

"It is my good fortune to tell you all," Sir Archibald continued, "that Miss Deering-Dolittle has consented to be my wife."

Gasps.

Polite applause.

A fork clattered.

"Bravo, bravo," Mrs Albright announced.

The door clattered shut: Captain Caruthers was no longer in the Dining Room.

Charlotte had lost the ability to close her mouth.

"You are a lucky man, Sir Archibald," said Monsieur Jacques.

And all the time, although she studiously avoiding looking in her direction, Earnestine was all too aware of Georgina's icy, horrified expression boring into the back of her head.

Earnestine smiled, a tight, teeth-grinding expression, hoping that no-one would see her scar white against her face as her complexion burned with shame.

Mrs Merryweather

The traitorous arch-strumpet Earnestine flounced up to the main table waving to everyone, the centre of attention, her face flush with victory. She didn't even have the common decency to look in Georgina's direction, her thoughts now clearly on greater things, no doubt.

The future Earnestine, Lady Reevers.

Georgina wanted to pick up her fork so she could drop it again. Or stab someone.

Instead, she smiled, clapped politely and said, "Excuse me, I must feed my daughter."

She went out along the deck, startling Captain Caruthers.

"Gina..."

He flicked his cigarette away and the fiery ember arced down to fall on the waters of the Great Bitter Lake – extinguished. This was the second of two passing points going south, and the stretch of the canal they'd just traversed accepted northbound traffic once more. Boats manoeuvred and jostled for position, trying to gauge which way the wind was blowing.

"It's Mrs Merryweather."

"Of course, Mrs Merryweather."

"One was... I was married *first*."

"Yes, I beg your pardon."

"Well, don't you forget it."

"No, of course not, I–"

"I'll say good evening then."

Georgina hurried along the deck, found her cabin, dropped her keys in her rush, and accidentally tried the Library key in the lock, before she managed to get inside. The paddles of the steamer thrashed the water, churning the froth to make progress, its constant engine noise threatening to overwhelm her senses.

"I'm perfectly capable," she said, sharply, but the Captain hadn't even followed to see that she reached her cabin safely.

Pippa was asleep.

It had been the Derring-Do Club forever.

Not now.

Not ever again.

With their father being lost up the river, it fell to Georgina as the married member of the family to act in his stead, so, Earnestine should have warned Georgina... no!

Miss Deering-Dolittle should have warned *Mrs* Merryweather that Sir Archibald was going to ask for Mrs Merryweather's permission to ask for Miss Deering-Dolittle's hand in marriage.

Just because Earnestine was older and more autocratic did not give her the right to take advantage of Georgina's overly kind nature and overturn the natural order.

Georgina turned on the desk light and glanced at her notes.

Nine suspects: Earnestine, number eight on the list.

Her sister had been flirting outrageously with that Mister Djehuti in Tanis only to be interrupted by the brave and reliable Mister Rake. Obviously, driven by jealousy and lust, Earnestine – who couldn't account for her presence when the shot was fired – had murdered Mister Rake, then seduced Sir Archibald so that he would persuade the committee of the Royal Expeditionary Society to fund a lavish lifestyle, and... and... she intended no doubt to carry on with Mister Djehuti, Monsieur Jacques, poor dear innocent Captain Caruthers and Uncle Tom Cobley and all.

And she'd do anything she pleased.

Anything *one* pleased.

Oh Lord, Georgina thought, her hand to her face, her sister had done it.

Earnestine had been at the stern of the ship, waiting, simply hanging around.

Everyone else had been in the Smoking Room or their cabins, and once Captain Caruthers had moved away, it would have been a simple matter to slip back to the Library. No-one would have seen. She could have tempted Mister Rake inside with the promise that she would be amenable to any proposal of marriage (which she'd keep secret from her sister). Earnestine was clearly a right Kali with numerous hands to give out in marriage to any man she met.

The engines seemed to increase in volume to match the churning rage Georgina felt pounding in her heart.

That scarlet woman, and she wore dark burgundy, had been in some man's cabin for his revolver. That would be easy enough.

Oh good grief! Earnestine had a set of lock picks.

After Earnestine had done the deed, she used these devious bits of metal to close the bolt – Georgina wasn't entirely sure of the details here, but Earnestine's set had shiny sharp pieces of steel for any lock, so surely someone in Sheffield had manufactured some device for a simple bolt – and then she'd casually slipped back to the stern.

Once the shot was heard, she had returned, acting all innocent, just as she had acted all innocent about her recent engagement.

Georgina felt an icy trickle down her spine.

Doctor Timon had offered Earnestine smelling salts!

Earnestine would never faint, she was made of sterner stuff, and the only reason anyone would think she needed smelling salts would be if Earnestine had pretended to swoon.

It was quiet now, quieter than it had ever been on board, as quiet as an Egyptian tomb.

Motive (with Mister Rake out of the way, Earnestine could marry to her heart's content), Opportunity (she was loitering at the stern right near the Library) and Method (she was a dab hand at lockpicks).

In the utter silence, Pippa woke.

But even with her baby's interruption, and as she cooed her child back and forth across the confines of her cabin, she felt tears trickling down her cheeks. She dug out her child's picture book and, as she flicked to the right page, Georgina realised that she knew everything.

"Once upon a time," she began, trying to conjure up as much false jollity as she could, "a man called Prince

Husain travelled to Bisnagar in India to buy a carpet. We're going to India, Pippa. Shall we buy a carpet? A magic carpet?"

Pippa loved being read stories.

But the murder of Mister Rake was no bedtime story. Georgina's investigation was over. She knew the truth. Earnestine did it!

Miss Charlotte

Charlotte went out onto the deck for some air.

She was going to be a bridesmaid again.

At Georgina's wedding to Captain Merryweather, Charlotte had got to wear an army uniform, stand in for their father to give the bride away, eat cake and get her nose covered in Champagne froth.

One of the crew shouted, a wailing refrain, and the engine gave an almighty crack. The boat juddered and the funnel emitted a belch of steam. Embers from the engine flitted upwards into the evening sky like fireflies.

Captain Caruthers, leaning on the railing, lit a cigarette.

"It's quiet," Charlotte said.

"I don't really want to talk, if you don't mind, Lottie."

There was more shouting, consternation from the front of the vessel. Other passengers appeared from the Dining Room: Mrs Albright, Sir Archibald, Monsieur Jacques, Earnestine...

The paddles at the side of the boat stopped.

Everyone was so used to the mechanical noises and the endless sloshing of water that they could no longer hear the racket, so the silence had a deafening quality.

Everyone talked in whispers.

"What's happened?" Sir Archibald asked.

Everyone listened, their heads turned to one side and clear expressions on their faces – silence.

"One doesn't know," Earnestine said.

Captain Caruthers stiffened: "Only one way to find out," he said before he marched smartly off towards the bridge.

"We've reached the Great Bitter Lake," Mrs Albright said.

Sure enough, the water on the starboard side spread out before them, the setting sunlight catching the ripples.

Unless it was a mirage, of course.

Charlotte knew they had those in the desert. She'd read about them in *1,001 Nights* and *On the Alexandrine War*.

Everyone was leaning against the railing on the starboard side, enjoying the cool air after the day's blistering heat and marvelling in the change of view.

"We've stopped," said Mrs Albright. "Then we have to consult with Amenemope."

Amenemope? One of the Egyptian crew perhaps, Charlotte thought.

"Very well," Sir Archibald agreed.

"Tonight."

"We are so close."

"Mademoiselle," said Monsieur Jacques, sidling up to Charlotte, "I see your sister is not here. Perhaps I could teach you some more French customs."

Customs like the unstoppable French cavalry charging the unbreakable British square at Waterloo.

"No, thank you," she said, counting herself lucky to have escaped more French homework.

Captain Caruthers returned: "According to the Skipper, we've broken down."

"Broken down!" said Sir Archibald. "Well, I never."

"Lucky it was once we'd reached the lake," Caruthers added. "Otherwise we'd have blocked the canal traffic."

Lucky indeed, Charlotte thought.

"Now what?" Sir Archibald demanded. "I have appointments to keep."

Men and their boring appointments!

190

"We're to drift to the shore and make repairs," Captain Caruthers announced.

"How long will that take?"

"These wallahs don't really do schedules, even if they knew the nature of the problem."

Just then, shouts came from the land.

Everyone moved around, or through, the ship to the railing on the port side to see the activities. It was as if they were on a balcony watching a piece of theatre. Lines were thrown from the ship and workers pulled to bring the vessel towards the shore.

The ship scrunched, the hull touching the bottom, and then everything listed to port before righting itself. Mrs Albright screeched in alarm, which made Charlotte giggle. A slight tilt to the deck remained, not much, but enough to be strange. It was as if they were caught in a wave that had yet to wash over them.

They tied up, not upon a proper jetty or harbour, but just around rocks and boulders.

"Have we reached tidal waters yet?" Pandit Singh Maçon asked.

"Not until we're south of the lake," Earnestine said. "It's tidal from there to Suez."

Pandit Singh Maçon nodded.

"I was hoping to make a connection."

"Charlotte, go and fetch your shawl," Earnestine said.

"It's hot."

"And it's getting cool now."

Charlotte made a face.

A gangway was run out from below, heaved out into the space between the boat and the shore, wavering as it seemed to search forward for dry land.

And then it thumped down connecting them to the bank of the lake.

"Well," said Caruthers, "that's that."

"Charlotte," Earnestine said, "it's going to be dark soon."

"So?"

"So best fetch your shawl."

"I'm fine."

"Charlotte, shawl."

"I'm going."

And Charlotte went to find her shawl.

CHAPTER XI

Miss Deering-Dolittle

"We need a fifth," Mrs Albright insisted.

The American grabbed Sir Archibald's arm and pulled him to one side near the aft of the ship. This corralled Earnestine into the curve of the railing there. Earnestine didn't fancy stepping on the hatch to the hold; even if it didn't give way, it would be a treacherous step now the sun had set. The lights on the SS *Karnak* barely lit them.

"Not to worry," said Sir Archibald, "my fiancée will suffice."

Fiancée!

Sir Archibald turned to face Earnestine with a grin.

Earnestine had no idea what to say.

"My dear?" he said to her, smiling.

"Of course," she said. Oh, that was the very phrase that had put her in this predicament. 'Of course' hadn't been sufficient. Should she say 'dear', 'dearest', 'darling'... another word beginning with 'D'?

"Excellent," said Sir Archibald. "I have it arranged with the Captain."

"With Caruthers? Arranged what?"

"With the Captain of the SS *Karnak*, Captain Abdul," Sir Archibald explained and he held up a key. "We'll use the Library."

"I see," she said. "The Library?"

"It's dark now," Mrs Albright said. "Almost time."

"Almost time for what?"

"Contact with the other side."

"Can you do that?"

"I'm a Priestess in the Hermetic Order of the Golden Dawn in Chicago," Mrs Albright explained.

"Chicago?"

"Our fine temple is dedicated to Thoth-Hermes."

That couldn't be right: "Egyptian and Greek?" asked Earnestine for clarification.

"We are here to commune with the Secret Chiefs here in Egypt, the land of mysticism and spirituality."

"You are?"

"Yes."

"Can you?"

"Oh yes, we brought an Egyptian emissary with us."

"Farouk."

"Farouk?" Mrs Albright was suddenly confused.

"The Guide."

"Oh, good heavens no. I mean the High Priest, Amenemope."

Earnestine glanced at the hatch to the hold. "The man in the sarcophagus."

Mrs Albright narrowed her eyes and examined Earnestine carefully. "You have the gift?"

"I... that is... Sir Archibald... Secret Chiefs, you say?"

"Absolutely."

"Aren't Secret Chiefs rather Red Indian, Buffalo Bill and all that?"

"Nonsense... all religions are a dim reflection of the one true Hermetic Order of the Golden Dawn," Mrs Albright announced. "You will join us?"

"In Chicago?"

"We have temples in London, Paris, Bradford and Weston-Super-Mare."

"Really? Weston-Super-Mare!? London?"

"The temple to Isis-Urania – quite appropriate – and the Order treats men and women as equals."

"You mean you've full suffrage?"

"Absolutely."

With that, Mrs Albright scuttled away, her stick tapping along the deck as she went to collect her paraphernalia, and she took such a long time, that Sir Archibald, Pandit Singh Maçon, Monsieur Jacques and

Earnestine had all gathered in the cramped passageway outside the Library.

Mrs Albright appeared in a whirl with a carpetbag.

Sir Archibald had the key to the padlock.

Once inside, they set the table up in the centre as if for bridge and Mrs Albright wafted a quite disturbing cloth onto the green baize. It was black with a five-pointed pentangle stitched in gold thread. A heavy silver candlestick became the central feature. The men all reached for their matches.

Mrs Albright took charge pointing with her stick.

"Miss Deering-Dolittle... and congratulations by the way."

"Thank you."

"You will sit here between Sir Archibald and the Pandit. I will sit here. Monsieur Jacques... if you would sit between Sir Archibald and me."

"I am unsure about these strange beliefs," said Pandit Singh Maçon.

"Don't worry, everything will be fine."

Monsieur Jacques held Mrs Albright's chair for her: "Madame?"

"Merci," Mrs Albright said, "merci beaucoup."

So, thought Earnestine, she can murder the French language as well.

Monsieur Jacques took her stick and leant it against the bookcase.

Mrs Albright lit a candle and the flickering light cast its spell upon their faces.

Oh no, Earnestine realised, it's a séance!

Georgina had once been to a séance and had told Earnestine about the wires to move the table, devices to make noises and a maid who had wafted cold air onto the backs of their necks.

However, this room was sealed. No-one could sneak around them wailing and moaning. No-one, except perhaps the murderer who had somehow escaped this very room.

"Hold hands," Mrs Albright directed. "Please..."

Pandit Singh Maçon's grip was cool and dry, whereas Sir Archibald's was pudgy and damp. She should pull away now; say there had been a terrible mistake.

Yes, that was the sensible thing to do, she thought, and there was no time like the present – *carpe diem!*

Mrs Albright droned on: "...do not under any circumstances break the circle..."

Grasp the nettle.

"...it can be very dangerous...."

Bite the bullet.

She took a deep breath. Break it off now. It was kinder: "I– *ow!*"

"Excusez-moi," said Monsieur Jacques.

The wretched Frenchman was playing footsie under the table with his long legs.

Earnestine wanted to rub her ankle. "Quite all right," she said.

"Please," Mrs Albright said. "We are gathered here..."

Oh lummy, Earnestine thought, what had she done? Only accepted a proposal of marriage. She needed to talk to someone about this. Mother! But her mother was lost up a river on an expedition. Perhaps Georgina, who had been married, might explain, although Earnestine imagined that her sister would never speak to her again.

"...to raise *Amenemope to life,"* Mrs Albright's voice changed pitch, becoming mesmeric, *"so that he can ask the High Chiefs..."*

The problem, and this American putting on a funny voice wasn't helping her mood, was that... wait a moment, they really did mean the mummy in the hold: "Amenemope!"

"Shh..." Sir Archibald hissed, gripping her hand even tighter.

"Yes," Mrs Albright agreed, *"the Great High Priest, Amenemope, himself. He will be our Spirit Guide to the afterlife..."*

The candle flickered.

Mrs Albright rolled her eyes, entering a trance state: *"...your followers from the temples of Thoth-Hermes, Isis-Urania and Ahathoor are here,"* she chanted, getting quite carried away. *"Aid us in our quest to commune with the Secret Chiefs. Assist us in bringing back from the spirit world your servant, Amenemope. Avail us to grant us our wish for the Book of Thoth."*

The others mumbled in reply: "Aid us... assist us... avail us..."

"Oh Thoth-Hermes, Oh Isis-Urania, Oh Ahathoor..."

They repeated the names of their gods. Earnestine mumbling, because she wasn't sure how to do any of this. It wasn't as if it was printed in the Book of Common Prayer.

"...we of the Hermetic Order of the Golden Dawn, beseech you."

Aid, assist and avail... now 'beseech' – they were working through the alphabet.

Mrs Albright nodded to each in turn: Sir Archibald Reevers, Pandit Singh Maçon, Monsieur Jacques, but shook her head slightly when her attention reached Earnestine.

"Your false prophet," Mrs Albright continued, *"Samuel Liddell MacGregor Mathers, has withheld the secret of communion with our Secret Master and consorts with the Satanist, Aleister Crowley. Instead, oh High Ones, give us a ritual beyond the Red Rose. Grant, oh High Ones, a ritual beyond the Golden Cross. Gift us, oh High Ones, a ritual of Se-akh..."*

Sir Archibald grunted in approval.

"...so we may raise the mortal remains of your servant and High Priest, Amenemope. As it was written before time, give him life, so he may walk amongst us. Give him

the gift of tongues, so he may talk to us. Give him wisdom, so he may tell your servants the secrets."

In the long silence, Earnestine heard the creaking of the boat, a wind outside murmuring from the desert wastes. The candle flame grew steady and bright.

Mrs Albright moaned.

Earnestine nearly jumped out of her skin.

"*I feel a presence,*" Mrs Albright intoned. "*Who speaks to us?*"

Sir Archibald could contain himself no longer: "Is it... is it?"

"*Who speaks?*"

This was jolly disturbing, Earnestine thought, and–

"*I speak.*"

Another voice, a croak as if from a throat wasted by centuries of decay and decomposition. But it was also speaking English, Earnestine noted.

"Who speaks?" Sir Archibald asked, taking over Mrs Albright's role.

"*I... Amenemope, once High Priest of Thoth.*"

"Grant us your wisdom."

Pandit Singh Maçon's grip became vice-like.

"*Ask your question.*"

It was Mrs Albright speaking, her mouth moved, her lips drew back in a snarl; she was a mouthpiece for the voice was from another world.

Sir Archibald stammered a question: "Where, oh wise High Priest, is the Book of Thoth?"

"*You wish to know where my book can be found.*"

The Book of Thoth, Earnestine thought... don't tell me, don't tell me.

"Yes, oh great Amenemope, where is your Master's book?"

"*The book with two spells...*"

Of course, Earnestine remembered: Ptolemy, hidden at the bottom of the Nile – not the Suez, obviously, they were still in the wrong place – and guarded by serpents and contained within a series of boxes like Russian dolls.

"...stolen thrice..."

Thrice... Nef-something and his ghost did something else.

"...stolen by the betrayer, Prince Neferkaptah, and hidden in his tomb..."

Neferkaptah! That was it. Not the bottom of the Nile... Neferkaptah's tomb. Could his burial site be near the Suez Canal?

"...stolen by Setne Khamwas..."

Who met Neferkawotsit's ghost! Earnestine knew this. It was all in the big red book with the gold lettering on the right of the middle shelf at home in Kensington.

"...and stolen again by Emrys Rake."

Yes, Nefthing's ghost frightened Setne Khamwas, who put it back into Thingy's tomb until... *Rake!*

"Where is it now?" Sir Archibald asked, his tone edged with desperation.

"Amenemope knows."

"Yes, yes, that's just what Rake said," Sir Archibald agreed. He glanced around the table at the others as if to say, 'I told you so'. Their faces were pale, petrified by these revelations. "Rake said, 'Amenemope knows'."

"Amenemope knows."

"Yes, Amenemope, but where? Where?"

"Amenemope knows."

"WHERE!"

There was a loud bang and the room seemed to swim away from them, a stomach-lurching movement, as if the world had become loose.

Mrs Albright screamed.

"Mrs Al... b-b-bright," Monsieur Jacques managed. "Are you all right?"

Mrs Albright looked about her as if she didn't know where she was, then she held up her hand. "The circle is broken."

Sir Archibald seemed to explode in rage: "Jacques, you bloody fool, you broke the circle."

"She was in pain."

"He was here," Sir Archibald insisted. "Amenemope was here and now he's vanished."

"Miss Deering-Dolittle, kindly calm your fiancé down," Pandit Singh Maçon insisted.

"Calm down!" Sir Archibald spluttered. "We almost found out where the book is."

"Sir Archibald..." but Earnestine couldn't think of anything to add. She wanted to find out what this was all about as much as he did.

Could this be how the murder was committed? Amenemope conjured into the Library with a revolver?

And all to get his book back.

Mrs Merryweather

Pippa finally dropped off to sleep again.

The tale finished, Georgina slipped some paper in as a bookmark and closed the storybook. She felt exhausted – it was night-time already and she should sleep – but her thoughts began to race.

For a start, the ship breaking down so conveniently suggested sabotage. Someone had deliberately damaged the engines to keep them in the Suez, but they had had the common sense to wait until they'd reached one of the passing places, the most southerly, before acting the Ned Ludd and throwing a clog in the works.

Earnestine had been to the hold, which was below decks and near the Engine Room.

Of course, she realised, if they'd become stranded in the narrow part of the canal, then the authorities would have no choice but to take action. Officials would be all over the ship and, with a murder having occurred on board, they'd all come under scrutiny. However, engine failure here, particularly in the largest of the three lakes that existed like stepping stones for the canal, meant that the Suez Canal Company could simply ignore them. It was not their problem.

Earnestine must want... but Earnestine had been in the Dining Room flaunting her good fortune, so she can't have been in the Engine Room sticking a spanner into the gearing. Unless it was delayed by clockwork or melting beeswax or some other instrumentality.

As for the actual murder, it was impossible to have murdered that man in the locked room. Utterly impossible, therefore it had not been done.

Unless it was a ghost.

Which was nonsense.

Therefore it had been done, but by some mechanism or cunning that she had not yet discovered.

She might never discover it.

No matter. It had been done, therefore it had to have been possible to do. Logically.

By whom?

Earnestine?

Getting betrothed behind Georgina's back, even though it was a mortal sin and a betrayal of sisterhood, wasn't exactly proof of guilt.

Georgina checked her list.

1. Sir Archibald Reevers, on deck, port.
2. Colonel Fitzwilliam, Smoking Room.
3. Captain Caruthers, on deck, starboard.
4. Pandit Singh Maçon, Smoking Room.
5. Doctor Timon, Smoking Room.
6. Monsieur Jacques, Smoking Room.
7. Mrs Albright, cabin.
8. Miss Deering-Dolittle, on deck, aft.
9. Miss Charlotte, levels.

So, Georgina thought.

When – witnesses had heard the shot, so that was fixed.

Where – the body in the Library behind a locked door.

How – a shot at point-blank range.

This left 'why' and 'who'.

Why – utterly inexplicable.

Who – a list of nine suspects.

The stewards had been present in the main Galley the entire time, so no crew could have gone aft without being seen.

Any of the passengers could have gone to the Library, performed whatever feat of prestidigitation necessary to flummox Georgina completely, and then return to the Smoking Room, the deck, their cabin or anywhere.

Any of them could have done it?

Except one must be lying.

But they had all lied.

One of them must be lying about the murder.

Perhaps the culprit was so devious that they would be the last she would accuse?

Who had she accused? Sir Archibald, Captain Caruthers, Miss Deering-Dolittle; so perhaps Colonel Fitzwilliam in league with Charlotte?

Or they took it in turns?

They were all laughing at Georgina, silly Georgina, who was vexed so by this puzzle. Like they had at the Eden College for Young Ladies: Amazo, Amazon, I'm-a-spot, am-as-gone, am-as-lost, as-an-ant, derring-do, derring-do.

Laughing and laughing...

...until she woke suddenly.

Something had made a noise.

A bang, a disconcerting feeling in her stomach... but it was gone now.

Pippa was still asleep.

Something flopped, snapped shut.

Georgina jumped!

It was just the book, only the book falling from her lap.

No, there was a creak also.

Not simply her book, but...

Georgina went to her window, pressed her face against the pane and stared along the edge. Distorted by the curvature of the glass and lit by the ship's lights, she saw figures clambering up the side of the ship, figures dressed in white rags, bandaged from head to toe, figures–

"Mummies!"

They were 'untoten', that ghastly Austro-Hungarian word that meant corpses raised from the dead. Georgina felt cold, a creeping chill that seeped into her bones. Her husband, poor Arthur... and these monsters were coming for her now. Her and her child.

Georgina banged on the wall.

"Mummies!" she shouted.

Pippa woke and became an alarm all of her own.

Georgina stepped out into the night onto the walkway. Ahead was nothingness and it seemed like the ship floated in an unfathomable darkness. To protect her child, she must get help, she must warn the men – they would save her baby.

Doctor Timon appeared, blinking his small eyes. "Mrs Merryweather, have you quite taken leave of your senses."

"Mummies! Attacking the ship."

"Do you have the hysterics, woman?"

"Look for yourself.... and get a gun, get help!"

"I am a Doctor, Madam. I have the Hippocratic Oath not to harm the living."

"These creatures aren't living!"

A figure appeared at the far end of the deck, bandaged – poor man – but no, only for a moment did Georgina think it was an injured figure.

"Mummy."

Doctor Timon took one look through his round glasses and then vanished into his room, a bolt clattering shut an instant later.

Coward.

The corpse shuffled towards her, shambling inevitably closer, but Georgina could not move. She saw the hideous bandaged face, but also the vile abominations that she had faced before. These unholy conjurings were like those that had robbed her of her husband.

It reached her, its breath full of stink and putrefaction, probing forward, trying to touch her. It was a creature from the afterlife, embalmed but alive, reanimated by unholy ritual, an undead, an untoten...

"Mrs Merryweather, if you should be so kind."

Georgina turned.

It was her late husband, standing there returned from the afterlife to save her... but no, only Captain Caruthers standing pointing his revolver at her.

He must have murdered Mister Rake and now he was going to kill her.

"Cap–"

"Fairly urgent, Gina."

"What?"

"Duck!"

Georgina dropped to the deck and Caruthers fired, two loud blasts that seemed to pummel overhead.

Caruthers stepped smartly forward, sidestepped her on the narrow walkway and stood solidly between her and the abomination.

"Are you hurt?" Caruthers asked.

"No... I'm... for a moment I saw Arthur."

"Arthur? You mean Merry?"

"Yes."

"I'm afraid I'll have to suffice."

"What are you doing here?"

"Keeping an eye on... Sir Archibald and Mrs Albright," Caruthers explained. "They're members of the Hermetic Order of the Golden Dawn and they are performing some ritual."

"They're raising these monsters!"

"Yes."

"But that's against everything that's civilised.   It's against Church of England doctrine. It's against natural history. It's against common sense."

"Steady now."

"I'm sorry... nerves."

Captain Caruthers nodded.

Pippa's wailing continued, a sharp distracting alarm.

Georgina felt foolish, allowing her panic to conjure up demons from her imagination when reality generated more than enough monsters.

"You said 'monsters'."

"Oh Lord, yes, I saw dozens climbing onto the ship!"

"If you'll excuse me."

Caruthers reached into his jacket and pulled out another revolver. Holding both weapons raised, he went aft, and Georgina hesitated, then followed. She'd far rather stay with the brave Captain than wait in the dark alone.

Wait!

Caruthers had two revolvers!

There was a shriek.

A commotion above.

Another monster appeared, lurching along the deck. There was no brave Captain to rescue her this time. It reached her cabin door and glanced towards the innocent babe wailing within.

"Here, here!" Georgina shouted, waving her arms.

It saw her, lurched towards her past the doorway. Her child was safe, but she realised that she wasn't. Georgina scampered to the central stairwell and went up to the deck above.

Wait, she was leaving her daughter behind.

But she had to, she had to draw the creature away.

And the Captain could have used one revolver to kill Mister Rake and the other as a decoy. No wonder she hadn't smelt cordite.

She smelt it now.

Another bandaged figure clambered onto the ship right near her. They were playing levels like Charlotte.

Caruthers was nowhere to be seen.

Other mummies followed, lurching up like a plague. The undead had returned, just like the monsters who had killed her dear Arthur. Georgina froze again, petrified by the recurring nightmare made real again. She could see was her late husband's face, pleading, and those vile abominations of the Austro-Hungarians. These horrors still visited her at night, but this was no dream. These ancient Egyptians had returned to destroy the living.

Georgina's breathing became rapid, uncontrolled.

A monster looked towards her, its dead eyes catching the light of the oil lamp.

It growled.

Still Georgina could not move.

Colonel Fitzwilliam stepped up, suddenly: "Back! Back!"

He lashed out with his stick.

The creature ducked, struck the old man and then grasped the Colonel's neck. The two tumbled over, landing awkwardly, the poor Colonel letting out a howl of pain as his war-wounded foot thumped against the hard deck.

The other creatures swarmed to the staircase and descended like the damned returning to hell.

Gunfire! Caruthers further along the deck.

Farouk appeared: "Away! Away!"

The Colonel and Farouk struggled with the monster on the floor, bandages unravelling, a fez knocked away to roll across the deck, a clattering stick, then the creature shoved them away.

It lumbered off, running.

"How can creatures from the dead move so quickly?" the Colonel shouted.

"Does it matter," Georgina shouted. "They can!"

Colonel Fitzwilliam struggled to his feet and helped Farouk up. "Perhaps we should regroup somewhere."

"The Smoking Room?" Farouk suggested.

They clustered together and retreated into the interior of the ship.

There were monsters in the Smoking Room.

"The Library?" Farouk shouted.

They rushed to the Library – it would be locked, she realised – she'd had a key, but where? She struggled for her purse, but it wasn't there.

Luckily the door opened, lamp light beckoning them to safety.

"Sacré Bleu!" Monsieur Jacques shouted.

"Damn it, no bolt," the Colonel said.

The Colonel was jolly nimble and he knew to lock the bolt, just as the murderer must have!

Already inside, gathered around a table decked with a Satanic cloth, Georgina saw Sir Archibald, Mrs Albright, Monsieur Jacques, Pandit Singh Maçon and *Earnestine!*

"Help me pull the chaise across," the Colonel commanded.

Monsieur Jacques and the Pandit shifted the chaise to block the door. It was already stained with the blood of one dead man: Mister Rake. He'd died here. They were all going to die here. Because of this ritual.

Georgina turned on them: "What is going on?"

"Mrs Merryweather," Sir Archibald explained in reasonable tones, "we are simply conducting a ritual to contact the dead."

It was too much. Georgina exploded. "Earnestine Deering-Dolittle, what were you thinking, raising mummies from the dead?!"

"One wasn't," Earnestine said.

"*You* were!"

"*I* wasn't."

"What do you call all those untoten attacking the ship?"

"I beg your pardon."

"The untoten – mummies – all over the place."

"Excusez moi," said Monsieur Jacques. "Pourquoi do you use the German word for 'mort-vivant', the 'undead'?"

Georgina rounded on the Frenchman. "None of your damned business."

"Georgina," said Earnestine. "There's no need for such language."

"Yes, there is."

"Mrs Merryweather," Mrs Albright said. "We are a responsible group. The Order of the Hermetic Dawn–"

"Are raising the dead."

"Absurdité," said Jacques, "there are no mummies here to raise."

Earnestine coughed.

Georgina examined her sister, eyes narrowing in contempt.

"Sir Archibald has one in the hold," Earnestine explained.

"And you are engaged to this man."

"Amenemope," Sir Archibald said. "Has our spell brought him back to life?"

"It has," said Mrs Albright. "We have raised the dead. Hallelujah."

"Then we can ask him directly."

"Ask him what?" Georgina demanded.

"Mrs Merryweather," Mrs Albright said. "I must protest. You can't go interrogating us like this."

"Of course, I can. I'm the Investigating Officer."

"Of the murder, not this."

"I will be the judge of what I can and cannot investigate, and you are hiding in this... room of the deed."

"Shhh..." Monsieur Jacques insisted.

They were silent immediately and stared at the Frenchman. He leant against the door, listening.

"What is it?" Georgina asked.

"I simply wanted you all to stop shouting."

"I can–"

"In case the creatures hear."

Georgina said nothing.

"Where's Caruthers?" Earnestine asked.

"Out there," Georgina said staring at the solid door. "Saving our lives from your sacrilege."

"I better go and help," said Monsieur Jacques.

He opened the door, automatic at the ready.

"Right ho," said the Colonel, hefting his stick.

"Colonel, perhaps..."

"Don't count this war horse out just yet."

"I will fight with you," said Pandit Singh Maçon. He drew a blade from his walking stick.

"Ah, a gupti, jolly good," said the Colonel.

The three men disappeared, and Earnestine went to follow him.

"No," said Georgina.

"But–"

"No."

"I have a gun."

"A gun! Earnestine Deering-Dolittle, what do you have one of those for?"

"In case."

"In case... what sort?"

"A Webley, so I'll just go and–"

"No, Ness, it's a job for the men."

Earnestine glared at Georgina and then glanced at Sir Archibald, her fiancé, still seated at the table, and said nothing.

Georgina heard the 'bangs' and 'phuts' beyond the door. Such frightful sounds. Sounds that had been heard when the murder had occurred *and her sister had a gun.*

Miss Charlotte

There was a battle going across the ship. Mummies clambered along the ropes that tied the stricken vessel to the shore, struggling along the gangplanks and hoisting themselves aboard. They appeared suddenly as they stepped from the night into the lamplight.

The defenders fell over each other, hampered by the narrow deck on either side of the cabins. Some fled fore, others retreated aft, neither knowing truly if they were advancing or retreating. There was no clear front line.

It was dreadful and Charlotte had been missing it.

She'd dithered in her cabin to remember her stupid shawl as if that would be useful.

But now she was on the top deck, so she grabbed the railing and jumped over, swinging away from the ship.

"Lottie!" Caruthers shouted, apparently frozen in the act of reaching to save her.

This was just like a game of levels and at the last moment, she came in, caught the deck with her toe and propelled herself upwards. Her right foot reached the railing and then she was clambering onto the roof.

She dropped prone, waved her hand downwards.

"Gun!"

"For goodness sake, Lottie!"

The reassuring lump of metal appeared in her hand.

"Shells!"

Rounds were thrust into her other hand and then she was on her feet scooting along the flat roof towards the stern. The Captain transferred his other revolver to his right hand.

A mummy appeared, its bandaged head stuck above the parapet as it reached up.

Charlotte fired.

A black hole appeared in the thing's evil visage and it vanished.

Another... *bang!*

She reached the back of the cabins and stood to overlook the Sun Deck, with its lines drawn for deck tennis.

Two mummies crossed from right to left.

Bang! Bang-bang!

The awkward angle meant she'd had to use two rounds on one of them.

An angry wail drew her attention to her rear.

Three mummies this time, one fully on the roof already. These were fast, faster than any reanimated corpses ought to be.

She raised the weapon: a Webley Mk 1, service revolver, top-break, .455, which took six rounds, so she'd have to be careful and make every shot count.

Aim... *click!*

Captain Caruthers must have fired two rounds already.

She hadn't checked: cadet error.

Click, click... yes, empty.

She broke the chamber open and flicked the spent cartridges out across the deck. The shells in her left hand weren't arranged neatly, so it was a struggle to reload.

The enemy shambled forward, almost running towards her, and entering the darker centre that the lamplight from below didn't reach. Its colour bleached away in the moonlight.

Three in, she closed the gun, dropped to one knee.

It was on her, arms out, reaching to clutch her.

Click, bang!

Its chest exploded spraying her with black ichor.

She threw herself sideways.

The creature kept going and careered off the roof tumbling.

She fired from her lying position – *bang!* – and missed.

She took her time, fired again – *bang!* – and this time she found her mark.

But the third one – it was too close.

Even as she reached to open the revolver and the seconds seemed to stretch, she knew she didn't have time.

But the monster slipped, its footing thrown by a spent cartridge rolling underfoot, and it fell to the floor.

Charlotte jumped up and kicked it as hard as she could, her boot catching it just under its chin.

She recoiled backwards, awkwardly.

It fell the other way, bounced, and then disappeared over the edge with a scream.

She reloaded the remaining four rounds and this time ensured that the first chamber was one with the start of the ammunition. At the port side, she saw where the creatures were attempting to board and she fired, four easy shots – *bang... bang, bang... ... ...bang* – and then she lay on the roof again to look at the deck below.

Apparently upside down, the defenders fought heroically.

Captain Caruthers fought with his fists, Monsieur Jacques fired with an automatic, Pandit Singh Maçon flashed his gupti back and forth, and even the poor war-wounded Colonel lashed out with his walking stick.

"Captain," Charlotte said. "Could I trouble you for some more ammunition?"

"Ha, ha, Lottie, I am rather busy at the moment."

"In your own time."

Charlotte tucked the revolver into her belt and flipped over the edge to swing in behind the Captain.

"Right pocket," he said.

She reached inside and brought out the whole box. She managed to get six rounds in this time.

The Captain was holding his own, so she leaned over the side and took a few pot-shots at the mummies crawling along the ropes, fore and aft. They got the message and retreated.

"May I?" Caruthers asked. "I dropped the other one."

"Be my guest," Charlotte said handing the revolver back. "Two shots."

"Right ho."

He fired twice, and then passed it back without looking, knowing that Charlotte would take it.

She reloaded.

That was it for the ammunition.

She checked over the side, but there were no more reinforcements of ancient Egyptian undead.

"Gun, Lottie."

"All clear port and aft," she said, handing the revolver back. "Only five rounds, the last of the ammo."

"You stay clear."

"Me?"

"For once, obey orders."

"I always obey orders, Sir."

"Of course you do, Lottie."

"Qui est cette fille?" Monsieur Jacques asked, shaking his head.

"That's Charlotte... oh!" Captain Caruthers realised what the Frenchman had meant. "One of the Deering-Dolittle sisters. They have this... club."

"Non! Ces filles? Le Club Derring-Do?"

"The same."

"Mon dieu, the stories are true."

Charlotte could not stop smiling.

A growl, some guttural sound behind her and she turned to see a mummy, coming from nowhere, brandishing a knife.

She knew that neither man had his gun ready.

Charlotte whipped her shawl from around her shoulders. She clasped something from her pocket, dropped it into the fold and whirred the thing above her head.

The mummy seemed to chortle at this yellow-haired apparition, then Charlotte loosed the slingshot.

Her aim was true.

The mummy's head snapped to one side, blood splattering its comrades and then, almost lifted from the deck, it fell backwards.

Caruthers and Jacques re-entered the fray now, given the diversion and the change of odds. They fought side-by-side, then back-to-back, with their walking sticks, one using Bartitsu and the other a fencing posture.

One of the creatures called out, growling a foreign word, and, suddenly, the mummies vanished into the night.

Even the bodies had gone, alive again to flee or carried away by their undead comrades, except for one, lying injured on the ground.

Charlotte recovered her slingshot from nearby.

"Where did you get that?" Caruthers asked.

"I... found it," said Charlotte.

"Lottie?"

"I found it in your crate," she admitted. "I was investigating for Georgina."

"We better check on her," the Captain said. "She's in the Library."

But Georgina appeared, coming in the wake of Sir Archibald and Earnestine, with Pippa in her arms.

"Everything under control? Captain? Colonel?" Sir Archibald demanded.

"Yes, Sir," Caruthers replied. "Mrs Merryweather?"

"Captain."

"Did you give Lottie here permission to investigate the hold?"

"Charlotte, did you?" Georgina said.

"Yes," said Charlotte.

"And when was I going to get a report?"

"I was going to, but we were attacked by mummies."

"There's always an excuse, isn't there?"

"That's not fair!"

"May I have it back," said Caruthers. He held out his hand.

Charlotte handed it over.

Captain Caruthers took out his handkerchief and wiped the blood from its cogs, then checked it over for damage.

"It's not a 'tank', is it?" Charlotte said.

"Tank?" said Georgina.

"In the hold, the Captain's crate says it contains a 'tank'."

"Well, Captain?" Georgina asked.

"It's a tank."

"I'm the Investigating Officer."

"Hardly pertinent to your enquiry."

"I will be the judge of that."

"If you must know, it's a code word," Caruthers explained. "We use it occasionally when transporting items that we'd rather no-one knew about."

"Secret things."

"Not at all."

"What else would they be?"

"They could be things that we don't have a name for yet."

"What if your code word stuck? Your precious secret invention would end up being called a 'tank' – wouldn't that be silly?"

"It would," Caruthers agreed. "But that's hardly likely to happen."

Georgina snatched the brass 'tank' part off Caruthers: "This is a gear for a Difference Engine."

"I think not."

"Yes, it is," Georgina insisted. "I've seen the diagrams. Charles Babbage's Difference Engine. He never finished it, but he manufactured some parts back in... over fifty years ago."

"I wouldn't know," Caruthers replied, retrieving the gear. "And neither do you."

"And you are charged with protecting this?" Georgina asked.

"I am."

"And how far would you go?"

"As far as necessary."

"Would you kill a man?"

"A man has been killed by it tonight."

"An undead, and that's not what I asked."

"I do my duty."

Sir Archibald came up to them, puffing himself up to regain his authority: "What has happened here?"

"We've killed a mummy," Caruthers said.

"A mummy? What of Amenemope?" said Sir Archibald and he rushed away heading towards the staircase to descend to the hold.

The creature on the deck moaned.

"I'll finish it off," said Caruthers.

"Wait!" It was Earnestine.

"It's a reanimated corpse," Caruthers explained.

"No, it isn't," Earnestine said. "Look at it."

Someone held a lamp closer.

It was a reanimated mummy, still moving in writhing spasms, its bandages stained with spreading blood.

"We brought these servants of the Secret Chiefs back to life," Mrs Albright exclaimed. She clapped her hands together and skipped with delight, her beads clattering. "How wondrous. It proves the Kabbalistic tradition is the true path to enlightenment."

"It's madness," said Georgina.

"You Natural Historians with your fixation on proof," Mrs Albright said, chiding. "You should have a little faith. How can you doubt, when you can see the evidence of your own eyes?"

"Yes, I rather can," Earnestine said.

"The long-dead brought back from the spiritual world in corporeal form."

"Or not."

"Or not?"

"The bandages are wrong," Earnestine insisted.

"Wrong..." Mrs Albright stared at the suffering mummy writhing on the floor. "What do you mean?"

"It is the undead, Miss," said Farouk. "The Pharaohs returning to rule us once more."

"Nonsense."

"How can you doubt!" Mrs Albright shouted, gesticulating at the evidence with her stick.

"The bandages are wrong. Proper mummies, like Amenemope down below and all the ones I've seen in museums, have their bandages going... so," Earnestine explained with that tone of patience wearing thin. She demonstrated, angling her hand to show how she would wrap herself.

"You cannot say this," Farouk countered. "I am Egyptian. I know when the Pharaohs rise again to enslave us."

"I've seen many mummies."

"I have seen more, Miss."

"I doubt that," Earnestine said. "There are more mummies in the British Museum in London than there are left in Cairo and the whole of Egypt."

"Only because you stole them."

"For study, to learn, to understand, so we can know when it's a pharaoh back from the grave and when it's just a man dressed up."

They looked.

"Let's see," said Farouk, his anger lending him bravery. He bent down and pulled the bandages free.

It was a young man, but bald, an Arab or Egyptian by his skin.

"He's injured," said Georgina. She handed Pippa to Charlotte and bent to help him, feeling his quite plump flesh beneath the bandages. Her fingers found the wound, the man gasped in pain and his sticky lifeblood seeped across her hand.

He grabbed her shoulder and pulled her down to listen to him speak.

Georgina pulled away, but even as his life waned he held on. As he did so, he rasped in her face as if his place in the afterlife depended upon it.

"I don't know what you want," Georgina said.

"It's Arabic," said Farouk.

"I always thought mummies would say bird, wavy lines, Eye of Horus, man standing funny," said Charlotte, as she jiggled her struggling niece up and down.

Farouk leant forward, partly to pull the clawed hand off Georgina and partly to hear.

The man spoke again, softly, his life leaving him.

Georgina tried to calm him with nonsense words, "There-there."

The man realised she didn't understand and switched his grip to Farouk's garment. He spoke again, the same unintelligible speech repeated.

"What does he say?" Earnestine asked.

But Farouk ignored her, concentrating on the wounded man's words.

The man spoke again, the same phrase, but then choked, spat blood; his eyes looked upwards to stare into the unfathomable unknown and then he was truly gone.

"Allah protect us," said Farouk. He touched the man's eyelids, and thankfully the stare was hidden.

"What did he say?" Georgina asked.

"It makes no sense, but he repeated it... I am certain of what he said, but it makes no sense."

"What did he say?"

"With his dying breath?"

"Yes?"

"He said 'I am not the god Thoth'."

CHAPTER XII

Miss Deering-Dolittle

"Tell me," Sir Archibald shouted.

Earnestine found him in the hold.

He was leant forward, his underlit face appeared both aghast and spellbound, his ruddy jowls close to the grey ruins of the High Priest. He caught the mummified remains by the bandages near where the throat had been and shook as if he had grabbed a rival by the coat lapels.

The creature stirred, rose up, shaking, its fragile limbs flailing and breaking. Dust rose and a cloud formed shapes in the air. There were monsters, genies, terrible visions, but then Sir Archibald coughed, fell back and it was nothing more than a trick of the light.

Anything supernatural had gone – if it had been there at all.

"Sir Archibald?"

Sir Archibald blinked wildly trying to recognize her in the gloom: "Miss... Deering-Dolittle?"

"Yes, Sir Archibald."

"He didn't come to tell us."

"What are you looking for?"

"Eden."

"What are you looking for really? It's not the Garden of Eden."

"No, not the actual Garden of Eden, but the secret of the Garden of Eden."

"I beg your pardon."

The President of the Royal Expeditionary Society held out his hand as if to hold a stone: "The Tree of Life."

"Any tree would be long gone."

"Not the Tree of Life," Sir Archibald said. "How could that die? But perhaps it did. Do you see? The world is six thousand years old and there are fossils. This

219

process of living matter becoming rock is slow and gradual, perhaps taking many decades, but trees eventually turn to stone."

"One supposes."

"But not just any stone. Part of it, broken off, became the Philosopher's Stone."

"Able to perform alchemy and turn lead into gold."

"My dear, a piece of the Tree of Life, even turned to stone, can prolong life indefinitely," Sir Archibald said, placing his hand upon hers. "How else does one explain the Wandering Jew?"

Earnestine raised an eyebrow quizzically.

"Or Methuselah."

"I think you are mixing your New Testament with your Old Testament."

"My dear, let me explain."

I wish you would, Earnestine thought; she nodded.

"There are many tales, because such people who found the Philosopher's Stone have lived so long and under many names. They are signposts on the journey back to the Garden of Eden. Someone, the Wandering Jew, Methuselah, Thoth, call him what you will. Maybe all of these are the same person. Nevertheless, someone defeated the cherubim and re-entered the Garden of Eden. They stole from the Tree of Life, possibly part of the tree itself and gave it life somewhere else."

"You mean a cutting?"

"Yes – a cutting."

"So, an Egyptian god involved in horticulture."

"It is the root of the myth of the Philosopher's Stone."

"That turns base metal into gold."

"Grants immortal life," Sir Archibald insisted. "Just one bite from the forbidden fruit and you are immortal?"

"Or it's a way of growing apples."

"Apples imbued with immortality."

Earnestine could imagine it. Just as the legends and myths of Troy had led archaeologist Schliemann to uncover the lost city, so too could the tales in the Bible lead to the Garden of Eden.

"I see from your eyes that you know it to be true," Sir Archibald said.

Earnestine's reply was a mere gasp: "Yes."

"Thoth found it in the East and brought it to Egypt, where he lived ever since with his book. He hid the Stone, or the tree, in a hidden tomb."

"Between Eden and Egypt?"

"That's it."

To the east was the Euphrates and the Tigris, and to the west, the Nile, and in between was the Suez Canal. "Hereabouts," she added.

"There are two shrines that indicate the route."

"The route?"

"It's hidden in the Book of Thoth."

"The book of... which Mister Rake stole?"

"It gives great knowledge and Mister Rake communed with the spirits. Amenemope knows."

Earnestine shivered, remembering Mrs Albright speaking in tongues.

"But Amenemope does not live again," Sir Archibald concluded, glancing angrily towards the desiccated corpse.

"Sir Archibald?"

A cough echoed behind them, polite and quiet, and insistent.

She turned.

"Ah, Captain Caruthers," Sir Archibald said. "Everything well?"

"Sir Archibald," Caruthers said. "We've discovered that these fake mummies searched the cabins."

"I see."

"We wondered if you'd check your belongings and let me know what might be missing."

"They won't have the book," Earnestine said, thinking aloud. Was that what they had been looking for?

"I hope not, my dear," said Sir Archibald, and he went past the Captain out of the hold.

Earnestine felt awkward: "He wanted to know that his mummy was all right."

"Running to his mummy at the first sign of trouble."

"Quite."

Earnestine went to leave. "I'd better check our rooms."

She passed him and Caruthers didn't seem to want to follow her.

"Good night, then," she said.

"You called him 'Sir Archibald'," Caruthers observed.

"That is his title and name."

"Not 'Archie'."

Earnestine glanced back at him as if he was mad. "Don't be absurd," she snapped. "He is the President of the Royal Expeditionary Society and deserves respect, even if... even if..."

"Even if he is your fiancé."

Earnestine's jaw tightened and her face reddened such that the long scar on the left side of her face appeared to stand out white.

It was cold outside.

The sky was clear, the waxing moon a day away from full and the Milky Way arched overhead. The ancient Egyptians thought this was the celestial mirror of the life-giving Nile. There ought to be a new trail of stars for the Suez Canal, she thought, as she rested on the railing on the port side to stare at the darkness. It seemed flat, calm and the moon's saucer reflection rippled on the desert. That didn't seem right.

She pinched the bridge of her nose and was about to look again when she heard Caruthers' footsteps behind her. She didn't look round.

He paused and then walked on.

Clouds drifted over the moon. The mirage in the desert had gone. Earnestine felt a sense of loss, something important slipping through her fingers like sand.

This land was where the Pharaohs and the High Priests lived, where the Gods Ra, Horus, Set and Thoth ('I am not the god Thoth' – what did that mean?) had once walked... where they walked still, if Sir Archibald's theory was anything to go by. Was that possible?

And a book containing all knowledge.

Two spells, if she remembered rightly.

Thoth, so the legend had it, invented writing and begat himself.

Mister Rake had not struck Earnestine as someone who communed with the spirits. He was far too pedantic and condescending to believe Mrs Albright and her Hermetic Orders, but, apparently, he had said that Amenemope knows.

The only thing to do was to go back to the hold and ask the High Priest, which seemed absurd.

There was no-one watching her, so she slipped down the stairs and along the passageway. The lamp was still there, foolishly alight. As soon as she stepped inside and looked down the row of crates, she knew.

According to legend, the Book of Thoth had once been hidden in a series of boxes, and so it was again. The crate, the outer sarcophagus and the inner sarcophagus. The lid was not nailed down properly. Sir Archibald had probably left it like that without realising that Mister Rake was no longer available to tidy up after him.

Earnestine pushed the various lids aside to look at Amenemope. The mummy was a wizened object, but he must have been knowledgeable and active in life. The High Priest of Thoth. Close to the divine, but, like the dead man on the deck, not the god Thoth.

She searched under the corpse and her hand touched it at once.

It was big, heavy, a weighty tome indeed, kept within another box made of teak with a clasp. Someone had gone to a great deal of trouble to keep this precious artefact safe.

She wasn't going to open it here in the hold with water dripping from the ceiling. Ancient artefacts required reverence and care.

She expected to be stopped on return to her cabin, but the others were all busy and no-one noticed her scurry inside. Her cabin had not been searched by any fake mummies, she noted. Odd, but she had no time to think about it.

She lit her lamp, locked the door behind her and put the teak box down upon her writing desk. It was exquisite, beautifully constructed, and locked.

A little fiddling with the right lockpick and *hey presto!*

Inside was a cloth tied with string that carefully folded around...

"Oh, my word!"

...a rectangular object, a book, obviously, it couldn't be anything else hidden within the material.

The Book of Thoth.

The actual, ancient Book of Thoth.

Mister Rake had found it, held it and died. He had met his end in a locked room, just as Earnestine had found and held this sacred book in a locked room.

She put it down.

Perhaps there were some things that should remain secret... no, arrant nonsense.

Earnestine picked it up again, felt the object within, and then she untied the string holding it closed, unwrapped it and slipped the contents out carefully, like a longed-for birthday present.

Here it was, the real 'Book of Thoth', an object unseen for centuries and now she held it in her hands.

Reverently.

With care.

There were the symbols that Thoth himself had invented to record his own name: the sacred ibis on standard, small bread loaf over two diagonal strokes and finally a seated god.

Thoth!

The actual Book of Thoth.

Except, it had a label, printed on a foolscap-sized hardback book with faint lines, margin and manufactured in Paris.

She frowned.

The Wandering Jew? Methuselah? Thoth? None of these would have written in such a modern book.

What was an archaeologist like Sir Archibald Reevers doing trying to locate a modern book? Why all this secrecy? Why... oh, just bother, why?

She'd always imagined life as a great explorer and archaeologist, travelling long distances across hazardous terrain to find a lost temple. Entering the dark gloom with her trusty lantern, being the first to navigate the ages-old passageways, perhaps overcoming traps and solving puzzles, to reach a fabled treasure. To hold in her hand, weighing the historical importance as much as the sterling value, some votive object, a discovery that would rewrite the history books and make the name Deering-Dolittle resonate down the ages.

But all she found were things that made no sense.

Perhaps the answer to this riddle lay inside.

She opened the book and sure enough, this too made no sense.

Whatever secrets might be contained within the book, they were written in ancient Egyptian hieroglyphics. She had studied her Jean-François Champollion, *Lettre à M. Dacier relative à l'alphabet des hiéroglyphes phonétiques* as translated by Rhys Bryant. She knew how to read this, except quite soon Earnestine's head was awash with buzzards, vultures, sun with rays, sun without rays, ripples, diagonal strokes, ovals, gateways with serpents, scribal kits and seated queens holding flowers.

She shook her head, mentally berating herself.

She knew she could translate this, most of it, maybe some of it, that section there possibly, but it would take her weeks and weeks. And it just went on, pages and pages of it, in neat, tiny pictograms.

She realised what it was.

It was a copy.

Someone had written down the hieroglyphs from the real Book of Thoth. The secrets, and surely the knowledge, were more important than the actual artefact, just as the history more vital than any shiny gold statuette. Those were still hers for the taking. To know what Thoth himself had known–

Earnestine gasped.

It made sense.

Apple trees can be moved, replanted, cuttings taken. They had done the same in their garden in Kensington to plant the Bramley. Perhaps this held the secret of immortality. Imagine living forever. The places she could visit. She could explore the whole of the Amazon basin, all the way up the Nile, the great Mississippi, even the river that her parents had explored only to disappear without a trace. All these wondrous places to visit *and the time to do it.*

Sir Archibald Reevers wasn't such a fool.

He wasn't looking in the wrong place as she'd first thought; he was looking for the map.

This was a treasure map!

Her eyes alighted upon a phrase within the book amongst the animals, birds and people. Just as a foreigner on the train might suddenly say, 'Paddington Station' amongst all their gobbledegook, there, plain as day, were the French words 'Canal de Suez'.

No, wait, so this couldn't be a copy of an ancient book.

'Canal de Suez', so it had to be after 1869.

Unless it was some book of revelation that somehow foretold the building of the canal from the Middle Sea to the Red Sea? In French. There a perfectly good Egyptian hieroglyph for a canal, two horizontal lines with slashes joining them rather like a section of bent railway line.

So, was this a coded piece of French espionage?

Earnestine felt quite put out.

It was an adventure – no, not an adventure, she had promised her mother – but nonetheless a sightseeing of a different hue.

Except, why not encode 'Canal de Suez'?

Even the French would not create a code without the letters 'a', 'c' to 'e', 'l', 'n', 's', 'u' and 'z'.

She flicked further and it suddenly became blank. The last quarter hadn't been used.

On the last written page, another word jumped to her attention – a jolly familiar word: 'Earnestine'.

What was her name doing in the copy of an ancient book?

Foolish of her. It wasn't an ancient book. She knew that much.

At least the author had spelt her name properly. It vexed when people missed out her 'a'.

The secret to the Garden of Eden was hardly likely to go bird, flying bird, say, 'ask', snake – this was making some sense to her – with that determinate it meant 'nubile young woman' next to 'Earnestine'.

'Nubile young woman' indeed! Nubile? This was coded salacious prurience.

Who would write such tittle-tattle about her in Egyptian and French?

Bother.

In the drawer of the writing desk, she found paper and a pen. Quickly, but carefully, she copied the last page making sure to include all the odd lines. It was strange to write her own name amongst this menagerie.

She wrapped the book back in its cloth and retied the string.

Where to hide the box?

She looked round her cabin.

Hers hadn't been searched, which suggested that the fake mummies where looking for something specific. She resolved to find out which rooms they had ransacked. However, it did seem obvious that modern mummies would be after a modern version of an ancient book.

It was really her duty to give the book to Sir Archibald.

In the morning.

So, devoid of any better idea, she hid the box in her unmentionables drawer next to her revolver.

After loosening her corset, she lay on the bed to let sleep take her.

She dreamt of a sacred baboon with a chevron moustache courting an ibis bird, that was somehow Earnestine herself. There was a tree and a snake all arranged neatly between faint lines. Mister Djehuti was there with an apple.

Mrs Merryweather

Pippa couldn't settle.

Georgina walked up and down, "there, there", half asleep on her feet. She was exhausted and jittery, her nerves frayed from the attack, and these symptoms vexed her child.

"There, there."

Oh, she was tired.

"There, there."

What was the matter with the girl?

"There, there."

It was the 'there, there' itself that conveyed far too much desperation.

Pippa wailed.

Someone banged on the wall and screeched about having one of her heads.

Georgina grabbed her notebook and took Pippa for a walk. The crew were patrolling the deck, everyone careful after the attack. They ended up in the Smoking Room where it was warmer. How the temperature dropped in this country.

The two of them were the only ones there.

"Right, Pippa," she said. "Let's solve this."

Pippa paused and smiled.

Oh, how she could forgive the child anything for that smile.

"The game's afoot," she said. "My dear... Watson, we need to organise things. Let's make a boat."

Almost before she'd realised what she was doing, she'd plonked a few books in a line along the table. *The Gods of Egypt* and Charlotte's own steamport book went next to each other in a line. They could be the Library and the Smoking Room. *Mrs Beeton's Book of Household Management* would make a good Dining Room.

She tipped out the chess pieces from the wooden box and consulted her list.

1. Sir Archibald Reevers, on deck, port.
2. Colonel Fitzwilliam, Smoking Room.
3. Captain Caruthers, on deck, starboard.
4. Pandit Singh Maçon, Smoking Room.
5. Doctor Timon, Smoking Room.
6. Monsieur Jacques, Smoking Room.
7. Mrs Albright, cabin.
8. Miss Deering-Dolittle, on deck, aft.
9. Miss Charlotte, levels.

"Sir Archibald can be a white king," she said.

Pippa reached for it, so Georgina let her hold the President of the Royal Expeditionary Society. Sir Archibald had been in his cabin, so Pippa's mouth could represent that.

"Oh, no, Pippa, no, dirty."

She put the white king to one side, but Pippa insisted on having it back.

Captain Caruthers was a white knight and went on the starboard side of the adventure book.

Colonel Fitzwilliam... she'd used a knight, so... *ah ha*, he was a rock of sorts, so the white castle went atop the lurid cover to show him asleep in the Smoking Room.

Doctor Timon could be a black castle.

The black bishop would make an ideal Pandit Singh Maçon, and it was best to differentiate between the English passengers and the foreigners.

So, Monsieur Jacques was the black knight – most telling – and he went next to Colonel Fitzwilliam's white castle.

Mrs Albright spoke a sort of English, so she added the white queen as well. No, better still, the black queen as this left the white queen for Earnestine. The white queen was to marry the white king, after all.

Finally, and as there were no special pieces left, Georgina selected one of the white pawns for Charlotte.

All placed in their opening positions of the puzzle, and it did resemble a game.

Black knight (Monsieur Jacques) from book to cabin.

Black queen (Mrs Albright) from book to cabin.

She'd forgotten Mister Rake himself. He'd have to be the black king.

Black king (Mister Rake) from book to other book.

"Check," she said aloud, and then she knocked the black king over as if she was resigning in a real game of chess. "Mate."

Pippa giggled and dropped Sir Archibald onto the desk.

"Check-mate, yes, Pippa."

Farouk had said it was from the Persian: *Shah Mat* – 'the king is helpless'.

But which piece had captured the king?

Georgina moved the pieces about experimentally.

The white knight seemed poised, ready, on the starboard side. Earnestine's white queen could move on the port side without Caruthers seeing her. Or not, if the black knight, black bishop or black queen came from their cabins. The white castle could go straight to the Library, as could the black knight in a most un-knightly manner.

Georgina absent-mindedly took Monsieur Jacques off Pippa.

"You won't like that," she said.

Pippa gurgled, and bashed pieces of the puzzle hither and thither as she made up her own rules. Like Charlotte.

Method, opportunity and motive, these were the three legs of the stool.

Method was easy – a gunshot – and then the difficult trick of the locked room – oh, how, how, how?

Or had there been two shots?

Opportunity was tricky; it seemed every time she moved the pieces on the board, one could do it and another couldn't. Another arrangement and it was reversed, or different or impossible.

She checked her notes and returned the pieces to their starting positions.

Pippa was asleep.

Georgina's arm, holding her baby to her, was also asleep.

She went back to her cabin and got one of the crew to open her door.

She settled Pippa in her cot.

How she wished her Arthur could see their daughter.

The whole night's horror had been too much and it had brought back too many memories. Thank goodness, there had been two military men to protect her and her child. Captain Caruthers was a brave man, reminding her of her late husband, and the Colonel had been very able, hopping into battle with his stick.

She felt cold suddenly.

It was always coldest before dawn, particularly in Egypt, when the night's temperature could drop alarmingly low, especially in contrast to the unrelenting heat of the day. But this was something different.

The Colonel had not been trapped in his chair with his war wound. His injury came and went: if he needed a brandy, for example, or to step once more unto the breach. He was quite capable of killing Mister Rake. He'd been alone in the Smoking Room; the Library was only a few feet away and you didn't need to be that able-bodied to fire a gun. For an old soldier like the Colonel, using a revolver was second nature. And the trick with the locked bolt; well, he'd been to India where they could vanish up a levitating rope.

So, motive... there were some books stolen, but the only real excuse for murder was the events in the Punjab. The regiment, cornered, had sent for help and one Mister Rake, secretary to the local garrison, had prevaricated. Had he done so out of concern for the garrison's soldiers, the need to protect the civilians in his charge, to save money... or cowardice?

Without Mister Rake to question (and calling him up with a séance was something Georgina would not countenance), there was no way of knowing.

But the truth of the matter was irrelevant.

The Colonel blamed Mister Rake and therefore that was a motive.

Georgina imagined the Colonel sitting in the Smoking Room. She saw him asleep; an empty brandy glass perched upon his stomach. He seemed harmless, cuddly even, but she knew that his steel – particularly in his glory days before his war wound had rendered him a near cripple – made up his bones and fire flowed through his veins. He had faced the horrors of the Thuggee, fought against impossible odds and won through. A simple door would present a problem that could be solved.

And he'd hated Mister Rake.

He'd sat on his chair and seethed, waiting, watching, preparing and when the moment came, he had – with but a few short hops – struck!

With some trick, some wretched, unfathomable trick, but then that obstacle faced all her suspects. It had been done, therefore it must have been done. QED.

But knowing the Colonel had done it was not the same as proving it.

Georgina narrowed her eyes: how could she trick him into revealing the truth? Hide the brandy perhaps?

And this brutal logic applied equally to the Captain.

So, she hadn't solved it.

Levitating ropes indeed.

And the Colonel had been asleep.

Or pretending?

She must write this down.

The writing desk was just there, a pace away, with a chair that would be so wonderful to take her weight off her feet.

And, oh, the chair was so comfortable.

Miss Charlotte

It was strange to see the narrow highway of water replaced by a large lake, a blissful change of scenery from the endless desert of yellow to a flat surface of darkness.

After guarding the ship all night, the men had gathered in the Smoking Room.

Someone had placed chess pieces on the table around some books as if recreating a war scene, but Charlotte couldn't place the battle.

"There were hundreds of the thieving blighters," said Sir Archibald.

Captain Caruthers turned to Charlotte: "Lottie?"

"I'd say there were more than thirty, but fewer than fifty," Charlotte said. "Sorry I can't be more accurate, but it was dark and jolly confusing."

"Seemed more."

"They had the element of surprise and attacked on all fronts."

"So, forty, plus or minus. There's always uncertainty."

"The 'Fog of War'."

"Nice expression."

"Not mine," Charlotte admitted. "Von Clausewitz's *On War*."

"Fog of war or not, this is a fine pickle," Sir Archibald said.

"That's it, then," said Caruthers, "the authorities will have to be informed."

"Thieves dressed as mummies. We'll be a laughing stock."

"When will the authorities arrive?" Doctor Timon asked.

"Depends if they come by boat or camel train from Tanis," Captain Caruthers mused.

"Or from Suez?" Timon added.

"Tanis is nearer Cairo and there are more protectorate forces there."

"Boat, I'd have thought," said Colonel Fitzwilliam.

"All the traffic has turned around and is northbound through the canal," said Sir Archibald.

"For twenty-four hours," Captain Caruthers said.

"And sailing time," Pandit Singh Maçon added. "They may miss the southbound convoy."

"I doubt they'll accept Mrs Merryweather as Investigating Officer."

"Yes, that idea of yours seems foolish now," Sir Archibald added.

"She has twenty-four hours left, then."

"I need my bed," said Monsieur Jacques. He looked at Charlotte as if he thought she too might be tired, but Charlotte felt invigorated by last night's fighting and didn't feel like sleep at all.

Jacques went out.

"Come on, Lottie," said Caruthers, "we may as well see the sunrise."

"Yes, Captain."

"Take your parasol."

"There's no sun."

"There will be."

Charlotte followed Captain Caruthers on deck. It was cold, and she shivered until the Captain put his jacket around her. It was warm and comforting, particularly the weight in the right pocket. She checked, and he still had his holster attached to his belt complete with his service revolver.

He fussed around her until he'd fished out his cigarette case and matches. When he handed back the case and box, Charlotte placed them back in his pockets and took a moment to surreptitiously finger the weapon – yes, another Webley; she could tell by the shape of the butt and hammer.

The horizon was vivid, the sunshine almost scarlet over the sand.

What was that rhyme, she thought, red sky at night, shepherd's delight, red sky... probably a silly old wives' tale.

"Ness is getting married," Charlotte said, changing the subject. "He's a Knight of the Realm, so will it be in St. Paul's Cathedral?"

Caruthers didn't reply.

"The Surrey Deering-Dolittles will be invited."

Caruthers carried on staring steadfastly for the sunrise.

"They pull my hair."

"The hawkers are up already," Caruthers observed, leaning out on the rail. "I wonder how many of them were wearing bandages last night."

"There were forty."

"Forty thieves... apt for this part of the world. No doubt we'll find an underground hideout and need to say, 'Open Sesame'."

"I wonder where they went?"

Caruthers flicked his cigarette away: "Come on, let's find out. Parasol."

Once she'd collected the light blue monstrosity, the Captain led them to the gangway and across onto the bank. Such was their speed that they were halfway up the rise before the swarm of beggars realised. Caruthers barked something in foreign and the natives backed off, hands raised, full of mumbled apology.

Charlotte carried her parasol like a rifle at the ready as they marched through the shadow cast by the hill beyond the bank and up into the dawn light. There were tracks, plenty of tracks.

Caruthers bent over, hands on knees to stare at them.

"Mad scramble," Charlotte said.

"Someone routed them."

Caruthers always knew what to say to make Charlotte grin.

They followed on foot and out into the endless desert. After a few hundred yards, the tracks started to split into four distinct trails fanning out ever so slightly and then they just stopped.

"Rubbed out," said Caruthers after a closer examination. "There wasn't any wind to speak of last night."

"If there was, it would have obliterated all of it."

"There's sand in the depressions, something…"

"Common trick to brush away tracks."

"Yes, let's try a hundred yards ahead."

"Another trick would be to change direction or double back."

"Give me your parasol."

Charlotte handed it over and Caruthers stuck it in the ground where the tracks faded.

Charlotte counted as they strode back the way that had come.

"You go clockwise," said Caruthers.

They set off, examining the ground or glancing at the upright parasol to take a bearing. Charlotte used her thumb to ensure she stayed the same distance as she walked in a circle.

There were no tracks on the ground in her arc.

She met the Captain a hundred yards ahead of the parasol.

"Anything?" he asked.

"No, nothing."

"Let's try a little further ahead."

They walked together and then moved apart to check the area. After another 100 yards, they paused.

"There's nothing," Charlotte said.

She glanced back and saw the tiny parasol sticking out of the ground. Forty thieves! They must have run over the ridge, down into the desert and then... vanished.

"Picked up by a genie," Caruthers suggested.

As Charlotte and the Captain walked back, they glanced occasionally at the ground in case they'd missed something, but they knew there was nothing to see. Once they'd reached their marker, the tracks appeared again – and they were jolly obvious, even under their own additions. Caruthers pulled the parasol from the ground and gave it back to Charlotte. She jerked it to 'shoulder arms' and then moved to 'slope arms' to march alongside the Captain.

"The gun is Rake's," said Caruthers.

"Gun?"

"The one in my jacket," Caruthers explained. "I searched his cabin after he was dead. Found it. Didn't find what I was looking for."

"What was that?"

"Papers. They went missing on the night Rake got what he deserved. It must have been at the same time."

"You think Mister Rake stole your papers?"

"No, he was too busy being murdered."

"So, whoever killed Mister Rake didn't steal your papers."

Caruthers grimaced: "Heck of an alibi. I didn't steal your papers as I was busy committing murder."

"A bit of a coincidence, though."

"Rake was murdered as a diversion?"

"Maybe."

They crested the rise and stood for a moment to admire the view.

The SS *Karnak* dazzled as the sunlight shone horizontally. Their shadows were long and slender, pointing straight ahead, dark shapes flowing across like evil fingers reaching out.

"The papers can't have been removed from the boat," Caruthers said.

"And the murderer is still aboard."

"Unless it's you or I."

Charlotte's laugh died in her throat.

"Convenient that we broke down just here, wouldn't you say?"

Charlotte nodded, although to be honest she'd have found it more convenient if they'd broken down near somewhere selling ice cream.

They went on, through the hawkers and gawkers, and back aboard.

"Your jacket," Charlotte said as she slipped off the garment.

"You best keep the revolver," Caruthers replied. "Just in case. There's a box of spare ammunition too. Twelve rounds."

"And six in the chambers already by the feel of it."

"I'd rather you didn't tell your sisters."

"No fear."

CHAPTER XIII

Miss Deering-Dolittle

Shockingly, it was elevenses when Earnestine woke.

She wondered for a moment whether she'd forgotten to adjust her pocket watch to the bizarre Egyptian time zone. Why the foreigners couldn't just stick to Greenwich Mean Time like everyone else was beyond her. There had been other time zones in her dreams too, ages of history like chapters in a book or layers of archaeological remains, a Troy built upon another Troy, medieval upon Roman upon Celtic, Mister Djehuti's words layered with meaning and her hand upon his arm and his arm upon her and their lips–

Cold water! That was what was needed.

She washed as best she could and dressed.

As she did so, she decided to confront Sir Archibald, make him confess his part and then insist that the stolen property should be returned. She took the box containing the book with her to the Dining Room, sat opposite him and waited until he'd settled after rising upon her arrival.

"Sir Archibald."

"My dear?"

She handed it over. It wasn't hers. Nor his.

He didn't seem interested until he realised what it was.

"My dear, my dear, wonderful," he said, flicking through the book.

"Mister Rake stole it."

"It is of great historical and cultural significance."

"And a clue in a murder investigation."

"Indeed, a vital clue."

"And it should be returned to its rightful owner."

"By solving the riddle."

"Riddle?"

"Here it is," Sir Archibald said, reading the hieroglyphs. "The Riddle of the Sphinx... 'I journeyed from the Temple of the Ancient'..."

"Riddle?" Earnestine repeated.

"The Riddle of the Sphinx," Sir Archibald replied. "You are familiar with it?"

"Yes... what has four legs in the morning, two legs in the day and three legs in the evening?"

"A man."

Earnestine thought of Pippa crawling about the deck, her own stance and, uncharitably, Mrs Albright using a walking stick: "Or a woman."

"The answer is a man, I assure you, my dear."

"Well, never mind that, it should be returned."

"There are three markers to the Temple of the Ancient. We found the Statue of the Man and hope to find the Shrine of the Child."

"Where?"

Sir Archibald glanced to port: "Never you mind, my dear. And then we shall have the direction."

Not that she was interested: "Direction?"

"On the map."

That made her sit up straight: "Map," she said with measured nonchalance.

"Yes, but only the Statue of the Man is marked... whereas..." – Sir Archibald lapsed into frustrating silence as he perused the book, until – "...ah-ha!"

Earnestine waited with... oh, to bedlam with patience: "What is it?"

Sir Archibald quoted directly: "'I journeyed from the Temple of the Ancient back along the Riddle of the Sphinx in a straight line' – here it is, here it is, straight line my dear, straight line – 'towards the fundament of the Shrine of the Child and caught a boat where the Bitter Lake and the Canal de Suez join.'"

"That's here."

"Exactly."

"The boat stopping here can't be a coincidence."

"This is marvellous, simply marvellous. It tells me which one is the Child and so the path to the Temple of the Ancient is a straight line – of course, of course."

Earnestine nodded: "The book?"

Sir Archibald hesitated.

"For my sister, the Investigating Officer."

"You showed it to me first."

"I did."

"Then I am in your debt, my dear."

He handed it back, which surprised her, but then he had learnt what he wanted to know.

"It has my name in it," Earnestine said.

"Yes, my dear, yes," said Sir Archibald as he finished his tea. "There is much to do."

"Yes."

"Eat something," said Sir Archibald, standing. "If you'll excuse me, my dear."

"Of course," Earnestine replied.

She sat. After a long time, a waiter realised she was there, and she explained her order three times. Breakfast had, she gathered, been disorganised. It was the terrible business of last night. There were those who had been unable to sleep arriving early, many had overslept and did not appear at all, while the crew hadn't been organised for full English or the more exotic continental fare. Even stranger were the tiny yellow flakes of corn of Dr John Harvey Kellogg for the Americans.

Presently, Mrs Albright and Doctor Timon joined her.

"Your fiancé not joining you?" Mrs Albright asked, leaning her stick against the wall and sitting down for a coffee. Coffee at breakfast was positively decadent. It was bad enough that there were coffee houses and other establishments of disrepute in Covent Garden and–

"Your fiancé? Not joining you?"

What was this American woman talking about?

"Oh," said Earnestine, remembering. "No... Sir Archibald was here, but he finished eating."

"I believe Sir Archibald has taken advantage of our stop and gone for a walk," Doctor Timon said.

"Walk?"

"More an expedition."

"Expedition!"

Earnestine downed her tea and got to her feet: "If you'll excuse me."

"You've not finished your breakfast," the Doctor said, looking over his round glasses and disapproving of her untouched and unclean bacon and sausages. "Most important meal of the day."

"Yes," Earnestine agreed, absently. She was half-way to the door, and back to snatch the Book of Thoth off the table, before Doctor Timon had got to his feet.

"Lovers' tiff," Mrs Albright explained for the entire room in that loud American voice of hers.

Earnestine dithered as to whether to rush after Sir Archibald or grab her adventure – *no adventures, Mother had said* – kit, or return to the Dining Room to find out how much of a head start the President of the Royal Expeditionary Society had on her.

It can't be much, she thought, mentally adding up her first course of grapefruit, kippers, toast and tea, and totalling it into far too many minutes. And that didn't include the interminable wait to be served.

She went to her cabin, changed into her stout Oxford Street boots and grabbed her small kit bag. She added a water bottle at the last minute, the Webley from her unmentionables drawer and hoicked her umbrella out of the wardrobe. The book went in her bag.

Finally, at long last, and with only the slightest moment of ceremony, she put on her pith helmet.

She was on deck.

Map!

He had said 'map'.

The Statue of the Man was in the middle of a straight line, but where was that and where was the Shrine of the Child?

She made her way straight to Sir Archibald's cabin.

Luck was with her; there was no one about.

She knelt down, took her lock picks from her small adventure kit, and quickly tweaked the door open.

It was a man's bedroom, but she was a Deering-Dolittle and not afraid of the unknown.

She closed the door behind her.

It was much like her room; indeed, it was the mirror image of Georgina's cabin on the other side of the boat, but it had a certain aroma of shaving foam and cologne water.

Where to start?

She took in the wardrobe, travelling trunk, chest of drawers, writing desk and the... steel framed thing with a mattress up against the wall. There were some details about such things on wedding nights. A geography test or something; she resolved to ask Georgina about that once and for all.

On his bedside cabinet, she found a pair of reading glasses and a copy of the Bible. So, she was right, he was jolly well aware of the Garden of Eden's location. Sir Archibald had neatly placed a copy of some magazine called *The Pearl* underneath.

The man was meticulous; therefore, it would be in his writing desk. Concealed perhaps, tucked away amongst other papers or simply hidden in plain sight.

She pulled down the desk to reveal the little drawers for ink, pens and blotter. There were no papers.

There were the three drawers in the desk, of course, but... and she saw it, a faint ridge in the blotting paper.

Carefully, she removed the pink blotting paper from the leather surround and sure enough, like uncovering a new layer at an archaeological dig, she found a thick sheet, folded once, hidden underneath.

She opened it.

Oh, joy!

It was a map.

She smoothed it out reverently on the remains of the blotter and turned it until north faced away. It was in French, but 'Tanis', 'Canal de Suez', 'Le Grand Lac Amer' and 'Suez' were all very clear.

The SS *Karnak* was stranded just where the lake's upturned funnel fed north into the canal.

Earnestine's finger tracked across the featureless terrain.

"'Le sanctuaire de l'enfant'," she breathed aloud. "The Infant's Sanctuary."

It had to be.

She searched around this dot in an expanding spiral.

Ah ha!

A mark upon the map, a tiny dot with the legend 'L'homme' – the Man, the Statue of the Man.

Not far at all: thirty, maybe thirty and a tenth, according to the scale. Kilometres, of course.

She visualised a line from the Infant to the Man and continued it further into the desert to the east of the Canal. Sure enough, there was a mark. Someone, stabbing down, had rubbed at the surface texture and there was a tiny pinprick in the paper. Similar holes in the Man and Child betrayed the use of a pair of dividers.

So, if the distances were the same, the lone puncture would be the third sign, the old man, marking the exact position of the Temple of the Ancient.

Imagine, Earnestine thought, the actual Philosopher's Stone, hidden in that tiny hole, just... there! Just waiting for her to discover it.

She stood, checked Sir Archibald's room for anything else that might be educational, and then walked back and forth, thinking.

Her small adventure kit tapped against her hip.

Thirty kilometres.

Less than twenty miles.

However, she mustn't succumb to the family curse and 'go up the river'.

Except this was a canal and the prize was in a desert.

She so wanted to stride out exploring, instead of stomping about in this bedroom, but she had promised Mother: *no adventures.*

Mrs Merryweather

Georgina wasn't sure where she was for a moment. It looked like a ship, but it wasn't swaying.

Pippa was eating something.

As she picked the fallen book from the floor, Georgina remembered she was on the SS *Karnak*, grounded at the side of the Great Bitter Lake.

"What's that, Pippa?"

The child was fiddling with some paper. It was yet another example of her child being more interested in the wrapping than the present. She glanced around the floor looking for a fallen toy, but the carpet was clear.

"Let Mama see."

Georgina eased the paper away. It was gooey with slobber, but she wiped this aside.

"See," said Georgina. "This is all about a baboon god. A baboon! Baboon!"

Pippa giggled at the sound: "Bab... boo."

"Yes, a baboon," she said, shifted the page around so that she could read them properly. "...he has the head of a baboon. Baboon! When he is the god A'an. Of equilibrium."

Pippa struggled, almost wriggling from Georgina's arms and losing her equilibrium.

"And... he mediated power between good and evil. He was one, begotten and self-produced – begot himself, how bizarre – made calculations and established the heavens, set the stars and planets in motion. He once made a bet with the Moon and won five more days for the year, so that the goddess Nut could give birth to Osiris, Set, Isis and Horus. The Egyptians thought he invented all science, religion, philosophy and magic as well as writing..."

Georgina paused.

An awful dread came over her as she unfolded the top of the page to reveal a woodcut of a man with a bird's head. She didn't need to read to know what it was, but the word jumped to her attention: 'Thoth'.

The man, who had attacked the ship and died, had said he was not the god Thoth.

This was the missing page from the Library's Egyptology book and her child had had it.

Pippa was the killer!

No, that had to be nonsense. Pippa couldn't walk yet, let alone handle a gun, magically lock a door from the outside and rip pages from history books. So how could she possibly have this page?

The murderer had given it to her.

Georgina held Pippa close, hugging her to herself and crumpling the page further.

The killer had been next to her precious child.

She made her way over to the table, sat with Pippa on her knee and carefully flattened the page out as best she could.

She read, carefully, going over every word again, sometimes aloud to the fidgeting child, sometimes to herself.

Thoth was a god, invented writing, begot himself and mediated disputes; he had the head of an Ibis bird or a baboon (except that the ancient Egyptians didn't believe that literally) and he'd won an extra five days from the Moon raising the year from the mathematically sensible 360 to the awkward 365.

"Well, Pippa," Georgina said, sitting the child on the table so that she faced her. "Who gave you this page? Perhaps someone trying to frame you for the murder."

No, wait, she had taken the page from Mister Rake's wallet. She'd put the page in the storybook to save their place and it had fallen into Pippa's cot when she'd fallen asleep, and so dropped the book.

...so, it was Georgina herself.

Of course!

It was perfectly possible for an agile man or woman to clamber over the railing, lower themselves a deck, work along and then climb back up. Georgina in the Dining Room could have done this, passed under the Smoking Room by clinging to the side of the ship and then shinning up to... it wasn't a worked-out theory. She'd had to have had a gun, shot Mister Rake, locked the door, but essentially, those minor objections aside, she could have done it.

Georgina herself was the killer!

No, no, that was the most foolish theory yet. She was tired and not thinking straight. It was no good being a full-time mother, without a wet nurse or even a single maid, and an Investigating Officer. Earnestine may well go on about suffrage, but how were women going to cope with all the extra responsibilities?

Tea. She desperately needed a cup of tea.

Besides, the crew had witnessed her presence in the Dining Room.

"And," she cried out, "I'd have remembered."

Pippa looked shocked at this outburst and then chortled.

"It's a fifteen puzzle," Georgina admitted. It was clear that she wasn't going to solve this by thinking until her mental faculties hurt. She'd get one of Mrs Albright's heads.

She laughed: "Would you like me with Mrs Albright's head? Or the head of a baboon! Yes, baboon. Baboon!"

The God of Writing.

There was the *book code*.

Could this page be used to send encrypted messages?

There must be evidence contained on the page. Perhaps tiny pencil marks left as someone counted so many words in, or some marginalia or simply that the text revealed something incriminating. Supposing the description of Thoth included an antiquity rightfully destined for somewhere like the British Museum that had been stolen? These items were worth a fortune and Mister Rake, as Sir Archibald's personal secretary, would be in exactly the position to uncover such desecration.

That would – finally – be a motive.

Miss Charlotte

The Egyptian Skipper put guards on duty, men with rifles who positioned themselves at points along the port side watching the land, as well as men on shore to keep people from the gangway.

There was no further sign of their mummified attackers and the bodies of the fallen had been spirited away. It was almost as if it had never happened, except for the one corpse. They'd taken that to lie next to Mister Rake in the Cold Room.

Charlotte shifted her game of levels to starboard after making sure that Rake's revolver, the one Captain Caruthers had given her, was loaded and safely tucked in her pocket. Always best to be careful, she thought, as she swung out over the side and dropped down to the deck below.

People had gone ashore and everyone else, she thought, was in the Smoking Room, so this was a perfect opportunity to search everyone's cabins for the missing 'tank' papers.

But she didn't have to search every cabin, because not everyone could have stolen them.

She reached Sir Archibald's cabin, glanced left and right, and then fished out her lock picks.

Certainly, Charlotte had not stolen the papers.

Georgina had not as she was in the Dining Room and wouldn't anyway.

Under no circumstances would Earnestine go into a man's bedroom alone, so... wait!

There was movement within Sir Archibald's cabin; someone walking back and forth. Sir Archibald had gone ashore, so someone else was in there.

As quick as she could, Charlotte scuttled along one cabin and picked Mister Rake's door. She closed it ever so quietly and, on her hands and knees, crawled over to the connecting door. This was the starboard equivalent of Georgina and Pippa's rooms. Clearly, Sir Archibald had wanted Mister Rake at his constant beck and call.

She heard movement inside Sir Archibald's cabin again as a shadow shifted where the light shone under the door.

The plot thickens, she thought. Were they looking for the papers stolen from Captain Caruthers?

Her hand patted the revolver, ready to draw the weapon at a moment's notice.

So, who could be in Sir Archibald's room?

As Charlotte waited, she returned to her deliberations... where had she got up to... oh yes!

Under no circumstances would Earnestine go into a man's bedroom alone, so she couldn't have stolen the papers.

The Captain and the Colonel had not, because they were the ones transporting these papers.

Mister Rake had not either as he was being shot at the time and Captain Caruthers had searched his cabin – this cabin – and found only a revolver.

Therefore, and indubitably, this left Sir Archibald Reevers, Doctor Timon, Pandit Singh Maçon, Monsieur Jacques and Mrs Albright.

Elementary.

She didn't need her deerstalker and a pipe.

A Knight, a Doctor, a... Reverend – yes, that's what that meant – a Monsieur and a Harridan of a church bell.

She couldn't imagine Mrs Albright firing a gun and not getting one of her heads.

Well, it was the Frenchman then, wasn't it?

Except, if he did, then that excluded him from being the murderer and Charlotte had rather thought he was the most likely candidate for that.

Maybe there was a secret passage from Captain Caruthers' cabin through the Dining Room, Smoking Room and passageway to the Library, and then Monsieur Jacques could have stolen the papers, killed Mister Rake and then gone down another secret passage to his own cabin.

Though, she realised, she probably only suspected him because he still hadn't done her French homework.

She could set a trap: 'ooh, I've just dropped this sheet of vital paper that Captain Caruthers had' and then hide behind the curtains.

Except that the curtains in front of the ship's windows were not big enough for hide-and-seek. The Library hadn't even had any windows for curtains to hide behind, as Georgina's experiment had demonstrated.

There was more movement in Sir Archibald's room and then the door to his cabin clicked shut. Whoever it had been, they had just left.

Charlotte carefully tried the connecting door – it was unlocked. That was a stroke of luck.

Whoever had been searching Sir Archibald's room had been careful as everything looked in its right place.

So, where to look?

She glanced around the room: wardrobe, travelling trunk, chest of drawers, writing desk and his bed. Everything about it was bigger than Charlotte's.

She was thorough and quick: under the mattress, bottom of the wardrobe, carpet in the corner and so on.

Nothing.

There was the writing desk, but only a fool would hide papers there. It would be the first place anyone would look.

That eliminated Sir Archibald.

Next, she tried Doctor Timon's cabin. It was full of medical references and the inevitable Egyptology texts that everyone went on about. She should have asked Captain Caruthers how big these papers were and whether they could be disguised as a bookmark.

Mrs Albright was in her cabin.

"What is it?"

"I..."

"I have one of my heads."

"I came to see if you wanted a tonic or ointment?"

"Ointment!? Silly girl. No, I do not."

"Sorry."

Ungrateful harridan.

She had a good mind to pull out Rake's gun and fix her headache once and for all.

So, Monsieur Jacques and Pandit Singh Maçon. The former seemed dangerous to check with Georgina still on the prowl. As she approached the latter's cabin, she saw the Pandit himself going over to the stairs.

The Indian glanced left and right, furtively, before he descended towards the hold.

Hmmm... as she started to follow, Charlotte wondered what he was up to.

CHAPTER XIV

Miss Deering-Dolittle

Best foot forward (without showing an ankle) and the Derring-Do Club forever!

Derring-Do Club, indeed.

Such was her rush, she went to the starboard side first. A sheen of blue replaced the blackness of last night, water as far as she could see – the Great Bitter Lake.

On the port side, a lowered gangplank (which looked secure when one was using it, but, when viewed from the side, appeared to bend worryingly) led to the bank.

All Earnestine saw, beyond the makeshift village of tents, was the desert; sand as far as it was humanly possible to see. Sir Archibald could be miles and miles away by now.

Except there was a commotion.

Sir Archibald was talking with a native guide, who, in turn, argued with some natives, and their camels snorting and braying in a pen. Rather, he was shouting at some natives, while Farouk translated.

No, not Farouk, Earnestine realised, but another guide.

Clearly, an Egyptian group had been passing and could not believe their luck that a boatload of Europeans and Americans, with purses of sterling, francs and dollars were at their bargaining mercy.

Other natives ran off to spread the message. Soon a whole market of hawkers and peddlers would spring up. Earnestine realised that if she wanted to stretch her legs, now was the time before the crowds had organised.

Georgina was walking around the deck carrying Pippa and trying to handle a cup and saucer as well.

"Ness?"

"Gina, morning."

"I see Sir Archibald is hiring camels."

"Yes."

"They are arguing about the price and he's saying that he agreed terms weeks ago."

"Weeks ago?" It was almost as if he'd planned it in advance, Earnestine thought.

"Come on, Pippa, lunch."

Pippa complained.

"I have to eat, child, Mama's not even had breakfast," Georgina said. "Who's in the Dining Room?"

"Mrs Albright, Doctor Timon and Pandit Singh Maçon, I think."

"And the Colonel and Captain?"

"They've not appeared yet."

Over on dry land, they struck a deal and the natives began loading the camels. Sir Archibald waved a horsehair fly swatter to direct everyone.

"I'm going ashore," Earnestine announced.

"Is that wise?" Georgina replied.

"Of course."

"The sun–"

"I have my pith helmet and my brolly."

"It's not a parasol when it's black."

"It might rain."

Georgina glanced at the sky; it was blue and cloudless.

"I simply want to know what Sir Archibald is up to," Earnestine explained.

"You'll need a chaperone."

"Sir Archibald will be able to protect me," Earnestine said, trying to keep the long-suffering tone out of her voice.

"A chaperone from Sir Archibald. You are engaged."

"Engaged people are allowed to be in the same room."

"Out there is not in a room, it's in public!"

"Oh... oh..." Earnestine looked about. She saw a familiar red fez by the gangplank. "Farouk."

"Hardly suitable."

"Needs must."

Earnestine sauntered along to the Egyptian Guide.

"Why, Miss Earnestine. Good of the morning."

"Farouk, it's Miss Deering-Dolittle."

"I know who you are, Miss Earnestine."

"No, I meant... never mind. Why are you not Sir Archibald's guide?"

"Regrettably, he hired another."

"In that case, you are free."

"Alas, Farouk may as well be for all the *'oshr el-ersh* I am not earning."

"Excellent, I need an escort."

"You wish to walk once around the deck," Farouk said. "It would be Farouk's pleasure."

"Yes, that would be fine, but first, down there and along the bank."

"Ha, ha... I thought... you mean?"

"This way."

"But Miss Earnestine, you are a lady alone."

"Not if you keep up."

The boards of the gangplank were remarkably solid, it seemed, as she walked ashore.

Earnestine saw the Arabs openly staring, including one with scars all over his face, someone she vaguely recognized. To them, she must seem exotic, a strange red-haired maiden from a far-away, almost mythical land, rather than the sensible, level-headed young lady she knew herself to be.

"One also needs a guide," she said when Farouk caught up.

"Of course, Miss," Farouk said, and he peered about their surroundings, which were devoid of anything ancient or modern. "What do you wish me to explain?"

Earnestine headed along the shore and then up a rise to the top of some dunes. They could have been the sand hills anywhere along the East Anglian coast until they reached the crest. The view beyond was endless.

"So, Farouk, what sights are there to offer here?"

"Miss?"

"You are a guide. What should I be looking at?"

"Miss, there are no sights here... except the lake and..." he searched around, desperate for something of note. "Ah... a stranded ship."

She adjusted her pith helmet to shield her eyes from the sun. It was true.

The SS *Karnak* and the associated encampment were the only things in the whole landscape.

"Are there no relics here?" Earnestine asked. "Surely, the ancient Egyptians built something here."

"Unfortunately, no," Farouk admitted. "The Nile is the life of Egypt. Always has been, always will be."

Sir Archibald's expedition, some dozen camels, had crested the rise too – Earnestine checked the small lucky charm fixed to the chain of her pocket watch – heading northeast.

"Perhaps we could go further," Earnestine said. "Explore."

"Alas, no, we would be the food for the vulture before the day is out. Without water. Here, the lake is not..." Farouk motioned with his hand. It took Earnestine a moment or two to realise that he was miming drinking.

"It's not fresh water."

"That is so. The water here is the same as the Mediterranean and the Red Sea, but has even more salt, brought in by the streams that made the lake before the canal existed."

"Like the Dead Sea of the Holy Land?"

"Much like, Miss, much. But not so much. There are fish here, much fish, but they are the fish of the sea."

"I thought Lake Timsah had crocodiles."

"Crocodiles of the salt water," Farouk explained. "They swim here too."

Earnestine glanced back at the ship and then along the shoreline. Below that calm surface, there might be crocodiles lurking in wait.

"A dangerous place," she said.

"Yes, Miss. Farouk, he will protect you."

Earnestine led the way along the path.

"Miss, why do they talk behind your back of a club?"

Earnestine narrowed her lips before she spoke: "One's sure they don't."

"What is the 'derring-do'."

"A silly pun on our family name."

"Deering-Dolittle to Derring-Do."

"My sister, Charlotte, came up with it and we've never been able to shake it off."

"I see, Miss," said Farouk. "But what does it mean, this 'derring-do'."

"It's an expression to describe reckless and foolhardy behaviour."

"From one such as yourself?"

"Absolutely not," Earnestine insisted. "It's asinine slander."

"Farouk has heard this. You are sensible, Miss, and not like the Kent Deering-Dolittles."

Earnestine felt the muscles in her jaw clench. With effort, she corrected him, "We are the Kent Deering-Dolittles."

"Ah."

Sir Archibald and his 'ships of the desert' crested the ridge and plodded away towards the horizon.

"So," said Farouk, "back to the ship after our little adventure."

"Adventure! One does not go on adventures. Mother specifically and strictly forbade going on adventures. And, besides, five minutes ashore hardly counts as an adventure."

"No, of course not."

"Let's hire camels."

Mrs Merryweather

"Just look at your Auntie Ness."

"Ne-ne."

"What is she up to, Pippa?"

A welter of activity lined the shore, full of tents, Egyptians, Arabs, Bedouin, camels, horses, stores, young children running, always running, and even some European tourists come to view the stranded ship. Thomas Cook and Son of Fleet Street were making a roaring trade, no doubt.

In amongst it all, Earnestine sauntering along, as if she was walking down the promenade to hire a donkey ride on some English tourist beach.

Georgina shook her head.

The men stood when she arrived in the Dining Room.

She was jolly glad of another cup of tea and plate of the cold collation. There was also cake for dessert, which Pippa liked. It was strange to have the first choice of slice; Charlotte didn't seem to be around.

As she sat, spooning food back into Pippa's mouth from her chin, she thought about the passengers on the SS *Karnak*.

Strange that Sir Archibald and Earnestine were on the same ship, considering their connection: Earnestine was always going round to the Royal Expeditionary Society trying to secure funding for an expedition up that dreadful river to rescue their mother, father and uncle.

A coincidence too that Mister Rake had been in India at the same time as Colonel Fitzwilliam and Captain Caruthers.

Mrs Albright had travelled with Sir Archibald.

Doctor Timon, Monsieur Jacques and Pandit Singh Maçon seemed to be the only individual travellers unconnected to anyone.

They had met so many travellers on the journey. Most had departed for the cruise ships up the Nile. There had been that fat Frenchman or Dutchman on the Orient

Express. And that dear, sweet old lady who had knitted so much – thank goodness she wasn't present because murder wouldn't have done her nerves any good.

Only certain passengers had reached the SS *Karnak* and this ill-fated voyage south along the Suez Canal.

Fictional detectives, Dupin of *The Murders of the Rue Morgue* and that consulting detective in the *Strand Magazine*, always deduced wonders from the smallest of clues. It was, Georgina thought, ludicrous. She couldn't even deduce if her own child wanted more food, less food, winding, changing, putting to bed or whatever.

If the gunshot had two sounds, 'bang' and 'phut', perhaps she could narrow the gun down.

Captain Caruthers was there.

"Captain, do you have a penknife?"

"I do," he said, fishing one out of his pocket.

"Excellent... hold Pippa."

"I'd really rather not."

Georgina swapped her baby for the penknife as Pippa became grouchy and Caruthers became alarmed.

"Walk her up and down," Georgina suggested.

She still had the key to the padlock and found the Library something of a mess. The wonderfully preserved scene was now sullied with the remains of that evil séance; however, this wasn't what she was interested in.

She checked the angle, pretending to hold a gun by pointing her finger, and then she removed the sheet from the chaise. There was a neat hole in the dark stain. She felt with her finger, probing into the upholstery. She couldn't feel anything.

She pulled the chaise away from the wall and looked at the back. Perhaps the bullet had passed straight through.

Indeed, the chaise had an exit wound, a savage cross of damage.

The wall behind was clean and polished where the blood had been removed. Whoever had cleaned it had obviously smeared the mess wide and so the bright area was large.

Could the blood have gone one way as the bullet went another?

This didn't seem likely.

She was sure she'd checked this wall thoroughly when she'd been looking for a secret door.

"What are you trying to find?" said Caruthers.

Georgina saw him leaning against the door jam. "Where's Pippa?"

"I gave her to the Colonel. They're in the Smoking Room."

"Oh, is she all right?"

"Of course, though I can't say the same for the Colonel."

Georgina nodded. "Do you have your stick?"

"Stick?"

"Officer's stick."

"Swagger stick?"

"That's it, if you'd be so kind."

Caruthers frowned, but then stepped smartly away, leaving Georgina to her thoughts.

No matter how she restaged the events in her mind, it always came unstuck. It was that wretched bolt. Rearranging the chess pieces upon various books made no difference. That magic trick stumped her every time.

While she waited, she pushed the chaise back into its original position.

Eventually, the Captain returned and handed over his rattan stick.

Georgina flipped it over so that the silver head, with the regimental coat of arms, aimed away from the chaise. She inserted it into the bullet hole and pushed. It went through easily enough and finally poked out.

Glancing behind her as she crouched by the chaise, she double checked that the angle was indeed what she'd imagined it to be.

It made no sense.

Could the bullet have been fired from below and behind?

No, it could not. The exit hole must be larger than the entrance hole and the blood splatter must go with the direction of the shot.

"Oh."

"What is it?" Caruthers asked.

The stick pointed to a dent in the metal wall.

But there was no bullet anywhere.

She stood and handed the swagger stick back to the Captain.

"You found something?"

"Quite the opposite."

Miss Charlotte

Pandit Singh Maçon paused at the doorway to the hold. The jewel on his turban caught the light, a red flash of warning.

Charlotte waited.

He waited.

Why was he waiting?

Did he suspect he was being followed?

But then the man disappeared through the door.

Charlotte tiptoed forward, reciting a litany of excuses in her head: she had permission, she was lost, the head prefect had given her an errand...

She looked through the door.

She could see the sides of the crates, but there was no sign of the Pandit.

There was nowhere to hide either. She knew this. Unless one counted the sarcophagus of A-something-moppy or the Pandit's empty crate.

Why was he transporting an empty crate?

Charlotte stepped into the room tentatively, but then stood upright and amazed.

The Pandit had vanished.

Could he be some Indian mystic, able to disappear in one place to reappear elsewhere?

She made her way to the far side of the crates and looked along them.

If he could do that, then perhaps, using some Indian mysticism, he had murdered Mister Rake in the locked Library and then vanished into thin air.

"Miss?"

Charlotte turned around slowly.

The Pandit was standing against the wall, revealed slowly as the door swung shut. He was still, then touched his ring, as he calmly contemplated his catch.

"Can I help you, Miss Charlotte?"

Charlotte felt utterly embarrassed. To miss such an obvious trick was unforgivable. Honestly.

"Miss?"

"I was lost," she said.

"You? A member of the infamous Derring-Do Club."

"Oh, you've heard of us."

"I do my research."

Charlotte grinned. She felt so proud.

Then the Pandit slapped her across her cheek.

"Ow! That hurt," she complained. "Really..."

She touched her face, feeling a slight dampness. When she looked at her hand, she saw the faintest of traces of blood.

"You cut me!"

The Pandit showed her his empty hands and a ring on his finger caught the light. It had a sharp, complicated setting that looked like brass.

"...your ring, it..."

There was something wrong with the light.

Men appeared behind the Pandit like shadows forming.

She fished in her pocket and drew out the revolver that Captain Caruthers had given her – Rake's gun, although much good it had done him. She tried lifting it, but it wouldn't move properly. She knew how to grip the handle; how to aim and pull back the hammer; how to line up the rear notch, fixed front blade and target; the right pressure to apply to squeeze the trigger and not to pull the aim from true; and how to kill with it.

But her fingers misbehaved.

The Pandit swatted it easily from her grasp. It arced away to crash and skitter across the deck, before coming to rest in the corner.

And then her legs folded under her.

The deck plating was hard.

Comforting.

She tried to close her eyes.

Feet moved across her field of vision.

More people coming into the hold.

Bandages.

Someone was trying to administer first aid on her cheek by bandaging her entire head.

And body.

Her heart pounded suddenly.

She could barely move.

Despite the weight of her arms and legs, they lifted her aloft so easily.

Many hands.

She tried to struggle.

The bandages held her tight, legs together, arms against her sides. Writhing made her bonds tighter, constricting her movements, but desperation made her fight back.

The top of the sarcophagus yawned.

They lowered her in.

Dropped her the last half foot.

No, NO, no, no, she was being mummified alive!

She twisted, saw the many faces staring down at her through the slit between two swathes of wrappings.

Please, please... she'd be good.

The lid of the sarcophagus blocked the light as it descended.

Anything, please no.

It slammed home.

She screamed.

The fabric muffled the sound.

It tasted of baking soda and incense.

Darkness.

She heard the crate's lid clunking into place.

Sorry, sorry... I'm so sorry...

A pounding detonation, so close and overwhelming.

And another.

Ness, Gina... Mummy...

Hammering.

Again.

Coffin nails.

And again.

She kicked.

Shouted.

Struggled.

Sobbed.

The final nail.

CHAPTER XV

Miss Deering-Dolittle

A short reconnoitre, Earnestine promised herself, just to look at the terrain and see if catching up with Sir Archibald was possible.

Nothing more.

Earnestine and Farouk reached the merchants, shooed the ever-present boys away and finally came to a man hiring out transport. There were horses and camels.

The camels looked exciting from the ship, but close up they looked awkward and angry. And they smelt.

"I'd like to hire a horse please," Earnestine said.

"Very good, very good, wonderful day."

"A horse, if you please."

"Sunshine, wonderful."

"No... look, horse... that!" she insisted, pointing. "How much?"

He looked doubtful.

"A penny? Threepence?"

He perked up as soon as money was mentioned: "For you, such a lovely lady, ten of the English pence, a bargain."

"One's only hiring it."

"Pardon. I not understand English."

"You know perfectly well, five."

"I have fifteen children's mouths to feed."

"Ridiculous... five."

"I–"

"All right, two."

"Two is lower than five."

"English and mathematics... five."

"Eight and my children will starve."

"Three."

"Three is less than five, Madam."

"Eight is more than five."

"Seven."

"Five."

"Six?"

"Four."

"Four is still less than five, Madam. You cannot haggle downwards."

"Five."

"Not five."

"I raised by one, four to five is raising by one. Now you lower your six by one to five."

"Five?"

"Done," said Earnestine. "Do you have change for two threepenny bits?"

"Pay the man six," said Farouk.

"Six for two horses."

"Two horses!" said the man. "That would be twenty."

Earnestine glared at him.

"I would be honoured to hire them to you, Madam, for ten."

"Five! One haggled to five."

"For one horse."

"I am a young lady. You can see that. Obviously, I can't go on my own, so obviously we were haggling for two horses."

"Me!" said Farouk. "I can ride a camel. A horse is far too fast for my digestion."

"Five for a horse and a camel."

"Ten."

Earnestine looked at the two multisided coins resting in her palm.

"Six."

The dealer beamed: "Done."

The next issue was that the dealer only had a man's saddle. The concept of side-saddle, and indeed, women riding horses, seemed to elude him and Earnestine's skirts proved awkward. The man went to help her – "Do you mind!" – so his women came to help. These women, dressed in head to toe in black, giggled as they aided, but mostly abetted, Earnestine to clamber onto the horse.

"Thank you," Earnestine said through gritted teeth. "What's it called?"

"Bucephalus."

"You're joking."

"As Allah is my witness."

Sir Archibald's expedition was well out of sight over the rise. Once Earnestine had guided her steed to the top, she could just make out a smudge of dust in the distance.

She glanced back at the SS *Karnak*, marooned on the shore. Workmen were unloading crates, including Sir Archibald's, so clearly, some passengers had given up on the voyage and were intending to continue to Suez overland.

Including Sir Archibald?

She knew nothing of this.

"I thought you said, 'no adventures', Miss," Farouk said when his camel caught up.

Earnestine looked up to him; his perch was far higher than her saddle. "I did."

"What is this, if it is not an adventure, Miss?"

"It's not... it's... merely... a stroll in the park."

"The desert is not a park. The sand, it must be respected. Feared. And we don't have any water, Miss."

"I have a water bottle and it's only a few miles."

"But, Miss, we are in the desert."

"It's less than Lyme Regis to Charmouth and back, and we walked that looking for rock creatures."

"Rock creatures?"

"You have crocodiles," Earnestine shouted up, "same thing."

The horse made steady progress at a walk. Earnestine reckoned it would take a little over an hour to reach where the dot of the 'Le sanctuaire de l'enfant' marked the map.

She decided not to mention that there was a second and third leg to this journey.

Farouk was talking to himself: "Only the British would go out in the sun. You live in a land forsaken by Allah, where it rains all the time. As soon as you are in Egypt, you all go mad. You ignore afternoon sleeping but prefer to strike out into the desert with no idea how to find water, guzzling drinks that burst into flames and letting the power of the sun god burn your skin until it turns red and resembles parchment."

"One thinks you are exaggerating."

"Really? Here I am with a young lady of your Empire. You. A woman who wears black with armoured underwear–"

"Please!"

"Tightened such that you cannot breathe, your pale face bare to the sunshine, your hair visible to all and coloured like fire. You wander about as if you own the place."

Earnestine was confused. "But we do own the place. And Her Majesty's Government has the majority of the shares in the Suez Canal Company."

"Sometimes, I think it would be better if the Pharaohs did return," Farouk said. "Then we would at least be enslaved by our own kind and I wouldn't have to dress up in this pantomime cliché just to get tips from tourists."

"We British don't enslave you."

Farouk simply raised an eyebrow.

"Well," said Earnestine, "you wouldn't want to be ruled by the French."

Farouk sighed.

"Their attitude to women is woefully foreign."

"Like Egypt?" Farouk said. "We Egyptians keep our women safe, properly dressed–"

"One is properly dressed," Earnestine retorted. "My ankles cannot be seen."

"–covered from head to toe and kept indoors."

"Prisoners."

"Assets."

"Slaves."

"Knowing their place."

"You should learn about Universal Women's Suffrage," Earnestine yelled back.

"Universal... what?"

"Everywhere I go, the same foolish arguments. Women should have the right to vote."

"Vote? Vote! What is vote?"

"And own property and... we should form a union for social and political change for women."

"I have no idea what you are talking about, Miss."

"Then pay attention!"

"I am. Your words are not ones Farouk knows."

"Women should have equal rights to men."

Farouk blinked rapidly. "Women have more rights than men."

"I beg your pardon!"

"Women are protected by men."

"Words desert me."

"I doubt that has ever been your problem. Men do not like women who..."

"Who what?"

"Argue."

"Argue! Argue? How dare you say I argue?"

"You would have men and women the same?"

"No, of course, not," Earnestine admitted in a loud hectoring voice. "Men and women should dress differently, powder their noses in different rooms, and a man should wine and dine and woo and ask a woman to marry her."

"Has anyone wined and dined you?"

Earnestine's hand flew up to her left cheek hovering to hide the vivid scar down her face. "One is engaged."

"Who is the lucky man?"

"The one who went off on an expedition without me."

"Sir Archibald?"

"He wouldn't have done so if men and women were treated as equals."

Farouk shrugged in an exaggerated manner.

"Women," Earnestine insisted, "will have the vote and then you'll see."

"How are you going to achieve this madness?"

"By chaining myself to the nearest railing."

Farouk looked about the featureless desert. There was nothing to see now in every direction. If a breeze blew, the fabled Khamseen or a Samoon wind, then all their tracks would vanish in a moment.

"We must go back, Miss," Farouk said, "otherwise we will be lost."

"Lost!?" Earnestine retorted. That settled it, she thought, there was no way she was turning back now. "One is a Deering-Dolittle."

Mrs Merryweather

"What now?"

"I'd like you to shoot the chaise."

Caruthers raised an eyebrow: "What has it done to you?"

"Captain, I'm serious," Georgina said, pointing to a place on the chaise away from the existing bullet hole. She stood back. "Stand there and aim here."

Caruthers flipped his swagger stick under his left arm, adjusted the diagonal strap of his Sam Browne belt and unbuttoned his holster. The gun looked jolly big and frightening.

He aimed: "Are you sure?"

"Quite sure, Captain."

She jumped when the ghastly thing exploded. The sound in the small confines of the Library was shocking. The chaise burst open and linen wadding puffed outwards.

The bullet had gone straight through and dented the metal wall.

"IT MADE A BIGGER HOLE."

"You don't need to shout."

"I'M NOT SHOUTING... oh, I beg your pardon."

Her voice sounded strange as if she was lying in a bath full of water. The smell of cordite hung in the room.

"Could you shoot the chaise again," Georgina asked, "but give me a few moments to reach the Smoking Room."

"I'll shout."

"That would be acceptable."

"Door closed again or open?"

"Closed."

Georgina made her way to the Smoking Room. Pippa was asleep on the similarly unconscious Colonel. It was a wonderful sight.

She chose a comfortable chair where she had an excellent view through the glazed top half of the Library door. This had to be the chair that Earnestine had sat in.

Presently, Captain Caruthers called, "Ready?"

She kept quiet but nodded in an exaggerated way.

"After ten."

One... two... she stopped counting. The door closed with a jolly distinctive *clang!*

Bang!

This sound she heard, rather than it pummelling through her chest as a shockwave.

Caruthers appeared. "Did that work?"

Georgina snuck to the Smoking Room door. "Yes... now with the door open."

"Really?"

"Please."

Georgina returned to her seat. She could see the Captain through the open door of the Library take aim. There was a bright flash and then the detonation.

BANG!

Even sitting down, she jumped again.

"What's going on?" the Colonel exclaimed, waking and catching Pippa. "I heard a shot."

"It's all right, Colonel," Georgina explained, rescuing her still sleeping child. "I'm investigating. The Captain is shooting the chaise longue."

"Investigating by shooting furniture?"

"I'm testing a hypothesis."

"Right ho."

Doctor Timon arrived. "I heard a shot."

"It's all right," Colonel Fitzwilliam said. "Young lady getting the Captain to shoot things."

"Shoot things?"

"No need to be alarmed."

The Captain reappeared. "Is that it?"

"Your revolver," Georgina asked, grateful that it was safely stowed in his holster, "is that a high calibre?"

"Point 455, Webley, standard army issue."

"And that's a high calibre?"

"I'd say."

"And Monsieur Jacques's automatic?"

"It's an FN Browning M1900, takes a .32 round."

"Smaller and therefore quieter?"

"A little."

It seemed to Georgina that 'BANG!' and 'bang' were very different noises; one loud, and the other muffled by the closed door. The room had been locked, so the latter must have been the case. So, how then had everyone come running at the sound of the shot, just as the Colonel and Doctor Timon had appeared when Caruthers had fired the third test shot?

Monsieur Jacques automatic would have been even quieter. The 'phut' might have been the lower calibre, or it might simply be because the listener was further away.

Conclusion: the door had been open when the murder occurred. In the seconds following, the murderer had simply closed the door and then locked it from the outside.

Or locked it from the inside, but then they'd still have been inside.

It wasn't so much two steps forward, one back; rather, half a step forward, half a step back.

Monsieur Jacques had described hearing a 'phut' or a 'poof'. His explanation had been that his cabin was the furthest from the Library, which was indeed the case, but if a 'bang' sounded like a 'phut' in the Smoking Room through the closed door, then surely, when heard through two doors and the length of the deck, it would sound like nothing at all.

Others had described a definite and loud 'bang'.

And, Georgina noted, Sir Archibald, Pandit Singh Maçon, Monsieur Jacques, Mrs Albright, Earnestine and Charlotte had not appeared now, despite the loud gunshot.

Sir Archibald and Earnestine were on shore, Mrs Albright no doubt had a headache, but Charlotte – jolly strange for her not to be around when there was gunfire.

"You've discovered something?" Caruthers asked.

"Not as such."

Miss Charlotte

Charlotte lay for a long time as still and silent as the grave she was trapped within. She felt sick. The sarcophagus smelt of dust and decay. There had been a body in it for thousands of years!

She panicked again.

Amenemope was still there, feeling and probing her back with his skeletal fingers.

She screamed and then choked.

But her back was against the solid base of the sarcophagus. The corpse had gone. Risen and attacking the living, she feared.

She needed to calm down.

Coughing wracked her lungs, as dust particles penetrated the tightly wrapped bandages covering her face. She was suffocating.

She'd fallen in the coalhole once. What she wouldn't give to see sisters laughing at her now.

Deep breaths.

She could feel the muck filtering into her like smoke from a fire with the flue closed.

Shallow breaths.

Air just in and out.

What if it was airtight?

Rapid breaths.

Calm down – think of something else.

She had to get out – where was the little cord to pull the bell? She'd been to graveyards and seen the little bells that the recently dead used if they woke up inside their own coffins.

Could she not use astral projection and contact Mrs Albright?

Haunt the bounder who had entombed her?

If she could just curse.

Pandit Singh Maçon was behind everything. He'd killed Mister Rake, obviously, and stolen the Captain's papers and now he'd buried Charlotte alive.

Egyptian mummies got a curse, didn't they?

"Pan*thit thing mathhh..., I curth...*"

All she got was a mouthful of bandages.

Wood splitting above.

What was that?

Thank goodness, it was the crate's lid coming off – she was saved.

Except it was followed by a crunching, metal noise and for a moment she thought she was back in the coalhole with tons of anthracite cascading down upon her, crushing her. But nothing struck her, despite a seemingly endless cacophony, deafening and all-encompassing.

273

It softened, came again, and each time the echo was less and less.

Then the nails hammered in again: each bang moving further around in a clockwise direction.

They'd taken the crate's top off again to fill the crate around the sarcophagus with every nut, bolt and nail they could find.

Why?

And then she was moving, floating, bumped and thumped. There were shouts and strange guttural cries that seemed more and more distant.

She crashed to the ground again.

The wood splintered once more.

Shouts in Egyptian and the clatter of metal, noises like cymbals and bells, but dull and muffled.

Suddenly she was hoisted upwards as if she was ascending to heaven, then a hard bump and this time she stayed still.

Charlotte felt her ears pounding, her skull full of pumping blood and she thought she must be tilted, her feet higher than her head.

She heard a voice speak English: "What do we do?"

She tried to shout, tried so hard, but she couldn't make a sound. Pins and needles in her arms gave way to a numb sensation.

A reply came: "Bury it."

CHAPTER XVI

Miss Deering-Dolittle

Earnestine felt she was gaining on Sir Archibald. Even so, the President of the Royal Expeditionary Society reached the Shrine of the Child first.

When Earnestine approached, she saw a small, simple stone building, not much bigger than the outhouses at home in Kensington. Sir Archibald was already examining the find as her horse and Farouk's camel plodded up to the entrance.

It was clearly Egyptian and rather splendid for Earnestine as it was the first, the absolute very first piece of ancient Egyptian history that she'd ever seen in-situ.

So jolly exciting.

"Miss Deering-Dolittle," Sir Archibald said. "And Farouk."

"Sir Archibald."

The archaeologist was standing before the shrine, with the other Arabs and Bedouin staying some distance away on their camels. One of them stared in her direction, his face a leer of scars. Earnestine had seen him somewhere before... Aaron... no, Haroun al Rachid.

"What do you think?" Sir Archibald asked.

Earnestine dismounted, a heroic swing of her leg around, so she could jump down, though its balletic motion foundered when she sank into the sand. She waded over to join Sir Archibald.

"Early, I'd say," she said, "perhaps Old Kingdom or First Intermediate. No, wait, that cartouche is Userkaf, so Old Kingdom, twenty-four or twenty-five hundred before Christ. Fifth Dynasty. The Ra symbolism is noticeable. No columns, just the suggestion in relief. There are jackals or baboons, an ibis, all pertaining to the god Thoth, and... oh my! A map."

"A treasure map, indeed. Would you be so kind?"

Earnestine wondered what he meant, but then she saw the notebook he had thrust towards her.

"Of course."

She took the hardbound book and checked Sir Archibald's progress. It was a simple matter to finish his diagram and add the hieroglyphics associated in her best calligraphy. There was a straight line of Child to Man to Ancient with additions signifying north, stars and the rising of Ra, the god of the sun.

This was truly marvellous. She was engaged to this man – she'd almost forgotten – and now here she was engaged in scholarly research too. It would be dynamite soon, she knew it. She'd be Lady Reevers. Imagine!

The Adventures of Lady Reevers had a certain ring to it, unlike the Deering-Dolittle surname with all its connotations. As if she'd ever had a moment's peace to 'do little'. She'd be free of that wretched Derring-Do Club millstone too.

No! Not Adventures.

The Sanctioned Expeditions of Lady Reevers – much better – and a suitable title for a memoir in three volumes.

She'd be up there with the great explorers: Livingstone, Bates, Everest, Neumann and, of course, her own heroines, Isabella Bird and Mary Kingsley. Think of it, she thought, Bird, Kingsley, Deering-Dolittle... oops, Reevers, obviously, née Deering-Dolittle.

A dot in the eye and a crossed ankh to finish – done!

She strolled after Sir Archibald to circle the building as if the two of them were going once around the deck. Back at the front, she peered inside, but her eyes were accustomed to the dazzling sunlight and so the darkness within appeared absolute.

"My dear?"

"Wonderful, so interesting," Earnestine replied. She leant forward to examine the carving. Despite the centuries in the desert, she could still make out the signs and symbols: bow, run, fly... strange, she thought. It reminded her of something someone said: a straight path from child to adult to wise... and tests. 'Bow' could be 'humble oneself'... or 'duck'? And that could be 'as softly as Sheut'. It vaguely reminded her of something she was supposed to remember.

"You should see Cheops and Karnak. Like this, but ten thousand times more impressive."

Earnestine felt a lump in her throat.

This was her future now. Travelling and discovering, and all officially, so they wouldn't count as adventures.

"This shrine," Sir Archibald said, "is merely passing through history. Its stone will become sand. In a few thousand years, it will be gone. Whereas, I will be immortal and go on and on."

Earnestine was coming to realise that Sir Archibald enjoyed going on and on.

"This is the first point on the route to Thoth's temple," Sir Archibald continued.

"How do you know all this?"

"I've been corresponding with Thoth for eighteen months now."

"I beg your pardon?"

"Oh yes," he said. "Mrs Albright might have carte blanche with séances, secret chiefs and spirit guides, but I've found it much easier to communicate using the postal service."

Earnestine scoffed: "And just for the cost of a penny lilac."

"Exactly, my dear," Sir Archibald said as he recovered the notebook. "May I have the Book of Thoth, too?"

"It should be given to my sister, Mrs Merryweather."

"My dear."

"Oh, very well," Earnestine said, fishing it out of her bag.

"Thank you," Sir Archibald said. "Enjoy the shade, my dear."

"I beg your pardon."

"You can't stay out here. In this heat, you wouldn't last two hours."

"But I'll be on my horse."

"No, no, no, I can't have you following me."

"But... Sir Archibald, I must protest. I should come with you."

"You?" Sir Archibald looked perplexed and shook his head.

"Aren't we engaged?"

"Yes, but this is men's work," he said. "You must count your blessings, my dear. I am doing you a favour. Through me, you will be held in high esteem, even though you will age and wither, whereas I will be immortal."

"Isn't that the point of marriage?" Earnestine asked. "Doing things in concert as we grow old together."

"You're a plucky young lady, I'll admit, but you'll only slow me down," Sir Archibald explained. "This is too important to foul up."

Earnestine's jaw tightened so much she couldn't object.

"Bring her horse and leave the excess equipment," Sir Archibald instructed loudly.

The men dumped a variety of items in a heap outside the shrine: water canteens, boxes of food, archaeology poles, canvas, firewood and a variety of paraphernalia. All the survey equipment joined it; Sir Archibald wasn't going to record the site properly and this incensed Earnestine as much as abandonment.

Sir Archibald shouted, "Farouk, you are with me."

Farouk took his fez off, holding it like a beggar. "Sir, I should protect the young lady."

Sir Archibald laughed, "If you are here, she'll only persuade you to take some awful risk on her account."

Farouk glanced at Earnestine.

She was still grinding her teeth.

The Guide trudged over and clambered aboard his ship-of-the-desert. Earnestine's horse, tied to Farouk's camel, jerked forward and then settled into step with the rest of the caravan.

Earnestine took a bearing – north – and made a note of this on her map. She had her copy of the last page of the Book of Thoth too, for all the good that would do.

Typical of men to leave her behind. So much for Sir Archibald's proposal of an alliance.

The herd of camels and her horse dwindled. They stayed on the same compass heading – still directly north – even when they became a mere shimmer in the distance.

It was hot in the sun.

Earnestine gathered up some water canteens and food before she retreated into the Shrine. The air inside was cold, enjoyably so, and she even shivered.

Outside, it was an oven.

Even with the water, food and her Kendal Mint Cake, she wouldn't last long in that heat.

How long would her supplies last?

Plenty of time, she could be here for days.

But even inside, without water, she would die eventually.

Nonsense.

Sir Archibald would come back for her. They were engaged. Although, that was turning out to be less advantageous than she'd anticipated.

Mrs Merryweather

Doctor Timon made his apologies.

"I have a task to complete," he said, bowing before he turned to the Smoking Room's door.

Unfortunately, Monsieur Jacques chose that moment to arrive and they collided.

A large jar crashed to the floor, spilling its contents across the deck: coins of silver and gold.

"Timon, imbécile– Madame, Colonel... and Captain, I did not see you there," said Monsieur Jacques.

"Rather let the genie out of the bottle, Jacques," Colonel Fitzwilliam said.

"Genie?"

"Geneih... the Egyptian pound, it's... it was a joke."

"Oh," said Monsieur Jacques, bending down to collect the coins. "Was it?"

"Obviously not."

"What are you doing?" Captain Caruthers asked.

"Mon Dieu, what does it look like?"

"It looks like you are scrambling around for money."

"I need... I have business ashore."

"With money in a jar?"

"It's the only thing I could find to carry it all."

"I see. Carry on."

Georgina left them to it and took the opportunity to take Pippa to their room. As she went, she wondered what Monsieur Jacques was up to. Everyone needed coins, bits of brass and tin for the inevitable beggars, but in the Frenchman's jar, there had been flashes of silver and gold. There were many items to be bought cheaply here and sold at home for a handsome sum. Foreign parts, she understood, exchanged their trinkets for other trinkets. Business indeed.

With Pippa settled in her cot, Georgina made her way to the Cold Room.

As she went by the cabins, she saw Monsieur Jacques leaving the boat, his jar now hidden in a bag.

The murderer had removed the bullet to hide the calibre of the firearm. That much was obvious. Knowing the gun might identify the culprit: .455 would be the Captain or somebody else with a similar gun; .32 would be Monsieur Jacques or somebody else with similar; and finally, any other size would be somebody else. Or possibly the Captain or Monsieur with a different gun.

She didn't seem to be eliminating anything, let alone narrowing in on the implausible.

The sight that greeted her in the Cold Room was depressing and chilled the bones. The three bodies lay next to each other with sheets pulled over them. Sad to see such life, Mister Rake and even the man who was not Thoth, cut down in their prime. Poor Mister Rake, poor whoever, poor... *three bodies!*

Three?

Someone else was dead.

A chill settled upon her that had nothing to do with the stacked blocks of ice. She looked away and saw only a brace of bloodless chickens.

With effort, she forced her feet to step closer, reach out with trembling fingers and finally pull back the first sheet: Mister Rake.

The second sheet was the bald Egyptian, or Arab, still in his fake mummy wrappings.

Finally, under the third sheet... she hesitated. Did she want to look?

Charlotte... oh no, where was she?

Mrs Albright had had one of her heads for an age; had anyone checked on her?

Perhaps Sir Archibald hadn't gone on an expedition.

Maybe Earnestine hadn't followed.

Where was the Pandit?

Her hand shook as she tugged at the sheet.

The corpse was... she gagged, snatched her hand back and reeled in shock.

Miss Charlotte

Dazzling light.

Charlotte winced, tried to turn away, but the brightness was such that she could see orange through her closed eyes.

"There's only a mummy."

"Nothing else?"

"No."

"Then only the crate had parts."

Charlotte turned to see who they were, forcing her eyes open.

Desperate shrieks – "It's alive! *It's alive!*"

Charlotte convulsed, trying to kick her bound legs such that she could sit up and see over the edge. Blinking, she caught sight of Egyptians on their knees, praying, bowing, prostrating themselves.

"Amenemope is alive!"

"Allah protect us."

"Save us."

The view was sand everywhere and then Charlotte toppled backwards again into the open coffin.

"Non, it is not the High Priest back from the dead," said a familiar, accented voice. "It is the Deering-Dolittle girl. Azim! Ce n'est qu'une jeune fille."

An Egyptian face filled the sky as it peered down at Charlotte, fearful and then delighted.

"Une fille, une fille... you stupid fools, it's only a girl."

The other men got up from their knees.

"Ma chérie," Monsieur Jacques said to her, "you have been inquisitive."

Charlotte spat and tried to shout.

"Why is she there?" Azim asked.

"The Pandit said she poked her nose in when the crate was being loaded," Jacques explained.

"We have to shoot her. What is your expression, put her out of her misery?"

Charlotte tried yelling.

"Mais non," Monsieur Jacques said. "I may be – how you say – a cad, but I am no bounder."

"Then what? She knows too much."

"She knows nothing."

"We'll sell her to the Arabs."

"Mon dieu."

"Or shoot her then, your choice."

"P'ah." Jacques made an offhand shrug.

"Mon... sieur," Charlotte mumbled, plaintively, trying to get the bandage away from her mouth.

Jacques paused a moment and then shook his head slightly.

The man Azim came closer.

Charlotte tried to pull away, but she was trapped inside the sarcophagus. He tugged at her bindings, pulled them away and they loosened. Blood pumped into her arms and legs threatening pins and needles. Finally, she could breathe properly, and she simply delighted in her coughing and retching.

Azim leered down at her, his mouth open to show his crooked teeth, "You are a pretty beauty, such a fruit to be plucked and–"

But Azim had stepped within range.

Charlotte kicked him between his legs with both feet still bandaged together. She got an elbow free, pushed herself up and shouldered him to one side. She fell face first into the sand.

Men screamed, still believing that she was a mummy come back to life.

This gave her a few moments to wrench her arm free and yank at the bindings around her ankles.

Azim was up on his knees, blinking precious water away from his eyes.

Charlotte kicked him again and fell over, the loose wrapping still around her thighs, then she fled, used to running with encumbered outfits; but she stumbled, her legs leaden.

"After her!" Azim screamed.

The other Egyptians replied, then he screamed even louder in their language.

Charlotte scarpered, wrenching off more bandage and nearly tripping as she did so, going sideways along a ridge, planning to cross further along.

Except there were figures dressed in black approaching, the material of their cloaks flapping in the breeze. They herded her back and then, when she froze, seeing the men approaching, they fell upon her like vultures descending upon their prey. They were women, and tricks like kicking where it hurt a cadet, did not work.

Monsieur Jacques had watched everything, amused.

"Take my property to the tent," Azim ordered. "Prepare her. Change her into something more appealing."

Jacques shrugged.

Azim yelled again in Egyptian.

Charlotte struggled, but the women carried her like a roll of carpet.

Until they dropped her on a rug inside a tent.

By this time, Charlotte was furious.

It was bad enough being bullied by her own sisters.

A cackling voice issued a stream of commands, sharp and distinct from behind a cloth mask.

"One's most awfully sorry," Charlotte said in her best Earnestine voice, "but one's got absolutely no idea what you are talking about."

That put them in their place, because–

"Owww!"

The woman had slapped her across the face.

Something foreign, the harridan insisted, waggling a warning finger.

"One..." Charlotte started again, but then the hand came up and Charlotte changed tack: "Very well... er... I still don't know what you want."

The woman hit her again.

Another of the women stepped toward, came over with gentle hands in front of her and began tugging off the last bandages and then Charlotte's clothing.

"What... oh, you want me to change."

Charlotte undressed, divesting herself of her dress, skirts, her corset (no loss there) after her gestures finally explained how to undo it, her petticoats, and they even wanted her unmentionables. She had to dress again in a set of light and comfortable undergarments, although the bloomers were tight drawers with leggings made of a silky, transparent material, and the vest didn't come down very far.

She put out her hand for the next layer.

The kind woman simply nodded.

"Yes, lovely, er... but where are the other clothes? Underskirts? Dress? Blouse? Jacket?"

The face-covering hid the woman's expression as she clapped her hands.

Another woman came forward with jewellery: bracelets for her wrists, bracelets for her legs, armbands, chains that dangled coins around her forehead, and earrings that they discovered she couldn't wear as her ears weren't pierced.

Charlotte felt like a jewellery stand.

She clattered when she moved to slip her feet into the tiniest of slippers.

Then they bustled her out of the tent and presented her to Azim and Jacques.

"Magnifique," said Jacques. "Bravo."

Azim licked his lips, clapped his hands and shouted.

The women pulled her away, increasing their pace, and Charlotte felt the tiny slippers start to slip and take on sand.

They all went over a dune.

Below, spread out like a picnic, was a Bedouin sitting upon a carpet. He reminded Charlotte of the caterpillar from *Alice in Wonderland*, so strange was the appearance.

Someone jabbed, shoving at her exposed shoulder blade to push her onwards.

The Arab sat in opulence upon his fine carpet, sadly rucked all around the edge; red with a diamond pattern weaved in gold. The hookah near the edge was of extraordinary proportions, although he puffed on a smaller one in the centre of the carpet. There was also a central table set with a bowl of fruit. He was bald; a standalone canopy protected him from the sun.

Azim walked forward and the two men talked to each other, or rather, at each other. She caught a confusion of French for a moment, something about the 'parlour view' and then, finally, a single word: "English."

"Yes, I know English."

"Ah, then we haggle in English."

"The English do not haggle."

"They are uncivilised."

Azim waved towards the women, an angry gesture of impatience. The women pushed Charlotte forward.

"See, see," said Azim. "Yellow hair. Much sought after. She is worth twelve, her skin is in excellent condition."

"I never look a gift horse in the mouth."

"You are wise, Master Zaid. She is not a horse, but still a fine piece of expensive merchandise. Look at her, look," said Azim. He grabbed Charlotte by her cheeks, like an awful aunt or uncle, and waggled her head about. "See her teeth. Excellent condition. If she were a horse, she'd be worth much gold. See, nice legs, blonde and fair skin, worth much. And..." – he slapped her on her behind – "...good backside."

Such was Charlotte's shock that she completely failed to punch him in the face.

"I don't know," said Master Zaid. "I've got girls."

"Not like this one."

"True, but can she dance?"

"Of course."

"I can't," said Charlotte, truthfully.

"Such modesty, she dances like an angel, danse du ventre and those exotic English waltzes, worth much," said Azim.

"Can she cook?"

"Great English delicacies like the fish and the chips, the spotted dick, the roast beef, all the masalas of the Raj, the pudding of Yorkshire."

"I'm not keen on foreign food."

"She could learn to cook kofta, mahshi, sheep's eyes and make a shawerma."

"I can make a sandwich," Charlotte admitted, "but that's it. Not that other weird stuff."

"Ha, ha, such spirit, worth much. Also, English girls know how to make tea. They know their duty."

"Can she write?"

"Read, write, recite – the three 'R's.'"

"In French?"

Oh lummy, Charlotte thought, she was never going to escape French homework.

"Of course, oui, oui, vaut beaucoup."

Jacques snorted to himself, but said nothing.

"She's very skinny," the Arab said. "Can you fatten her up?"

"She's on a diet of cake already. She'll balloon like a beautiful hippo. Worth much."

The other man grimaced doubtfully. He didn't seem to want to buy her; Charlotte didn't want to be sold, but even so, she felt put out.

"You buy now, I throw in... rug. Good rug."

"I have a rug," said Zaid, gesturing to his carpet. There was a smaller rug on his carpet almost hiding the central diamond pattern.

"I drop price, eleven genieh."

"I'm not sure."

"It's a good price."

"Five?"

"Master Zaid, at that discount I'd risk being drummed out of the White Slaver's Cartel. Very bad, big risk, but for you, I take that risk. I practically cut off my own arm. My wives, they will be furious. My many mothers-in-law, oh my! I will miss payments to the Thieves' Guild."

"What else can she do?"

"I'll find out," said Azim and he came over to Charlotte. "What can you do?"

"Climb trees."

Azim glanced around the desert: "What else?"

"Oh..." Charlotte kicked him right where it really hurt those cadets.

Azim yelped and keeled over.

As he fell, Charlotte yanked his gun from his belt, cocked the hammer and pointed it back and forth between Azim, Jacques and the buyer, Zaid.

"Azim!" Zaid complained.

Azim groaned.

"Azim, you fool, why didn't you tell me she can handle a gun. That is worth much."

"Oh, do be quiet," Charlotte ordered. "You! How do I get out of here?"

"Six, Azim, I will offer six."

"No, you won't," said Charlotte.

"Nine," Azim managed with a strangled expression.

"Seven," said Zaid, "my final offer."

"I have seven wives to care for," said Azim, getting up to his knees.

"Then you are seven times lucky."

"And seven mothers-in-law, three with their mothers."

"Eight?"

"Done."

The Egyptian spat on his hand and then shook Zaid's hand to seal the deal.

"Aren't you forgetting something," Charlotte said, brandishing the gun.

"There are no bullets in that," Azim said.

"What?"

Charlotte glanced down to check. There were bullets, she could see the lead points in the chambers. Stupid man didn't know his gun was loaded and–

She had a mouthful of sand before she realised and then she was knocked off her feet. Her head rang from the blow.

Azim had the revolver back too. "Behave for your new master."

Charlotte spat the coarse grains from her mouth.

Zaid smiled: "She has spirit, Azim, here is the eight we agreed."

Azim bowed and accepted his handful of coins. "You won't be sorry."

Jacques just stood there.

"How could you?" Charlotte demanded.

"You would not that time, ma chérie."

"What time?"

"In my cabin."

"That was homework, which you didn't do, and you let him sell me for only eight guineas," said Charlotte.

"It's not guineas," said Azim. "It's genieh."

"But that's only a few shillings," Charlotte whined.

"I wouldn't know," Jacques said. "It's half a franc, maybe."

"Welcome, sweet English rose," Zaid exclaimed. "I am Zaid the Eunuch. Care for a smoke?"

"No, I would not," Charlotte said.

Master Zaid shrugged: "Put her on the carpet."

"Excuse me, but–"

Azim grasped her upper arm and dragged her along, much as various teachers had dragged her along school corridors.

"Ah... ah!"

"My Master will be pleased with his prize," Zaid said. "Bring her."

Azim yanked Charlotte again and pushed her onto the carpet. Zaid fiddled with the large hookah and all its pipes, puffing smoke from the apparatus.

The hookah *blooped* and *whooshed*.

"Sit!" Zaid commanded.

"I'd really–"

The eunuch, still standing upon the firm ground, struck her on the back of her knees and she crumpled to land face down on the luxurious pile. He grabbed her hair, yanked it.

"Sit and look pretty," he whispered in her ear.

But Charlotte was not so easily defeated. She wriggled away to escape, until Zaid gave her a sharp slap on her rump.

"*Ow!*"

"Stay still."

"Yes – *ow* – sorry."

"Don't answer back."

"Sorry, I–"

He hit her across the face. It really smarted.

She glared at him.

He grabbed her by her hair and dragged her across to the low table. In trying to keep up, she grazed her shockingly bare-looking knees on the rough carpet. The gauze offered no protection whatsoever.

"There," said the man, "unpleasantness over."

She struggled to sit, leaning on one elbow.

The small table jiggled as if preparing to dance, and the fruit rolled about in the bowl as if the carpet stirred beneath it.

Charlotte ignored this, because nearby was a corked bottle, a bowl of fruit and some cheese. There was also a small, elegant knife with a carved handle and curved blade ready to peel an orange, core an apple or gut the eunuch, stab the smug Arab right in his stomach and twist, to disembowel his entrails all over his precious carpet.

"Don't get any ideas," Zaid said.

Charlotte tore her gaze from the weapon and sat upright properly.

The eunuch laughed: "Arise, carpet!"

With a strange sibilance and billowing, cloud appeared from nowhere. The carpet came alive, it bulged, shifted and rose upwards!

Rose! Up! Actually, off the ground.

Surely not?

Charlotte found herself lying in a divot made by her weight as they hovered inches above the ground. Clouds surged around, spreading outwards to evaporate like an early morning mist in the sunlight, and it was like a boat, but one that floated upon the air.

"Let us away," Zaid commanded as he clapped his hands three times, sat down, cross-legged, and reached for his hookah.

The thing rose higher.

Charlotte was only just beginning to take it in.

A storm of clouds fogged all around them and then they were off – flying!

Charlotte blonde hair streamed behind her and she felt a cool breeze on her face as they picked up speed.

It was fast.

"What do you think of my carpet?" Zaid said, seeing her astonished expression.

"Extraordinary," Charlotte said. It was exhilarating. One in the eye for Georgina's insistence that everything was explainable and scientific – this was real wizardry!

Charlotte rolled onto her side to get a view.

The dunes zipped past at much the same speed as if she were travelling within a train carriage, but the action was not that of an agreeable clackety-clack, side-to-side motion, but more of a rippling flow.

And, she noted, they kept low, clearly to avoid being observed from afar.

Zaid spoke: "Yes, my Rose, we fly through the air."

There was no doubting it – they were flying.

On a carpet.

Magically.

CHAPTER XVII

Miss Deering-Dolittle

Best to keep occupied, Earnestine thought.

Her small kit bag contained a variety of items and she circulated through them to find something like a trowel. She even risked venturing outside, but Sir Archibald hadn't left anything actually useful for archaeology. Her notebook might suffice, she thought, but in the end, she used her hands to push the loose sand away to reveal the far wall. She knew that proper archaeology required a study trowel, a thick and a light brush, and sticks of dynamite but needs must.

The hieroglyphs were just about readable.

She mumbled to herself as she became engrossed in translation: "Shrine of the Child... honour the lives of Thoth... who begat himself... wife Ma'at... become a man... 'become a man'?"

They needed suffrage here.

"...won five days..."

This sent a shiver down her spine. Was it coincidence that they were in the middle of this intercalary week before the first day of the Ancient Egyptian year? The first of the five days had been when they were in Tanis, then Mister Rake had been murdered, so today was the third day – a full moon too. It felt like time was running out.

She brushed away more sand. A portion of the plasterwork disintegrated, so she had to skip that section.

"...the straight way to the Temple of the Ancient."

Given that the Egyptians had lost the meaning of their own ancient language, this would have been a perfect way to keep a secret. If it hadn't been for the Rosetta stone, recovered from the French a hundred years ago, then it would still be an enigma.

"...five tests – or was that puzzles? – for each of the five souls. Ren, Bâ, Ka..."

Those were 'name', 'personality', 'spark', and next to them were 'choose', 'prostrate', 'run', but the sand hid the others. She expected to find Jb and Sheut, the heart and shadow, deeper down, so she dug further into the ground to uncover more and–

Earnestine jerked backwards.

Her mouth opened and closed twice, then: "What!"

Now she felt a chill seeping through her veins.

"What?"

It couldn't be, could it?

"What?"

She dug, on her hands and knees pulling the sand away, digging down into the cold, compacted ground. When she'd revealed enough, she went sideways, desperate to prove that this was only here, only in this one spot, perhaps a repair, perhaps just an aberration, perhaps... something other than the obvious.

But there it was.

Wait! The Romans had built the Parthenon with this. It simply meant that the dating had to be Cleopatra's era rather than the earlier Pharaonic kingdoms.

Except this was Old Kingdom, Fifth Dynasty.

And Roman buildings had burned lime and pozzolana.

She's seen Smeaton's Tower in Plymouth. They'd had a tour of it after that dreadful business with the skybattle. They'd all climbed to the top to look out over the devastation wrought by that adventure. Mister Jackson, the tour guide, had shown her how to differentiate the new with its use of hydraulic lime, from the powdered brick and pebbles variant used by the ancient Romans.

This was not that.

Instead, this was... there was no doubt about it.

The base of this ancient Egyptian shrine was made of good, solid, dependable, modern 19th-century concrete.

The Shrine of the Child was a fake!

Mrs Merryweather

Georgina forced herself to look.

The corpse was desiccated, a wizened old collection of rags and bones. What could have had such an appalling effect? She knew of nothing in Natural History that could possibly reduce a body to such a state, so quickly.

Was she infected?

She checked her hand.

Should she stay away from her child?

It was as if the body had been mummified for thousands of years.

And so, suspicious, Georgina looked again.

The mummy wrappings looked correct if Earnestine's mimed actions, when she pointed out the dead attacker's costume last night, had been right. Georgina had no doubt that Earnestine knew what she was talking about. If this was a real mummy, then, there was one obvious candidate.

She shifted the sheet further down.

High Priest Amenemope had been dead for centuries. His wizened, bandage-wrapped body lay in front of Georgina with a seemingly mocking expression.

Mummification meant that they had removed his brains, via his nose with a special spike, breaking the ethmoid bone and then wiggling the instrument until the brain liquefied. The result was thrown away. Only the lungs, liver, stomach and intestines were saved, stored in Canopic jars, as well as the heart, the organ of thinking, according to the ancient Egyptians, which stayed with the body.

Those would have decayed long ago.

What was Amenemope doing here in the Cold Room?

Had someone killed him again?

She backed away.

He'd come to life, then someone had killed him in the attack and moved the body here with the other poor unfortunates.

And if he came to life once, then he could do again.

She shivered. The cold wasn't helping matters.

The warmth of the passageway didn't help either. A High Priest's curse would follow her until the end of her days no matter where she fled.

And if not a killed re-animated corpse, then what?

With stiff legs, she traipsed back up the stairs to the light and heat.

Mrs Albright was enjoying the shade and the magnificent sunset.

"These people, terrible that they've lost all their history and their connection with the mysticism of their past... what is it?"

Georgina just wobbled her head.

"You look like you've seen a ghost."

That snapped Georgina out of her trance. This spiritualist wanted to see ghosts, foolish woman that she was.

"Amenemope seems to have moved."

"He's come back to life!" Mrs Albright's face flushed with excitement despite the archaeological layers of foundation.

"He's in the Cold Room."

"Is he? I must talk to him, offer sacrifice."

"No, I mean his corpse is in the Cold Room."

"He'd died again... what did you do?"

"Nothing."

"But he came back to us!" Mrs Albright said, her hands aloft in halleluiah.

"He's dead," Georgina insisted.

"But he came back and walked amongst us."

"To the Cold Room?"

"The spirit world is mysterious."

"Not half as much as everything else. Where was he before this?"

"In the hold in his sarcophagus."

"Right."

Mrs Albright was so busy waving her hands that Georgina was at the top of the stairs before the woman started to follow. She caught up, once Georgina had reached the hold.

"Where?" Georgina demanded.

"There!" Mrs Albright said, pointing to a gap at the end. "His sarcophagus has gone to the spirit world too."

I wish you would, Georgina thought. "No, it's been stolen."

"If it's been stolen," Mrs Albright said, "then Amenemope will never rest easy."

Georgina understood why someone would steal a mummy. They were valuable commodities amongst collectors. Any museum worth its salt had to have an Egyptology wing nowadays, complete with genuine Egyptian mummies. So, why leave the mummy and take the crate it came in?

"Fetch Captain Caruthers."

"I will commune."

"Fine, but after you've found Captain Caruthers and sent him here."

Mrs Albright stared at her wide-eyed: "I will."

Once the woman had left, Georgina set about searching the rest of the hold. There were three crates: the infamous 'tank' of Caruthers, Mrs Albright's collection of madness, and Sir Archibald's half-empty collection of expedition equipment.

She looked for clues and found a hammer, a crowbar, an unlit lantern, pieces of straw, lots of straw, and oil and water spilt upon the deck.

A thought struck her, and she took the crowbar to Captain Caruthers' crate. She pushed the wedge end under the lid of his crate. The wood split and the nails squealed in complaint, but it would not shift.

She leant her weight on it and succeeded in bruising her hand.

"What are you doing?"

It was Captain Caruthers, his expression stern, leaning against the door jamb.

"I'm..." – *don't say lost, don't say lost* – "...investigating."

"Likely story."

"Oh, do shut up and open this crate."

"There's nothing to see that will affect your investigation."

"Open the crate," she said, thrusting the crowbar towards him. "That's an order."

Captain Caruthers sighed loudly, took the crowbar, but made no move to open his crate.

"Some crates have been unloaded," Georgina said indicating the gaps in the hold.

"I was watching the unloading the entire time, just to be certain that this remained here," Caruthers said, putting his hand on his own cargo. "Only Pandit Singh's and Sir Archibald's were taken ashore. They're to be taken overland. No-one knows how long we'll be stranded here."

"But one of Sir Archibald's crates was emptied before they unloaded it."

"Nonsense," said Caruthers. "It had High Priest Amenemope in it."

"The one they tried to contact the other night with that unholy ceremony?"

"That's the one."

"A mummy that's just been unloaded and smuggled *into Egypt.*"

"Yes... ah. Yes, I see."

"The same mummy that is currently in the Cold Room lying next to Mister Rake and that dead, fake mummy."

"Are you sure?"

Georgina gave him such a look.

"Of course, you're sure."

"So, Captain, the sarcophagus must have been empty."

"Why would anyone take an empty sarcophagus?"

"Why indeed," Georgina said. "They might steal the mummy. They are jolly valuable to collectors, but the point is that they are worth more in their original packaging."

"Yes."

"But perhaps they didn't steal an empty sarcophagus. Perhaps they took the mummy out to put something else in it."

Captain Caruthers blanched.

"Yes," said Georgina patiently.

Quickly, the Captain turned the crowbar on his crate and wrenched the top off by both yanking nails free and splitting wood. Finally, he plunged a hand inside and felt around in the straw.

"Empty."

"So, it is just a crate."

"There's only straw here."

"Why are you–"

"But there were parts here."

"Parts that would easily fit inside a sarcophagus," Georgina said.

The Captain glanced to where the sarcophagus had been, sizing it up in his mind: "Not completely."

"Then they took some in the sarcophagus and some another way."

"Possibly."

"Captain, someone has stolen your Difference Engine."

"How did you know?" Caruthers demanded.

"I investigated."

"Who?"

"Whoever unloaded the crates."

"Workmen. Egyptians. The Skipper oversaw it. I thought Sir Archibald must have left instructions. They organised camels. He must have been planning this all along and killed Rake to achieve it."

"Why would Sir Archibald kill Mister Rake to steal your crate?"

"I don't know. It makes no sense."

"It makes sense, just not to us."

"Right under my nose," Caruthers said. "I'll have to..."

"Yes. I'd have thought so. As quick as you can."

Captain Caruthers jumped to the door and his rapid strides took him down the corridor.

Georgina wondered about returning the crate to its former state, but that seemed like hard work and risked a hammered thumb. The horse had bolted after all.

She'd have to follow, but first, had she missed something here?

She glanced at the floor and then systematically checked back and forth. Everything was as before, except she saw something against the bulkhead in the corner. She had to kneel down to fish it out of the oily water.

It was a gun.

Perhaps even the murder weapon?

It was one of those revolvers favoured by British officers. Charlotte would know what kind. Where was Charlotte? She was never around when she was needed.

Whoever had killed Mister Rake had hidden it down here where no one would look. Or if they did look, then there was no way to connect it to the murderer. It made sense; hiding it in their cabin risked its discovery and the culprit's unmasking.

She wiped it as best she could with her handkerchief and then threw away the ruined cotton. Just as she was secreting it in her purse, she noticed that there were initials carved upon the handle: 'SR'.

Sebastian Rake.

He must have killed himself.

No, ludicrous.

How could he have brought it down here after he had shot himself and locked himself inside the Library?

She still did not have the answer.

Miss Charlotte

Charlotte had seen flying vehicles before. She'd flown and controlled a Zeppelin, which had been magnificent, and she'd seen Earnestine take off wearing a Haversham Mark III Rocket – oh, she was so jealous of that and, of course, Earnestine had not let Charlotte have a go. Then there had been the Skycraft, great whizzing aerial machines that she'd flown about the skies above Devon.

Those were all great fun.

They had been machines; all gas balloons, metal gantries, controls and engineering. All explicable; hydrogen lighter than air and propellers like a ship, a controlled explosion like a Chinese firework and finally the engineering marvel of the Skycraft with its spinning machinery.

But this was different.

It was a strange, ethereal experience like floating on a cloud, and more akin to magic than mathematics. It just floated without gasbags or motive power, and it moved without propellers.

They sped on.

Lying down – trying to look pretty, but she was bored of that – all Charlotte could see was the sky.

The carpet undulated beneath her as the wind cooled her face and her blonde locks streamed out behind her. Unlike the Zeppelin and Skycraft, this was open to the elements. She'd stuck her head out of a steam train's carriage window once as it sped through the English countryside – this was as fast.

Now she had a chance to view the carpet and better understand it in operation, she realised that the pipework was not a hookah. It was an elongated set of tubes, jars, gubbins and wotnot. They'd obviously caught a genie and trapped him inside a lamp with tubes and pipes to give him extra room. The genie must conjure clouds for the carpet to ride upon.

It was cold too. A frost dusted the apparatus as if a pinch of fairy dust had been cast upon it.

"It will replace the camel," said Zaid.

"That's no bad thing," Charlotte replied.

"It can go anywhere."

"Can it take me home, please?"

Zaid laughed: "Such spirit. We make the mistake of bringing up our daughters in protective boxes. It brings men such pleasure to break in a wild horse."

"Lovely, I'm sure."

Her sister, Earnestine, had always warned her about this sort of thing. Warned and warned – *yawn, yawn* – but it wasn't her fault that when she was alone with men, they went mad. Always going on about getting her into bed, when it was they who should be locked in bedlam.

She smiled to herself – that was clever.

"You enjoy it," said Zaid. "We ride on a pillow of clouds. We can cross the desert or traverse the waters, faster than a horse."

The sun was setting; the stars appeared as bright pinpricks and the river of the Milky Way shone in a magnificent arc above them.

"I'm a little cold, actually."

He looked at her. It was indeed a strange thing for her to have said, this being the desert and usually so jolly hot. However, they'd insisted she wear the thin and rather short night attire, sit by a magical icehouse and then whizz along in a biting wind. No wonder she was shivering, and her bare arms were all goose-bumpy.

"Here, have my binnish," he replied. He took off his simple overcoat and gave it to her.

Charlotte wrapped herself in it gratefully.

"Cold in Egypt, eh?" she said, teeth chattering.

"It is hot during the day, but at night, it becomes colder than ice."

"No clouds."

"Yes."

"Except under your magic carpet."

They continued into the night, away from the last glow of the evening, the stars and the full moon lighting their way when they dipped into the shadow of a dune. The night sky was much brighter without the competition of gas street lighting. The horizon was blade-sharp, dark, with the occasional shape, a camel or a solitary palm tree silhouetted against the orange fire of the rippling sun.

They wafted down a slope and turned to follow the course of an ancient wadi. As they did so, the wind caught the binnish and made it flap, billow out with air and threaten to lift her off her feet. She fought with it as she would with a sheet on the washing line or a kite in Kensington Park.

And she laughed.

"We will be there in an hour."

"Good."

She struggled to stand.

To one side, there was a small building, a dark shape like silhouette pictures cut from black card, and as they turned, Charlotte moved her binnish to catch the wind again as if it was a mainsail. The force was strong, and she was lightly framed, so it was enough.

She flew from the magic carpet: "Byeee..."

Wow.

Like going down a helter-skelter to bump onto the mat.

The magic carpet circled as she hurried up a dune and then lay flat, the black binnish pulled over her.

The cold was biting, even lying hidden on the warm sand. She had to reach the building and its warmth, but first, she had to avoid recapture by Zaid the Eunuch.

Each time he circled, she waited until the sound dipped before she moved, keeping low, trying to stay in the shadows and not break the horizon with the red tinge of the last glimmer of the sun, while holding the dark binnish between herself and any searching eyes.

Then the noise increased.

She dropped to the sand again; the material over her to hide her bright, white skin. But the magic carpet was upon her. His search had brought him to exactly where she lay. It was too late; the strange vehicle hurtled right over her.

There was a blast of wind like an Arctic northerly that brought snow and ice, and it buffeted her about. She screamed, but the sound was whooshed away by the thick clouds that gathered beneath the flying carpet.

And then it was gone.

The binnish too, wrenched away from her grip by the sorcerous tempest.

There was frost on her eyelashes.

She waited, listening, shivering, but Zaid must have given up. She couldn't understand why he hadn't simply flown upwards and looked down to see her. Perhaps someone bought for only eight genieh was not worth the bother.

She walked towards the distant building, her bare feet sinking in the soft sand, but she forced herself on. She had to get there before the sun truly set completely and everything became pitch black. Perhaps the full moon would light her way. It would be bliss inside, like a warm cup of cocoa on a winter's day, and that thought kept her going.

Finally, she hiked up and went inside.

It was warm and pleasant, dark inside where the final rays of daylight couldn't reach, except... there was a presence. Her skin crawled, and she knew that someone watched her from the shadows.

She tried so jolly hard to keep the tremor from her voice: "Who's there?"

A shadow moved, pulling itself from the gloom.

"I said 'who's there?'"

A gun cocked loudly.

CHAPTER XVIII

Miss Deering-Dolittle

"Charlotte, what are you wearing?"

It was beyond belief.

Earnestine lowered her gun.

Here Earnestine was, wrong-footed by that charlatan, Sir Archibald Reevers, angry with herself for being such an appalling explorer and vexed by it all, when in walked her sister, without so much as a water bottle, pith helmet, fly swatter or parasol on her.

"They're sort of pyjamas... Ness? How? But?"

Charlotte was indeed wearing an outfit that was shameful, even if she had been wearing a dressing gown over it and the bed linen pulled up to her chin, and the whole arrangement covered with an extra blanket. She did not even appear ashamed – she was flaunting.

"Never mind that. Have you anything to change into?"

"No."

"So, you're stuck wearing that?"

"I didn't choose it," Charlotte replied, indignant. "They chose it for me."

"And you agreed?"

"I didn't have any choice."

"You can see your legs and middle and... everything."

"You can't see my ankles."

"A few bangles on your ankles doesn't make up for the lack of the rest of it."

"I didn't want it. It was for the bedroom, they said."

"Then you should have asked for a sensible nightshirt. Anyway, you're not in the bedroom, you're wandering about in the desert in the middle of the night. I can see your tummy and it's quite obvious you're not wearing a corset."

"I don't like corsets."

"They aren't designed to be liked."

Charlotte made a face.

"You'll have to wear something of mine," Earnestine said. She tugged at her own clothing as if trying to select something off a dressmaker's rail.

"I don't want to wear that."

"You're jolly well going to have to... oh!" Earnestine realised there was only her own corset, blouse, skirt, single underskirt, small bustle and no cage crinoline! It had been hot, so she had deliberately underdressed. "If you wear this, then I won't be decent."

Charlotte made a face.

"Where's your sunhat?"

"Where's yours?"

"Pith helmet."

"Is this an adventure?"

"No."

They faced each other as if waiting for the other's biscuit to crumble. Earnestine was not going to be the one that cracked first.

"How did you get here?" Earnestine demanded.

"Magic carpet."

"Lottie," Earnestine warned.

"No, really, a magic carpet. It flew. There are these Bedouins–"

"You've been consorting with men!"

"No, they captured me."

"You let them capture you!"

"I escaped as soon as I could."

"Clearly not soon enough."

"It wasn't my fault."

"It's never your fault, is it, Charlotte?"

"No, it isn't."

There was a truce of sorts in the conversation; the cut and thrust of the telling-off exhausted. Neither was in the mood.

"That gun's still cocked."

"I know."

Earnestine carefully released the hammer and placed it back in her kit bag. She took out a candle, balanced it on a stone and lit it. The light flickered before casting its weak light into the room.

"How come you're here?"

Earnestine tightened her jaw and handed over the map.

Her sister held it up and moved into light. "Oh, you didn't."

"I may have done."

"Honestly, you? Ness, you of all people, believing in a treasure map."

"Please. Don't. One's embarrassed enough."

"You're always saying they aren't true."

"Yes," she hissed. "One's jolly well aware."

Earnestine lips narrowed further.

"What is this place?" Charlotte asked.

"This is 'le sanctuaire de l'enfant'."

"Oh, this is French homework again."

"The Shrine of the Child," Earnestine continued. "And over there somewhere is the Statue of the Man. It's the Riddle of the Sphinx."

"The baby, man and old man thing?"

"Yes, this is the baby, then the man and finally, the old man further away in the middle of the desert. They line up, but it's all fake."

"Fake?"

"This shrine was constructed less than twenty years ago," Earnestine said and she pointed. "That's modern concrete. Who would build a fake temple?"

"Loads of people," Charlotte replied. "Everyone's building a folly on their land."

"It also means that Sir Archibald *is going the wrong way.*"

"Oh," said Charlotte. "But, if this is a new temple, maybe that's what it means – a baby temple."

"But all temples were new when they were built, and these clues were left centuries ago. They are supposed to form a line to the Temple of Thoth–"

"Thoth?"

"The ancient one, apparently he's... can I tell this?"

"Please."

"Where was I?"

"Lost."

Earnestine's jaw tightened. "So is Sir Archibald. This shrine must have been built to queer the pitch."

"So, he'll..."

"He was going to come back for me, although he's taking his time," Earnestine said. "But he's stubborn. He'll travel on and on until his supplies run out."

"So, we're going to die here, aren't we?"

"Yes."

"The cold and then the heat," Charlotte said. "You won't believe how cold it gets here."

"Especially if you're wearing practically nothing."

"Not my fault."

"Whose fault is it?"

"I think he was called Azim."

"Azim! That's a man's name."

"He was a man."

"Charlotte!"

"Monsieur Jacques was with him."

"Then how come you were kidnapped?"

"He just stood by."

"Typical French."

"He has to be the murderer."

"And he's a man, Charlotte."

However, there was no venom in Earnestine's jibe.

For her part, Charlotte ignored her, and Earnestine didn't care. Instead, the youngest sister went over to the candle to look at the map again.

"Is this the wrong shrine then?" Charlotte said.

"Yes."

"It's not like you to go to the wrong one."

"It's the right..." Earnestine sighed. She might as well own up. "The shrine is a marker, start here and head in a straight line between this and the other marker, 'The Man', and it leads straight to the Temple of Thoth, the 'Old Man', and the secret of immortality."

"The secret of immortality?"

"Sir Archibald Reevers believes that the god Thoth is Methuselah and lives forever because he has the Tree of Life... transplanted, probably with an herbaceous border."

"Why?"

"You wouldn't want to live off nothing but apples, particularly if you were immortal. They'd become tedious after a few centuries, I expect."

"They become tedious half-way through the scrumping season," Charlotte said. "Why does Sir Archibald believe this?"

"He's been corresponding with the god Thoth for months, apparently."

Charlotte sat down, and Earnestine followed suit. There was a marked temperature difference between the top of the small room and the lower half. It was cooler on the modern concrete floor. There was heat still, dry and enveloping, but the temperature was turning.

Earnestine tried to collect her thoughts. "Charlotte, do stop jiffling."

"The floor's hard."

"If you were wearing a modicum of skirts."

Surely, someone would come looking for them. Captain Caruthers could be depended upon, but there was the whole of Arabia to search.

"This is concrete," said Charlotte.

"Please, Charlotte, one's trying to think."

"And this wall and the roof are an ancient building."

"Clearly not," Earnestine explained. "The basic principle of archaeology is that lower levels are older. Newer material lies on top."

"Unless it's been turned upside down."

"Then all the hieroglyphics would be upside down."

"Unless it was moved."

Earnestine opened her mouth but said nothing.

"Like Marble Arch," Charlotte continued. "That was moved from Buckingham Palace at the start of the Queen's reign."

"But why would you move an Egyptian shrine?" Earnestine said. "There are theories that they are placed to emulate the stars in the heavens. The Great Pyramids are the Belt of Orion. Father thought–"

But Charlotte prattled on: "If you did move it, then you'd want a firm foundation."

"Lottie, honestly, think. Why would you move it?"

"You might if it was in the way of building a canal."

"What canal... oh my," Earnestine said. She stood up. "This has been moved."

"Told you."

Earnestine quickly flattened out her map.

"But from where?"

"How far to the canal?"

"About six and a fifth miles."

"What's that in kilometres?"

"Not sure," Earnestine replied. "About... *exactly* ten kilometres."

"It was built by the French, so perhaps the Monsieur in charge simply told some workers to move it ten kilometres, and they did exactly that."

"And they'd have done it in a straight line."

If the shrine was put back in the middle of the water, then the line from the Shrine to the Statue would go northeast, not due north. Earnestine checked her copy of the last page of the Book of Thoth: yes, a straight line, if that squiggled snake, that squinted eye and that leaning tower meant what she thought. Her name was there: *Earnestine* – keep on the straight and narrow. Sir Archibald could have as much head start as he wanted:

he'd go to the Man and then carry on in a straight line – the wrong straight line.

Earnestine, however, now knew the correct bearing.

Except knowing didn't help them; they didn't have any horses, so they were still trapped.

"All right, we're here," said Earnestine.

"That's true. That's always true."

"And we need to be…" – Earnestine turned in the small shrine getting her bearings – "…there."

Charlotte looked at the wall her sister pointed towards.

"But it's night," Earnestine concluded.

"Indubitably."

"Lottie."

The distance to the canal and the distance to the next shrine were both too far. In this cold, they'd freeze, but if they waited for daytime, they'd shrivel up and die. Heat exhaustion, dehydration and madness were all they could look forward to if they ventured forth during the day.

The shrine was cool during the day, the bedrock seeing to that, and during the night, with the sky devoid of any clouds, it would keep its heat.

Earnestine knew that she might make some progress at night, but Charlotte would freeze in that ridiculous, pantomime outfit; whereas, she would have problems during the day in her sensible corset and Charlotte would burn in the unrelenting sunshine.

They were trapped.

They could survive huddled together for warmth perhaps, but in three days' time, the thirst would kill them.

Earnestine took a deep breath. "This is going to involve a lot of construction."

"You mean we're going to have to engineer the Mrs Jones out of this."

"Charlotte, language please."

Mrs Merryweather

Like a man possessed, Caruthers went straight to Sir Archibald's cabin, broke the door and started searching the writing desk. He'd done a lot of damage in the five minutes Georgina had delayed.

"There must be a clue," he said.

"Stop."

"Here somewhere."

"Captain, stop now and think."

"Think?"

"Did he kill Mister Rake in order to steal your engine parts?"

Caruthers stopped. "Rake. It'll be in his cabin."

The Captain went outside and along the deck and Georgina soon heard the crash as he put his shoulder to the door.

She went through the unlocked connecting door to confront the Captain.

"I've searched here," Georgina said. She put her purse down and it landed with a heavy clump.

"Yes, so did I."

"What did you find?"

"Nothing to tell me what he was up to."

The Captain searched Mister Rake's writing desk, flicking through the papers, but barely skim reading them. Clearly, he didn't know what he was looking for.

Georgina could hear Pippa's distant wail through the walls accompanying the crash and clatter of searching.

"Stop! I order you."

"Order me?"

"Yes, Captain, as the Investigating Officer."

Caruthers stopped and seemed to realise what he was doing. He looked delightfully sheepish.

"Yes, Ma'am," he said.

"Good."

He put the papers down.

"When was the cargo unloaded?"

"This morning."

"A good twelve hours or more ago."

He nodded.

"Sir Archibald took equipment from one crate to go and search the Garden of Eden."

Caruthers snorted derisively: "Garden of Eden."

"Ness thought it mad too, but he's looking for something. Ness followed him. Without a proper chaperone."

"She seems to have lost her mind. Engaged to Sir Archibald – madness."

"That may be... and Charlotte's bound to have tagged along, but the point is that Sir Archibald didn't unload his other crate."

"No."

"So, someone else did."

"It was a suitable container."

"If I hadn't found the mummy, we still wouldn't have known."

"I have to get it back."

"I'll see to a babysitter."

"You can't come."

"I'm the Investigating Officer, so I don't think you can tell me whether I can or can't."

"Look, a joke's a joke," Caruthers said. "It might be dangerous."

"Then you'd better make sure you protect me."

So, Caruthers went to find Farouk, only to discover that he'd gone with Earnestine.

"I'll get Jacques."

"We can't go now," Georgina said. "It's night."

Caruthers stared over the railing. Above them, everywhere, the heavens were a tremendous swirl of wondrous constellations. Beyond the fires of the camps on the shore, the world was a black void.

Georgina knew common sense: "We'll go in the morning."

Miss Charlotte

Charlotte was unimpressed by Earnestine's first step in the survival plan; they dug a hole outside. The moon was full, so they could see what they were doing.

"Hard work..." she gasped.

"Never hurt anyone."

"Can't we just wait for rescue?"

"From Sir Archibald. Never! He left me here."

"Why did you agree to marry him in the first place?"

"It just happened. I thought he was talking about something else and then, before I could put him right on the matter, he announced it."

"You didn't say he'd made a mistake."

"I didn't want to make a scene," Earnestine said. "And despite my great restraint in that regard, he left me here."

"But he is coming back, isn't he?"

"Left me – *me!* – when he went on an adventure... expedition, I mean. We have to get the Book of Thoth back."

"Book of–"

"Yes, it holds the key," Earnestine insisted. "Get it back at all costs, Charlotte."

"I hear you."

"Do you?"

"Yes, get the book back at all costs," Charlotte agreed. "I understand."

"Sir Archibald has it."

"I'll get it."

An angry Earnestine dug faster, Charlotte realised, so all she had to do was push some sand to one side to prevent it from falling back into the small pit.

"And help me!"

"Yes, yes, I am, I am, but, this digging uses water."

"Nonsense."

"We're sweating."

"We are not. Young ladies do... not... even perspire."

"I am..."

"Then concentrate on your decorum."

The sand cascaded back into the hole, so Earnestine collected fallen masonry to create a partial wall. Finally, they finished: two feet deep and two feet in diameter.

"Why are we doing this?"

"This sand is hot, but it's cooler underneath."

Charlotte shivered. "But we need heat."

The sand had been soft, and, unlike the beach, lacked any water to make it hard; even so, Charlotte's hands hurt.

"Now what?"

"We put the water in the bucket in the hole."

They did so, ferreting through the supplies to the occasional blink of Earnestine's precious Misell Electric Flashlight.

"I can't see."

"I don't want to waste the batteries."

It was done, so they stood back to admire their handiwork.

"What was the point of that?" Charlotte asked.

"Usually you have a metal lid that goes over it during the day."

"You've not answered my question."

They made a fire inside using packing paper, broken up crates and archaeology poles – "Don't be so profligate with the matches, Charlotte" – and thank goodness, because the night had turned truly icy as if they had been transported from the sun-baked desert to a dark cave in Norway. The smoke made them cough, as there was no proper chimney, but it did warm the shrine.

It was dark outside, except for the glorious display of stars she could just see through the open doorway. The celestial sphere turned slowly, the stars rising from the floor and setting behind the lintel. For a while, the full moon shone an eerie glow through the doorway, a band of silvery light that gave no warmth. Once, a shooting star flashed past, a moment of wonder, but mostly Charlotte just shivered.

Earnestine held on to her.

She held on to Earnestine.

In the morning, the light was dazzling.

"Come on," Earnestine said to a groggy Charlotte.

"What?"

Charlotte stumbled after her sister, outside where it was still chill, to the hole they'd dug.

The water was frozen.

Frozen!

"Old Roman trick," Earnestine explained. "They used to make ice cream in Africa. I read it in... doesn't matter, come on."

They went back inside the shrine.

"We have to get moving," Earnestine insisted.

"Can't we wait until it warms up a bit?"

Earnestine consulted her fob watch: "No, it's already six fifteen... on the fourth day of the intercalary week."

"The what?"

"Never mind, let's get on," Earnestine said, sorting through her kit bag, taking things out, putting them back in. She hesitated when she came to the heavy revolver. "We have to travel light,"

"We take the gun," Charlotte said.

"Yes, and my opera glasses and... oh, everything."

Charlotte tried to help, but her limbs didn't work properly: she was so cold.

"Drink," Earnestine ordered. She did first, using the only container left that wasn't full of ice in the well. Charlotte followed suit and Earnestine splashed water over herself, dampening her dress and even her blouse.

"Do the same," Earnestine said, taking the container back and drinking more herself.

Charlotte stepped forward and Earnestine poured water over her.

"Arrrggh..."

It was like the cold shower at the Eden College for Young Ladies – brutal and cruel.

"Freezing," Charlotte managed. Her teeth chattered, her arms were goose-bumped.

Earnestine soaked all their clothes: the sun hats, her pith helmet, and even the scarves. They were like two drowned rats when they finally emerged.

Earnestine pulled the ice bucket from the well, the canteens and the sheets too. She attached the mess to two of the archaeology poles to create a wooden contraption that suddenly made sense. It was a stretcher.

Charlotte took one end.

"No, no," Earnestine said. "We drag it."

They both took a pole each and Earnestine pushed her umbrella up to create a canopy with the sheets to cover them. It was like standing in a tent that they could drag along.

Earnestine checked the horizon: "This way."

Earnestine had only one pair of goggles, which she wore to protect her eyes from the blowing sand. They set off, trudging away, and, because they were surrounded by canvas, all Charlotte could really see was the sand beneath her bare feet. There were tracks.

"Isn't this the way you said Sir Archibald went?" Charlotte said. "And you said he was going the wrong way."

"He was going from here to the Statue of the Man and then straight on. To find the right direction, we have to find the Statue and extrapolate from where we think the Shrine of the Child used to be."

"Oh."

Charlotte pulled, glad of some exercise in the icehouse they'd made. Her breath condensed in front of her like a cloud.

As she walked, her bare feet sliding about in the shifting sand were so cold they were numb, and she felt a chill upon her neck, the hairs standing on end despite the cold water dripping down.

Beside her, Earnestine counted their steps, chanting numbers like a marching song, and on 500, she'd take out her fob watch, check her lucky charm compass and shift their direction by a degree or more.

On the quarter hour, they drank water. The ice was melting, and they were spilling the precious liquid onto the thirsty sand.

"We're too slow," Earnestine announced.

"We're walking on sand."

"Hmmm."

Charlotte's feet were first to heat up. With each stride, she sank a little into the soft sand, now warmed by the rising sun. It was strange to be warm afoot and chilled to the very insides of her skull.

"Cold," she said.

"Walk faster."

They picked up the pace, tramping along, turning to take the ridge of a dune, rather than have to go down and then up again. Charlotte doubted they could move the sled up too great a slope with the sand avalanching downwards.

By the proper time for breakfast, an uncountable number of water stops–

"Twenty-five," said Earnestine.

–they ate the last of the food. Even the 'only for real emergencies' Kendal Mint Cake.

"Can we just stop to enjoy this?" Charlotte said of the delicious, sugary confection.

"No."

"Please."

"If we stop, we die."

Well, Earnestine was just a spoilsport. They trudged on, eating as they went.

It seemed absurd: they were hot and cold, such that Charlotte's body didn't know whether to shiver or glow in a ladylike fashion.

Two or three, or twenty, drink stops later, the ice had melted and the last of the water dripped past their throats, so they abandoned the sled, keeping only the protective canopy.

It was jolly hot now, approaching the hottest part of the day. Charlotte sweltered beneath the covering that flapped in the dry heat as if the oven door had just been opened. There was no cake to eat, just the grit blown into her mouth and eyes.

"We should have stayed in the shrine," Charlotte said. "Someone would have found us."

"Not fast enough. Reevers will beat us to the prize."

"Prize?"

"Discovery."

"But what is it?"

"Only one way to find out."

They struggled on, the sun now so bright that the sand looked white, as white as snow, except that it burnt Charlotte's feet.

This was mad.

So hot.

Charlotte giggled.

"Lottie?"

"It's just... mad English... out in the... sun."

Earnestine chortled too.

Presently, Earnestine seemed to be ahead. This was fine, Charlotte wanted to rest, her feet following a more zig-zagged route than her bossy sister's compass direction.

"Charlotte! Charlotte!"

She tried to answer but her throat was dry.

"Come on, if you fall behind, you'll die."

Charlotte tried to wet her lips, and then water trickled in from a canteen. Earnestine had been hoarding, wicked girl, nasty, horrible, bossy and other words that came to Charlotte, far easier than 'left', 'right', 'left', 'right'.

"I can catch up," said Charlotte.

"No, if you fall back, then I'll be resting while you catch up and you'll never catch up."

"That makes no sense."

"Come on, we can do this," Earnestine said. "Baroness Wentworth, Anne Blunt, crossed the Arabian desert in 1879."

"Anne Blunt… isn't she Lady Lovelace's daughter?"

"Yes, that's her."

"Wasn't Lady Lovelace something to do with Charles Babbage?"

"So?"

"Captain Caruthers has a Difference Engine," Charlotte said. "Is that something to do with Charles Babbage?"

"Her daughter's explorations are far more important than machines. She was the first woman to cross the Arabian Desert."

"Didn't she have lots of bearers though?"

"A minor consideration. Come on."

Earnestine dragged her, pinching her arm as they went. Charlotte struggled, pulling away.

"Are you angry with me?" Earnestine asked.

"Yes."

"Then use that to keep going."

Charlotte did. She'd show Earnestine, the always sensible, always in charge, always… never considering Charlotte ever – the horrid Earnestine.

Vultures!

They circled above as if they knew by some mysterious power that the two sisters were going to die.

And flies.

Charlotte swatted at them, but they were giant, great winged birds, made of flapping material, that were so large that they blocked out the sun.

Ra!

The sun.

The ancient Egyptian god of the underworld.

They'd stopped walking.

Charlotte found this fact incredible. Surely, it was impossible. They had been destined to walk for all eternity.

"Lottie, Lottie." Earnestine shook her.

"*Ow!*"

"Lottie."

"What?"

She heard a sound like a radiator complaining about air trapped, or a new-fangled automobile engine cranked and misfiring, or an old colonel snoring in his favourite chair.

"Camels," Earnestine explained.

They raised the material and stared.

Earnestine's navigation had brought them to a spot perhaps 500 yards to the east of the Statue of the Man. Camels sat in the shade of a palm tree and a gigantic sculpture.

It looked unreal.

A mirage?

Charlotte simply couldn't believe it.

CHAPTER XIX

Miss Deering-Dolittle

The Man lay in the sand, much like the statue of Ozymandias. It was huge, now lying on one side, the head cracked, and a piece fallen to the sand. It was hollow inside. It may have once stared across an empire or guarded this secret road through the desert, but here it was serving only as a windbreak for a small gathering of Bedouin.

"Look on my works, ye Mighty, and despair!" Earnestine said to herself as she pulled off her goggles and pushed them up around her pith helmet.

There was no-one on guard or even looking in their direction, for it was impossible to simply stroll across the desert.

"The Man," said Charlotte.

"We're on the right track."

"On the right track on a *treasure map.*"

"Yes, but think of it. An actual map showing the lost statue of whoever, leading us to the secret Temple of Thoth."

"But you said... you always said, treasure maps are–"

"Yes, yes, there's no need to crow," Earnestine said. "We'll go and demand horses."

"They only have camels."

"Camels then. If we must. And we'll get some clothes for you."

Earnestine raised her finger to attract attention.

"Ness," Charlotte hissed. "No."

"We need their help," Earnestine explained. "These are the men from Sir Archibald's expedition."

"They are also the men who bought and sold me."

"Are you sure?"

Charlotte made a face.

"Oh," Earnestine whispered.

They both ducked down, hiding beneath the material they'd brought to protect them from the sun.

"Gun," said Charlotte.

Earnestine handed it to her.

"Spare ammunition."

"I don't have any," Earnestine admitted.

"But there's far more than six of them!"

Earnestine slipped her kit bag off her shoulder and left it with her umbrella. They shimmied along to look over the crest of a dune. "Why are they here? Sir Archibald is going on from the Statue to the Temple."

"Maybe he doesn't trust them."

Earnestine nodded, understanding this. She couldn't get her head to work properly. After walking for so long, it seemed utterly bizarre to be still.

"I can move around and outflank them."

"No, you can't. You're not dressed."

"I've got trousers on."

"That material is invisible," Earnestine pointed out. "Only you could fall for rampant bloomerism *and* flaunt your naked legs."

"They only gave it to me because I was a girl."

"And your... *you know*, are displayed by that... top... whatever."

"I didn't want these you knows... they get bigger by the week."

"They do not, you've finished growing."

"But it's not fair," Charlotte wailed.

"Stop moaning."

"I don't want to be a girl. I want to be a boy and join the army and win medals."

"Don't be ridiculous."

Charlotte collapsed into a heap and looked just like a child who had broken her favourite toy.

"Charlotte–"

"I don't want to grow up."

"Lottie," Earnestine said in her best attempt at a reasonable tone. "You're a young lady, whether you like it or not, and so there are certain... standards."

Charlotte made a face.

"I'll let you outflank them."

"You're just saying that to make me feel better."

"Well... yes, that and not wanting to die in the desert."

"All right," Charlotte said, sniffing.

"There."

"Better if I just sneak up," Charlotte said. "They won't be expecting an attack from this direction."

Earnestine nodded: "There are a lot of them."

"Twenty-two, probably more in the tents."

"Do you think?"

"Yes."

Charlotte let go of the material and launched herself forward, stepping from the stifling heat of moveable tent into the furnace of the outside. She had energy now, of course, probably because she was doing something she liked, but even so, she stumbled, her legs unable to sprint as fast as she wanted. So instead, she skulked towards the encampment with the gun held ready.

Earnestine followed, abandoning their survival apparatus, and her heart leapt with joy as she saw where Charlotte was heading.

Several rifles leant against the palm tree, muskets, blunderbusses and a few stolen British rifles, proper Lee Enfield .303s – bliss.

Charlotte snatched one up, checked it expertly, her exhausted fingers knowing where to go, what to do: bullet engaged and rifle cocked before she handed it to Earnestine.

It felt heavy and comforting.

Charlotte took the other, checked that, moving quicker now. However, she hadn't anywhere to tuck the revolver, so she put the rifle around her shoulder by its strap.

"Oi!" Charlotte yelled. "Stand and deliver!"

The Bedouin sitting in the shade startled at these apparitions. They glanced about looking for camels, but saw only Earnestine and Charlotte's approach: two English young ladies out for a stroll in the middle of the desert.

No wonder they gibbered to each other in shock and confusion.

"Will you stop that appalling babbling," Earnestine demanded. "SPEAK ENGLISH."

One of the men stood slowly, nervously, and replied in remarkably good English, proving once again that it was the best language. "Madam, you are... how did you get here?"

"We walked."

"Walked!" He jabbered to the others; they repeated his gibberish phrase back to him with the same tones of incredulity.

"Right, guns down, over there."

One of the men objected to the leader, who replied with his arms wide and–

"In English!" Earnestine demanded.

"How can they be stealing our women," he repeated in English. "They are women."

The other men chattered on, wanting to know what he'd said, like a shouted version of Chinese Whispers.

Charlotte moved sideways, a flanking manoeuvre, the revolver steady, until she stood in the shade.

Earnestine followed.

There were tents beyond the shrine, eyes staring out at them through the canvas and hide flaps, hidden by all-over clothing.

"I am Miss Deering-Dolittle, this is my sister, Miss Charlotte."

The man's gaze was all over Charlotte's scantily clad body. "I am Azim and I know your sister already."

Earnestine glanced briefly at Charlotte. "You do?"

"He... sold me," Charlotte explained.

"Sold you!"

"I got a good price," said Azim.

"Did you haggle?" Earnestine demanded.

"I wasn't buying me," Charlotte complained.

"I'd have got more if I'd known before the sale that she could handle a gun," Azim added.

"She can also play the pianoforte."

"Ness."

"What?"

"I can't really."

"If you practised, Charlotte."

"Aren't we getting off the point?"

"Quite," Earnestine agreed. "You, Azim, we need water and camels."

"That's not my decision."

"Whose is it?"

A man stood, his face divided by a deep scarring pattern. "I am Haroun al Rachid."

Earnestine recognized him from Tanis. He'd been talking to Mister Rake.

"No doubt you want a guide back to your ship," Haroun al Rachid said.

"We know the way," Earnestine replied. "We are Deering-Dolittles–"

"Of the Derring-Do Club," Charlotte said brightly.

"Yes, of... never mind that. So, we don't need a guide."

"And in return for this service?" said Haroun al Rachid.

"You'll be paid."

"Anything I desire?"

"Just money."

"Much money?"

"A quarter of that."

"Half."

"Done."

"In that case, I'll help one of you, but not both."

"I beg your pardon."

"One help for half."

"No, half for both of us."

"Oh look, just..." said Charlotte. She hefted the gun aloft and fired into the air. "Stand and deliver!"

The Bedouins got the message.

"Azim!" Haroun al Rachid shouted. "Fetch water and camels. Enough for two."

A shout: "Miss Deering-Dolittle! Miss Charlotte!"

Earnestine glanced across to see Farouk running towards them. Charlotte's attention immediately snapped back to cover the Arabs.

"Farouk?" Earnestine said.

"Miss Deering-Dolittle... how... I... Miss."

"Farouk, how much of a head start does Sir Archibald have?"

"Miss? Many hours. He set off this morning."

"Water. Transport. Something for Charlotte to wear. And we'll be on our way."

"Back to the boat?" said Farouk.

"Possibly."

"You cannot mean to follow Sir Archibald."

"No, well, he's going the wrong way. But get the camels and supplies ready."

"Yes, Miss."

Farouk hurried after Azim.

Haroun al Rachid stepped forward. "The wrong way?"

Earnestine flinched when he came nearer. The man's aspect was worrisome; the craquelure on his face spoke of violence.

"These scars," he said. "They frighten you?"

"Nonsense."

"I am ugly, no?"

"Well, you hardly appear respectable."

"You would not agree to be my sixth wife?"

"Certainly not... and one's betrothed anyway."

"You have a scar too," he said, pointing.

Earnestine couldn't let go of the rifle to tug her curls over the left side of her own face.

"These scars I received from my father," al Rachid said proudly, "as he was scarred by his father, as our ancestors did back to the time of the Pharaohs. One day, I will take another woman. She will give me a son and I will beat him to make him strong."

"That's cruel."

"It makes us strong."

"You wouldn't last five minutes at the Eden College for Young Ladies," Earnestine said. "Besides, this was from a duel."

Charlotte pipped up: "It was a fair fight... sorry. I said I was sorry."

"Charlotte, watch them."

"Yes, Ness."

"What are you doing out here?" Haroun al Rachid asked.

This was the tricky question, Earnestine knew. "We're British young ladies from the SS *Karnak* and we're trying to prevent antiquities from being stolen."

"Stolen?"

"Yes. By certain... well, it's the French."

"It was Monsieur Jacques and Pandit Singh Maçon who stole me, and he sold me to... someone else," Charlotte added.

"Jacques and Singh Maçon! I dare say he'll ask for his money back," Earnestine said.

"No receipt," al Rachid said.

"You didn't give him a receipt for Charlotte?"

"I can't write."

"Let the buyer beware indeed."

"Monsieur Jacques and Pandit Singh Maçon were stealing something from the ship."

"What was he stealing?"

"I don't know, he stole me first," Charlotte said without looking at Earnestine. "They wrapped me in bandages and–"

"Yes, I'm sure it was awful," said Earnestine. "He must have been stealing that Egyptian mummy Sir Archibald was bringing into Egypt."

"Odd that they're smuggling the wrong way."

Haroun al Rachid grunted, "You British admit that you steal our antiquities?"

"That's quite different," Earnestine insisted.

"Our history is taken from the land of the Pharaohs."

"And kept safely in glass cases in the British Museum. I've seen them. I can attest to the care they receive."

"Like the French."

"Not like the French, at all," Earnestine said. "Look, the French shot the nose off the great Sphinx at Giza. That shows they have an enormous disrespect."

"Just as you threaten to shoot off my nose here."

Earnestine realised she was pointing her rifle at the man, but before she could put him in his place, Farouk reappeared, leading a camel and her horse, each loaded with supplies.

"Those cost much," said al Rachid.

"You stole my sister and profited by that, so we'll call it even."

"She's only a woman. These are camels and a horse!"

"Get the difference off Sir Archibald."

Farouk searched through the bags strapped to the animals and brought out a canteen of water and some clothing.

"No, Farouk, the clothing first."

"But I'm dying of thirst," Charlotte said.

"Then get dressed quickly."

Earnestine covered them with her rifle, while Charlotte took a white shirt and buttoned it up.

"That's a man's shirt," Earnestine said.

"It is one of Sir Archibald's," Farouk replied.

"Could you not get something feminine?"

Farouk glanced towards the tents. "Farouk cannot go into the women's tent."

"Could you not stand outside and ask them to hand out a corset and dress?"

"Farouk cannot."

Earnestine tightened her jaw. "But that's my fiancé's shirt and it barely covers her at all."

"It's big, it comes down my legs."

"Down to the top of your legs cannot be classed as 'down your legs'," Earnestine observed. "Farouk, water now."

Charlotte covered the Bedouin as Farouk handed over a canteen. Earnestine drank, forcing herself to do so slowly and carefully, despite the wonderfully refreshing taste of the tepid water. She handed it back to Farouk, recovered her rifle and then nodded to Farouk. It was Charlotte's turn and she guzzled back the precious liquid.

"Lottie! Not too quickly."

She'd spilt enough down the front of her borrowed shirt for it to become semi-invisible, like her gauze trouser legs, but Earnestine bit back pointing this out.

Charlotte paused, then sipped.

"Farouk, what about you?" Earnestine asked.

"I have had tea."

"Oh, tea," said Earnestine. That would be refreshing.

"And cake?" Charlotte asked.

"Sheep's eyes," Farouk said. "Very tasty."

"Isn't that just to shock Europeans?"

"Still tasty."

"Let's get on," said Earnestine.

"I ride this camel. You have your horse."

"And Charlotte?"

"She rides with me."

"I hardly think so."

"Ness," said Charlotte, "I can't handle a firearm and control a camel."

"Oh..."

There was no other choice; where was a chaperone when you needed one?

Earnestine recovered her kit bag and her umbrella. Other supplies had been added to their rides. Farouk helped Earnestine onto her horse, then brought the huge camel down to its knees. He got aboard and leaned down to pull Charlotte up.

"Ready?" Earnestine asked.

"Yes, Miss."

"Ready, Ness?"

"By the way, Lottie, 'stand and deliver' – really?"

"It was the only thing that came to mind."

"But, honestly, we're not highwaymen."

"I know that," Charlotte said. "There's no highway and we're not men."

"That's not quite what I meant."

The camel rose up, far higher than Earnestine sitting on the horse. They rode away with Farouk guiding them towards the East.

"We go to the canal and follow it to the ship," he yelled. "That way we cannot get lost."

"I'm a Deering-Dolittle," Earnestine said, checking her lucky charm. The needle was adamant about north.

As soon as they were over the first dune, she took another bearing and she steered her horse to one side.

"This way?"

"Miss, we cannot follow Sir Archibald."

Earnestine glanced up from her lucky charm compass. "We're not."

She turned north, her horse leaving hoof prints amongst the line of disturbance left by Sir Archibald and those few he trusted. Three camels by the look of it.

She rode for another thousand yards and then, with a check of her compass and map, she turned them north-east heading into the great empty space.

"Miss Charlotte," Farouk implored.

"She's making sure those Arabs can't follow us."

"I understood that," the Guide said. "I mean, why are we going deeper into the desert?"

"Don't worry," Charlotte shouted. "She knows the way."

It made Earnestine feel so proud.

And then Charlotte ruined it by adding, "It's an adventure."

"No," Earnestine insisted, "it isn't!"

Mrs Merryweather

Georgina and Captain Caruthers, Doctor Timon and Monsieur Jacques reached Sir Archibald's excavation in good time. They'd hired horses. Georgina did not know much about archaeology, but she did know enough to know that this was the right place. Archaeological equipment was strewn all over the place and a hole dug on one side.

The structure itself was a small, unassuming building, more of a shrine than a temple.

"They lit a fire," Caruthers said, coming out of the doorway.

Georgina sat higher in the saddle of her chestnut mare. "There's no-one about now."

"Perhaps they went somewhere else."

Monsieur Jacques had finished a circuit. "Madame, there are tracks leading away."

Doctor Timon helped Georgina down and she went to the excavation. Why had they dug there? She didn't know – perhaps the hieroglyphics had directed them to do so – but the tracks that led away included a pair of sharp lines. It was obvious to everyone that Sir Archibald had dug up some artefact and then dragged it north on a sled.

If he'd found whatever he was looking for, then why had he carried on and not brought it back to the ship?

Should they press on or return to the SS *Karnak* themselves, Georgina wondered? She had enlisted both Colonel Fitzwilliam and Mrs Albright to look after Pippa. The Colonel would no doubt be asleep and Georgina didn't trust Mrs Albright, who was bound to have some strange ideas about bringing up children being both a spiritualist and an American.

One of the guides shouted.

Georgina didn't understand the word, but the pointing was clear. She scanned the horizon, her hand shielding her eyes from the sunlight. In the afternoon heat, the land shimmered, as unreal as mercury spilt from a thermometer.

"There!" Doctor Timon had seen something as he stood upright in the stirrups.

There was a smudge, dark amidst the near white of the sand and sky.

It was mesmerising as it grew in size and stature, split into shimmering shapes and then smeared into one image. The picture started to resolve as daguerreotypes did when subjected to the right chemicals. Slowly, from the quicksilver of mirage, shapes imperceptibly formed.

In the shimmering heat, finally, she saw a hint of colour. It was many shapes and then one as the distortion of rising heat still played tricks on them, but they could see detail materialising.

For a moment, the surface became like water and it appeared like three ships were approaching, tacking back and forth as the light dissolved and shifted.

Then, it changed again, and the wavering vessels became ships of the desert.

Three camels like the wise men approached.

Miss Charlotte

Earnestine glanced at her compass yet again.

Charlotte could see her easily; the extra height of the camel meant she towered above her sister. The camel was in front, its long legs making it the tortoise to the horse's hare.

Charlotte shifted round again – Farouk sitting in front had given up complaining – and scanned the horizon. It was desert as far as she could see. On a ship, there was always that moment when the land could not be seen in any direction and everything was the sea. This was like that, except that the waves were dunes and the white horses were sand whisked into the air by the wind.

She was hot under the shirt, the cuffs folded back three times, but she did know that in this sun she'd burn.

It was worrying.

They'd have to turn back.

They plodded up a large dune, gaining height. At the top, they'd be able to see even further. If there was nothing, then there'd be no choice. Perhaps their estimate of the original position of the Shrine of the Child was wrong, or maybe going around the Statue of the Man to obscure their route had pointed them askew.

Their camel crested the brow and the dunes stretched in both directions like a sculpture of a wave.

"Miss?"

Charlotte jiffled around again. "Farouk?"

"Look."

She craned around the large Egyptian, but all she could see was his grey waistcoat. "You're in the way."

Farouk shifted to one side as far as he dared given the uncomfortable moving seating.

A temple jutted out of the next wave like a sinking ship, almost invisible given that it was half-covered in sand and the stone was the same oppressive ochre as everything else. It was part of the wall of a valley, or gorge, made long ago by a wadi that had not seen water for centuries.

"Ness!"

"Lottie?"

Charlotte pointed, almost pushing Farouk overboard.

Earnestine sighed with relief.

Farouk tugged the reins to make the camel drop to its knees.

Charlotte had not been ready for this – she'd never ridden a camel before – and she toppled off to land in an ungainly heap.

The camel snorted.

Given that she was wearing practically nothing, it was extraordinary how the sand got in everywhere.

Earnestine had dismounted too and led her horse to Farouk, who saw to both animals.

There were two dark openings carved in rock, flanked by statues. The figure to the left was a monkey and the right was guarded by a bird.

"Is this it?" Charlotte asked. "It must be it."

"The Temple of the Ancient," Earnestine replied. "Ibis and Baboon, emblems of the god Thoth."

"So, this is it?"

Earnestine turned, her face catching the sun so that it gleamed. "We're the first to find this temple in thousands of years."

"And there's this Philosopher's Stone, Tree of Life thing."

"Thing?"

Charlotte shrugged.

"But which entrance?" Earnestine mused.

Farouk came up alongside them. "Miss, you cannot be thinking of going inside."

"Why not?"

"It will be dangerous."

"Nonsense."

The two of them moved forward going down into the old wadi, Earnestine eager and Farouk nervous.

Strange, Charlotte thought, that Earnestine didn't see it. She was probably just excited like when there's cake and you couldn't see anything else.

"Ness."

Earnestine paused.

"Ness, if it looks like soup and it tastes like soup..."

"What do you mean?"

"Before it was moved, the shrine, the statue and the temple were in a straight line. They aren't that far apart. We can't be the first. Lots of people want the thing–"

"Thing?"

"Ancient artefact that turns lead into gold and makes you live forever, so... well..."

"Well, what?"

"When you want to ambush an enemy force, you draw them onto what's called a 'killing ground'," Charlotte explained. "This is a trap."

"How can you say it's a trap?"

A guttural bellow: "STAY WHERE YOU ARE!"

"Oh, I see."

Charlotte's Lee Enfield and Earnestine's Webley were still stowed on the camel.

Haroun al Rachid and his Bedouin lined the top of the crest, weapons at the ready, pointing down.

Charlotte, Earnestine and Farouk were stuck in a wadi with no cover or line of retreat.

Earnestine gasped: "How did they find us?"

Haroun al Rachid smiled, his scars shifting as if changing from one complex hieroglyphic to another. He pointed to the sky.

Charlotte shaded her eyes with her hand: tiny black arrowheads circled high overhead.

"Vultures," al Rachid said. "They follow those about to die."

Chapter XX

Miss Deering-Dolittle

Earnestine swallowed awkwardly.

The Bedouin were silhouettes on the crest above them.

Behind her, a low cliff of stone protruded from the sand and cut into it were the two entrances; dark chasms that promised and imperilled.

Maybe they could run for it.

"Lottie, Farouk," she whispered, but it was too late; the shadows marched down towards them.

"You," said al Rachid, "go first into the temple."

"Me?" said Earnestine. Her breathing quickened; all her life she had dreamed of this. To be an explorer, setting foot where no-one had trod for thousands of years, to be the first modern human to set eyes upon what marvels, to be– *ow!*

"Get a move on!"

"One was just preparing oneself."

"You are afraid," Haroun al Rachid sneered.

"Of course not."

"You want to follow your family tradition, Deering-Dolittle. There! Look! Certain death. Go! Explore!"

"My family are explorers, but when they went up the river, it wasn't to their deaths."

The leader laughed at her: "This is the tomb, the great tomb, it is *death!* It is the mother and father of *death!*"

"Well, of course, it is," Earnestine replied. "It's a tomb. All tombs are about death. It's implied in the word 'tomb'."

"But it is *death!*"

"There's no need to be melodramatic about it."

"You will raid the tomb, find the Philosopher's Stone and bring it to me."

Earnestine was shocked: "Raid the tomb?"

"Yes, you will be our tomb–"

"One most certainly will not," Earnestine asserted. "For one thing, – and I know everything there is to know about ancient Egypt, so I say this with authority – this isn't a tomb, it's a temple, clearly from an early dynasty. I'd say the–"

"It is a tomb," Azim said. "The Tomb of Thoth."

"The tomb of someone who lives forever. Really?" Earnestine said. "And for another thing, we're not raiding it, we're exploring."

"Hardly exploring, Miss," Farouk said, trying to calm her down.

"Well, granted, but raiding implies deliberate damage, whereas we're simply sneaking within and taking the valuables. We're more like robbers or burglars."

"I have found it," al Rachid announced.

"I'd like to point out–"

"Please don't," said Farouk. "Miss."

Earnestine was incensed: "But it's a man taking credit for a woman's discovery! Again!"

"I think other men have found this temple."

There were skeletons in the entranceway, men in the rags of Arabic garb and some in the remains of European clothing.

"Yes," Earnestine admitted, "but could they do it in a corset, long skirt and heels?"

"Do you think another man could have found it?" al Rachid said. "No. I, Haroun al Rachid will be the first to win the prize."

"Prize?"

"The Secret of Eternal Life."

"Oh, that."

"Your pompous Archibald, with his superior attitude could not find it. Do you think your father could have got this far?"

"My father?"

"Earnest Deering-Dolittle."

"Oh yes," Earnestine said. "But he'd have organised a proper expedition and entered the temple at the proper time. He'd have had no truck with all this desperate running, jumping and shooting."

"All the proper equipment did not help Archibald. We let him live only because he could read that stupid book."

"Book?"

"The Book of Thoth. In hieroglyphics. But we don't need it anymore. We will have our revenge upon Thoth. The false god lives in there like an evil Djinn hoarding his secrets. We will go in, we will find him, make him tell us, and then kill him and take what is rightfully ours."

"Rightfully yours?"

"By the right of the sword."

"Go on then."

"What is it you English say, 'ladies first'?" al Rachid said.

"I'd rather not."

"When in the British Protectorate, do as our British Protectors do," al Rachid added. "In case."

"In case of what?"

"We sometimes drive goats over the desert to find the sinkholes and the quicksand."

"Ah."

He smiled, his scars accentuating the lopsided grin, and pointed toward the two entrances.

So, there was a choice: left or right, ibis or baboon...

Choice, that rang a bell.

"And if I don't," Earnestine said, "or if I find the secret and keep it for myself?"

"I kill your sister."

His men grabbed Charlotte, yanked her arms back and tied her with rope. The poor girl struggled, she even managed to floor one of these thieves with a jolly accurate kick, but they were too strong. They trussed her up and dumped her in the shade of the camel. The thieves had their rifles, camel and horse, her pack, her umbrella – everything.

"I'll need Farouk."

"Why?"

"One's a young lady out alone in a strange land, so obviously I need a chaperone."

"There is no-one else in the tomb. No-one still alive."

"Then... as a guide."

"Farouk has never been in this tomb before."

"What if I see something of note and want it explained?"

"You said you knew everything about ancient Egypt."

Earnestine tightened her jaw. She was going to have to bluff: "One doesn't know quite everything."

Al Rachid's facial muscles twitched and then relaxed. "Take him, I don't care."

"And my umbrella."

The man's eyes narrowed as he contemplated this request. Farouk had made sense, but this seemed a petition too far.

"Why?" he said.

"It might rain."

Haroun al Rachid looked heavenward at the bright, cloudless sky, and then into the dark interior of the temple.

"Great and honourable al Rachid," Farouk said. "She's British."

Haroun al Rachid tossed the umbrella to Earnestine, who caught it deftly.

"And my pack?" Earnestine said.

Haroun al Rachid had had enough. "No."

"To solve a riddle, one always traditionally has three things. I only have Farouk and my umbrella."

"It might have something in it that you'll find useful."

"That's the idea."

"I meant to escape."

"You don't want me to come out of the temple?" said Earnestine with one of her scathing tones. "If you are worried, check it."

The man nodded and opened her small kit bag: he rummaged, found the revolver straight away and confiscated that before turning to the other items.

"What's this?"

"Mine."

"What is it?"

"A whistle."

"And this?"

"Lockpicks."

"This?"

"A peg."

"What's it for?"

"Hanging up laundry and keeping one's nose pinched in sewers."

"And this Tabasco sauce."

"It's spice in case your foreign food is too bland."

Haroun al Rachid looked at her as if she was mad: *as if she was mad.* How dare he?

Farouk stooped and held his hands out placatingly.

"Take it then," al Rachid said.

Earnestine carefully placed the items back into her kit bag, slipped it over her shoulder and then swung her umbrella like a walking stick.

"Come on, Farouk," Earnestine said as if she was suggesting a brisk walk to Hyde Park.

"Azim!" al Rachid ordered, "take Lisimba, Chumba, Moshe and some of the others, and go with her."

Azim stepped forward, a dark, bearded man leading three reluctant thieves, and he nodded to al Rachid.

"I don't need so many to watch a woman," Azim said.

Except that Earnestine had already departed from the correct course.

"Lottie," she said, going over to her sister, "are you all right?"

Charlotte's face was covered in sand: "I'm fine."

"Excellent, if..."

"First chance."

"Be careful."

"Always."

"Find the Book of Thoth."

"Right ho."

"I'll just..."

Charlotte struggled to sit up and nod back.

Earnestine had to admit things did not look good.

"There will be traps, Azim," al Rachid said. "Let her take the risks."

And they weren't getting any better.

"As you wish, my Master," Azim said. "Come! Come, woman!"

Earnestine smiled bravely down to the tied-up Charlotte. Charlotte grinned back, so Earnestine made her way over to the temple entrance.

Haroun al Rachid clapped his hands. "The rest of you, put up the tents."

Despite the sudden activity behind her, Earnestine concentrated on the two temple entrances.

Left or right, ibis or baboon... women turned right in tombs so that when they emerged to the afterlife, they could stand on the man's left and process out together.

"Miss, what do we do now?" Farouk asked. He stood to her right, keeping his voice low.

"Shout 'Derring-Do Club Forever' and then do something foolish."

"Derring-Do Club forever?" Farouk mumbled.

"That's the spirit."

As they clambered under the entranceway, the figure of the baboon reared overhead as if pouncing down upon them. The four thieves followed like delayed shadows.

Everyone paused in the entrance to light their torches.

Earnestine took her goggles off her pith helmet and put them into her bag. She rooted out a candle and melted the wax to form a blob in the peak of her headgear. She squidged the candle down firmly.

"There."

They stepped inside, forcing their light to push against the darkness. Earnestine held the lantern up to inspect the walls and illuminated a series of pictures.

"You need to decode the secrets of the tomb," Azim ordered, his voice echoing.

Earnestine felt her jaw tighten: "Quite."

Farouk came over to help. "But why did you ask for Farouk, Miss?"

"To save you from the thieves."

"But Miss..."

"You didn't want to stay with the thieves, surely?"

"No, this is true, but the thieves are with us, and I also did not want to go into a tomb that no-one has ever come out of alive."

"Really? But it's exciting. Where's your adventurous spirit?"

"I take your Mother's advice."

"My Mother's advice... oh, yes. No adventures. It's good advice."

"But not advice you heed."

"Well... needs must."

"And why did you ask for the umbrella?"

"It's mine, not theirs. I bought this especially from Edward and Thomas's Fine Tailoring of Raynes Park."

"Is it a trick umbrella with a blade like a sword stick?" Farouk asked in a whisper, glancing back at the entrance and the four silhouettes watching them carefully.

"It most certainly is not," Earnestine replied. "It's a Fox's Paragon – never inside out."

"Farouk does not understand."

"Never inside out... it means that if the wind blows it stays in shape to keep off the rain."

"It does not rain here, we are indoors and there is no wind."

At that moment, the air shifted as if the rock breathed. The cavernous space howled and moaned, echoing, as the draft funnelled sudden wind like a gale playing along the tops of chimney pots in an old house.

"There's a passage somewhere."

"Farouk doesn't like this."

"Well, Earnestine..." She stopped herself. It was bad enough speaking of oneself in the third person, but to do so on first names terms was too much. "Miss Deering-Dolittle doesn't either."

"People have died in here," Farouk said. "There are stories, many stories of men lost."

"Yes."

"We could hide here, pretend," said Farouk. "And then, maybe when they've gone, come out."

"There's nowhere to hide, they're watching us, and they have my sister."

"They'll send her in next."

The wind blustered outside, and a flurry of sand swept into the antechamber. An eerie noise whistled onward, betraying the depths of tunnels beyond like a siren's call. And yet the walls seemed solid.

"Then we better make sure they don't need to," Earnestine's eyes twinkled in the lamplight. "Let's go in."

Mrs Merryweather

"They're here," said Georgina, her sigh of relief far too loud.

And still the expedition was an unfathomable distance away, but finally, after much squinting and staring beneath raised hands, the group arrived.

The native at the front moved to one side and Georgina saw Sir Archibald.

"Good afternoon!" she shouted.

"Madam."

"Thank goodness you are all safe."

"I am safe, thank you."

The camels fanned out as Sir Archibald came to a halt, flicking his reins like an expert.

"Where's Earn– I mean, Miss Deering-Dolittle and Miss Charlotte?"

"I don't know about Miss Charlotte," Sir Archibald said, "but my fiancée is here."

Caruthers harrumphed.

"No, my sister is with you," Georgina said.

"I left Miss Deering-Dolittle here at the Shrine of the Child yesterday."

Georgina turned around and looked at the Egyptian building: a shrine, quite possibly.

"She's not here now."

"Well, dash it, she's probably found her way back to the SS *Karnak*."

"No, we've just come from there."

"She'll have gone to the canal and worked her way along while you crossed the desert more directly," Sir Archibald said.

"I think she would have gone straight across," Georgina replied. "She's quite capable of reading a compass."

"If you say so."

"And Miss Charlotte?"

"I've not seen her."

"What?"

"She's not here, Gina," Captain Caruthers said.

"But Ness was here."

She looked about at the featureless desert all around them. Earnestine could read a compass; so could Georgina, but she doubted she could navigate this void. Only the most foolish would try to go across – the most foolish and, sadly, also the most stubborn and headstrong.

"Could she have followed you?" Georgina asked.

"We saw no-one."

Georgina went into the shrine. Only Doctor Timon followed.

It was dark, particularly so after the brilliance of the desert sun, but Doctor Timon had a lamp ready. There had been a fire here, partially burnt expeditionary material attested to that, and the badly cooked food – Earnestine had certainly spent time here and she'd only light a fire at night.

Sections of the wall had been cleared away, the sand recently piled to one side and the hieroglyphics revealed. This she did not understand.

"Fetch Sir Archibald, please."

Doctor Timon brought Sir Archibald inside.

"Sir Archibald, what does all this mean?"

Sir Archibald harrumphed, but replied nonetheless, "The god Thoth is wonderful, begat himself, gifted humanity writing, etcetera, etcetera – all along here – until he wins five days from the moon and then Thoth and the Goddess Ma'at – in the underworld your deeds are measured against Ma'at's feather – blah-blah... tests for the unwary and the need to choose, prostrate oneself, run and so forth."

"And this, Sir Archibald?"

"This wall talks about the Temple of the Ancient, the Statue of the Man and the Shrine of the Child."

"The Shrine of the Child?"

"This is the Shrine of the Child."

"And the others?"

"We know where the Statue of the Man is," Sir Archibald explained. "It's north, and beyond that, supposedly, is the Temple of the Ancient."

"Which is?" Doctor Timon asked.

"The resting place of the god Thoth."

"And?" Doctor Timon insisted, the light of his lamp flickering in his glasses.

"Supposedly where the Philosopher's Stone is hidden."

"You don't mean the magical alchemical object that turns lead into gold?" said Georgina, not knowing how much to scoff.

"And the secret of immortality," Doctor Timon added.

"They are in a straight line, it says so here. Like the constellations, equal measure, praise to Thoth, etcetera, but I've been north a full day and night, and it's simply not there."

"Perhaps you missed it."

"I am the President of the Royal Expeditionary Society, Doctor. I don't miss anything."

"What's this?" Georgina asked, pointing to where the wall had been uncovered despite a singular lack of inscriptions.

"That?" Sir Archibald said, glancing down. "Foundations. Nothing important."

Outside, back in the blazing heat, Georgina did a circuit of the small, square building. The only noteworthy observations were the tracks leading north and the hole.

"Sir Archibald," Georgina said, "what did you drag on a sled?"

"Sled?"

"Here! See. These parallel lines."

"I have no sled, everything's on the camels."

It had been her sister then, Georgina deduced. Earnestine had dug something up, possibly interpreting all the 'blah-blah' and 'etcetera' that Sir Archibald hadn't bothered to translate properly, and then dragged it north. The wind was obscuring the tracks, certainly, but they were still present, and yesterday they would have been clearer.

So, the only way Sir Archibald could have missed her would have been if Earnestine had veered from the path deliberately.

Georgina said, "Miss Deering-Dolittle dug something out of the ground here."

Sir Archibald barged forward. "She did!"

"Perhaps your route works the other way round and goes from the ancient to the child," Captain Caruthers suggested.

"Nonsense."

"How big is this Philosopher's Stone?" Caruthers asked, miming holding an object in his hands, an object that could easily fit in the hole.

"She has the Stone!"

"And then," Georgina said, "she dragged it north. Why would she do that?"

"The heat must have affected my fiancée's wits," Sir Archibald said.

"Perhaps you shouldn't have abandoned her in the middle of the Arabian desert," Caruthers said.

Sir Archibald objected, "Hardly the middle, we're only half a dozen miles from the canal."

"Perhaps," Georgina mused, "she was taking the Philosopher's Stone to this Temple of the Ancient."

"Why would she do that?" Sir Archibald said. "The whole point is to get the blighter out of Thoth's temple."

Miss Charlotte

"Do you find me attractive?"

Charlotte did not.

The man's face was covered in scars, his teeth were rotten and his breath worse than a night soil man's. He leered, his eyes bulging in his sockets as he gazed at her helpless, trussed-up body.

As much as the ropes allowed, Charlotte recoiled.

She had been dragged into a hastily constructed tent, surprisingly opulent considering it came out of the packs strapped to their camels, and then she had been dumped on a thin carpet. Sadly, it did not fly.

The Bedouin leader, Haroun al Rachid, came in soon after to ogle her.

"You know of men?" he asked.

Oh boy, did she know about men! Yes, she did. She knew every sort: infantrymen, cavalrymen, guardsmen, fusiliers, marines, cadets, not to mention the officers. You name it, she thought, she knew all about them. She personally knew Captain Caruthers, Colonel Fitzwilliam, Major Dan, Captain Conway and lots of others in their regiment.

"I will teach you about men."

There'd be homework, she knew it.

"You will enjoy it, and come to call me Master, once I have destroyed our god."

Destroyed their god?

But wasn't Allah the same god as God, who was the same as Jehovah. Or Yahweh? Charlotte frowned; she wished she'd paid more attention in Sunday School. But really, once you'd read about Malchizedek, Israel against the Amalekites, the destruction of the Canaanite cities, the Battle of Jericho, Joshua against the Ai, the storms that defeated the Amorites, the wars with the Midianites, most of Judges, the civil war, Perizzites, King David (apart from all the psalms), Egypt sacking the temple, Assyria, Babylon... and then there was the New Testament, which despite having Romans in it sadly didn't feature any battles. Not even Masada.

But no, the Reverend Long had skipped all that and instead gone on and on about Genesis and how the ungodly Darwin had had a monkey's uncle, and how there couldn't have been dinosaurs. But they'd been to Lyme Regis, and she'd seen the twirly things with her own eyes and she'd even pretended to listen when Georgina had explained all about them.

"Isn't that jolly ungrateful," Charlotte ventured. "With Him creating the world and everything."

"He did not create the world," Haroun insisted. "He merely stood by and chronicled events as the Ogdoad and Amun parted the waters of Nu. Huh and Hauhet, Kuck and Kauket, Amun and Amaunet..."

Charlotte sighed inwardly. None of it made sense to her, but she knew a sermon starting when she heard one. She stifled a yawn.

"...and yet Thoth stood by during the three great battles—"

"Battles?" She tried to sit upright, wriggled and struggled against her bonds, and managed it.

"The first between Ra versus Apep, the second was Heru-Bekhutet against Set, and finally Horus defeated Set."

"Oh, just one against one."

"And Thoth stood by, just as he did when Egypt was conquered by the Greeks—"

"Ooh, I know this. Alexander."

"And then by Rome, the Sasanian Empire, the French and now the British pigs."

"I know this too... ooh, don't tell me. Admiral Seymour and Lieutenant General Wolseley. The battle of Tell El Kebir, before I was born, but on my sixth birthday we had cake and Uncle Jeremiah told me about it and gave me a toy ironclad battleship, which I've still got but the masts broke."

"Quiet!"

"Sorry, but how can you destroy a god?" Charlotte asked. "He's immortal."

"Gods are not indestructible. Set killed Osiris, why not Thoth? Why not all of them? And, as the British have proved, nothing can stand against the gun."

"Oh yes, the Lee Enfield .303, muzzle velocity 2,441 feet per second and—"

Haroun struck her across the face and she crumpled like a dropped coat.

Why was he allowed to go on about his pet subject while she had to keep quiet?

It was so unfair.

"I will have the Philosopher's Stone," al Rachid ranted. "I will turn base metals into gold and become the richest man alive. Me! Haroun al Rachid, the son of a goat herder. Ha! I will buy the British. I will buy guns. I will buy fierce fighters and we will oust the infidel from our lands."

"Oust the infidel?" Charlotte said. "Seriously? Why?"

"We will kill the British redcoats."

"Oh no, the uniforms are lovely."

"I will be like a Pharaoh from the old days with a great army," al Rachid said, gesturing out of the tent towards his men.

"You can't call that rabble an army!" Charlotte was incensed. They were just a bunch of lanky men with scruffy beards, running around with stolen Lee Enfields and ancient weapons – muskets for goodness' sake – in long nightshirts. There wasn't a single handsome moustache or polished button amongst the lot of them.

The British Army had proper uniforms with medals and everything, and why wouldn't they let her wear one? What had they said? 'Your feminine charms would get in the way.' They hadn't when she'd fought the Austro-Hungarian army of the dead. Nor had they during the sword fighting to save London from the Chrononauts. They were no problem during that Tartan King business. And they hadn't when she had sky-battled to save the Crown Prince and the Empire from invaders... and some of that had been single-handed.

Just a uniform.

That's all she wanted.

Haroun al Rachid leaned in close, his stinking breath caressing her bare shoulder like a miasma from a cesspool. "Prepare yourself for me," he whispered, and he licked the side of her face.

Charlotte wanted to be sick.

Then al Rachid stood, adjusted his belt, belched and strode out of the tent.

Charlotte struggled against her bonds, but they held fast.

CHAPTER XXI

Miss Deering-Dolittle

Earnestine finished her examination of the walls. They listed the gods of Ancient Egypt, each in their own raised oval.

"There is a gap around the writing," Farouk said.

"Yes," Earnestine agreed. "I think the cartouches are switches."

"Should we try one?" Farouk reached for the nearest.

"No, no, I think not," Earnestine said. "One will be right, the others will be ill-advised."

"What do you mean?"

"If it looks like a trap, smells like a trap and feels like a trap, then on no account step in."

"Miss, we already did."

"Quite." Earnestine scratched her head: what to do? "Shame there's no magic beacon to shine on the right path."

"Yes, Miss, and it is a shame we cannot save this moment with a magic spell, try each cartouche, and if it is a trap, then we could return to this minute to try again."

"Try, try, try again, except each attempt may be our last."

"Miss, may you solve the riddle on your first try."

"There are dates," Earnestine explained as her index finger tracked along hieroglyphics always travelling in the direction the birds faced. "This is the origin of the universe in around 28,000 BC. There are solar eclipses mentioned and... there's one due here next year in November, I think. Maybe we have to wait for the total eclipse. Gina... Mrs Merryweather would know how to work it out, but we'd need something that can do a vast number of mathematical operations a second."

"Where would we find that?"

"I've no idea."

"Then we are stuck."

"We could use dynamite."

"That would bring down the roof."

"The answer lies in these hieroglyphics."

"Farouk does not know how to read hieroglyphics."

"How could you lose your language?"

"I have not lost my language."

"Writing is the single most important advance in any civilisation – given to you by Thoth himself according to your legends – the very definition of culture, and you went and forgot what your hieroglyphics mean. Not once, but twice. Both hieroglyphic and demotic. To lose one writing system may be described as a misfortune, but to lose both looks like carelessness."

"Farouk is sorry."

"Hmm, hardly your fault."

"My ancestors have a lot to answer for."

Earnestine's hand paused over the symbols, searching, dithering, until eventually, she chose one. She pushed and the whole cartouche, three hieroglyphics contained in an oval, disappeared into the wall.

A section of solid stone swung away, and the air rushed inwards with a desperate moan.

"Miss, how did you know?"

"The cartouche looked worn."

One of the thieves rushed forward, "She has discovered the treasure."

Azim shouted after him, "Moshe!"

"There is nothing to fear," Moshe replied, and he hurried through a gaping hole into the passage beyond. The light shining from the opening pulsed as the lantern swung, bright and dark, and, with each step further, its glimmer faded.

The cartouche popped back: it spelt 'Dhwty', which was an ancient variant of the god of writing, "Thoth."

"What was that, Miss?" Farouk asked.

"The name of the god... five tests and the first was Ren and it asked me to choose."

"Choose, Miss?"

"Yes, and the other tests? It was written in the Shrine," Earnestine said, trying to think above the concrete. "Ren was to choose the right name, Bâ was 'bow' or 'prostrate', Ka was 'run'... oh, but the heart was further down, and I don't know what the heart calls for."

"Is it important?"

"And there's the other one I can never remember," Earnestine said. "Remember, remember... I've been told this. The right name, a time to be humble, running or was it flying? And softly like a shadow. I will remember. Oh, but what?"

"Come!" Azim ordered.

Earnestine disagreed: "Yes, but, perhaps..."

However, Azim was already leading them inside hurrying to catch up with Moshe. The others formed up to follow.

The opening led to a long corridor cut into the rock. It was narrow, perhaps wide enough for two people and Earnestine was near the back, trying to get past and missing the excitement. So much for leading this expedition, she thought.

A scream leapt out of the gloom, a sharp, high-pitched note and then sudden silence.

A thief pushed ahead, "Moshe, Moshe!"

"Leave him, Lisimba," Azim said. "He's dead."

"Miss... look away," said Farouk.

Moshe was transfixed by a rack of spears that projected from the wall, their sharpened points jutted from his chest: he was quite dead, his eyes white and staring upwards.

If he had bowed low as he entered the temple, then the spikes would have missed him. One had to prostrate oneself before the god. Earnestine glanced at the other wall checking for a clue.

"Ah!"

Pinned by another collection of vicious spikes was a second body, a skeleton: European judging by his rags, leather satchel and boots. A pith helmet lay nearby. Earnestine picked it up.

"He has been dead a long time, Miss."

Earnestine nodded. "He was an explorer... Woods, Doctor Woods."

"Doctor Woods?" Farouk asked.

"The famous Egyptologist missing for nine years."

Farouk looked at the skeleton. "Are you sure?"

"It's written in his hat." She showed him the pith helmet and the clear capitals inked within the khaki interior. "I suppose we've solved a mystery. Sir Archibald will be pleased."

Azim emerged out of the gloom: "They say a man survives if his name lives on."

"His Ren, yes," Earnestine agreed.

Farouk stepped closer: "Miss?"

"In addition to one's Ha, one's body, the ancient Egyptians believed one has five... souls," Earnestine explained. She counted them on her fingers. "Bâ, Jb, Ka, Ren and – oh, I know this... Sheut. That's personality, heart, vital spark, *name* and, finally, his shadow."

"All that's left is their names."

"Their Ren, yes, and also their Bâ perhaps, if you believe the superstition. The Bâ leaves the body after death as a human-headed bird to go to the afterlife. If the heart weighs less than the feather of Ma'at, the wife of Thoth, then they live on in the afterlife. If they've been good."

"I didn't see any human-headed bird," said Azim. "And Moshe was not a good man. He was not even a good thief."

"Well, they have their Ren."

"Moshe will be forgotten soon enough."

"Doctor Woods was a famous Egyptologist."

Azim took the pith helmet, checked the inside and then discarded it with a derisive snort, "We go on."

Earnestine dug out her notebook and jotted down a few notes before starting a map.

"Ladies first," said Azim.

Earnestine gave a tight smile and then picked up her lantern and umbrella, edged past the corpses and led the way into the fog of cobwebs that trailed from the ceiling. The gossamer tendrils caught on Earnestine's pith helmet and red curls. The passage took them deeper into the rock, down an incline as they descended under the desert.

"Miss?"

"Farouk?"

"Stay still."

"What is it?"

"Spiders."

Farouk used his fez and patted away at Earnestine's shoulders.

Once he had finished, Earnestine flicked several crawling shapes off his clothing with the handle of her umbrella.

They moved on; both smirking to each other when a Bedouin behind them shrieked in alarm.

The corridor split right and left.

When solving mazes in the garden of English country houses, the trick was to keep to the hedge on one's left hand. One walked along every path, but one would eventually reach the centre. Or the right hand, the trick worked either way, so long as you picked one and stuck to it.

Right or left?

She tapped her notebook with her fountain pen as she considered it. There wasn't enough information in the layout she'd recorded to decide.

Male pharaohs were buried in tombs that required a left turn: female burial chambers were reached by a turn to the right. Was it to be this choice every time? She was female, most explorers were male and all explorers entering this tomb had perished.

Right or left?

But there was death here.

It wasn't so much right or left, but right or wrong – live or die.

Traps set millennia ago were as sharp and deadly as ever, and the unwary, and even the wary, could easily fall foul of them. Devious, cunning and yet... why have tunnels unless this was a puzzle to be solved? Why set tests, unless it was to exclude the ignorant and admit the enlightened?

"What is the holdup?" Azim demanded.

"There's a fork in the road," Farouk shouted back.

"Then pick one."

"We are," Earnestine replied through gritted teeth. She pointed. "This is 'man' and this, 'woman'."

"Like the water closets on the SS *Karnak*," Farouk said.

"Quite."

"Right then."

Earnestine turned right and Farouk followed.

"You two, follow them," Azim said. "You with me."

"Azim... I..."

"Lisimba, go with Chumba. I'm not going the woman's way."

"Master," said Chumba.

So, Earnestine thought, the odds were changing in their favour from three-to-one to one-to-one.

Further ahead, the quality of the masonry changed. No longer was this a passage hewn from the living rock, but constructed from large, interlocking stone blocks. She added this detail to her map. It also made searching for traps – which Earnestine did by swinging her lantern around clockwise to examine ceiling, wall, floor, wall and ceiling again – much easier.

"The walls."

"I beg your pardon, Farouk."

"The walls."

She stopped so that the lamp's swinging subsided; however, the shadows continued to shift. At the base of the wall, with a noise like teeth grinding, a pebble bounced and jiggled. It caught against the stone, splitting suddenly. The pieces powdered like sea salt in a mortar and pestle.

"They are moving," Farouk said.

Earnestine shone the light to the other wall, it too moved closer and down the corridor, the pale rectangle at the far end was thinning noticeably.

The whole corridor was shrinking, and they'd come a long way. Going back would be suicide.

What was that advice in the shrine? Oh yes!

"Run!"

She sprinted forward, her lamp clanging in her grip dangerously.

She reached the far end, which opened in both directions, and collided with the far wall such was her haste.

Behind her, Farouk called out, "Miss! Miss!"

She turned.

The man's larger frame squashed between the two walls. Behind him, the two thieves pushed to no avail.

Earnestine dropped the lamp, grabbed the swatch of material acting as Farouk's belt, and pulled.

"Miss, I–"

"Breath out!"

He did, and popped out like a cork from a bottle.

They fell on the floor together in a heap.

Lisimba and Chumba jumped over them.

Earnestine recovered her dignity, somewhat bruised, and her lamp, which was thankfully still intact and lit.

"Miss?"

"Farouk?"

"Would you shine the light upwards?"

"Certainly."

The corridor they were in, with the way they had entered gone, was high and–

"Run, Miss."

Farouk, agile for his size, scrambled to his feet and set off. One of the thieves followed him as Earnestine queried his choice of direction, but then she too started running.

The other thief ran after them.

Earnestine could see over Farouk and the thief, Chumba, to where their long shadows leapt and cavorted in the ever-diminishing space, sometimes they danced upon the ceiling, which continued to descend, inexorable and uncaring.

"Move quicker, move quicker," begged Chumba.

Sand, like water, ran between the joints as the masonry sank lower.

Farouk bent low, the thief too and Earnestine had to do the same. Her knuckles, holding the lamp aloft, scraped across the stone ceiling.

Farouk was through.

Earnestine bent double.

Chumba was through.

Earnestine, constrained to her hands and knees, threw the lamp and umbrella forward and crawled towards the flickering light. She got a hand over, around the stone doorframe, pulled. Someone caught hold of her wrist – Farouk – and yanked her towards them. Her Oxford Street boots scraped against the floor and her heels touched the ceiling.

She was through!

The two men turned to grab the thief behind her.

With a deep, sonorous percussion like a bass drum, the gigantic stone block slammed down. Dust whipped around as the blast of air swirled in the enclosed space. The massive block hadn't even paused in its descent, as if there had been no obstruction at all.

Earnestine stepped away into the gloom, but something pulled her back.

There was no-one behind her, just a solid wall. Earnestine couldn't even remember the flattened man's name.

A metal sound echoed in the confines as Farouk rammed the bolt of a rifle home and pointed it at Chumba.

The thief struggled and pulled out a revolver.

They faced each other, shaking, but determined.

"Are you going to kill me," Chumba said, "guide to the infidel?"

"If I must," said Farouk.

"We outnumber you," Chumba said.

"Not here, you don't."

"Gentlemen, please," Earnestine said. "Might one make the observation that we are all trapped in this temple. Any animosity we may have felt outside has little bearing on our survival in here."

The two men stood for a moment and then lowered their weapons.

"Truce?" Farouk suggested.

Chumba nodded.

"Jolly wise," said Earnestine.

"My gun?" Chumba said.

"I'll keep the rifle," said Farouk.

Earnestine handed him one of the lanterns. "Shall we press on?"

"And we'll take it in turns to step into the lion's den," said Farouk. "It is not right that Miss Deering-Dolittle takes all the risks."

"Thank you, Farouk."

Chumba glanced to where the tunnel had once been. There was no gap between the massive stones. It looked like the wall had always been there.

"Let me say a prayer for Lisimba."

"May Allah protect his soul," Farouk said.

All three of them bowed their heads for a moment.

"I'm sorry about Lisimba," Earnestine said.

"His name means 'lion'," Chumba said. He'd kept his gun in his hand, but he pointed it down the tunnel.

"You go," Farouk said.

Chumba set off, and, rifle at the ready, Farouk followed, but as Earnestine stepped forward, something tugged her back. Her skirts were firmly trapped by the masonry.

"Farouk," she said, "one appears to be stuck."

Farouk came back, put the lamp down.

"Miss," Farouk said, and he propped the rifle against the wall to reach down to grab her skirts.

"What are you doing?"

"I go to rip your dress."

"I beg your pardon! Get away from my ankles."

"You could remove your skirt," he suggested.

Earnestine gaped for a moment: "I beg your pardon!"

"It is simple, just undo and step out of–"

"It is not simple, it will not undo, and I will not step out of it."

"Then you are stuck, Miss."

"I am not, Mister Farouk," Earnestine explained. "You must lift the stone."

"Me?"

"And you?"

Chumba startled: "Me?"

"Yes, you... what's your name?"

"Chumba."

"Chumba, yes, both of you together."

"It is impossible."

"For goodness sake," Earnestine said reaching into her small kit bag and realising she was ill-equipped. "Look around and find a lever."

"A lever?"

"Yes, with a lever and the proper fulcrum one can lift the world."

Farouk and Chumba made a pointless show of looking around.

"Very well, Mister Chumba turn around and–"

"Azim said I should watch you," Chumba pointed out.

"Turn around! Now, Mister Farouk, please remove the minimum of material *without looking!*"

Farouk examined the task: "Miss?"

He had to look, but Earnestine felt she had made her objection clear.

It ripped.

When she stepped away, free at last, her right Oxford Street boot was showing all the way up its seven lace holes to the very top, and then a horrifying inch of stocking was clearly visible.

"Are you injured?"

"Appallingly," Earnestine said, "and please look at me. I'm up here, not at my ankles."

Farouk looked her in the eyes: "We must go on."

"Quite."

Chumba had the rifle pointed at them both.

"I have the upper hand now, don't you know," he said in a mocking, public school English accent, "so you will do as I say."

Earnestine grabbed the weapon off him in one easy motion. "Mister Chumba, for goodness sake!"

They went on and reached another T-junction.

"Always two directions," Farouk said. "I have lost my sense of direction."

"Luckily, I have not," Earnestine replied. She handed the rifle to Chumba, fished out her notebook and made a few additions to her floorplan of this changing labyrinth. "We did a lot of running, so I'll count that as a pace and a half."

"We crawled out of the last tunnel."

Earnestine thought of her niece, Pippa, escaping across the floor, which always seemed jolly rapid.

"Perhaps half a pace for each crawling motion."

"Is this accurate?"

"I hope so. Best I can manage in the circumstances," Earnestine said. She was terribly aware that they'd chosen, bowed and run, which brought her to the advice she'd not read in the Shrine of the Child. What was one supposed to do with one's heart? "These walls seem jolly thick."

"It is well made," said Farouk, "good Egyptian building."

"Your ancestors certainly knew how to make tombs."

"Let us hope their descendants know how to escape from their tombs."

"You know," Earnestine said, "I think left here is the way out to the Ibis entrance, whereas the right will take us to the heart of the temple."

Farouk took a step towards the exit.

"No," Earnestine said. "We must go on."

"We must steal the Philosopher's Stone," said Chumba. "Don't you wish to live forever?"

"Farouk wishes to live this day."

They did go on deeper into the temple and a hundred yards further along, the floor dropped away.

Farouk grabbed Earnestine as she teetered on the edge. Just as it seemed they would both fall in, Chumba pulled them both back.

"Thank you, much obliged," Earnestine said, once her Oxford Street boots were on a firmer footing.

"We can go no further," said Farouk.

"We must backtrack to the other route," Chumba agreed.

It did appear to be too far to jump, as the passage didn't afford much of a run-up.

Earnestine searched her pockets and found a few coins. She cast them into the pit, as she would wish in a well. The brass caught the light briefly it as spun downwards. She counted, slowly, in elephants, until eventually, it sounded prettily.

"Hmm..."

"Deep," Farouk observed.

"Seven times thirty-two is two hundred and twenty-four feet."

"We cannot climb down," Chumba said, "and if we could, we could not climb back up."

"We can swing across," Earnestine said. She pointed with her umbrella at a wooden pole that spanned the gap between the walls on either side.

"I cannot reach that," said Farouk.

"We swing across with my umbrella."

"It won't take my weight."

"It's a Fox's Paragon."

Earnestine gathered their equipment and flung it across the hole. It landed and slid away making tracks in the light covering of sand.

"Who goes first?" Chumba asked. "It is like that riddle with the jackal, the sacred bird and the bag of grain."

"Don't be silly," Earnestine said. She took the rifle off Chumba and gave it to Farouk, then drew the revolver from Chumba's belt and tossed it across the gap.

"That was mine," he said.

"You don't want it to fall out down the pit, do you?"

"No."

Next, Earnestine reached up, hooked her brolly over the pole, hocked herself back – and swung across. She landed – just – and held onto the umbrella.

"Catch when I swing it back. One, two–"

"On three or–"

"Now!"

Chumba lent forward, overbalanced, lurched forward and caught the tightly furled cloth of the umbrella. He swung, chaotically, but Earnestine caught his clothing and tugged him safely across.

"Farouk, now you," Earnestine said.

Farouk shook his head: "Farouk cannot."

"Come on, Farouk."

"Miss, you know Farouk cannot. Too much basbousa."

Earnestine did know it; he was too plump.

"Wait for us," Earnestine said. "Maybe check that passage to the Ibis entrance, but be careful."

Farouk held the rifle tightly. "Farouk will be careful, but you be more careful, Miss."

Earnestine nodded and picked up the revolver from the floor. "One's always careful."

Chumba managed to unhook her umbrella.

Amusingly, Earnestine now carried the revolver, Farouk had the rifle and Chumba had her umbrella.

They moved on, cautiously, Earnestine first, and then she indicated that Chumba should go first.

"You are leading."

Earnestine waved the revolver at him.

"I could do with the gun," Chumba said.

Earnestine contemplated this for a moment. "I could do with two guns."

Chumba went first.

A bell *tinged*.

"What was that?"

Chumba stood stock still, rigid with fear. "Miss."

"Chumba?" Earnestine asked, stepping towards him. "No!"

Earnestine stopped.

Chumba held his hand against his body and jabbed downwards with tiny movements. His foot caught against a string drawn taut across the passage.

"I felt it," Chumba said, his voice trembling, "and heard the bell."

It was like the bell to call their maid at home; a wire that travelled above the picture rail from the Drawing Room pull to the Kitchen bell. This trip went across about three inches from the stone-littered floor.

Earnestine checked her kit bag. The only object with any weight were the opera glasses. She cautiously knelt down and pushed the glasses against the twine by Chumba's foot.

"Kindly bring your foot back, carefully," she said.

"Carefully, yes, carefully."

Chumba moved away, the string shifted, but the glasses held it in position.

"Back away slowly."

"Slowly, yes, slowly."

The glasses were about an inch from the floor. Earnestine lowered them, but the string caught on the focusing wheel. She repositioned the cord – another distant *ting* sounded – and finally put the glasses down. They slid slightly, so Earnestine searched around and found a broken piece of stone lying to one side. She put this against the glasses.

"Something moved," said Chumba.

"Yes... in a moment," Earnestine said, carefully releasing her grip – it held.

A shadow moved across Earnestine and then she realised that Chumba had moved his lantern to shine down the passage.

"There!"

Still kneeling, Earnestine looked and saw something black creeping in the shadows. It had legs, pincers and an angry tail. Another appeared crawling out of a gap in the side of the wall.

And another.

"The bell alerted them," Chumba said. "Like a dinner bell."

There were many more now, creeping forward.

"Why did it have to be scorpions?" Earnestine said. "Why couldn't it be kittens?"

"You are afraid of scorpions."

"Of course, they can kill you."

"Yes, Egyptian scorpions, very deadly."

Earnestine stood slowly. "What do we do?"

"We keep away."

Earnestine glanced behind her and then at the creeping carpet of black shapes. Her choice was to brave the scorpions or face the thieves.

They backed away.

The scorpions hesitated when they reached the cord; the leader's pincers tugged and rang the bell. An agitated quiver flowed through the horde. Another scorpion clambered over her opera glasses, leading the way.

Why was there a piece of stone lying on the floor?

She checked the roof and found that there was a ledge leading all the way around, high up on the wall like a picture rail.

"It's fly, fly, the answer is fly. We can use that to go over the scorpions," she said. "Hand over hand."

Earnestine hoisted her pack over her shoulder, slipped her umbrella horizontally into the straps, attached her lantern and jumped up. But she couldn't reach the ledge.

"Chumba, if you'd be so kind."

He got down on his hands and knees, so Earnestine had a leg up. Her fingers just reached the edge and she hoisted herself up.

Chumba scrambled to his feet and hooked the lantern to her pack.

"Hurry, please."

Earnestine's jaw tightened. "I am hurrying."

Earnestine crabbed along the wall, keeping herself away from the rough surface by pushing her feet against the blocks.

"Go, go..." he said as he backed away from the scampering of many, many legs.

"Come on, Chumba."

She heard him jump up and his sandals scrape across the stonework.

She heard other scuttling too.

Had she gone far enough? She looked down on both sides, but all she could see was the handle and point of her umbrella.

"Am I clear?"

"Go further."

She shuffled on.

At the corner, she could see down to the floor without her umbrella obstructing her view.

This corridor was only a yard across, less than that.

With stinging fingers, Earnestine shuffled around. Her arms ached. She checked downwards, but it was point and handle again.

Holding on by one hand, she could just about look straight down in front of her.

There, illuminated by her swinging lantern, scorpions snapped their claws.

She went on.

All sensation in her arms had gone and she was going to get hands like a maid's if she went any further.

She stopped, one-handed again, and looked down – scorpions... fewer, she thought, but she had to swing back as she began to slip, and could not check thoroughly.

More hand over hand.

Charlotte did this sort of climbing for fun. Silly girl!

Earnestine paused again, breathing hard.

Looked down.

Scorpion... scorpion and... oh, it hurt.

She tried again.

Yes, two scorpions, but it only took one to pump its venom into her blood to kill her.

She held on again with both hands and, walked up the wall so that she could see down through the slit, between her stretched skirts and the wall.

Two, just two.

"Here boy, here boy," she sang softly.

The two evil creatures shuffled to look her in the eyes.

She dropped.

Right and left soles of her Oxford Street boots found their targets in a popping squish of unpleasantness.

It felt as if her arms had actually dropped off.

Numb.

No time to waste.

Earnestine turned and... something caught her fast.

Another trap!

No!

And scorpions behind her!

Chumba dropped beside her.

"I'm trapped!" Earnestine screeched.

"It is all right."

"Get me free! Get me free!"

"It is your stick caught against the walls," Chumba said. "Here. Turn sideways."

Earnestine did so, as Chumba yanked the umbrella free; she shuffled sideways along the narrow passageway.

Another two hundred yards and the way opened out to a large space. It was obviously the inner sanctum, wide, spacious and at the far end was a raised area complete with an altar. Caught in a shaft of sunlight, a shining canopic jar gleamed temptingly.

Chumba went forward.

"No!"

Earnestine put out her hand to prevent him.

"It is gold," Chumba said, "there for the taking."

"It might be," Earnestine admitted.

The jar did look like gold and it had the head of a baboon.

"The jar," Chumba said, "is the image of Thoth. This must be the Philosopher's Stone. See, it has turned that jar to gold."

"The canopic jar with the baboon is the image of Horus's son, Hapi," Earnestine said.

She glanced around the room as she fished out her compass. The altar was to the north. If it was a canopic jar, then it was correctly positioned. Hapi was the baboon-headed god, whose jar contained the lungs of the mummified corpse traditionally placed to the north.

They were at the south.

"Let us get the gold," said Chumba.

"Wait... there have been traps. It's foolish to think that this room is undefended."

"I bow to your wisdom... ladies first."

"Chumba," Earnestine warned, waving the revolver in the thief's direction.

In response, Chumba raised Earnestine's umbrella.

She smiled and turned her attention back to the problem.

The south should have the likeness of the god, Imsety, and a jar containing the liver. She couldn't see one. Unless Chumba stood in for the human-headed god; he had a human head.

To her right should be the jackal-headed Duamutef and a jar with a stomach, while her left, the west, should be Qubehsenuef, whose falcon-headed jar contained the intestines.

She couldn't even see the puzzle, let alone a solution.

Except that the god Thoth could be a baboon as well as an Ibis. So, the jar might not be a canopic jar, but simply a container protected by Thoth.

That made more sense.

Except she expected Thoth, the keeper of records, to have a library.

"Let's..."

"Let's not," Earnestine said. "If it smells like a trap, looks like a trap, let's not find out if it kills like a trap."

"You are afraid," Chumba said. "You are a woman. That is understandable."

"Hmmm," Earnestine agreed. She wasn't really listening. It was a moot point. They had to return with the prize if they were to live and save Charlotte.

Or they could stay here.

D-worded if they did, d-worded if they didn't.

Or there might be a backdoor through a vestry, perhaps behind the altar, that led to the desert behind the rocks.

"Let us tread carefully," she said, and she swapped the revolver for the umbrella.

She poked the ground, tapping with her brolly's ferrule to test each small flagstone, in case it gave way.

Poke-step, poke-step.

She sensed Chumba following.

Poke-step, poke-step, poke–

Something whizzed past her eyeline like an angry hornet to thud into the wall nearby, where it stuck out like a nail ready for a picture hanging.

Chumba stepped backwards. "We don't need a statue."

"You are forgetting Azim and those lunatics outside."

"I am not, but..." he gingerly peered at the embedded dart. He reached out. "It is coated in some substance."

"Don't touch it!"

Chumba snatched his hand back.

"Poison," Earnestine explained.

The thief nodded.

"It's this type of flagstone," Earnestine explained. "The stones here and here seem safe."

"If you say so."

"But these are quite deadly."

"Yes."

"You stay here."

"If you insist, Miss."

She handed her umbrella over, but Chumba kept the revolver. He held out his hand for her kit bag.

"I need this to carry the jar."

Chumba nodded.

So, best foot forward, Earnestine thought. Like a dance in a ballroom, there were steps she could take and those she couldn't, but it was straightforward: one, two, three... one, two–

Overconfidence nearly made her unbalance and fall.

A quick two-step and she skipped up to the altar.

The golden statue of a baboon was tantalisingly close, she could simply reach out and touch it, snatch it from its resting place and then... leave with it. Back down the passageway, swing across the gap, take that long passage to the Ibis entrance and it was done.

Easy.

The baboon head looked in her direction, seeming to bore into her very soul – or all of her five souls – with its painted eyes.

Something was wrong, jolly wrong.

"Take it," Chumba shouted across the room. "What are you waiting for?"

She held her breath and reached forward, adjusting her fingers to take hold...

Hapi, Canopic jar... lungs.

She pulled her hands back.

And breathed out.

She glanced over her shoulder to mentally rehearse her sprint back. The pressure points in the floor would be designed to shoot their poisoned darts at someone sneaking into the temple, rather than someone fleeing at speed.

Or would they?

Only one way to find out.

Chumba crouched low, his expression hungry, and raised his hands as if he was about to reach across the yards of space to pick up the statue himself.

Earnestine turned towards the prize.

Was the altar booby-trapped?

Booby – a foolish person, although buckets of cold water poised above a door in the dormitories of the Eden College for Young Ladies often caught the sensible as well as the stupid as Earnestine herself could attest.

Trap – oh dear...

She reached again, and saw her own eager face, distorted into a gargoyle by the surface of the shining gold sculpture in front of her.

Surely, they were searching for the Philosopher's Stone. Sir Archibald reckoned it was a fossilised piece of the Tree of Life from the Garden of Eden. A rock that turned lead into gold seemed like silly superstition; whereas, there was documentary corroboration for a petrified tree with supernatural powers.

The golden statue (had it once been lead?) was jolly beguiling.

She touched it, the tips of her fingers feeling the cold surface. It would be heavy and worth a fortune. Enough to fund several expeditions.

Her hands cupped around it.

Ready.

She picked it off the altar and held it in her grasp. A breath escaped her lungs – trapped in a jar, no... just a premonition, an idle fear unworthy of her.

This was truly a prize. Not the gold, or any price in mere guineas, but with this, she would make her mark. They'd enter her in the rolls of the Royal Expeditionary Society. Her Ren, her name, would be recorded and so her reputation would live forever.

She turned to Chumba, who was smiling with a huge, white toothy grin that was so obvious within the canvas of his swarthy skin.

She called to him, "I–"

But something shifted with a grating sound, stone grinding on stone.

She wasn't sure.

The room seemed different: no longer poised but pouncing.

Chumba stared at her, his eyes seeming to widen as he watched her. His fear was evident, petrified by something that had to be behind her.

She glanced over her shoulder.

Before she fully comprehended what was happening, she was already running, her Oxford Street boots smacking the hard stone as darts shot from concealed tubes, behind her, catching her bustle, hitting the steel ribs of her corset... and she ran.

Chumba had fled.

The entire stone edifice was collapsing!

The rage of the god tore everything asunder to destroy those who dared desecrate his temple.

She reached the narrow passage, sidled along it as rapidly as she could and then turned a wider corridor, just in time to see dust covered scorpions scuttle away into their mouseholes in the wall.

She ran on, a few turns and then she skittered to a halt.

It was the pit.

Ahead, a massive piece of masonry was descending inexorably from the ceiling to seal the way out.

Chumba stood on the other side of the hole, holding her umbrella. Her thrown pack landed at his feet.

"Throw me the umbrella," Earnestine shouted.

"Throw me the Philosopher's Stone."

"Throw me the umbrella!"

"No time to argue. Throw me the stone."

Earnestine did so.

Chumba caught it.

"Throw me the umbrella," Earnestine shouted.

Chumba casually dropped the brolly. "Toodle-pip."

He ran to the closing gap and ducked to escape beneath the stone.

Nothing for it.

Earnestine took four strides backwards and then, with all the puff she could muster into her corset-constrained lungs, she hurtled towards the gap and sprang forward.

For a moment, she seemed to hang in the air, almost collided with the wooden pole across the passageway, and then she hit the side of the pit. Her hands caught the edge, slipped, scrabbled – the sand and stones loose – and then she just managed to heave herself up.

The ground shook, she grabbed her pack, umbrella and a lantern, and scuttled under the lowering weight.

In the passage, living pillars of sand cascaded from above as chambers emptied to cause the massive stone blocks to shift and move and descend.

She reached the T-junction.

Ahead was the route to the Ibis entrance – she hoped.

Chumba stood by the wall, his eyes staring without seeing, and stakes jutting out of his chest.

The golden jar lay at his feet.

Earnestine snatched it up and slipped it into her small kit bag as debris from the ceiling cascaded downwards. For a moment, she thought the roof was coming down.

It was!

A massive stone door descending to obscure the long corridor ahead.

She ran, lost her footing, stumbled and sprinted, as she used her umbrella to swat away the growing cloud of plaster dust.

She had to reach it.

She must.

She did, throwing herself onto the floor, flinging the lamp underneath without due regard and then rolling herself under the massive stonework.

She made it.

The stone door a mere few feet, two, one...

Where was her *umbrella!*

She'd dropped it.

She reached back – her knuckles grazed the underside of the stone – and whipped it through to safety.

Just in time!

The stone struck the ground with a bone-crunching shudder. It was like a wall now, so solid that it was hard to believe there had ever been an opening.

Ahead, across a chamber that was five yards wide by a near impossible twenty yards long, another stone barrier began to descend.

She seized the lamp. The precious flame fluttered and complained, but held. She swung it forward to light her way as she took a step forward and then, at the last moment, wrenched herself back.

The floor had shifted.

She hadn't proper hold of the lamp. It slipped from her fingers and arced through the space, tumbling, as darts zinged through its sweeping spotlight like Haversham Mark III Rocket powered hornets.

One struck!

The lamp jerked to one side from the piercing impact, then it hit the hard floor and shattered.

More darts, activated by the lamp striking the floor, whizzed across the room from both sides.

Every step activated these deadly missiles.

Earnestine pushed herself back against the newly lowered wall behind her, trying to stay under the door lintel and not have a single part of her within the lethal room. The stone felt reassuringly solid, except that she needed to be on the other side and through the closing gap.

The lamp still burned – incredibly – and its light shone on the yawning chasm of safety as it shut.

Only half the opening left.

How could she cross twenty yards without touching the ground?

Fly?

The lantern itself resembled a wounded hedgehog, covered with spines. The flames fluttered. A dart jutting from the metal fizzed as the poison coating ignited.

Think, think...

A third of the space left.

Dried wood on the floor next to the fallen lamp caught fire, burned briefly...

A quarter gap.

...and went out.

A fifth.

The oil flared, burning brighter as the contents spilled.

A sixth.

Brighter and faster.

An eighth.

Turning red as the fuel thinned.

The barest sliver left and then gone with a thud.

Finally turning blue, like brandy burning on a fruit pudding, the lamp's flame spluttered and went out.

Darkness.

Silence.

Mrs Merryweather

Logically, they could not go out into the desert to look for Earnestine. The area to search was far too great to search and they didn't have the water for a trek anyway.

So, it was decided that they should return to the SS *Karnak*.

"She may well be there," Sir Archibald assured them.

He clambered aboard his camel while a native kept the evil creature on its knees.

The others followed: Doctor Timon, Monsieur Jacques and then Georgina herself. Captain Caruthers was the last to turn away from staring north into the shimmering mirage.

And there was still Charlotte to find too.

And the murderer.

"Captain?"

"Mrs Merryweather."

"What were you doing on the deck just before the murder?"

Caruthers shook his head, "That I won't tell you."

Georgina did not feel like an officer, investigating or otherwise, but merely a pawn, a slice of cake to be moved up or down a plate, or a biscuit going soggy. There wasn't just one thing going on, but, just like Charlotte's pastimes invented for the long journey, there were other games being played.

The line of horses and camels continued to snake across the desert on the long trek back to the ship.

One amongst them hadn't stuck to the rules.

But which one?

Rules were there for a reason: knife and fork here, spoon there, ladies first, sandwich before scone, up the ladder and down the snake, dunk the biscuit all the way into the tea and so on.

It was rules that held the Empire together, that made the difference between civilisation and barbarism. 'Port to the left' and 'horse and carriages to the left' always turned out to be sensible. It gave everyone a fair share and enabled traffic to proceed safely. Port could be passed to the right (although the hint was in its nautical name) and driving could be European, a silly idea of Napoleon's that seemed to have caught on elsewhere in the ex-colonies, but it wasn't the proper way.

The logic was inescapable.

Men were right-handed, or at least those who didn't succumb to opium and poetry, so the sword, like the mightier pen, was held in the right hand. Thus passing to the left was more natural, and men drove carriages with their traditional placement being to the right of the woman, who, on account of her more delicate frame, should be the passenger. The man stood to the right, because it freed up his sword arm and he could use his shield to protect his spouse. Women could be shield bearers and thus had to stand upon the left.

It was the natural order.

An order upset by suffragettes and murderers.

Miss Charlotte

Charlotte heard such a commotion outside, shouting in Arabic or Egyptian or possibly French.

Still bound at the wrists and ankles, she wriggled like a worm until she reached the edge of the tent. She kicked the canvas up and then squirmed round to put her face to the gap, so she could see what was going on.

The yelling outside increased in vehemence.

She could see Azim, dark and cruel, and that nasty al Rachid arguing.

Farouk was there, nervously throttling his fez between his hands, and...

She twisted to look further.

...no-one else.

She remembered Haroun al Rachid ordering Azim to take doodah, whatsit and thingumabob with a few others into the temple. They weren't there now. Ha, she thought, things had not gone well.

But where was Earnestine?

Were they shouting at each other because Earnestine had tricked them?

That seemed jolly likely.

There was usually a lot of shouting where Earnestine was concerned. Usually by Earnestine.

Probably a good idea if I escaped, Charlotte thought, otherwise Earnestine would shout at her: *Charlotte, you were in that tent without escaping for how long?*

She shuffled back and then wriggled round to sit up. She jangled as she did so.

Her first task was to untie her hands and feet.

There were so many types of knives: dinner, fish, fruit, steak, fillet, salad, butter, cheese, tea, dessert, bread, bayonet... how were you supposed to remember them all? Heaven forbid she ever use the wrong one for the wrong thing at the dinner table. *Don't use a khukuri for Red Leicester, Charlotte, honestly.* Or something like that. So many knives and yet she couldn't find a single example in the tent.

Her hands were tied behind her and her feet were fastened together such that the various bracelets and anklets were divided by the thick rope. Her legs looked strange: she wasn't used to seeing them bare. Or, more accurately, barely covered in a wispy gossamer. She wiggled her toes. Her shoes had fallen off some time ago.

The knots weren't that complicated, but she needed her hands to be able to undo them. Her hands were behind her back and she couldn't see the quality of field craft that had tied that rope, but she imagined it was the same.

Someone was looking at her.

She shifted round.

It was a boy, younger than Charlotte and dressed in simple robes with his head shaven. He smiled as children do when they know something but aren't telling.

"Good afternoon," Charlotte said.

He tilted his head to one side as he contemplated her.

"I'm Charlotte."

He considered this and then nodded.

"And you are?"

The boy said nothing.

"Could you help me?" Charlotte asked, lifting her feet up to show him she was trussed up.

The boy just looked at her as if she was a child.

Charlotte bumped along on her behind rather like Pippa and then stopped. "Please."

The boy smiled, beatifically: more a choirboy than a cadet, she thought.

"Look," she said, "who are you?"

"I am not the god Thoth."

Chapter XXII

Miss Deering-Dolittle

In haste, Earnestine felt around for her kit bag.

No, no, no... calm down, get a grip.

A few steadying deep breaths were needed, but she coughed. Stone dust from the huge stones grinding downwards still floated unseen around her.

It was so dark.

She leant her umbrella in the corner of the recess.

Her kit bag was against her hip, heavy with the golden jar. She worked around that knowing she had to be careful. If she dropped something, it would be lost. There was absolutely no way she could feel around on the floor without touching pressure points and the poison darts would find their mark even in the pitch black.

By touch, Earnestine felt around the Tabasco bottle to find her matches. Her fingers searched, touching a peg, goggles and all her other useless items until she found the comforting rough sandpaper edge of the box. She brought it out, careful not to lose anything else.

But which way up was it? If she opened it and the matches cascaded to the ground...

She shook it.

There was no way to tell.

She had to open it ever so slightly and feel which way was up and which was down. With the box surrounded by her right hand, she pushed the inside outwards. It shifted, she felt, her finger probing into her own grip to find the open end.

It was upside down.

She turned it over.

And opened it further.

She heard the matches shake as her body trembled.

She found one, closed the box safely, and struck it along the sandpaper edge. The match flared, dazzling her, and she let the flame take hold. It was fascinating, beguiling like the flame that attracts a moth to its doom.

And it burnt her fingers and went out.

"Damn."

The d-word, no... she must calm down.

She extracted another match, struck it and then reached over her head to find the candle stuck by its own wax to her pith helmet.

She should have taken it off first.

By touch, singeing herself, she–

Dropped the matchbox.

"Damn!"

The shadows danced in celebration.

Her quivering touch found the wick.

It burnt.

The light held.

She could see properly.

In the flickering light, she saw the dread truth. Her prison cell was five yards wide by twenty yards long. The walls solid except for the miniature arrow slits on either side, each a mouth ready to spit death. The floor was a mass of small, irregular stone shapes like a floor covered in broken tiles, each one, a hair-trigger.

She remembered the skeleton she'd found, that long-dead explorer who had fallen foul of the devious nature of this temple complex.

As she had.

It was a tomb.

Her tomb.

She leant forward, stretching against the pressure of her corset, to pick up the matchbox. It was out of reach, just... a little... further. Wax splattered down onto the precious box, Bryant taking the brunt of it on the 'Bryant and May' lettering. Her fingers touched it, held it, brought it up and then carefully opened it.

Three matches left.

That cold night in the shrine, Charlotte had used match after match lighting the fire. If only the girl would do as she was told.

Earnestine cut at the cardboard on one flat side with her fingernail to mark the top. She could feel that. It went back in her kit bag.

She doubted she'd use them. Once the candle was gone, how long would a few matches last? There were no spare candles. A bottle of Tabasco, a peg, goggles and all the useless items, when what she needed was a spare lamp.

Let the candle burn to save the matches.

Put out the light to eke out the candle.

Diligently, she examined the room, three walls (she daren't step forward to view the one behind her), ceiling and floor, the position of the destroyed lantern... and then she took off her pith helmet and blew out the candle.

A tiny smudge of orange remained in her vision and then it shone only in her imagination.

She put her helmet back on.

Even the smell of the smoke dissipated.

She struck backwards in frustration, but her head didn't strike the wall. Instead, her pith helmet rose as the back connected.

A lever!

If she had a lever, then, as Archimedes said, she could move the world.

It wasn't the world she wished to move, just the block of stone weighing tons and tons behind her.

Except all she had was her trusty umbrella, but even a Fox's Paragon would crack under the strain.

She could do nothing, and standing still meant that the cold stones leached the heat from her body. Her shoulder blades ached, stiffened, but she daren't move. She was conscious of her breath spreading out, condensing unseen in front of her.

Perhaps, if she opened the umbrella, the thin fabric might deflect the stinging darts and allow her to cross the room to the far side.

Except the darts fired from both sides.

The other end's sealed doorway would be just as impossible as the one behind her.

She blinked, amused by the foolishness of closing her eyes in the darkness and bothering to open them again.

Was she swaying?

Like being on the ship again, the ground was unstable, moving, or it was her upright body rocking back and forth.

Was this what it felt like before ladies swooned?

She should light one of the matches. It would be warm, she would be able to see and face death standing upright. She couldn't do that often, there being only three matches left, but at least for those vital seconds, she'd be alive again, instead of this nonexistence.

It was worse than death, this waiting without hope.

Going mad.

No, the cold stone behind her was so jolly solid. The motion was only fear.

She breathed a sigh of relief.

The air was dying, she knew. How long would it last as each of her breaths depleted the precious oxygen? She was like the white cockatoo in *An Experiment on a Bird in an Air Pump*, a painting by Joseph Wright that hung in the National Gallery. Earnestine had been appalled, Georgina fascinated, and Charlotte had wanted to see the paintings of battles. Uncle Jeremiah had taken them one rainy afternoon. His watch was in her pocket, engraved *'For the Future'*, but there was no future for Earnestine. No trips to art galleries, no adventures, no exploring – she would follow her mother's advice, finally and posthumously. If she ever went to a museum again, it would be as an exhibit: 'Unknown skeleton, circa 1900, found in the Temple of Thoth'.

'Unknown' – her Ren gone too.

Would a visitor in the far future, view her remains and wonder who she was, before moving on to the lovely café with its choice of teas and its fine selection of cakes?

A Kendal Mint Cake wrapper.

A peg.

There must be something she could do with those.

Think, think!

Kendal Mint Cake – Quiggin's since 1880 – was mostly sugar, 'glucose', 'fructose' and 'sucrose', Georgina called it, and powdered, it would burn jolly brightly, generating light, except that she and Charlotte had shared the bar between them.

All these items and she'd eaten the only useful one.

On the SS *Karnak*, Mister Rake had met his end in a locked room and the killer had escaped. Earnestine imagined looking around the Smoking Room again: Georgina, Colonel Fitzwilliam, Captain Caruthers, Sir Archibald, Monsieur Jacques, Doctor Timon, Mrs Albright, Pandit Singh Maçon and finally Charlotte. One of them had committed murder, but, more importantly, that person knew how to get out of a locked room.

Work out the murder, work out the escape.

Not Gina.

Not Charlotte.

She couldn't believe it was brave Captain Caruthers – he wouldn't turn away from rescuing her.

Or the Colonel.

Mrs Albright was too interested in contacting the dead to kill the living.

Who did that leave?

Sir Archibald, Doctor Timon, Monsieur Jacques, Pandit Singh Maçon, Jacques... Timon, Maçon, Reevers... Jacques. Who? Who was it? Who had the trick of it?

Sir Archibald had expertise on ancient Egypt. Could that have been used to leave a room in a ship in Egypt? What was a minor puzzle about modern door made of metal with a flimsy bolt that was impossible to slide from the outside compared to a cold, dark, stone-built mausoleum buried under hundreds of feet of rock?

But she'd forgotten someone. She was sure of it. In the room, when she had accused them all of murder, there had been another presence. Someone she'd missed.

Amenemope!

He'd been in his sarcophagus in the hold, staring upwards all the time at their trivial goings-on, his cold, empty eye sockets examining them as he waited – as he had waited for three thousand years – until he struck. His mind reaching out to kill and kill and kill.

Earnestine struck the back of the wall, her hand stinging as her fists connected to the unyielding stone.

Bringing her round.

Clearing her head.

Toppling her forward.

"Arr*ghhh...*"

She waved her arms, snatched up her umbrella and twirled it about like the long pole of a tightrope walker about to tumble to the safety net.

Except there was no safety net.

Flailing.

Desperately.

The heels of her Oxford Street boots floated above the ground as her toes tried to grip through her insoles.

She thrust forward with her umbrella, stabbing the ground, and darts zinged across, so close to her face that she felt the points pass through her ringlets as they snagged at her hair.

Balanced again, the reassuring solidity of the icy stone steady against her back, her trusty brolly gripped in her hands.

She was so cold.

Come to Egypt and freeze to death.

But someone would save her.

A man.

A hero would arrive in the nick of time: Caruthers, Djehuti, Holmes, Quartermain, Thoth, someone – please, even Sir Archibald – even if they had to rise out of the pages of the Strand or a penny dreadful to save her.

No-one.

The age of champions on white chargers saving damsels in distress was long gone.

Even Thoth, the arbiter of conflict, was dead.

She was going to die!

She might as well accept it.

But surely not one of the Derring-Do Club?

Surely not... except Captain Merryweather had died.

Just died.

There one minute, full of life and possibility, and then *bang!* Gone.

And they died all the time in Egypt: fighting, old age, tuberculosis, smallpox, malaria, plague, locusts, starvation, the Wrath of God. She was the first born. There were mummies buried all around, death piled upon death, hidden underground in secret chambers.

One came to Egypt to see tombs.

She was in a tomb... temple! Get a grip, stiff upper lip. It was an ancient Egyptian temple. She knew all about those. She knew all about the fallen civilisation. She'd read books and been to lectures.

Sir Archibald had said that women turn left and men right at the end of the entranceway.

Signore Belzoni, the Great Belzoni, Giovanni Battista Belzoni, had said that there was nothing left to find in the Valley of the Kings.

Except that her own father had reckoned he knew where the tomb of Tutankhamun could be uncovered.

And Queen Nefertiti in a secret chamber behind that.

Just like this secret chamber with her father's princess, his brave little girl, sealed inside.

There were tears on her cheeks.

This was succumbing to hysteria, wasn't it?

Her father had sat his daughter on his knee and filled her head with tales of expedition, discovery and adventure. Yes, adventure, the forbidden word that had led her step-by-step along the tiny lines of all the maps to this fate.

She'd die soon.

Would her soul be able to navigate its way out of this labyrinth?

Coins! *Coins!* She scrabbled in her pocket and found that collection of metal to toss at the ground to stave off beggars. There were more than two: enough to have one for each eye when the time came.

Except in Ancient Egypt, she had many souls.

One's Ha, or physical body, contained five elements: Bâ, Jb, Ka, Ren and – oh, why did she always get stuck with the shadow... Sheut.

Her Bâ was her personality, but one knew jolly well that one didn't have a personality. Others did, but Earnestine was straightforward and not affected by such frivolous affectations.

Her Jb, her heart, survived death if it was lighter than the feather of the goddess Ma'at, the wife to Thoth. Her heart felt so heavy, so unrequited. As if the very absence of light was weighing her down, and her leaden heart was a few hundredweight versus those ounces of feather.

The Ka was her vital spark... it was colder... so cold.

Her Ren was Earnestine Jemima Deering-Dolittle.

The fifth element was her Sheut, her shadow, but it was so dark that hers had already succumbed.

She knew she would fall.

She felt herself sway, the dark robbing her of a sense of up and down. Exhaustion would take its toll and then she'd drop to the floor, the stone floor would move, and the darts would fire, finding their target easily enough even in this absolute darkness.

She'd thought that already, so she'd gone in circles like a lost explorer.

Perhaps she should step forward and get it over with.

Perhaps she already had, and this was purgatory, Christianity's waiting room.

Wasn't there supposed to be a light to guide you to heaven, and she'd do anything to see again?

Or perhaps she should just sit down, scrunched up in this doorway, and wait. She could compose herself in some suitable posture so that when a future archaeologist discovered her, she might pass on some secret. Die to leave a skeleton pointing the way to the exit.

That explorer would thank their unknown predecessor and be saved.

She pointed now, her hand feeling nothing in the stygian inkiness.

Except she didn't know the way out.

And she wouldn't be found trapped in this tomb.

Her tomb.

Her mind had circled again to that inescapable fact.

A sacrifice to Thoth.

Because the weight of the doors was such that it would take explosives to shift them.

Or a pulley system connected to a steam engine.

Or the right weighting and probably chains.

Or a lever.

Or a magical flying carpet to lift them.

She laughed, a noise that sounded hollow.

"Good day!" she shouted.

Again, the echo, and another, and another – mocking.

"Help!"

A queue of Earnestines, each tinnier and seemingly more desperate, called for someone – anyone – but the next echo was the only reply.

And then silence again.

As silent as the grave.

As cold as a sepulchre.

As dark as a tomb.

Mrs Merryweather

Where was Earnestine?

It was just so typical of Earnestine to leave her in the dark. Woe betide anyone who left Earnestine in the dark, of course.

She must be on the SS *Karnak*, Georgina thought, along with Charlotte. They were probably having tea and cake and playing that silly game of Charlotte's, moving the scones up a level and the Battenberg down a plate. How Georgina looked forward to chiding them.

Her horse followed the one in front and she rocked back and forth in her saddle.

They were nearing the canal, she hoped.

"Just over the next rise," Caruthers shouted.

She smiled, a wan attempt.

Jutting from the sand was a huge doll. It was fascinating, a face staring at her, and so it was some time before she thought to ask.

"What's that?"

Caruthers turned in his saddle. "What's what?"

Georgina pointed.

"It is nothing," Monsieur Jacques shouted.

"No, it's a figure."

"Rien. Ce n'est rien."

"Is that the Statue of the Man?"

"The Statue of the Man is miles behind us," Sir Archibald called down from his perch upon a camel. "That's... my word, a mummy."

The expedition wheeled around to investigate.

Once they were nearer, it was obvious that it was a sarcophagus, just lying on the sand, much like a forgotten picnic basket on the beach.

Everyone dismounted, handing the care of their rides to the native guides. The Egyptians themselves didn't seem interested; if anything, the European fascination with their ancient, and dead, culture bemused them.

The two Englishmen, the Englishwoman and the Frenchmen went closer. Doctor Timon hovered, somewhere between the superstitious guides and the enlightened tourists. Georgina remembered that these were her suspects; one of them could have murdered Mister Rake. There were only a few on her list absent.

"Fascinating," Sir Archibald said as he reached the sarcophagus. "Second Intermediate or possibly Middle Kingdom. A High Priest no less... and his cartouche, let me see, *ah-ha*, here it is. This is a High Priest of Thoth."

"I am not Thoth," Georgina said. "That's what that fake mummy said."

"Yes, yes, and this contains the High Priest of Thoth, the most educated and blah-blah... Amenemope!"

"Isn't Amenemope that High Priest you tried to conjure?" Captain Caruthers said.

"Yes, this is my mummy. What's it doing here?"

"Didn't you order it unloaded?" Caruthers asked.

"I did nothing of the sort."

"Then did it come to life and transport its coffin back to the desert?" Monsieur Jacques said.

"Nonsense... unless Mrs Albright's conjuring is real."

"The mummy's not there," Georgina said.

"Of course he is," Sir Archibald insisted. "I checked the packing myself in the British Museum."

"It's not."

"One way to find out... Tarik, Tarik! Yes, you, get this lid off."

One of the guides, presumably Tarik, ran over, realised what was being asked of him and retreated, shaking with fear.

"Oh, for goodness sake, Tarik, there's no curse," Sir Archibald said. "Must I do everything myself? Captain?"

"The mummy's not there," said Caruthers.

"Nonsense, get the top off."

The Captain shrugged and then hefted the lid of the sarcophagus off. It slid to the ground to reveal the interior.

"Empty!" Sir Archibald shouted.

"We did say," Georgina said.

"How... he rose again? Yes. The conjuring worked. It worked. He will show me the secret of the Book of Thoth. Something I missed." Sir Archibald fumbled in his bag and brought out a hard-backed, foolscap notebook. He opened it. "Oh Amenemope, guide me."

"Is that a copy of the Book of Thoth?"

"This? This is the actual Book of Thoth."

"A modern notebook? Surely not?"

"It is, I assure you. I recognize the handwriting," said Sir Archibald and he showed Georgina the inside pages. There was a mass of birds, men with sticks, eyes and all the other strange, doodled symbols.

"How can you recognize Thoth's handwriting?"

"I have been in communication with Thoth himself."

Georgina scoffed: "By spiritual séance?"

"Not at all. By letter. We've been exchanging correspondence for eighteen months now."

"With the god Thoth?"

"Yes," said Sir Archibald. "And this was his High Priest, Amenemope."

"Amenemope's mummified body is on the SS *Karnak*," Georgina said. She was trying not to smile, trying so very hard, but she saw the smirk on Captain Caruthers face, and she just couldn't help herself.

"You've spoken to him?"

"He's in the cold store. Still quite deceased."

"Then why is his empty sarcophagus here?"

Captain Caruthers' expression fell. "Why here? Why empty?"

Georgina realised, "Oh."

Where was the Captain's machinery, his Difference Engine cogs and wheels, if it wasn't in the sarcophagus?

Miss Charlotte

The boy undid Charlotte's ropes.

"This way," he said.

He led her to the edge of the tent and they crawled underneath, pushing the sand away to make a burrow.

His robe seemed clean; whereas, sand covered Charlotte's pyjama outfit and borrowed white shirt. She brushed it away.

"Now..." Charlotte began, but he had gone.

There were no tracks on the ground.

She glanced about, ducking down to avoid being spotted by the thieves. Her choices were to steal a camel (which she wasn't sure she could control on her own), follow Earnestine into the temple or go with the boy.

Earnestine would probably need rescuing: there were thieves following her after all.

Except the boy was waving to her from behind some rocks about thirty yards away.

She went over.

"Now, perhaps–"

He signalled her to be quiet, then nodded in a direction along the wadi.

Once upon a time, a river had cut this craggy valley in the desert. From a distance, it was invisible, but the temple had been cut into the rock face. The boy led her along one side of this ravine.

"Perhaps you could tell me who you are."

"I am not the god Thoth."

"And I am not Queen Victoria."

"Glad to meet you Miss Victoria Notqueen."

"No... look..."

They came to a section of rocks that jutted out, but instead of going around them, the boy turned into the crag.

"It's a tight squeeze," he said.

"I can manage."

It was a tight squeeze and required her to lean to one side as the narrow opening wasn't vertical. She would have never found it the boy hadn't shown her.

The passage became progressively darker, as they moved away from the blinding sunlight, and the boy disappeared again.

Charlotte paused.

"Excuse me," she whispered.

A hand appeared and pulled her into a side passage.

They made a right-angled turn and then it opened out into a wide corridor, but Charlotte only knew this from their movements and the fact that the walls were further apart.

A green light pulsed in time to a strange sloshing noise.

Once it was strong enough, Charlotte could see the boy shaking a jar that glowed with enough ghoulish illumination to see their surroundings.

The rock had been natural, but it was now square enough to suggest that it had been worked.

Earnestine made such a fuss about being careful about entering a temple, traps and such nonsense, and here was Charlotte just strolling in. She looked forward to seeing Earnestine's gormless expression when she just turned up again. It had been so funny to see her so flabbergasted at the Shrine of the Child. And Charlotte had solved the mystery of the concrete foundations. It would be marvellous to save the day again, except... Earnestine had given her strict instructions.

"Stop," said Charlotte.

"Miss?"

"This leads into the Temple of Thoth, doesn't it?"

"That is correct," the boy replied. "This passage leads to the Alchemical Workshop."

"Alchemical Workshop, fascinating, but the thing is," Charlotte said, "I need... or rather my sister needs help."

"She does?"

"Yes, there's this book."

"The Book of Thoth?"

"That's the one."

"You know where it is?"

"Sir Archibald has it. So, you see, I can't go into the temple until I've found it. Ness, my sister, would be jolly angry."

"We need the book."

"That's it."

"Is Sir Archibald back at your ship?"

"No, he's... somewhere in the desert, north of the Statue of the Man."

"He went the wrong way."

"That's it."

"I have a flying carpet."

"Excellent."

They didn't go the same way out, but instead took another passage and Charlotte was quite turned around when they emerged into the bright sunshine again.

There were half a dozen carpets arranged in a line. Each had a hookah arrangement of pipes and tubes at the back with controls.

Hang on, Charlotte thought, one of these belonged to whoever had tried to buy her. She hesitated, and this gave something away.

"What is it?" the boy asked.

"I was going to be sold to a man with a carpet like that?"

"Zaid the Eunuch?"

"That was him."

"He was buying you for us."

Charlotte backed away: this was an ambush.

"To save you from Azim and his thieves," the boy added.

"Really?"

"Did not Monsieur Jacques explain?"

"No, he didn't," Charlotte said. There had been others around, so he hadn't had the chance to explain. So,

Monsieur Jacques wasn't quite the bounder she'd believed. Or a cad and not a bounder.

"He is in our employ."

"Oh, is he?"

"Such men do anything for gold."

Charlotte checked the surrounding rocks, wondering about escape routes, but even if she could climb up the steep sides of the wadi, where would she go? The thieves were camped at the front of the temple.

The boy walked onto the carpet, stepping over the ruck around the border, and went to the hookah-like apparatus. He turned a tap and the jars and pipes gurgled and belched.

Charlotte paid attention this time and saw the sense of the machinery. It wasn't magic, but rather something that generated clouds underneath the thick material to lift the carpet. The hospital corners created a turned down edge that further trapped the escaping gas and aided the upwards force. Finally, a nozzle could expel some of the gas backwards, controlled by use of a tiller and this propelled the carpet forward.

"Which way?" he asked.

Charlotte pointed: "North from the Statue of the Man."

"I'm afraid north from the Statue of the Man would be thus," the boy explained, indicating a direction differing by a right angle from Charlotte's finger.

"Yes, that's what I meant."

"How will we find them?"

Charlotte smiled. "Vultures."

The boy looked up at the evil birds circling high above.

"Sir Archibald will have the same scouts tracking him," Charlotte explained.

"Climb on," the boy said, easily. Too easily.

"I think not," said Charlotte, backing away.

"I insist."

"No."

Charlotte turned and ran down the wadi, back towards the camp. There were camels and horses. Which were quicker, Charlotte wondered – magic carpets or racing camels?

She could find Earnestine and ask.

Charlotte skidded to a halt.

The very rocks surrounding her came to life, hands appeared, bandaged and filthy, as every crevice gave up its dead. The mummified corpses moaned, clawed towards her with grasping hands, and swivelled their dark eyes in her direction.

Charlotte screamed.

CHAPTER XXIII

Miss Deering-Dolittle

The black, oily waters of the Styx washed over her. She was as light as the feather of Ma'at and yet she sank to the depths. Cook bustled about in the kitchen and then started to feed a baboon.

Earnestine drifted closer and saw that the monkey's feast was her own pickled lungs. Her stomach was in a pie cooking in the oven and a dog stood by, salivating. A man fried her liver and a falcon picked at a plate of tripe.

She felt hollow because they'd taken out her insides.

"One needs those in the afterlife," Earnestine said. "They should be in jars."

The man turned around.

"What does your name mean?" Mister Djehuti asked.

Earnestine shook her head: "I can't remember."

"Are you serious?"

"One's afraid so."

"If you can't remember your name, then I can't write it down, and if I can't write it down, then it won't last forever."

"Oh," Earnestine replied, "and one's forgotten one's shadow."

Captain Caruthers scraped his chair back – "I am not the god Thoth," he said – and left.

"Don't go!"

Earnestine started.

She'd fallen asleep standing up.

For a moment, she didn't know where she was – the gas light wasn't lit – but then she remembered. She was in a room of traps and she was going to die.

When, finally, her Bâ flew away as a human-headed bird – the cold of the stone seeped into her shoulder blades, so she wouldn't even feel her wings growing – no-

397

one would remember her name, her Ren, or that of Doctor Woods. It was too dark to write them down in her notebook.

Poor Doctor Woods, who had entered the temple, lumbered about setting off the traps and abruptly died.

Poor Earnestine.

Except, Doctor Woods had entered this temple some nine years ago. The Royal Expeditionary Society, the *Explorers' Gazette* and *The Times* had published his obituary when he was presumed dead, which was surely a record of his Ren.

There must have been others before Doctor Woods too. There were many explorers who vanished without a trace – her uncle, father and mother, for example, who had gone up the river – and some of those must have followed the line from Child to Man to Ancient One.

Yet, the temple had been ready for Earnestine.

Someone had reset the traps!

Unlike the tombs in the Valley of the Kings that had been broken into, looted and then that was that. This temple's protection remade itself.

As Thoth begat himself.

Earnestine pointlessly closed her eyes, "Of course."

This temple was utter nonsense. The poison would have lost its venom over the centuries, the wood of the crossbows hidden in the walls would have rotted away, even in this dry climate, to say nothing of the tensioned gut that made the bowstrings. This temple must be maintained. And the workers, even in a country without any regard for the health and safety of its workers as this land, would not risk coming through the corridors. There must be another maze of tunnels, running alongside just like their servants' staircase at home in Kensington.

But knowing the secret didn't help.

It still trapped her.

Except the walls had been jolly thick.

Just as pointlessly, she opened her eyes again and looked sideways to view the darkness in that direction.

Jolly thick, she thought, because of the hidden passages in the walls.

She crouched down carefully and took out her box of matches, feeling for the scar her fingernail had made in the cardboard. It was the right way up. She took a match out.

This time she removed her pith helmet before lighting the candle.

Three matches, half an inch of wax – she'd have to make every vital spark count, both in terms of the phosphorus and her own Ka. She lit the candle and secreted the precious box of matches in her bodice.

The room was as before, but the dust had settled.

The doorway formed an alcove away from the deadly floor. She reached and touched the wall with the openings like arrow slits. Hitting and punching did nothing, so she took her kit bag from around her shoulder, repositioned herself and got a good kick in with her Oxford Street boots.

And again.

At least the exertion warmed her up.

The apparent stone suddenly gave way revealing the mud construction beneath. Thank goodness, it wasn't a supporting wall, but just a wattle and daub divider covered in plaster and painted to look like solid stone.

She stabbed it with the end of her umbrella and the point penetrated, and moved freely after the third attack as the end went right through to the other side.

Flipped over, she used the Paragon's handle to tug pieces out. The debris fell to the floor.

A dart zipped across the room as a fallen chunk activated a trip.

Careful, she thought.

The gap was larger now, so she could reach inside with her hand and pull great wodges free. If the lump stayed together in her hand, she flung it into the room and heard the zing of darts.

When she thought that the hole was large enough, she moved her kit along the floor. There was no chance of a run-up, so she just dived into it, scrambling desperately to get through and yet keep her feet off the floor.

Beyond was a small room with crossbows positioned in a wooden frame and wires to control them. If she could just get through. An unlit lantern hung darkly from the ceiling and–

Her pith helmet hit the top of the opening and snuffed out the candle immediately.

She wriggled through in the dark, losing her protective headgear as she did so.

There had been a lantern, she was sure.

She put her hands out as if she was playing blind man's bluff in the nursery, but everywhere seemed colder.

Eventually a crack on the head, painful but delightful, rewarded her.

She ferreted in her bodice and retrieved the box: two matches left.

She struck one, let it catch and then lit the wick inside. It took, fuelled and ready for whenever the servants scurried here to re-arm the deadly traps.

The lantern was stamped *Made in Birmingham.*

Gingerly, she recovered her pith helmet, the brand-new appearance now ruined by dirt and wax.

With her umbrella, she leant back into the space that was so recently destined to be her burial chamber and hooked the strap of her kit bag. It was heavy; the golden jar was more than a few troy pounds in weight.

Earnestine put the lantern down, put the precious box of matches, with its single occupant away, and went through her kit bag.

She had a notebook with some of the temple mapped, but sadly, most of that had been sealed. She had sprinted through other passages, but far too quickly to map or even remember. There were many levels too. She hadn't been prepared for that when she'd started drawing and she'd gone far further east than she'd anticipated, so those corridors were squished up against the edge of the page making a mockery of her scale.

Her compass told her that north was ahead, which led deeper into Thoth's kingdom.

She checked the golden jar and wondered about opening it. If it was fragile, here was not a good place, and it could be a further trap for the unwary. Also, this didn't feel like the prize, but more like a gaudy trinket added to bait a trap for the greedy and stupid. The Philosopher's Stone would be something plain.

If only there was some beacon to show her the way to her objective.

She set off north, skirting to one side as the direct path became impossible.

Rooms betrayed mechanisms to drag walls to one side, chains to lower ceilings, nasty looking spikes primed to spring into action, giant blades poised to swing through narrow slits and many other fiendish contraptions.

Presently, the ground echoed as she walked, and she realised that the rough ground had given way to a polished surface. A faint illumination grew in strength and she came to an elegant, palatial corridor that led to a crossroads lit by lamps set high in alcoves.

A young boy walked past, and stopped suddenly to stare at this apparition of an English young lady. Earnestine realised that she must look a sight, covered as she was in dust, grime and wearing a quite outrageous mix of clothing: burgundy and khaki. And she had one ankle showing!

His robes, by contrast, were monastic, simple, yet well made, and his young head was completely bald. He was clean too, betraying none of the ubiquitous sand that got everywhere in this benighted country.

She raised her finger. "Excuse me, but do you... speak English?"

The boy said nothing.

"Or at a pinch Latin or Greek? Or Egyptian?" She prayed he didn't know French, and her Egyptian went as far as ordering a glass of water and asking for the salt.

"Yes."

"Yes?"

"I know English, Latin, Greek and Egyptian."

"Do you?"

"Yes... are you?"

"Am I?"

The boy frowned. Clearly, she was the strangest thing he had ever seen.

Earnestine rubbed her forehead and pushed her red hair back to give her time to think. Introductions were always tricky, particularly when there wasn't a mutual acquaintance to perform them, and she felt she needed to make a good impression. He might be able to help her.

But, just as she was about to say something, the boy took a breath, "Are you Miss Derring-Do?"

Earnestine felt her jaw muscles tighten: "It's Miss Deering-Dolittle."

"Earnestine, yes."

She wracked her brains, but she was certain she'd never seen this youngster before. "You know me?"

"We met at... forgive me," he said. "You did not meet me at Tanis."

"No, we did not. I'm sure I would have remembered."

The boy smiled as if everything was now understood.

"But you still know me?"

"Yes, Miss Deering-Dolittle," he said. "This way."

"Thank you."

He turned and walked along the corridor, so Earnestine followed.

"By the way, who are you?"

"I am not the god Thoth."

Mrs Merryweather

Earnestine was not on the SS *Karnak*.

Neither was Charlotte.

Where were they?

They'd gone off adventuring, that's what they'd done, leaving Georgina stuck on the ship.

Colonel Fitzwilliam was glad of a brandy once he was rescued from Pippa. Mrs Albright had suffered one of her heads and had retreated to her cabin.

"Where are your sisters?" Colonel Fitzwilliam asked.

"Sir Archibald?" Captain Caruthers said.

"Well, my betrothed has obviously wandered off," Sir Archibald replied. "Clearly, I shall have to have words with her. I mean, where is she when I need her assistance logging the results of my expedition. And I must re-examine the Book of Thoth. There must be a mistake in the translation, perhaps distance, or the direction to the Temple of the Ancient. It's perplexing."

"I could be of assistance," Doctor Timon offered.

"Well..."

"I am a qualified doctor."

"Very well."

Georgina sat with Pippa, trying to keep her calm. Everyone had gathered in the Smoking Room: Sir Archibald, Colonel Fitzwilliam, Captain Caruthers, Doctor Timon, Monsieur Jacques and Mrs Albright.

Six suspects.

There should be nine.

Georgina felt the absence of her two sisters keenly.

"We need to find Earnestine... Miss Deering-Dolittle and Charlotte," she said.

"Ne-ne, Lot-lot," said Pippa, her face screwed up in dismay.

"They're not on board."

No one said anything.

"Someone needs to go and find them!"

Sir Archibald spoke, "Mrs Merryweather, we can't–"

Pippa began crying, a gathering storm of upset threatening to break.

"Find my sisters," Georgina ordered.

"We can't," Sir Archibald said reasonably.

"We have to try."

"Even if we went ashore, where would we look? We did search. Farouk is with them. Mrs Merryweather, you have to understand, the desert stretches for hundreds of miles."

"He is right, ma chérie," Monsieur Jacques said. "They are gone."

"As he said, the Guide is with them," Doctor Timon added. "We have to consider the safety of everyone else."

"I would go, bien sûr, I would. Bien sûr."

Georgina rounded on them: "You are all spineless."

The men were unable to look her in the eye: Colonel Fitzwilliam, Captain Caruthers, Monsieur Jacques, Doctor Timon and...

"Who else is missing?" she demanded. She couldn't think straight.

"Perhaps a lie-down," Doctor Timon suggested. "I have the little sedatives I prescribe for Mrs Albright."

"Who else is not on board?"

"They are very soothing. Just a powder."

"Where's the Pandit?" Georgina asked.

There was silence, even from Pippa.

"Last I saw, he was supervising the unloading of his crate," Captain Caruthers said. "He needed to transport it to India. He had a schedule and we don't know how long we're going to be stranded here."

Sir Archibald harrumphed: the sort of noise someone makes when they've a good hand and their bridge partner has played the wrong card.

"If the sarcophagus was empty," Georgina said, her words cheerfully directed to keep Pippa happy, but intended for the room in general, "then–"

Caruthers was ahead of her. "His crate!"

"I was thinking."

"Gina... Mrs Merryweather's right."

"What's the Pandit done?" Colonel Fitzwilliam asked.

"The cargo... we have to get the ship moving," Caruthers said. "The man has a head start, but overland. We could catch him."

It was Sir Archibald's turn for a bad card as it were: "Hum, ah, well, perhaps I can do something about that."

Sir Archibald put down his brandy, tugged his waistcoat down pointlessly and made his way out.

"Do you know what he meant?" Caruthers asked the Colonel.

"Dashed if I know," said the Colonel.

"I think – don't I, Pippa – that Sir Archibald wanted to explore this part of Egypt," Georgina explained, "so he arranged for the ship to stop here."

"He bribed the Skipper, that Abdul chap," the Colonel said. "I said they took bribes. I said, didn't I?"

"Yes, you did, Colonel," Caruthers agreed.

With a sudden grinding, the engine started up. From the chimneys came thick belches of black smoke as the boiler lurched and complained, before the huff-huff of white steam. The heavy pistons groaned and complained before the first splash. Crew shouted and ran to port, the lines were cast off and drawn in, the ends wet with salt water from the Great Bitter Lake. Finally, they drew in the gangway separating the ship from the land.

On the shore, people waved.

Everyone went on deck to watch.

"Captain, what's going on?" Georgina demanded.

"The Skipper has *fixed* the engine," Caruthers explained. "We're to make up time."

"Captain!"

The Captain's face shone in the light of the afternoon sun, washed-out like an overexposed daguerreotype.

"My duty," he said, and then he swallowed, "is to protect a certain delivery."

"What about Ness and Lottie?"

"Gina," Captain Caruthers started, "Gina."

"Not Gina to you!"

"Mrs Merryweather, I have my duty."

"I'm ordering you."

"You can't."

"I'm the Investigating Officer."

"You can't."

"Captain, it's family or duty."

"My regiment is my family."

Georgina was half-way across the deck to the door before Captain Caruthers had finished. She swept into the Smoking Room. The deck lurched suddenly, a disturbing motion after so long stationary. They were turning; the shadows seemed to rush to the side as if they were trying to abandon ship.

"Colonel!"

"Oh, ah, yes, my dear," Colonel Fitzwilliam replied, moving his brandy glass to one side.

She handed Pippa over without asking.

On deck, the shoreline was already hundreds of yards away, far further than the width of the canal, but then they were on the Great Bitter Lake. Even so, Georgina rushed towards it, channelled by the Sun Deck's rail until she reached the stern.

The encampment on shore was breaking up; tents dropped and disappeared, camels snorted as they stood to amble away, and the ubiquitous beggar boys ran along the shore keeping pace with the paddle steamer. Soon, it would be as if this town had never been there.

Beyond all the activity was the endless, empty desert.

Even if her sisters made it to the shore, they could not reach the ship now.

The Red Ensign fluttered as if waving goodbye.

Miss Charlotte

Charlotte sprinted back.

The boy stood by the controls of one of them, adjusting the main valve to generate clouds beneath his magic carpet.

"Mummies!"

"They are my friends," said the boy, his calm face surprised for once.

"What?"

It had been a trap!

Charlotte hurtled towards him and jumped onto the carpet. Like a mattress, her landing caused the boy to spring upwards. She pushed him, and he tumbled backwards to fall into the rippling clouds generated by the sorcery. Her thin, borrowed shirt was no protection from the icy blast and she felt the cold.

At the hookah of pipes and controls, she pulled the handle, twisted the tap and the carpet started to move. By turning the tiller, she spun the carpet, and the whooshing exhaust blasted white gas over the approaching mummies, like a raging steam funnel.

The creatures recoiled.

The carpet leapt forward, hit the wall of the wadi, crumpled and then bounced back, sliding uncontrollably.

"Go forward!" Charlotte shouted at it.

The monsters tried to outflank her on both sides.

The force of the gas increased – she'd got the sense of the controls – and the carpet glided off leaving the mummies to scatter in the white wake. The gossamer on her legs and the white shirt billowed and flapped, and her blonde hair streamed behind her as she sped away.

The mummies rushed towards the other carpets.

She had a head start, but she knew they'd give chase.

Trying to go as fast as she dared, she weaved along the route of the ancient watercourse. Long ago, water had cut deep into the rock, winding in big loops, splitting – *that was close!* – and re-joining. Boulders littered the route like those infernal machines laid by the Russians in the Crimean War to catch Royal Navy ships.

The walls were too steep and sharp to escape.

And soon enough, the pursuit appeared.

At first, it was a single flying carpet overhead, rushing along the top of the canyon to catch up on her right. It must have taken a straight line across the desert to intercept her: her route curved one way more than the other.

Another carpet appeared behind her carrying three bandaged mummies, and it was gaining.

And another.

Her head start had gone, and her pursuers knew it. On both sides, other carpets raced to come alongside.

Surely, she should be faster, she thought, because her craft was lighter.

But the monstrous crew acted like yachtsmen leaning out to prevent a boat from heeling. They knelt at the front to force the bow down, whereas, on Charlotte's carpet, the weight was at the stern, so the front rode up and the gas pushed forward, counteracting the propulsive force. She needed to stand at the other end *and operate the controls* – some tiller extension perhaps.

One of the mummies behind her leaned over the edge and grabbed a stone.

Charlotte ducked, as she just managed to thread her carpet into a gap in the rock cut by the wind.

The top of her control clanged, a stone ricocheted off and rolled along her carpet.

She glanced over her shoulder – glanced forward, turning as the wadi forced her along its ancient route – as they threw things at her!

Two carpets behind her, coming alongside, tried to box her in. A mummy reached out to grab a trailing tassel. Others readied themselves to board her vehicle.

The carpets touched, the endless stream of white gas becoming a geyser-like wall of rushing force. The edge, deformed under the pressure, and then suddenly they locked together.

Mummies rushed across, their steps tilting the undulating surface such that the rush of gas reappeared. The jet caught a mummy halfway across and flung him upwards, his arms flailing as he was tossed into the sky.

Everyone else struggled to find their balance.

Charlotte steered into the opponent and lowered the pressure, so her carpet slipped beneath the other like a knife under a tin top. Then she hit the power. Hers rose, lifting the opposition, and the mummies on her carpet stumbled back.

Freezing white clouds engulfed everything; a whiteout, as the other craft clambered over, and then, its downward force split between her carpet and the desert, so the thing flipped over.

It spun, cartwheeled to create a spiral of whizzing white in the air, stuck in the ground, deformed and then bounced away, before connecting against the wall in a blizzard of debris.

The thick mist cleared instantly.

Two mummies on her carpet faced Charlotte as she stood by the hookah-like apparatus. They spread out, hands upward, clawing the air as they rehearsed snatching her away and ripping her to shreds.

She turned the craft again.

Something in her expression must have given it away.

The lead mummy's eyes widened, the whites almost flashing with light, and he turned and screamed.

An overhanging rock.

Suddenly only one mummy stood on her carpet.

It grabbed at her, caught hold and tugged her away, but she slipped out of the big white shirt.

Two other carpets came up, gaining, as Charlotte's craft lost speed. They sandwiched her between them, the rush of vertical gas shooting up once more.

Charlotte ran across, threw herself through, like jumping into an upturned waterfall. For a moment, the shock of the cold stunned her.

She landed on the other carpet, fell forward and rolled, coming to a stop just at the edge.

She leapt to her feet.

The carpet's pilot didn't know what to do.

Charlotte shoulder-charged him and he disappeared into the white exhaust.

She took control of this craft.

The walls of the wadi had collapsed ahead forming a ramp.

She aimed at that.

Up she went, quick, and out on to the open desert.

Other carpets followed. Each carpet left a long trail of white, a long line showing its passage, and they made huge circular loops, swirling fogs that crisscrossed and evaporated.

Those chasing closed in.

Faster too.

No longer did they need to dodge the obstacles in the wadi, so this was worse. In the desert, there was nowhere to hide, no obstacle to manoeuvre around, no trees, no overhanging rocks, no twists and turns.

High above and far behind, Charlotte could just see the specks that circled: vultures marking the Temple's position.

She set course for the sun.

Except the other carpets flew after her.

Both sides: Charlotte glanced right and left, and they both appeared about to smash into her.

One did; the turned down edges acted to cushion the bump, but a mummy jumped across.

Charlotte let go of the controls, grabbed the attacker and pushed him. That, and his momentum, caused him to fly over towards the carpet on the other side.

She had hold of the end of a bandage.

The mummy spun in the air as his disguise unwound before he landed awkwardly.

Back at the controls, she looped the bandage around the hookah's frame just in time.

It snapped taut.

Her vehicle slalomed to one side, the attachment causing a quick turn.

On the enemy carpet, the mummy jerked and flailed as he was tugged, and unravelled as the distance between them increased.

Another carpet came between them.

Charlotte steered, and the long bandage stretched across to catch that pilot unawares. The strip flexed before pinging him off the back of his craft.

The bandage rippled in the air like a streamer.

When it went tight again, Charlotte's carpet seemed to stop in mid-air.

She tumbled forward, rolling, until there was no more deep pile to support her. For a moment, she was airborne and in the next, she had a face full of sand.

Half-on, half-off – she struggled to drag herself to safety.

The carpet bucked.

At the engine, the collection of tubes and pipes spluttered. The bandage had yanked it out of shape. A bubble of clear air forced itself around the contraption, squeezed along by the force of the vapours, to join with another trapped pocket of atmosphere.

Charlotte rolled back to the controls.

It was running out of steam and there was nowhere to shovel in more coal.

The carpet hit something and buffeted Charlotte from side to side. It was lower; the clouds generated beneath couldn't raise it as high as before, and so she no longer glided smoothly over the terrain.

Other carpets were surrounding her again. There were trails of smoke criss-crossing the desert as if dozens of steam engines had hurtled off the rails.

Balloons rose if you threw things out!

But there was nothing to jettison, except herself.

Shouts!

She could hear them over the reduced volume of the apparatus.

Two carpets came up in line astern.

Could she?

There was nothing else for it.

She gave the control a last, desperate twist, it gasped, burped the air out and the fog pea-souped behind her.

Charlotte jumped.

As she vanished through the jet, she felt a glorious cooling, a relief from the oppressive heat, then she hit the baking sand and rolled, throwing herself as flat as she could.

The next magic carpet went right over her.

Like a snowball down the back of her neck, the arctic blast of the downward jet chilled her to the bone. The force pushed her into the ground, cooking her underside.

Then it was over.

She jumped up, pulling her legs up high to clear the next magic carpet as it slid majestically beneath her.

The two men on the vehicle saw her come out of the cloud and their jaws dropped in unison.

She barrelled into the pilot, striking him and gaining his forward momentum to stay on the carpet, while he cannoned off into the volatile space behind.

With no-one at the controls, the magic carpet veered wildly.

Charlotte lost her footing, bouncing around like a child jumping on a mattress.

She kicked at the other man, but he was too large to be thrown off. So, they fell, struggled and fought, until they tumbled apart, taking up opposite corners as if they were prize-fighters.

Charlotte jumped as high as she could and came down on the corner.

The carpet rocked; the opposite corner see-sawed to bump the mummy aloft.

Charlotte hit him like a battering ram and, suddenly, he was no longer there.

She saw a figure struggling to his feet as she grabbed the levers to regain control.

This magic carpet had considerably more *oomph*.

Except, she'd just run out of endless desert!

The canal!

The other carpets had cut off any possible escape left or right.

She was going too fast.

There weren't any brakes.

She couldn't stop!

It was too late.

The flying carpet reached the embankment, lurched dangerously downhill and then sped into the water. Charlotte took a deep breath ready for the inevitable dunking. Perhaps she could swim across the canal, her wispy outfit wouldn't soak and drag her under, but the channel was wide and probably treacherous, full of crocodiles and poisonous snakes.

And yet she was still dry.

The carpet had bent in the middle, briefly, before straightening, as the vehicle shot across the water like a stone skipping over the surface.

This craft worked over water!

She turned the carpet, casting a spray of water in a wave, to head south along the canal towards the Great Bitter Lake.

Without bumps, slopes and treacherous rocks, the going was smoother and faster, much faster, but only as quick as the pursuing carpets.

Chapter XXIV

Miss Deering-Dolittle

This was the second person she'd met who was not the god Thoth and for the second time, she admitted to herself that she was not Queen Victoria. She corrected herself: in fact, she had met many, many people who were not the god Thoth or indeed Queen Victoria. Indeed, all the people she had ever met fitted in both categories.

The boy took her to a large room with columns along the walls suggesting further alcoves hidden away behind ornate curtains. Sunlight poured in from skylights above. In the centre was a pool of water and an ibis bird waded across like a peacock in the gardens of a country house.

"Master," said the boy, "may I present Miss Deering-Dolittle."

Out from somewhere, Earnestine didn't see where, stepped the dazzling form of Mister Djehuti.

Earnestine startled, not knowing whether to hide her ugly scar or the wanton display of ankle.

"Miss Deering-Dolittle?"

"Mister Djehuti."

He bowed, and Earnestine saw that his head was smooth. She realised that this was not natural baldness, but rather that he shaved his head like the boy's. She glanced at the boy: they were priests.

"Ah," she said. "Mister Djehuti, I understand. You are both followers of Thoth."

"Not exactly."

"Then pray explain."

"I am the god Thoth."

Mrs Merryweather

"Ahoy!"

Georgina went up on deck to see what the commotion was about, carrying a wriggling Pippa.

Captain Caruthers was there, Doctor Timon and Monsieur Jacques from one direction, and Sir Archibald and Mrs Albright from another.

She heard the whooshing noise first.

Astern – Georgina blinked in amazement – speeding towards them was a magic carpet!

It flew low along the lake from the canal to the north. Its direction was obvious because the magic carpet left a condensation trail behind it leading all the way to... other magic carpets!

"Look!" she shouted.

Pippa pointed.

Caruthers had seen: he checked his revolver.

The others followed suit.

"Sacré bleu."

Georgina looked around but couldn't see Monsieur Jacques.

A woman on the carpet waved. "Captain!"

"Lot-lot," said Pippa.

The carpet came alongside the ship, hovering on clouds trapped beneath it, and a Jezebel stood at the back about to smoke a hookah.

"Gina! Gina!" the harem girl shouted, waving.

"Lot-lot," said Pippa, waving back.

Georgina was about to shift around to prevent Pippa from seeing such a shameless display, when a second shock stunned her senses.

The girl was... but... and... but without question... and wearing practically nothing.

"Charlotte," Georgina whispered, trying not to attract anyone's attention, "you're wearing nothing."

Charlotte shouted back, "What!?"

Captain Caruthers leant over the railing. "Lottie?"

It was too late now, everyone had seen her. Everyone was ogling her. Even the Egyptian crew.

"Charlotte Deering-Dolittle!" Georgina yelled. "What are you wearing?"

"They're pyjamas."

"I can see... and also... and... what about sunburn?"

Charlotte looked away to make a face.

"Just stop that and come up here."

"I can't."

"Of course you can."

"If I stop," Charlotte shouted, "then the carpet stops flying."

"That's a good thing."

"And then sinks!"

"That's... oh."

"Captain," Charlotte shouted, "I need a gun."

"Lee Enfield or Webley?"

"One hand," Charlotte said with a wave.

"I only have my own revolver."

Georgina fussed in her bag. "Captain, I have this one."

Caruthers took it. "Rake's gun," he said.

"Throw it here," Charlotte yelled.

"Overarm or underarm?"

"Just chuck it."

Captain Caruthers checked it, loaded it and then flicked it down. It spun as it fell before hitting the middle of the central golden diamond.

Charlotte reached across, the magic carpet juddering as she let go of the controls, but she snatched it up in time.

"Now the book!" Charlotte shouted up.

"What book?" Caruthers asked.

"The Book of Thoth. Sir Archibald has it. Rake stole it for him."

Georgina needed to correct her: it's *Mister* Rake, Charlotte; but Georgina's teeth were chattering. It was cold. Why was it cold? It was the middle of the day in Egypt. These clouds under the magic carpet must have

416

been teleported from a higher altitude. Boats and ships made sense, but flying on a rug should be confined to nursery make-believe.

"Nonsense," insisted Sir Archibald. "It's my property."

"I'm sorry, Lottie," Caruthers shouted down.

Charlotte throttled back on the artificial clouds and the magic carpet idled. "It's for Ness."

The Captain straightened up. "Sir Archibald."

"It is mine, I say."

"Hand it over," Caruthers said.

"I will not."

The Captain grabbed Sir Archibald by his lapels, yanking him around. There was going to be no argument. "I insist."

"It's in my room."

Captain Caruthers pushed Sir Archibald away.

A cry went up from the other side of the ship, "Mon dieu, repoussez les assaillants!"

The approaching storm clouds of the other magic carpets had closed in. There were mummies on them. Fake or otherwise, they looked dangerous.

Captain Caruthers took up the shout. "Prepare to repel boarders!"

He moved aft.

The carpets zipped past, then turned to circle. They were fast, faster than someone could run the length of the deck.

"Gina!" Charlotte was craning her neck trying to track the enemy. "Get the book!"

Georgina held onto Pippa. "Right."

Captain Caruthers worked along towards the bow, aiming, always aiming, trying to get a shot without wasting precious ammunition.

He fired.

Georgina ducked in fright and held Pippa tighter still.

Out in the lake, a carpet was hit. White gas shot upwards as if from a burst pipe. The force caused the flying apparatus to wobble and buck. The pilot struggled with the tiller, but then he regained control and the carpet carried on.

A man on the carpet raised his weapon.

Georgina saw the fire sprout from the barrel, but she didn't hear any shot above the splashing of the paddles and the grinding of the machinery.

"Take cover," Caruthers ordered.

Yes, she had to get Pippa to safety. She ducked into the connecting passage and hurried to the Smoking Room.

"Colonel."

"By George, but–"

With the child safely plonked on the Colonel's lap, Georgina hurried outside again and along to the cabins, conscious of the white clouds gathering like a fog rolling off the Thames to plunge day into night.

She knocked on Sir Archibald's cabin door.

"What is it?"

"Sir Archibald, it's Mrs Merryweather."

On the other side, Sir Archibald harrumphed, "This has no bearing on your case."

"For goodness sake, Sir Archibald, I am the Investigating Officer."

"You have no authority over the book."

"Open this door!"

"I will not."

The ship's engine changed note, the machinery becoming more desperate.

Georgina took a deep breath: it was an emergency after all. As Investigating Officer, she should surely investigate and nowhere should be out of bounds, even places beyond decency for a widowed woman to visit alone.

The door was locked.

Georgina put her shoulder to it and the bracket gave way.

"Mrs Merryweather!" Sir Archibald said, stuffing something into his jacket. "This is an outrage!"

"Yes," said Georgina fixing him with her best mother's glare, "but I won't report you if you hand it over now."

She held out her hand.

Sir Archibald hesitated, his hand fluttered by his lapel.

Georgina gesticulated savagely, "ARCH-I-BALD."

He took the object out of his jacket like a caught schoolboy.

Georgina snatched it off him, momentarily worried that she had damaged a precious historical document before she realised it was a modern hardback notebook.

"Is this it?"

"Yes, my dear."

It all seemed jolly unlikely. She flicked through the pages and saw that it was full of hieroglyphics, all Greek to her. Well, not Greek, which she knew a little, but ancient Egyptian.

"And I want it back, Mrs Merryweather."

Just outside the door, she met Doctor Timon, who blocked her way.

"You have the book?" he said.

"I do, Doctor."

"May I see it?"

"Seriously, we're under attack and I haven't the time."

He didn't move. "It is the secret of immortality. Imagine the good that could be done – that I could do – against the scourges of typhoid, malaria, smallpox, cholera, measles, mumps and rubella. Perhaps even the female hysterics."

Georgina could see his point. "I'm sorry."

"But Mrs Merryweather, I must insist," he said, and he snatched at the book.

She had taken enough cutlery off Pippa for her reflexes to be fast enough.

"Mrs Merryweather."

"TIMON!"

It was Captain Caruthers; thank goodness there were men on the ship ready to protect her.

"Thank you, Doctor," she said, and she made her way past.

The magic carpets chasing the ship were nowhere to be seen.

She reached the railing and looked down.

Charlotte had gone.

Miss Charlotte

Charlotte revved the tubes and pipes, and the freezing vapours surged behind her. The magic carpet lifted higher, shot forwards and then, with a push on the tiller, Charlotte guided it back around the front of the SS *Karnak*.

The other carpets were upon her.

Shots rang out from behind and above.

That cad Jacques ran along the deck firing his automatic.

Charlotte headed straight for the bank. The magic carpet had managed the transition from land to water, so she hoped the tactic would work in reverse.

A carpet followed her, but the others concentrated on the ship. There was so much white cloud now that it was hard to tell how many. The Great Bitter Lake vanished beneath the fog.

The SS *Karnak* was under full steam attempting to escape, but it was an uneven race. The heavy, sluggish steamboat heaved itself through the water, thrashing the surface with its paddles. The magic carpets, on the other hand, flitted with utter ease, barely marking the rippling water as they zoomed forward. They zigzagged, not for any reason, but simply to show off. They knew they could catch the SS *Karnak*. There was only the lake, and then another stretch of long canal ahead. Once there, the ship would not even be able to manoeuvre, and it was miles before the Gulf of Suez.

It was akin to greyhounds chasing a tortoise.

But she had her own problems.

Her carpet's bow was high, the problem with having no crew, so she managed to shift from water to land easily, dodged some panicked camels and made it over the rise.

The other carpet slammed into the shoreline, beached and tumbled.

With height gained, Charlotte's view of the lake was improved.

The SS *Karnak* turned, veering sharply to port.

A magic carpet, speeding alongside, did not realise, bumped against the hull by the stern and then smashed into the turning paddles of the steamer. The carpet shredded and tore as the wheel pulled it up and then into the paddlebox. The wood splintered, the foreign body threatening to jam the mechanism, but then the debris threaded through to be ejected out the front, pulled downwards and plunged underwater.

The lake seemingly boiled as the gas generation machine spewed beneath the ship with a force that caused the entire vessel to pitch alarmingly.

Another speeding carpet had time to veer away, but the gap between the steamship and the bank was not wide enough. Despite being turned, the carpet continued forward, and crashed into the side, smashing into the sand, but then climbing up the bank, turning and descending again to fly across the lake in front of the ship.

Charlotte turned to fly back to the water; she had to help.

The huge ship hit the bank, the paddles clattering as they thumped earth, and then they moved away. Even so, the gap between them and the land was too narrow for the magic carpets.

"To the starboard side!" Captain Caruthers shouted.

Charlotte zoomed back over the water and into the fray. She fired, accurate as ever, and the pilot of one magic carpet threw his arms aloft. He didn't so much fall as his vehicle slid from under him.   He splashed down, disappearing from sight.

Another craft hovered over the land, sliding next to the battered paddles on the port side.   Mummies jumped off, barefoot but sure, and scrambled onto the deck to be met by crew and passengers alike.

Charlotte came alongside, keeping away from the churning paddles of the steamer.   The big wooden construction was like a mangle, ready to chop her and her carpet into pieces.

Georgina appeared above her, leaning over the railing.

"Here it is," Georgina shouted, but then she hesitated. "I can't... I'll miss."

"Gina!"

"It'll blow away."

Charlotte realised Georgina was right.   The gun had been heavy, so it had dropped straight down onto the carpet, but the paper would catch the wind and the book would flap away like a bird.

And Georgina was hopeless at throwing.

It had to be weighed down with something, but what?

"Gina," Charlotte shouted, "jump aboard."

"I can't get on that, it defies natural history," Georgina hollered.   "And it's down there!"

"Jump!"

"Look, I think–"

"Jump!!!"

CHAPTER XXV

Miss Deering-Dolittle

"Thoth!"

"You are here," Mister Djehuti... Thoth said.

"Yes."

"I knew you would come."

Was the man really a god, Earnestine wondered? "Was it precognition?"

"You followed my clues."

"Clues?"

"The hints I gave you as we sat outside the British Residence in Tanis."

"Oh, yes..." Earnestine said. She bit her lip. She'd meant to write down his words, so she'd remember them, but one thing and another, and it had slipped her mind. "Those clues."

"Come, let us talk as we did in Tanis," Thoth said. "Eat, drink, become one."

"I must save my sister, Charlotte."

"There is no need to worry," said Thoth. "My servants are taking care of her."

"Thank you," Earnestine said, and she took the golden statue out of her kit bag. "In that case, this is yours."

He took it and handed it to the boy, without giving it a second glance.

"You'll be wanting to return it to its place once you've reset all your traps," Earnestine said. "It's bait."

Thoth nodded, "To tempt the unwary and the foolish. They find the entrance and the puzzles, and assume they are on the right path."

"The Philosopher's Stone and all the alchemy stories, aren't they simply myths?" Earnestine said. "My sister, Georgina, Mrs Merryweather, is quite sure."

"Are you certain?"

"I think.... yes."

"Alchemy has been used as an excuse by charlatans, it is true. However, it is truly the study of what one chemical does with another, and by extension, what forces and properties hold sway in the universe."

"Our expression for that is 'Natural History'."

"Or 'science'."

"Yes."

"We have discovered here that some chemicals create fire, others poison, others expand rapidly to create the gaseous material that our carpets fly upon, and so forth."

"You said 'we'. Who are the others?"

"Myself and those studying to become me."

"Your disciples?"

"I suppose."

"Those who are not Thoth."

"How astute," Mister Djehuti said, smiling. "How did you find the temple's puzzles?"

"Quite... exhilarating."

"The real secret is kept elsewhere."

Earnestine felt her mouth go dry. It was true. Here was the living proof of the Philosopher's Stone, a piece of the Tree of Life, somewhere here. The temple traps were a diversion, something to occupy the inquisitive and satisfy the greedy. The true prize was nearby.

"If you are Thoth–"

"I am."

"How old are you?"

"I am 78 centuries old."

Earnestine snorted: "How can you be... 1,800 years older than the age of the world?"

"Do you mean the Abrahamic theory of the age of the world?"

"The world is 6,000 years old," Earnestine said, glad that Georgina wasn't present with her theories about many thousands, or even millions, of years.

"Their faiths come somewhat after that of Ra, Isis and myself."

"But surely–"

"The Egyptians built pyramids a thousand years before the time of Abraham. And millennia before the Age of the Pharaohs, it was the Age of the Gods."

"Oh."

She had been so proud of her extensive knowledge of antiquity, and yet here she was talking with a man for whom everything she knew was modern history.

"You are thirsty," Djehuti or Thoth, she wasn't sure which name to use, said.

"I am."

"One Two Thirty."

"I am here, Master," said the boy with a bow.

"One Two Thirty, fetch water and fruit for my guest."

"At once, Master." The boy lowered his head again in supplication before he hurried away.

"Let me take your headpiece," Thoth said. He reached forward and took her pith helmet, as a kind host would do upon the arrival of a guest. He looked inside, saw her name and nodded: "Your Ren, I see."

"But the boy? He has no Ren, he's just a number?" Earnestine said. "One Two Thirty?"

"It can be a name. He is my servant," Thoth replied. "There have been many. They strive for a higher name."

"But One, Two... *Thirty*?"

"I count in sixties as the Babylonians did."

"Ah... so, er..." but Earnestine couldn't multiply sixty times sixty plus two times sixty and add thirty in her head. "A lot."

"Yes."

"But why not names?"

"I have had many servants. They look alike."

"Oh."

"Unlike yourself. You do not look like anyone else I have ever met. Fair skinned with red hair. I met a Viking once in Constantinople, Rangvald, but never one of the Norse maidens."

"When was this?"

"Recently, no more than a thousand years ago."

"Because of a piece of petrified tree?"

"Stone and paper, yes."

"But, if what you are telling me is true," Earnestine pondered, "how can you be immortal, due to something that grew nearly two thousand years after you were born?"

"Two thousand years?"

"The Tree of Life in the Garden of Eden."

"Yes, I remember," Thoth said, looking upwards as if to see the memory floating above him. "I walked there once, I recall my footprints in the mud by the river."

"And the Tree of Knowledge?"

"Yes."

"And the Tree of Life?"

"That too."

"Did you eat the fruit?"

"I was already immortal."

"Then it's true," Earnestine said. "As Sir Archibald deduced, the Garden of Eden has been transplanted here."

Thoth smiled. "It is an allegory, a story for children. How the world came about, the importance of caring for the animals, how men changed from hunters to farmers, and so forth. Not literally true. There are many other creation myths. The ancient Egyptians believed that it was Amun created everything from the waters of chaos. I myself made the calculations necessary to construct the heavens and the Earth."

"You?"

Thoth nodded, "And I was not born. I begat myself."

"How can you beget yourself?"

The boy, One Two Thirty, returned with a tray containing a copper jug, goblet and a bowl of apples.

"Please," said Thoth, pouring the water.

Earnestine put her pack and umbrella down, so she could take the goblet. She drank; it was the most wonderful drink she had ever enjoyed.

When she'd had her fill, Thoth handed her an apple: "From our own small orchard," he said.

Earnestine held the precious fruit in her hand, bit into it, and again felt the exhilaration of the taste. The juice dribbled down her chin, quite indecently.

"To beget myself is the secret of immortality."

"And you could make me immortal?" Earnestine asked between bites.

"You are already immortal," he said, smiling.

Earnestine swallowed the last of the apple, almost choking, before she replied, "How?"

"I will show you." He held out his arm to signify one of the passages that led away from the antechamber.

"You have the secret!"

"Bring your water."

Earnestine put her kit bag over her shoulder again, collected her goblet and her brolly, and walked after him. They passed through a heavy curtain.

"Then your notebook, the Book of Thoth, explains the secret of immortality."

Thoth laughed: "It is the secret."

"Are you saying that the book allows one to cast a magic spell?" Earnestine said, and she laughed too at the absurdity of it. "Does one just write one's name down and one lives forever?"

"Yes."

Mrs Merryweather

Georgina jumped.

Her skirts billowed outwards until she thumped into the centre of the magic carpet. It sagged as if she was an iron dropped onto a pile of laundry, and great gouts of white smoke surged around them. It might have been lovely to land on, like a mattress stuffed with cumulus, but the carpet had a tough weave.

The book fell from her grip and came to rest next to her on the central, diamond-shaped medallion pattern. The wind blew over its pages, flicking through them until it came to the last page with any writing. There was a word tucked amongst the eyes, birds and dancing men, a name written in the Latin alphabet: 'Earnestine'.

"That's odd," Georgina said aloud as she rescued the book.

She struggled over to Charlotte across the uneven surface.

"No, Gina," Charlotte instructed, "sit at the front!"

Charlotte steered them away from the ship in a large arc and then aimed directly towards the shore.

"Pardon?"

"You need to hold the front down, so I can get some speed."

"No... no, surely we want to go slower."

"Gina."

Georgina struggled back across the lumpy carpet, which seemed to come alive and bulge disconcertingly. She balanced on her feet, one foot higher than the other, until the pressure increased and the surface grew taut. Even then, floating a few feet above the water, it dipped under her weight. She made the few strides needed to stand dangerously close to the edge before sinking to her knees. The surface of the water, rushing under the fringe at the end, was jolly close. On a ship, you looked down on the waters from a position of superiority over the elements, not *sideways!*

They were so low.

Her fingers clawed into the upholstery almost trying to tear the fibres from the fabric in order to hold on.

"Further."

"Further? Don't be insane."

"Gina."

The edge was cold – she'd assumed that the clouds were steam from some miniature boiler, but they weren't. Whatever the propulsion, the vapour mixed with the froth of their bow wave and splashed upwards. The chemical apparatus must be generating gas that expanded, and so cooled the environment. A frost formed on her face. Someone had made some sort of vapour compression device that let out gas, which froze as it expanded. And they'd disguised it as sorcery from a fairy story.

"Now move further back," Charlotte commanded.

"Sorry?"

"Further back so that the front comes up."

"Comes up?"

"Because we're going onto land."

"Land?"

Charlotte yanked the tiller around, but the magic carpet was going at such a speed that it just turned and carried on in a straight line, going sideways.

"Lottie! Look out! Look out! We're going to crash!"

The shore, a vast edifice of sand and sharp rocks, hurtled towards them. Charlotte turned directly towards it. Georgina threw her hand in front of her face and staggered backwards.

"That's it," said Charlotte.

The bow came up as if they were about to shoot upwards into the heavens, but their flight transitioned from water to land, throwing Georgina about in a way utterly unlike boats, coaches or trains.

Georgina kept hold of the book and crawled to Charlotte. It was like trying to negotiate a bumpy mattress stuffed with fighting dogs.

"Do we lean?" Georgina shouted.

"What?"

"Lean... like on a safety bicycle?"

"I don't know."

Charlotte operated handles and taps; the apparatus gurgled and hissed sending a jet out backwards. It seemed

Charlotte knew what she was doing, standing there with her hair streaming out behind her and her gossamer bloomers fluttering in the breeze revealing... well, revealing.

"What are you wearing?" Georgina demanded.

"Don't start."

"I can see your legs," Georgina said, her voice high-pitched. "And those are technically trousers! Charlotte Deering-Dolittle, only you could flaunt your legs and commit rampant bloomerism at the same time."

"Oh Gina, it wasn't my fault. It was... never mind."

"Never mind."

"Ooh, look, a rock."

"Where... what!" Georgina exclaimed ducking down and hiding her head.

And then Georgina realised, she'd been had, and as she turned to berate Charlotte, she saw white plumes behind them in the desert.

Georgina screamed, "Mummies! Undead mummies on flying carpets!!!"

"Don't be a gulpy," Charlotte shouted back. "They're in disguise."

"Oh, that makes it so much better," Georgina said. "Why are they dressed as bodies raised from the dead?"

"I imagine it's to frighten people and give them an advantage."

"Well, I wish they wouldn't."

"Here take this," Charlotte said, "and keep that there and this right over."

"I can't fly a magic carpet," Georgina complained, but then saw how it all worked. She'd once driven a steam engine, after all.

She took the icy controls.

Adventures are all jolly fine, she thought, but should they put their faith in what was, after all, just tapestry?

Miss Charlotte

Charlotte checked her gun. Three rounds left – not good.

Just hold your breath, Charlotte thought.

The carpet slalomed under her feet.

"Steady, please."

"I'll give you steady... yes, of course."

The carpet levelled, more gas forced down rather than behind them, but it also slowed. That was fine, Charlotte thought, as she wanted to even the odds a little.

The Webley was heavy, and Charlotte's fingers were numb with the cold from the pipes.

The foremost carpet was close. The hookah at the back appeared as big as the foresight and the three mummies watched carefully.

Aim...

BANG!

She hit. With her first attempt too.

The enemy hookah burst open. The jet from the pursuing carpet no longer blasted out backwards, but shot out sideways as well. The vehicle slewed to the right and then, suddenly began to spin, whizzing around in a spiral of sand and venting gas.

Round and round.

Tiny figures tumbled away as if flung from a hare-brained playground roundabout, then it keeled over and became a huge expanding sphere of white.

"Tug that!" Charlotte commanded, pointing to the valve that controlled the rear jet.

She ran to the front, tracking another carpet.

The mummies realised and pulled away.

Her weight forced the front down and the carpet accelerated.

They whizzed over the dunes, blasting sand in all directions where the gaseous outflow escaped from the downturned edges of the carpet. The hookah arrangement at the back gurgled, and spat angrily, as Georgina adjusted a dial and the main tap. Even in the desert sun, frost formed where the jet appeared.

The pursuing carpets fanned out behind them, one taking a dune edge and overtaking.

"Gina! Go into the smoke."

"What? We won't be able to see."

"Neither will they. We're more used to pea-soupers."

Georgina pulled the tiller and directed the carpet into the gas trail of the enemy. Everything went white.

"Turn in!"

The whirlwind buffeted and chilled.

Charlotte struggled over to the back. "Two-dimensional thinking," she said. She found her sister, put her hand on the controls and forced back a lever.

"We need to–"

"Stop," Charlotte said, turning the tiller.

The carpet lurched, flew off a rise and then fell like a leaf into the dip.

"Down," Charlotte directed, guiding her sister down to lie on the rug.

The roar of magic carpet receded until it was quiet, like a still winter's night.

"Now what?" Georgina whispered.

"We wait until they've gone and then we follow them."

"Follow? Whatever for?"

"They came from where I left Ness."

"And what's she doing?"

"Exploring a tomb."

"Typical."

Hesitantly, Charlotte rose, looking around through the clearing mist. "Where are they?"

"I don't know."

There was no sign of their pursuit and the carpets left no tracks. Indeed, the downward blast obliterated any marks by sweeping the desert smooth.

Charlotte pointed.

"What?" Georgina asked.

"Vultures."

Georgina squinted to make out the tiny circling dots as Charlotte powered up the magic carpet. When they were aloft again speeding along, Charlotte kept the vultures to her centre-left.

"We need to sneak up," Charlotte explained, "so I don't want to just come over the hill and be spotted."

"But we might lose our way."

"We can't. There's a canyon and–"

The ground gave way suddenly as they came upon the wadi. Charlotte thought – hoped – the carpet would jump the gap.

It didn't.

Instead, it dropped, stomach-churningly, before it floated down into the gorge with the walls whizzing past, perilously close.

The clouds beneath them cushioned the fall, but the apparatus took a terrific knock. It split and gas gushed upwards, condensing out quickly to fall as snow.

Charlotte and Georgina stood looking at each other as the white flakes settled. It looked as if Charles Dickens had rewritten the *Arabian Nights* as a sequel to *A Christmas Carol*.

The two sisters couldn't help laughing.

"Come on," said Charlotte, wiping the snow off herself and flinging a portion at Georgina.

"What do we need to do?" Georgina asked.

"Sneak back to the temple, defeat the thieves, overcome the mummies and rescue Ness from a tomb of deadly traps."

"Oh... just that?"

"Yes... and give her the Book of Thoth."

"This?"

"Yes."

"Then we can all go back to the ship?"

"So you can solve the murder, yes."

"Oh."

Chapter XXVI

Miss Deering-Dolittle

"This is my Library."

The room was far more spacious and considerably brighter than the North Kensington Public Library on the corner of Lancaster Road and Ladbroke Grove. It would be hard to imagine this luxurious seating and profligate use of space in that cold, Gothic building.

As they entered, Thoth casually pointed to one item after another. She saw fossils, brass apparatus, parts manufactured in Birmingham, textiles from India, curiosities from the Americas, specimens from Asia, as well as a multitude of marvels she did not recognize. Another alcove displayed artefacts from ancient Egypt, scarabs, headdresses and jewellery. These Earnestine recognized, but they were far more wondrous than those on display in the dusty cases at the British Museum.

"My headdress," said Thoth. "Alas, it no longer fits me. I have grown in stature over the centuries."

Earnestine nodded.

The shelving was unusual too: pigeon holes for scrolls, places for clay tablets and neat shelves for modern notebooks.

Further on, bald-headed boys of all ages bent over their desks working studiously. They reached the nearest and Earnestine glanced over his shoulder. The student copied a book, open in front of him, duplicating the neat columns of hieroglyphs in fine penmanship. He wrote with a fountain pen.

"Ah," said Thoth, having seen what attracted her attention, "the construction of the first great pyramid at Giza. I remember."

The boy smiled as if he too remembered all that time ago before he returned to his labours.

"This is where I beget myself," Thoth explained. "When I have no more need of this vessel, I will move to another."

"So," Earnestine said, "your body does grow old, die and decay."

"This body yes, like countless ones before it, but my thoughts continue."

"But it's not the same."

"You are not the same as when you were a little girl."

"Of course I am."

"Your form has changed, your substance replaced by what you eat and drink. No element, fire, water, air, earth or otherwise from that child's body stands before me now."

"Yes, granted, but it's not the same, it's simply not... is it?"

"And yet, despite changing completely, you remember events from your childhood."

She did. As a child, Earnestine had sat upon the lap of her father, seen him trace a route of a river across the map, from one rectangle over the folds to another. She had imagined the folds themselves as mountain ranges and valleys. She had taken his compass to explore their home, 12b Zebediah Row, finding the hall ran to the north and the stairs were a clamber to the south, turning east after ten steps. These memories were clear to her, just as the encampment in the Amazon made from bedsheets, and the steamer travelling trunk had transformed into a ship to navigate the Orinoco. She'd seen brightly coloured birds of paradise that could not have been simply scarves or hats. These things had been real to her.

"You understand," Thoth said. She saw that he had been watching her. "Memories make us who we are. You write a journal – I see you do – then something you read within its pages, even if you have forgotten, becomes real again. If another reads it, they remember the moment as if it were their own. If you wrote enough and they were to read, and re-read it often, then they would think as you do, remember as you do, live as you do."

"But..."

Thoth smiled, as a parent smiles upon an errant child, who had stamped her foot, angry that – apparently – pixies do not live at the bottom of their garden, that the tooth fairy does not take away a molar for a shiny sixpence and that a place dreamed up is no more than a fancy.

"How?"

"I write down my thoughts and with my words I am immortal," Thoth explained. "It is not your soul, Miss Deering-Dolittle, not your hand or arm or shoulder, but your thoughts that define you. We find a child, many children, and they read the books, study them until their thoughts become one with Thoth. They think like Thoth, they become Thoth. As I am Thoth."

"Just like One... er..."

"One Two Thirty, yes. Just as I did and as I will again."

"Give me a child until he is seven and I will show you the man," Earnestine said. "Aristotle."

"I met him."

"But how do you know?"

"I remember," he said, touching his forehead. "It is written."

"But just because it's written," Earnestine insisted, "it doesn't mean that it actually happened to you."

"If not me, who else?"

"Or happened at all."

"It is what happened now."

"But it could have been changed."

"The future is mutable, why not the past?"

"No, no, history... happened. It can be proved by digging up tombs."

"So keen on facts. Ma'at was... and will be again, the goddess of Truth. I have chosen well."

"But it's a *story*... ah! Do you remember gambling with the Moon and meeting Anubis and Isis?"

Thoth nodded.

"But that's a fairy story, a myth."

"Is your country not bound by its myths?"

"No, we live in an age of progress and enlightenment."

"What of chivalry?"

"We're chivalrous, yes."

"Because of King Arthur and your Knights of the Round Table."

"Yes... no, oh, please understand."

"I do, Earnestine, I do. I am Thoth, the Keeper of Records, the man who begat himself from those very records. These books here, they are my immortality."

The edifice of books towered above her and Earnestine tried to picture the knowledge they contained. The thoughts of one man, or many men, distilled and recorded for thousands of years. Studied by the numbered acolytes carefully sifting through the tomes, copying and recopying, memorising by rote and understanding by repetition.

"If you write it down," Thoth said, "it becomes true."

So, Earnestine thought, if one read and knew every book here, would one really become the god Thoth?

"Could anyone become a god and live forever?" Earnestine asked.

"If they wrote and their writing was read."

And if one read every book in North Kensington Public Library, every book in the British Museum, everything in the Grenville Library and the Circular Reading Room, then what would one become? Perhaps more than a god?

"But the people of Egypt no longer worship you."

"I do not need the power of prayer to grant me life. I beget myself and eat as you eat, drink as you drink, love as you love."

"Well... quite."

"A god does not need to be worshipped," Thoth said. "A god simply is. You will learn this."

"I will."

"When you become a goddess."

"Me? A goddess."

"The goddess Ma'at, the consort of Thoth. It requires study," Thoth said. He showed her a wall of shelving, only partially filled with scrolls. "I have shelving here with the writings of the earlier incarnations of Ma'at, and enough space for another five hundred years of your journals as well."

"And then?"

"Together, we will put up more shelves."

"And I just add my journals?" Earnestine said, wishing she'd kept hers up to date.

"Of course, and study the previous volumes, so that you become an immortal goddess."

So, she had a choice between being a lady with Sir Archibald and becoming a goddess with Thoth.

"It was my plan," said Thoth, "but unfortunately only temporarily."

"How can you be immortal *temporarily*?"

"The latest of my journals is missing."

"The one stolen by Mister Rake."

"He tricked his way into my hotel, pretending to be intoxicated, and I only discovered its loss in the morning."

"Was it the only copy?"

"My servants copy out the texts, but the current volume must be written first before it can be duplicated and memorized."

"I see," Earnestine said. "I have a copy of the last page."

She fished it out of her kit bag and passed the crumpled page to Thoth.

His eyes lit up when he saw it – Earnestine felt overjoyed to have created such pleasure in such a man –

but it was short lived. He turned the page to find there was no more than half a scribbled side.

"It is incomplete," he said. "It lacks my account of when we fell in love."

"I'm sorry, I... I beg your pardon."

"I recall writing such. My feelings are literal."

"I'm sure they are."

"But if this vessel dies," Thoth explained, "then, when I beget myself again, I will know nothing of my feelings for you. This page is not enough. How can you be Ma'at, if Thoth himself has never heard of you?"

"Quite."

The boy priest ran up. "Sidi?"

"What is this interruption?"

The boy deferred to Thoth, and then bowed to Earnestine, before stepping up to whisper in Arabic (Earnestine guessed).

"In English," Thoth said, "for our guest."

"My apologies," the priest said. "Master, there are men breaking into the temple."

"Have the traps not been reset?"

"Master, they followed those returning on the levitators."

"Levitators?" Earnestine asked.

"Flying carpets," Thoth said. "Where are they now?"

"They are trying to enter the alchemical workshop."

"Raise the alarm," Thoth commanded. "Protect the Library."

"But they may reach the Treasury."

"It matters little. Let them find it. Let the lustre of gold turn them from what is important," Thoth replied. "Only the great Library and the books matter."

"My sister?" Earnestine said, collecting her kit bag and umbrella. "She is held by the Bedouin. If they are attacking elsewhere, then she will be lightly guarded."

"One Two Thirty, show Ma'at's sister the way and keep her safe."

The boy bowed, "Sidi."

"I'll get your book back," Earnestine promised. "The one Mister Rake stole."

"It is not just the last few weeks I would lose," Thoth said. "It is much worse."

Thoth stepped up to her, took her hands in his to look into her eyes and deep into her five souls. She gazed up at him, entranced, seeing in his eyes the knowledge and wonder of the ages.

"What could be worse?" Earnestine said.

"I risk losing you."

Mrs Merryweather

Charlotte's tight drawers and gossamer bloomers seemed to protect her from the sand, whereas the particles of silica easily found their way into the armour of Georgina's corset and unmentionables. She crawled on her hands and knees after her sister to the top of the dune.

"Is this really necessary?"

"They have guns," said Charlotte, scanning the vista in front.

Georgina could see two entranceways carved into the rock of the gorge's wall. Tents too, but the only signs of life were some camels and horses tethered on the shady side.

"There's no-one about," Charlotte whispered.

"Good."

"Yes, but where are they?"

"In the tents?"

"The flaps are tied on the outside."

So, no-one was inside... but Mister Rake's murderer had locked the door from the other side – this was not the time to think about that.

"I wonder if they've left any guns," Charlotte said.

"Best leave weapons to those with the expertise."

"Pardon?"

"Men handle guns."

Charlotte gave her such a face.

"Oh... just this once."

"Cover me," Charlotte said as she scooted over the hill.

"With what?"

Charlotte ran low down the hill, jingling on account of her wanton anklets.

How was the girl coping with the heat? It was unbearable. She was clearly made of sterner stuff than Georgina, and yet, after that day in Great Yarmouth, it had been Charlotte's pale skin that had blotched and peeled.

Charlotte reached the nearest tent, glanced about and then loosened a guy rope. This made a loose section of canvas and Charlotte squeezed underneath.

This was the Temple of Thoth, Georgina thought. A god who begat himself and gambled with the moon for five extra days. Georgina would like an extra five days. With her Arthur. She'd swap anything for five more days. Or five hours. Or even five minutes.

Charlotte had been an age.

The wind shifted, blowing sand into her eyes, and she heard voices echoing down the gulley.

Come on, Lottie!

Finally, the girl reappeared like a rabbit from a burrow. Thank goodness. And then, of all things, the silly girl turned around to crawl back into the tent. She wriggled about such that her Nancy stuck right up in the air.

Thank heavens there were no men around, except that a long shadow rippled over the canvas.

An Egyptian!

From nowhere.

Georgina's throat trapped the air from her lungs as she watched the man amble over towards Charlotte in all her vulnerability. Any moment now, he'd see Charlotte. Georgina daren't make a sound, and yet, somehow, she had to shout a warning.

The man came nearer.

Charlotte still squirmed about.

He walked past, then paused and turned, incredulous for a moment at the scene, before he leant back to admire Charlotte's shame, exposed upwards from her prone position. He licked his lips.

Finally, Georgina got her mouth to work, "..."

Miss Charlotte

A curved sword!

It was all she'd been able to find: a khopesh.

What possible use was a curved sword? She'd practised with that fighting machine ages ago with foil and sabre, both sensible straight swords rather than this over-sized cheese knife.

She imagined her sisters scolding her: straight swords for Europeans and curved swords for Arabs, and work inwards from the outside weapons.

What she really needed was a .303.

She wriggled out of the tent and found herself on her knees facing a Bedouin, one of al Rachid's men. The man smiled, showing his blackened and broken teeth. He held a thick rope, knotted at one end, and swung it casually.

"Little one," he said, "I shall break you like a mule and—"

Charlotte stabbed upwards, twisted, and then found she could slice up into the man's stomach using the curve of the blade to alter the angle.

The man dropped, the moisture-hungry sand already claiming his blood.

"Effective," she murmured to the khopesh with a new-found admiration.

Georgina appeared, flushed from running across. "Charlotte, what have you done?"

What was she on about? "It was a basic thrust."

"You murdered him!"

442

"Murder? He's a casualty of war. A soldier killed in battle. In the line of duty."

"But you're not a soldier."

Charlotte stamped her foot. "Only because no-one will give me a uniform."

"And are you going to go around killing everyone?"

"Of course not," Charlotte said. Once, Charlotte had read a book (she'd read lots of books), but this one was *The Art of War* by Sun Tzu. She had hoped for something about uniforms and medals, excitement, last stands, brave men in battle and even derring-do. Instead, it had been full of advice about strategy and tactics. "We can't attack unless we outnumber them ten to one."

"There are only two of us, so... there's no such thing as a fifth of a person."

"So, we switch to guerrilla tactics."

"No, let's just find Ness and get out of here."

Sun Tzu had a chapter on the use of spies, Charlotte remembered, although spies never wore uniforms.

"Yes," Charlotte said, "let's find out what's what first."

Charlotte guided her sister around the tent keeping as close to cover as possible. She stepped heavily over the guy ropes.

"Charlotte, what are those?"

"Those?"

Georgina pointed at her feet.

"Oh, boots, I found them in the tent."

"They're men's boots and they hardly go with that lack of clothing."

"My feet needed... *shhh....*"

Georgina ducked and whispered, "What? What?"

"Nothing. Come on."

Again, Charlotte guided them forward and then scooted over a gap to another tent. It was right at the end, so Charlotte pointed to the Temple with its two entrances. "Ness went in there."

"Which one?"

"That one."

"Yes, but which door? The one with the bird or the one with the monkey?"

"I don't know. I was tied up over there."

"Tied up!?"

"I escaped."

"We'll have to go in and rescue her."

"Lots of others went in there," Charlotte said, "and a lot of them died."

"Died!?"

"There are traps."

"What about Ness?"

"Let's find some guns," said Charlotte, and she passed the khopesh over to Georgina.

"I'd rather not," Georgina said.

"I can't carry it and get into the tent."

"Oh."

Georgina took the weapon. "It's still got... oh... yuck."

Charlotte undid a guy rope and crawled under the canvas.

Inside, it was strangely luxurious. These Bedouin seemed to bring comfortable cushions and expensive-looking carpets wherever they went.

There was a man inside.

"Farouk?"

He jumped up, his fez coming off his head, and he juggled it until he caught it properly.

"Miss Charlotte?"

"Where's Ness?"

"Miss Deering-Dolittle?"

"Yes."

"Farouk was with her, but the temple... traps."

"Ness... you don't mean..."

"She got over the pit, but alas, Farouk is not as able as he was when he was a boy."

"So she's still in there," said Charlotte looking in the direction of the temple entrance. "Where are the guns?"

"I am ashamed, but Farouk knows not."

"Oh, well, come on then."

Charlotte struggled out from under the canvas, and then went around to the front to untie the tent flaps.

Farouk appeared, grateful.

"It was only tied with string," Charlotte pointed out, "you could have escaped."

"Where would Farouk go? And... Mrs Merryweather, delighted, but it is dangerous here. You must both flee."

"We intend to, Mister Farouk," Georgina said, handing the sword back to her sister, "but we must find our sister."

"The Derring-Do Club's not complete without her," Charlotte added. "So, you're the Guide, guide."

"Oh, if only Farouk had a geneih for every time he'd heard that," Farouk said. "Alas, Farouk knows not where she is now."

"Let's try... over here," Charlotte suggested.

This was back along the line of tents. There were more than she remembered; perhaps the Bedouin had brought up reinforcements.

They saw one tent with a guard.

"Quiet," Charlotte whispered.

"We'd best be going," Farouk replied in a low tone.

"I've a better idea," said Charlotte and she readied her khopesh.

But Georgina put her hand out to stop her. "No."

"But–"

"We need to find out where Ness is."

Charlotte looked to Farouk for support, but the man just shrugged apologetically. The thing was that Georgina was too kind-hearted, and this dangerous situation needed bold action and... where had she gone?

Georgina had gone forward.

Wait, she didn't know anything about soldiering.

As Charlotte tensed to rush forward, Georgina tapped the man on his shoulder. The man turned around and Georgina caught his hand, twisting it until she was holding him down with his arm straight up.

The man managed a yelp.

"Now, Mister... what's your name?" Georgina said.

"Ja – *ah* – bari."

"Where is my sister?"

"Who?"

"Miss Deering-Dolittle."

"Who?"

"Earnestine."

"I know of no Earnest."

"Don't lie."

Jabari yelled again in pain, "You're breaking my arm!"

"Of course not," Georgina corrected. She shifted her grip. "*This* is breaking your arm, whereas... *this...* is dislocating your shoulder, but *this...* is tearing your tendons."

The man shrieked, squalled and screamed each time Georgina changed leverage.

"You see," Georgina concluded, "quite different sensations, you'll agree."

Charlotte looked on wide-eyed. "Gina, how do you know this?"

"I read a book on anatomy."

"Did you?"

"Yes."

"Did it talk about men's–"

"No."

"What about–"

"No."

"Or–"

"It most certainly did not mention that either!"

Jabari whined, "Please, please, have mercy."

"Oh, sorry," said Georgina, loosening her hold by a scintilla. "Where is everyone?"

"I cannot tell – *ah-ah* – my Master, al Rachid, curses be upon him, has gone down the wadi to attack the Temple. He's going to kill Thoth."

"Kill an immortal god that doesn't exist?"

"Yes, a thousand curses upon him for his blasphemy."

Charlotte bent down. "Where are the guns?"

"We have no – *oh, oh, oh* – they are in a chest inside."

Charlotte nodded, nipped inside the tent and found several chests closed with padlocks. She could have found something to stand in for a lockpick, but she found that the khopesh was effective at chopping the wood surrounding the metal clasp.

After two disappointing attempts that only revealed tawdry gold goblets and cups, she smashed open one with a treasure of Lee Enfields.

She found a belt for her khopesh and a bag for spare magazines. It was a struggle to carry three rifles out to the others.

Georgina still had Jabbering's arm in a lock.

"Farouk, get some rope," Georgina said.

Farouk looked around, and then used a guy rope still attached to the tent to tie the man's feet. After Georgina had deftly demonstrated an arm's ability to fold neatly behind the back, he tied Jabari's hands.

"You, Farouk," – Jabari spat – "I shall remember you."

"Farouk is being forced."

"You are not being forced."

"She has three rifles."

"She's just a girl, you coward Farouk."

"She is Derring-Do."

They each had a rifle now and worked their way along the wadi.

Charlotte remembered that she'd been this way before when she'd been rescued by the bald–headed boy.

They came across the Bedouin army around a bend and ducked back.

Haroun al Rachid was concentrating on a wall; he was shouting in Arabic.

Charlotte looked to Farouk.

"The entrance is here," Farouk translated at the merest whisper. "It must be. They went that way. Into the rock."

Charlotte jerked her head to indicate a tactical withdrawal.

"They can't get into the temple," Charlotte said to Georgina.

"Do they need to say, 'Open Sesame'?" Georgina asked.

"Something like that."

"We have to get past them."

"I don't see how."

"Farouk and I will rush them."

"Farouk?" Farouk asked.

"Yes, it's dusk, second best time to attack," said Charlotte. "We won't survive a night in the cold."

"If you'd remembered your shawl," said Georgina, half-heartedly.

"So," Charlotte continued, "best if you, Farouk, pick off the thief over by the camels and I'll take on the dozen back by the entrance."

"Yes... what? That seems rash."

Yes, Charlotte thought, Sun Tzu had talked about precision in your knowledge of the enemy. "Quite right, I stand corrected. Farouk, you take the one by the camels and I'll attack the *eleven* by the entrance."

Charlotte checked her rifle and then ensured that she could remove a new magazine from the bag with ease.

"What should I do?" Georgina asked.

"Cover us."

Georgina nodded doubtfully and struggled with the Lee Enfield.

"May Farouk ask a question?"

CHAPTER XXVII

Miss Deering-Dolittle

Earnestine went with Thoth along the peaceful corridors towards the intrusion. It seemed incredible that anyone would attack such a place. If one wouldn't dare cough in North Kensington Public Library, then how could anyone invade this sanctuary?

"Please, Ma'at... Miss. We can deal with this."

"I can help," Earnestine insisted, waving her umbrella to emphasize her point.

He smiled and led the way, but a returning priest intercepted them; another boy, or the same one? It was difficult to tell as they all had their heads shaved.

"Sidi."

"In English," said Thoth.

"Master, is this a test?"

"Miss Deering-Dolittle is here."

"My apologies," the priest bowed to Earnestine. All this formality, when there was an emergency. It was jolly admirable. "They have nearly broken through via the Levitator chute."

"Will it hold?"

"No, Master."

"Perhaps," said Thoth, "we should lay a trap."

"You can make a pit open or lower the ceiling?" Earnestine said.

"Set a trip wire to the alchemical transmutor," Thoth instructed. "We'll inundate the workshop."

"Master."

The priest bowed and ran off, his sandals flapping down on the marble floor.

"What will that do?"

"The levitators generate rise by using the expansion of dead air."

"Dead air?"

"All animal life, including men, cannot survive in such an atmosphere."

"Ah," Earnestine said, remembering the painting of the bird suffocating in the jar.

"It may also kill them with the cold. As the dead air expands, it cools."

Earnestine nodded, as if she understood, while she resolved to ask Georgina to explain. "This all seems sensible."

The priest returned. "All is prepared, Master."

"Most excellent."

The priest bowed.

Thoth took Earnestine's hand, quite making her heart flutter in surprise.

"It is time for us to measure their worth against a feather."

"I beg your pardon."

"You will be Ma'at, and if their evil causes them to enter our trap, then we will weigh them. If their tread is heavier than a feather, then they will not have been virtuous, and they will perish."

"One wrong step and boom."

"Indeed," Thoth said. "Our temple is our sanctuary and we will defend it."

Earnestine held her umbrella at the ready and nodded.

Thoth smiled. "We have but to wait."

Mrs Merryweather

Georgina knew that Charlotte was preparing for battle. It was all these dreadful books she read. She was going to rush al Rachid and his Bedouin, attack them from behind.

"Could we not simply sneak past?" Farouk asked.

"Don't be silly," Charlotte said. "We can't... oh, there was a boy who showed me into a tunnel."

"Boy?" Georgina said. "What sort of boy? How old? Does he come from a good family?"

"No, Gina, somewhere hereabouts."

Charlotte stood aside and searched the stone face of the ravine, working back the way they had come.

"Here," she said, and she slipped up to the rock wall of the gulley, and vanished.

Georgina went over.

It was a solid wall, tumbled where the stone had broken away and in shadow as the setting sun vanished. Nonetheless, it was completely impenetrable.

A hand appeared and gestured.

Georgina squeezed up and into an opening. She had to lean to get through and into a roughly hewn passage.

"Alas," said Farouk, "Farouk has had too many hot dinners."

"Then go all the way around..." Charlotte began, and then she squeezed past Georgina and went closer to the entrance. "Farouk, find a camel and get help."

"Yes, Farouk understands."

"And Farouk... are you there, Farouk? Farouk?"

"He's gone, Lottie."

"He won't be able to fetch help in time."

"No," Georgina said. "The SS *Karnak* is too far away, there and back, to bring help quickly on a camel."

"Too far on a magic carpet too," Charlotte said. "We're on our own. Come on."

Charlotte squeezed past and then led Georgina by the hand through the passage, sometimes taking a sharp right-angled turn. Georgina found her rifle catching against the rocks, something that didn't affect Charlotte's, of course, as her identical weapon must have been shorter, or something.

The passage changed.

It was no longer carved from the rock but became smooth and architectural. The design was certainly ancient Egyptian, and no doubt Earnestine would have been able to tell them the period.

"The boy said this is the way to the alchemical workshop."

"Don't be foolish, Lottie, there's no such thing as alchemy, so how can it have a workshop?"

"There's no such thing as gypsy fortune-telling," Charlotte said, "but there are still caravans of old women wanting silver."

"Maybe."

They came to a large room, more a factory space than a workshop, full of strange devices. Georgina could not make head nor tail of it, until she realised that these devices, jars and pipes were simply ornate versions of standard chemical apparatus.

Georgina pointed out a couple in turn. "This is for distilling and that's a gas condenser."

"See. It is an alchemical workshop."

"All right," Georgina admitted, "it's an alchemical workshop."

"Come on."

"We should tread carefully."

Miss Charlotte

Tread carefully indeed, Charlotte thought, in these clompy boots. But she always trod carefully. She may well go where angels fear, but she wasn't foolhardy. They weren't the Light Brigade at Balaclava.

She had her rifle aimed.

She moved on the balls of her feet – the 'borrowed' footwear sliding only slightly – and a flagstone shifted under her foot as she stepped slowly and deliberately forward.

Was that a noise?

"It's quiet," Gina said.

Charlotte nearly fired off a round, such was her sudden fright.

"Gina, *shhh...*"

"Sorry."

Yes, too quiet, Charlotte thought, at least until her sister opened her big mouth.

Jolly carefully, she turned her head left, then slowly to the right, checking up and down as she went, and finally, she repeated the process from right to left.

Her gun was fully loaded, ten rounds, and cocked.

It was nothing.

Her imagination?

Perhaps.

She stepped forward.

Click!

She had a moment to see a glass storage tank burst at a valve and spew forth gas, then everywhere was blizzard.

Chapter XXVIII

Miss Deering-Dolittle

Earnestine leapt forward, opening her Fox's Paragon with a quick deft movement.

The white clouds billowed towards them and she held her umbrella out like a shield, pulling the other two around with her free hand. The explosive rush of gas blasted against the thin fabric, imperilled the elegant stretchers, juddered the pole and threatened to tug the handle out of Earnestine's grip.

And all at once, it stopped, as if the storm had passed.

Georgina looked panicked.

"Slow, deep... *oh...* breaths," Earnestine said. "It's dead air."

"Car... bon... die... ox... stand," Georgina said.

"Uh?"

"Stand... up... up..."

They did, and then Georgina pointed towards a table. With leaden arms and legs, they clambered on and stood. Earnestine and Charlotte turning back to help Georgina up. The air was improved higher up, even though standing had made Earnestine wonder if she was about to come over all faint. They held on to each other and slowly the dark fug in her vision evaporated.

"You're safe," Georgina gasped. "You're... oh my..."

"What are you... doing here?" Earnestine said.

"I was... with Lottie... and..."

"You should have stayed on the ship... get your breath back."

"I had to... find you and Lottie," Georgina said. "Sir Archibald abandoned you in the desert... hardly... the actions of a gentleman."

"Quite."

Earnestine checked her brolly – a thick frost coated the black material. She shook it, and droplets fell from it onto the tabletop.

"When I packed for Egypt," she said. "I never thought I'd need my umbrella for snow."

"How did you know?" Georgina said.

"Both of you, yelling at the top of your voices. 'Quiet,' 'shhh' and 'sorry' – honestly. Enough to wake the dead... oh, sorry, Gina, I didn't mean anything."

"It's all right, I'm just glad you're safe."

"Did you bring the book?"

Georgina showed it to her and added, "We've come to rescue you from the mummies."

"I don't need rescuing."

"But the mummies are based here," Charlotte insisted.

Earnestine felt her jaw tighten. "We're on their side."

"Since when?"

Then the wall exploded.

Mrs Merryweather

Georgina half-ducked and half-fell behind the table.

Dust everywhere.

She'd dropped her rifle.

There were guttural shouts, men trying to gain access to the room through the debris.

"What happened?" she asked.

"Sir Archibald had archaeological equipment," Earnestine said.

"What does that mean?"

"The thieves dynamited the entrance," Charlotte shouted, as she hoisted her Lee Enfield into a firing position.

"Back this way," Earnestine shouted, and she grabbed Georgina, pulling her deeper into the temple.

Georgina ran, her hand stretched out behind her like an athlete in a relay race to grab Charlotte. She waved, reached further, and then looked back, but her sister wasn't behind her.

"Lottie!"

BANG!

Georgina jumped.

She glanced behind her and saw an attacker fall as others rushed in to fill the gap. They fired too, more out of gusto than accuracy, but it only took one bullet to find its mark.

Georgina pulled away, but Earnestine's grip was stronger, so they left Charlotte behind.

Miss Charlotte

Up, aim... *fire.* Retarget... *fire!*

Another two hit, down again, crawling along the table, quickly, doubling back.

That's... up, aim... *fire!*

Four rounds, three hits, six rounds left and only... ah, seven thieves, more behind them.

The thieves fired back, using mismatched weapons that blasted a multitude of calibres: bullets pinging and whining around where she had been standing. A blunderbuss peppered the wall above her.

The ricochets came from different directions.

The enemy must have split up, some going right, some left, given the angles of attack. They'd scrambled through the narrow opening, so any hope of holding them there had gone. This room wasn't suitable either. She'd have to fall back.

There was a lull, both sides hiding behind cover. More of them were sneaking through the gap. She heard the rocks shift and clatter, broken glass on the floor crack.

A man's voice cut across the workshop, "You cannot have more than five bullets left, little girl."

Charlotte winced: they were 'rounds', not 'bullets', she wasn't a little girl, he couldn't count and, worst of all, she had only six left. She'd lost her bag of spare magazines in the explosion. Curse these ridiculous pyjamas and curse all women's clothing for being pocketless.

A proper uniform – such a small request.

The man taunted again, "You have, maybe, five bullets. There are forty of us."

"There *were* forty of you," Charlotte shouted back.

"We have lost martyrs to our cause." It was al Rachid; Charlotte recognized his vile voice.

"Any more for martyrdom?"

"Ha, ha, such spirit. You will make a good slave."

"I'm British! We will never, never, never be slaves."

She leaned over the table and loosed off a shot. Foolish bravado, and she was a round down.

"Ha, ha, you missed."

"What do you want?"

"I want the Philosopher's Stone," said al Rachid, and then, after a pause, he added, "and with it, wealth beyond even my dreams. I will buy your British guns. I will buy mercenaries. I will have the secrets of the god Thoth, his alchemical knowledge, the sorcery of flight, and so... I will sweep you under the carpet. Ha! Sweep you all under the magic carpet."

Why was he talking to her and why did he pause?

Oh, she realised, they're sneaking up around the side.

Charlotte shuffled to the other end of the table, aimed and waited. The light shifted against the far wall and she fired. A cry, and some desperate backwards shuffling, rewarded her.

Over the other side, there was a movement in the crack below a wooden cupboard, so she put a bullet through that.

"You and you," al Rachid shouted, "go forward."

"Sidi, we beg you."

Two men hurtled forward, one stumbled because his leader had pushed him, but the other came at her full of fervour and desperation.

Charlotte took her time: *BANG... BANG!*

He'd thrown those men away she thought.

But al Rachid was laughing.

"You have lost, pretty girl," he said. "Azim, fetch the prize."

"Sidi, she–"

"She has no ammunition."

Azim came forward, but he pushed another thief ahead of him as a shield.

"Come here," said the thief. "Your gun is empty."

Charlotte couldn't see Azim properly and al Rachid was still in hiding.

"This," Charlotte said, showing him her Lee Enfield .303. "It's a rifle."

"Give it here."

Charlotte shrugged daintily and then blew his head off.

Azim came forward now, knife drawn.

Charlotte raised her gun and aimed at him.

"Lee Enfield, .303," she explained. "You can load the magazine when it's in position."

"We only had magazines for that, not spare bullets."

Charlotte grimaced. "They are rounds, or shells, or ammunition, not bullets."

Azim came right up to her, the barrel against his broad chest. "If you had, you would have killed me by now."

"Oh, well, I'm out now," she said sweetly in her best butter-won't-melt voice.

Azim knocked the gun to one side, grabbed her and yanked her head back by her hair.

"*Arrgh...*"

"Al Rachid, Master, let me cut her throat!"

Azim pulled back even further to stretch her neck and elongate her vulnerable veins and tendons. The dagger flashed in the lamplight, cruel and effective – a curved blade poised to strike.

"Wait!" said al Rachid. "I have a better idea."

Chapter XXIX

Miss Deering-Dolittle

It was a moment that chilled Earnestine's blood. Haroun al Rachid's hideous voice, edged with triumph, gloating. "Give me the Philosopher's stone or the girl dies."

"Shoot him," Charlotte shouted. "*Aaaa...*"

"Give me the stone."

Earnestine turned to stare at a terrified Georgina and at the calm face of Thoth.

The god shrugged. "Give them the stone."

Earnestine smiled – they had a bargaining chip.

Thoth turned to one of his boy priests. "Get the gold. You may run."

The priest bowed and hurried away.

"Men like this man see gold and then they see nothing else," Thoth said.

They were hiding behind a temporary barrier of furniture. Every priest armed themselves with a wooden shield and a vicious sword, or a bow and arrow, but their opponents had firearms. They'd fight well, Earnestine knew, they were loyal and devoted to their god: the god they were not. Fanatics might be a good description, but she'd have felt happier if the expert in military matters wasn't the one held hostage.

"Well," al Rachid shouted, "time is running out."

"We're fetching it," Earnestine shouted back.

"Hurry, she doesn't have much time."

"Release her," Thoth shouted, "and I, Thoth, will be merciful."

"You!" al Rachid responded. "You may be a god, but you are an ancient god. Old and weak."

"I have powers."

"You may be protected from arrows and spears, but let's see how you fare against bullets."

There was a volley of gunfire.

The barricade split and exploded as the shot smashed into the wooden chairs, tables and cabinets. They all threw themselves to the ground as the ricochets whistled overhead.

"This won't hold them," Thoth said. "Light the fuse."

Earnestine stared at him. "You can't. My sister."

"I have no choice."

Earnestine hesitated; she knew he was right.

She nodded.

"Five-minute fuse," he replied. "However, it is moot, we have no tinderbox."

Earnestine fished inside her kit bag and found her box of matches. One left. She struck it, let the wood catch after the initial phosphorous excitement, and then lit the end of the fuse. The black cord fizzed, the fire rushing along the length, speeding towards the charges set within the workshop.

Earnestine slipped the spent match back into the matchbox and deposited that into her kit bag.

She checked her pocket watch – five minutes was not long.

Knowing they were committed, she needed to save Charlotte, so she shouted over the barricade, "You release my sister and you can have the stone."

"You give me the stone, you can have your sister."

"If I give you the stone, then what's to stop you keeping my sister and selling her?"

"Nothing... you'll have to trust me."

"In that case, you release my sister *and then* I'll give you the stone."

"You don't trust me."

"I am an English young lady and thus above reproach."

"And you are saying I'm not."

"You don't even look like a young lady."

There were sniggers from the Bedouin until al Rachid turned and berated them.

The fuse now burnt upwards, along the wall and then the sparks vanished into an opening.

The priest, sent by Thoth, returned with the golden jar Earnestine had raided from the temple interior. It shone, a bright expensive bait for a trap. Thoth indicated Earnestine and the priest gave her the valuable, but worthless, item.

Earnestine placed the golden jar upon the top of the barricade, in full view of al Rachid and his men.

There was a collective out-breath from the thieves born of their greed.

"That is just a golden jar," al Rachid shouted. "The Stone is a stone."

"It's in the jar," Earnestine shouted.

"Show me."

Earnestine reached up and took the jar back, tried to open it, but had to hand it to Thoth. He took the lid off easily. It was empty.

"But–" Georgina began.

"Don't worry," Earnestine said.

Thoth had already picked up a suitable lump of rock, a fragment generated by the volley of gunfire.

Earnestine took it, held up the open jar in one hand and the stone in another.

"There! See?"

"I see," al Rachid shouted. "Bring it here."

"No, I'll put it here," Earnestine shouted, placing the stone into the jar and putting the lid back on it. "You release Charlotte, we'll back way and you can claim your prize."

"If you trick me..."

Earnestine couldn't see where the fuse was burning. Her fob watch was hidden in a pocket, but she knew it ticked away the seconds far too quickly. "I won't."

"Don't give him the Stone," Charlotte shouted.

"Quiet, Lottie."

Charlotte cried out, and then her footsteps sounded across the workshop floor.

"Come on, Lottie," Earnestine shouted.

Charlotte reached the barricade and clambered over.

Thoth indicated to his priests and they fell back quickly, their serenity slipping in their expressions.

"Ma'at," said Thoth.

"Yes," Earnestine replied, and then she shouted to al Rachid. "All yours."

They retreated further, Earnestine pulling Charlotte by the hand until they were well away.

"We need to hold the barricade," Charlotte said.

"I think not," said Earnestine, and she fished out her pocket watch – any moment now.

"Oh, lummy," said Charlotte, realising.

Earnestine glanced back; al Rachid's hand grasped the golden jar, pulling it down from the barricade.

And then the charges exploded.

Mrs Merryweather

Georgina hated explosions.

This one's deep percussion echoed, and re-echoed, down the labyrinth of Thoth's domain. Dust billowed along the corridor like a sandstorm.

Earnestine brushed herself down.

Something was going on between her and that Mister Djehuti character, Georgina could tell.

"That's that," Earnestine said, "we're trapped."

"Hardly," Mister Djehuti said. "We have a number of exits, but the main one must be sealed too."

"How do we do that?" Georgina asked.

"I have dynamite," Mister Djehuti said, showing them a bag of explosives. "Archaeologists bring such items when they discover my temple."

Earnestine dug out some sticks to put in her kit bag.

Georgina was aghast. "Do you know how to use those?"

"Of course, I've studied archaeology."

"But isn't archaeology just boring digging and pottery and books?" Charlotte said.

"After the explosions," Earnestine said.

Charlotte was incensed: "If I'd known that!"

"How many do we use?" Georgina asked.

"To be honest, I'm not sure," Earnestine replied as she finished packing her bag. "All my studies have concerned how much to use to uncover something. Burying it was rather beyond the remit."

"But if we seal ourselves in!" Georgina said.

"There are other ways out," Mister Djehuti reminded them.

"We'll have to get horses," Earnestine said.

"Or a magic carpet," said Charlotte.

"Oh, be serious, Charlotte."

"No, no, Ness, she's right," Georgina said, "we used a flying carpet to get here."

Earnestine glared at Georgina and then raised an eyebrow.

"Yes, really," Georgina insisted.

"But?"

"I know."

"Very well, give me the book."

Georgina handed over the modern notebook. Earnestine flicked through it, stopped at the last page and shook her head slowly.

"What is it?" Georgina asked.

"A god writing about me."

"A god?"

"Thoth."

The penny dropped: "Mister Djehuti is Thoth?"

Earnestine nodded.

Georgina leant closer to talk to her sister privately. This conversation about their future was always being put off. It wasn't her place, it was their mother's, but mother had followed father up the river.

"You and he…" but Georgina didn't know quite what to ask.

"He's asked me to be Ma'at, his goddess."

"And?"

"I do—"

There was a shot.

Miss Charlotte

Charlotte couldn't work out where it had come from.

And another sounded, followed by the whine of a ricochet.

Then she saw him – al Rachid, battered and bruised, but still alive.

"An immortal god, ha!" he shouted. "I have your stone. I am immortal now, Thoth."

Charlotte grabbed a bow from a nearby priest and loosed off an arrow.

The man jerked backwards, and then his shadow leapt across the wall and fled away.

"He got away," Charlotte shouted taking a quiver from the priest. "He must have been this side of the explosion getting the gold jar the stone is in. You shouldn't have given it to him."

"It was nothing," Georgina said.

"He's trapped in here."

"And we're trapped with him."

"Charlotte, keep him back," Earnestine replied. "Thoth, my sister is… *Thoth!*"

CHAPTER XXX

Miss Deering-Dolittle

Now Earnestine realised, that gunshot became the loudest sound she had ever heard. It had sounded through her chest more than her ears, such was the sudden force of the detonation. Her mouth opened, air escaped, and yet, she continued to live.

She'd talked to Charlotte, while behind her everything came to an end.

Thoth gazed back to her, his expression one of pain and regret. There was a hole in his chest at one side, through his ribs and a lung. As he held his side, blood oozed between his fingers and drained down his hip and leg.

"Rarely do I remember the pain of death," Thoth said. "It is merely an emptiness, a two-line gap, between this life and the next."

"It's going to be alright."

"My life is leaving me." Thoth coughed. Tiny specks of red touched where his breath reached. "Do you have the book?"

"Yes," said Earnestine, showing him the battered and damaged book. "I'm sorry."

Thoth dismissed her fears: "Everyone forgets things now and then."

"What can I do?"

"My Library."

"Yes."

Earnestine took his side: half-carried and half-guided him along the marble floor.

"Gina, Lottie... seal the entrance, find a way out," Earnestine said and she threw them her kit bag.

"Yes, yes," Georgina said, picking it up.

"I will show you both the way," a priest said, stepping forward.

"If I'm not there in ten minutes," Earnestine said, "go without me."

"If you are not there in ten minutes," Georgina said, "we'll wait another ten."

"And then ten more after that," Charlotte added.

"For heaven's sake, go," Earnestine said. "Just go!"

The two of them scurried off down the corridor, Charlotte ahead of the priest and Georgina glancing back over her shoulder.

Then she was alone with the fallen god, or at least Earnestine hoped so. Where was al Rachid? She heaved Thoth higher up: he was fading fast. She supported him as he faltered.

"The thief will find us," Thoth whispered.

Earnestine was already well aware of the trail they were leaving. It would not take a Bedouin, trained in desert tracking, to follow a vivid scarlet line on a white floor.

They reached the Library.

"The..."

Earnestine knew what Thoth meant. She placed the hardback notebook upon the desk, a piece of furniture that would not have looked out of place in 12b Zebediah Row back in Kensington, and opened it at the last page. Again, the English word 'Earnestine' jumped to her attention.

Thoth took up a pen and added a few characters, hieroglyphics of men and birds, each more injured and deformed than the last.

"I cannot," said Thoth.

"Cannot?"

"The problem with keeping a journal is that you never get to finish it."

"Just hold on."

"So many deaths... and I don't remember any of them."

He tried again, but his fingers fumbled the pen.

"Please, save your strength," Earnestine implored.

"Please write... for me."

"Yes."

"My exact words."

"Of course, but I don't know..."

"English is acceptable."

Earnestine nodded. She would honour this man – this god – with her best penmanship.

"She writes for me now," he dictated.

Earnestine wrote, carefully, but quickly.

"When I first saw her in Tanis, I knew," Thoth continued. "We sat under the arbour and talked about relics buried in the sand. Things cannot last. I told her that some things can last forever."

He had seen her in Tanis, as Earnestine had seen him, she realised. Noticed her. And she wrote on, becoming his conduit such that she did not hear him speak, but rather became surprised to see these words appearing as if divinely inscribed upon the lined paper.

'...she caught mine eye with her red hair. I love her for she has fire like Ma'at, so long ago. I was entranced by her nature when we talked in Tanis. She haunts my dreams. I love her for'

He paused, perhaps searching for the precise word.

"For?" Earnestine asked.

She had stopped writing and so saw, somehow for the first time, what was written.

He loved her.

The line ended with a blotch of ink marking the moment he'd stopped speaking.

"For?" she repeated.

But Thoth was dead, his head back and his eyes staring upwards to the heavens. Had she missed his Bâ leaving him as a human-headed bird?

He loved her... *had* loved her.

She felt alone, even as she heard a respectful footfall behind her. She could not tear her sight from his perfect form. To look away would be sacrilege. She did not believe he was a god, but he had been powerful and possessed the wisdom of the ages.

Now he was gone.

But she could gaze upon him forever and so hold him to this world.

The most delicate of coughs.

An acolyte had entered, like a visitor from a spiritual realm, his form indistinct as if seen through water. She'd glanced at the boy. When she looked back to the man, it was too late. Something had gone in that moment and there was only Thoth's Ha, his empty husk, left.

"Do not be upset," the boy said.

"I'm not... crying," she said. "I don't cry. Stiff upper... and... all that."

The boy gently took the notebook away from her. He flicked back a page and then, despite the horror and everything that had happened, he simply read, carefully, like someone studying for a viva.

Thoth was still lying beside her. He was pale, diminished without a Ka, the vital spark, powering him. She gently closed Thoth's eyelids.

"Goodbye," she said, and she kissed him on the forehead. When she had glanced away, the spell broke, and his Bâ must have flown when her gaze was broken. Where it landed, she did not know.

"You are Earnestine?"

"Yes."

She wiped her face and stood. She would be brave.

"I love you," the boy said.

"I beg your pardon?"

"I love you."

"How can you love me?"

"You haunt my dreams."

"No... that's only what you've read from the book. It's not real."

"It is written," the boy said. "It must be so."

"We've never met."

"We met in Tanis," he said. "I remember it well."

"We did? I don't recall," she said, and she didn't. She had been blinded by Thoth's beauty, enraptured by his words and his voice and those eyes. Perhaps that was why she hadn't seen this boy.

The lad spoke again, "We sat under the arbour and talked about relics buried beneath the sand and how things cannot last. I said that some things can last forever, and I was entranced by your nature."

But he was a boy, younger than Charlotte, strong of limb and well built, he would become as handsome as Thoth – her Thoth – but of a different ancestry. His eyes were not the same shade of deep brown and yet they were Thoth's eyes. They burned with the same knowledge and the same passion.

"But that was..."

His eyes seemed to twinkle. "That was me."

"But..."

"Yes, I am the god Thoth."

Mrs Merryweather

"We have to seal the main entrance," Georgina said.

The priest was ahead of them. "This way."

He led them along a wide passage and then reached a rougher corridor with rooms off, hewn from the rock.

"Anywhere along here," the priest said.

Georgina had Earnestine's small adventure bag with the dynamite. She set it down and knelt beside it. Three sticks of dynamite seemed to be inadequate to bring down the roof of a temple made of solid rock and yet, at the same time, far, far too dangerous.

The priest placed the charges in cavities in the wall and laid out the fuse.

Charlotte danced from one foot to another.

"What is it?" Georgina asked.

"We're being followed," Charlotte said.

"Find out."

Charlotte nodded and went forward, a strange figure in transparent pyjamas and holding a nasty looking curved sword.

Finally, Georgina found Earnestine's box of matches in the kit bag: it barely rattled.

"Oh, silly, foolish Ness," Georgina said, "she's only left one match."

But you only need one, she thought.

It was spent.

"No."

That was it, all over, except that there were oil lamps set into the wall.

Georgina took the end of the fuse cord and pulled it towards the nearest. She got within a yard before it stuck.

She reached out, just being able to touch the oil lamp, but it wouldn't move. Some glocky cove had cemented it into the rock.

The priest watched her patiently.

Looking around, she could see nothing useful, and then she remembered her handkerchief. She pulled it out, dangled it in the flames until it caught.

She held it against the fuse as the heat built up around her delicate fingers. The flame stroked the end and then, finally, the black gunpowder within the jute yarn glowed. She dropped the ruined handkerchief and blew on the glowing end of the fuse. It died between each of her breaths only to glow when she blew on it again, and then, finally, it took.

Suddenly alive, the fire fizzed and sparked as the energy leapt quickly along the length.

"...and retire to a safe distance," Georgina said to the priest. She wondered just how far that would be and how long the lengthy, but rapidly burning cord, would give them – perhaps a very few minutes.

Charlotte was blocking their escape.

And Haroun al Rachid was blocking her escape. "Little one, you have not deserted me."

Charlotte lunged with the strange bent sword.

And al Rachid simply swiped it aside with his own scimitar.

The blade swept back, slicing the air in twain, and Charlotte narrowly avoided the same fate. She bent backwards, fell and Georgina grabbed her.

"Keep away," said the Priest, stepping forward.

Haroun sliced downwards, the sharp blade carving downwards like a scalpel in a dissection.

Charlotte gasped.

Georgina got the message and they retreated, away from the swordsman and towards the burning fuse.

As they ran, Charlotte shouted, "I'm cut, I cut!"

She pulled her hand from her face and Georgina saw that it was clean.

"But–" – there was no time to ask.

They made it around the corner.

"Say I died in there," Charlotte said.

"What? No," Georgina said. "We stick together. Derring-Do Club forever."

"Go in there and shout that I've been killed," said Charlotte, pushing her towards the door.

Georgina hesitated, turned to argue, but Charlotte was nowhere to be seen. Except the curtains over an alcove moved, slightly.

Georgina backed into a storeroom full of boxes.

"HELP! HELP! CHARLOTTE'S DYING!"

Miss Charlotte

Charlotte heard the footsteps, heard them move along the passageway, pause, and then pad into the room. He'd be facing Georgina now, there to gloat over Charlotte's demise.

Charlotte forced herself to count three, long full-length elephants.

Then she stepped smartly out.

Haroun al Rachid had his back to her as he blocked the doorway.

"Serves her right that she is dying," he gloated. "She cost me many men, but I would have liked to have broken her... where is she?"

"Oh, er..." Georgina began.

Charlotte stepped in behind him and ran him through with her khopesh.

Haroun al Rachid turned, his scarred face livid. Blood gushed from his chest as he struggled in his pockets. He found the stone and tugged it out to grasp it in his fist. He held it against his chest trying to stem the flow of scarlet. It seeped through his fingers, pouring down his tunic.

"But... I am immortal... I... am... a god."

He slipped to the ground, stared at the useless stone held in his bloody hand in disbelief, and died.

"I seem to have broken him," Charlotte said.

"Something important just happened," Georgina said, her breathing heavy.

"I saved your life," said Charlotte.

"Yes, that too, but..."

"But?"

"Something about you being out there and me being in this room."

Charlotte glanced behind her and then back to Georgina. "What?"

"Oh... and dynamite!"

"Sorry... oh!"

Charlotte clasped Georgina by the hand and the two hightailed it from the storeroom, round the corner and along the marble floor.

A blast wave picked them up and flung them along the corridor.

Charlotte grabbed at Georgina as her sister grabbed at her, but Charlotte's Arabian pyjamas didn't give her anything to grip. All the time Georgina's mouth opened and closed as if she was trying to shout above the buzzing in Charlotte's ears.

Then they stumbled to their feet and ran on.

The ceiling started coming down, not in the stately, inexorable progression of a temple trap, but in a haphazard shambles of calamity.

Chapter XXXI

Miss Deering-Dolittle

Another deep rumble and sand fell from the ceiling as the stone above shifted.

Priests ran back and forth, messages passed on as the aftershocks continued. Earnestine hoped that Georgina and Charlotte were safe and then they arrived, dusty, but pleased with themselves.

"We sealed the entrance," Charlotte said.

"Oh... Ness, I'm sorry," Georgina said. She had seen Thoth's body.

They helped with the injured as best they could, and when there was nothing more they could do, they slept on cushions in the Library. Surrounded by the towering shelves of Thoth's life, Earnestine wanted to dream of the god and bring him back to life in her mind, but she was too exhausted.

When Earnestine woke, she found the boy watching over her. He had a goblet of juice for her.

"Thank you," she said. The drink tasted sweet.

"It is a sign of my love for you." It was his voice, that handsome golden man who had gone and come back as this boy.

"I'm sorry."

"There is no need. What visits me in my dreams is part of your Ka, your life essence. I will be honoured by the presence of your life spirit. In return, I will keep your memory safe in my Ib, my heart, and secure in my books. Your Ren, your precious name, will be forever recorded there and so you will survive in the afterlife."

"Thank you," Earnestine said. "Will you be all right on your own?"

"Do not concern yourself. I have my servants, like One Two Thirty-one here, and I will find you, wherever you are, and I will resurrect you."

"Me?"

"Ma'at."

So Thoth would find some other girl and educate her, she would read Ma'at's journals until those words became her own and she would become the goddess, begat as Thoth begat himself. At some time in the future, perhaps in many centuries time, Thoth and Ma'at would be reunited. Not Djehuti and not Earnestine, but another pair.

"He is a lucky man," Thoth said.

"Who?"

"Whoever," Thoth said. "We have many souls, because... how to explain? You say you should follow your head, not your heart, or your heart and not your head."

"Yes."

"Perhaps you should follow your heart *and your head.*"

"I don't understand."

Georgina and Charlotte arrived.

"We are so sorry about your... the man who led you," Georgina said.

"Do not mourn," Thoth said. "That is only my old Ha... my body. Here is my Ib, my heart, my Ren, my Bâ, my Ka... look, upon the ground, there is my Shuet, my shadow. I have begotten myself again."

Earnestine saw Georgina looking at her for an explanation, but Earnestine had none.

"I am the god Thoth," the boy said.

"Aren't you a bit young?" Charlotte said.

"I am 28,899 years old. Tomorrow is my birthday."

"That's a lot of candles on your cake."

"Isn't that the day after tomorrow?" Earnestine said. "There are five days."

Thoth smiled. "It is morning already. Tomorrow will be the First of Thoth. The first day of the Egyptian year. I know for I invented it."

"Did you?" Charlotte said.

"Yes."

"And today is the last day of the interwotnot."

"Yes. The last of the five days I won from the moon."

"The intercalary days," Earnestine said.

"Like our 29th of February," Charlotte said.

"I suppose."

Charlotte shrugged, "We don't have a present."

"You have saved my book and so my life," Thoth continued. "For that I am grateful. It is the greatest gift."

Next, Thoth turned to Earnestine, who stood quite still, without seeming to hear or see anything.

"Miss Deering-Dolittle."

Earnestine blinked.

"Miss Deering-Dolittle," Thoth said. "I realise this is difficult. I love you and so I must let you go. But, as it is my birthday tomorrow, may I break with convention and give you a present?"

"A present?" Earnestine said.

"I give you this day, the fifth day I won from the moon. It is yours."

"Thank you," Earnestine said.

"Thoth's eve for Thoth's Eve."

Earnestine made a shape with her hand as if to seize the day from the air between them.

She had Thoth's eve, but she was not to be his Eve; nor he, her Adam.

He smiled and bowed, taking his leave and going to supervise the care of the injured and the recovery of bodies. There would be bandages needed for the living and many more for the mummification of the dead.

A priest came and showed them the way out through passages that Earnestine did not see nor care about.

Otherwise, the temple was sealed.

Thoth and his followers had the great Library. They would rebuild and dig themselves out. If not, then in some time to come, a future archaeologist might uncover the Library, read the books and so Thoth would beget himself again. A world in which men did anything for money, one with thieves like al Rachid, mercenaries like Jacques and politicians like Sir Archibald, did not deserve such a God of Enlightenment. *'...To the Future...'* as the engraving on her pocket watch said.

The sunlight cast a long shadow and the old wadi was in darkness, but the sky was blue.

A carpet lay waiting for them.

Magic carpet, honestly, she thought, shaking her head.

A spiral of dust, blown out from the temple, caught the wind and churned around before flowing over them like a gritty version of a London pea-souper.

The three sisters crouched and ran.

Charlotte grabbed the controls, pumped the handle and started the hookah. White gas billowed up and outwards, driving away the sandstorm as it filled the carpet up to the hospital corners.

Then they were off, whizzing out from the gas and dust cloud, to shoot along the wadi.

They surprised the thieves' camp – al Rachid's men scattered and then ran for their camels to give chase.

"Go higher," Earnestine commanded.

"It won't go higher," Charlotte said. "It needs land to push against."

"Oh."

It was still exciting, a smooth rush, unlike the clatter-clatter, squeal-squeal and slosh-slosh of a steam train, horse-drawn carriage or ship.

"It will go faster," Charlotte said.

"Please don't," said Georgina, who was lying on the carpet holding on. "There's no need."

Camels raced after them, with Bedouin riders waving their stolen British guns aloft, screaming and cursing, firing in the air and in their direction.

"The Derring-Do Club won the day," Charlotte shouted. "Ness, isn't that what Thoth gave you... today."

"Yes."

Charlotte made a face: "Not much of a present."

"No, wait! Of course!" Earnestine said. "It's the best gift he could have given me."

"Why?"

Earnestine glanced at her pocket watch; there was still time. "We need to fly, Charlotte, fly like the wind."

"Are you sure?"

"Charlotte, as fast as you dare."

"As I dare?" said Charlotte as she adjusted the controls. "What is it?"

"It'll be an adventure, and... *woo hoo-oooo....*"

Mrs Merryweather

Georgina's worst fears were realised. "The ship's gone!"

They had zoomed over the desert, along the canal and then they'd flown the length of the Great Bitter Lake until they reached the final stretch of the Suez Canal.

There was no sign of the SS *Karnak*.

Charlotte zig-zagged the magic carpet between the ships, sometimes floating over land to get around, as they overtook one after another. There were no men on camels chasing them anymore.

Georgina wished they would slow down.

Earnestine shouted, "There!"

The next ship was the familiar paddle-steamer.

"Captain," Georgina shouted, waving.

The man stood upon the deck and his chevron moustache was nearly upturned, such was his smile.

"Ahoy there, Derring-Do Club."

Earnestine called out, "I have a day, and when in Rome–"

"Oh, never mind that," Georgina snapped.

They lowered a rope, and Earnestine grabbed it, handing it to Georgina.

"I'm not sure," Georgina said.

"You have to go first," Earnestine said. "They'll pull you up."

"If you insist."

Earnestine leant closer and whispered in her ear. Georgina thought it would be 'good luck', 'be careful' or even 'be brave', but instead she said, "And get some clothes for Charlotte."

Georgina bumped against the side once, then got her feet on the hull of the ship to keep her from swinging about. At the top, she was rather manhandled over the railing to land in an undignified heap.

Farouk was there.

"Farouk," Georgina said. "You made it back safely, good. But now please, fetch a dress for Charlotte."

"Farouk cannot go in a lady's boudoir."

"Of course you can," Georgina said as she rushed inside. She did realise that he couldn't, but she had her own task to perform.

Colonel Fitzwilliam was in the Smoking Room.

"Oh, my word," the Colonel said seeing her. "Mrs Merryweather, thank goodness you are here. You won't believe the trouble I've had."

Pippa looked up from the floor, her mouth smeared with cream and treats. Georgina could well believe the trouble the Colonel had had.

"Pippa!"

"Mama."

Miss Charlotte

Earnestine offered the next rope to Charlotte.

"I need to hold this," Charlotte said, keeping her hand on the controls.

Earnestine nodded, swung easily up against the ship and walked up the side.

Clothing landed on the carpet.

Georgina, holding Pippa on her hip, shouted down, "Put that on."

Put that on, grab the rope, hold on, Charlotte thought – always people telling her what to do.

She leapt at the rope, caught it and shimmed up, her conveniently bloomerised legs on either side of the thick, hemp line.

She grinned as she came up. "Farouk, you made it."

"Yes, Miss Charlotte. Farouk is sorry he did not bring help."

"We managed."

"Your dress!" Georgina shrieked.

They all looked back.

The magic carpet had veered away from the ship and then, as the pressure of gas subsided, the carpet settled and sank. A forlorn dress floated for a moment before the Suez Canal claimed that as well.

"It's not my fault," Charlotte said. "I didn't throw it in."

CHAPTER XXXII

Miss Deering-Dolittle

The city of Suez beckoned: not far now.

Her day was nearly spent.

Earnestine stood in the depths of the shade. The strong Egyptian sun cast a hard-edged shadow in which she skulked.

The others had returned to the Smoking Room, their cabins or hung about on deck. Georgina was at the bow, Caruthers to the stern, and Charlotte had probably clambered over the side.

Everything had finally settled down after their, frankly, ostentatious return. It had been like Piccadilly Circus when everyone had wanted to know everything about what had happened to them. Earnestine remembered that the statue in the real Piccadilly Circus was not Eros of Desire, but Anteros, the Avenger of Unrequited Love.

There were times to follow one's head and times to follow one's heart, Earnestine knew that (and there were times to throw caution to the wind), but one could follow one's head and one's heart. As Thoth had said.

She checked her pocket watch: less than an hour since they had returned so theatrically. The sunlight caught the legend engraved within. *'JJD, To the Future, CM'.*

The future, she thought, and snapped it shut.

The day was coming to a close, the day Thoth had gifted to her, but the last embers of the sun still searched through the layers of haze hovering on the horizon.

There was a story about choosing between a gold, a silver and an iron casket.

Thoth had been golden and would be again, but she would only be with him after another young lady had studied hard to become the goddess Ma'at.

Sir Archibald had silver, which paid for a good standing, fine living and even money for expeditions. Or perhaps that was thirty pieces of silver.

But iron?

When iron was fired in a crucible, it became something stronger and she had seen that steel.

She stepped from the shadows and promenaded aft along the deck.

"Captain Caruthers."

"Miss Deering-Dolittle," Caruthers said, turning towards her. "Fine weather we're having."

Earnestine ignored this. "Thoth gambled with the moon and won five days."

"With the moon?"

"According to legend. The year was 360 days long. The Babylonians liked that number. It divides conveniently. Anyway, Thoth gambled with the moon for five days, so that the goddess Nut could give birth to Horus, Osiris, Set, Isis and Nephthys."

"That's a lot of children in five days."

"It is, but it's a legend about the intercalary days needed to bring the year back into alignment."

"Like our leap year."

"Exactly, and at the end of their year too."

"February the 29th isn't at the end of our year."

"The Romans devised our calendar and they had the Kalends of March at the start of the year, so the extra day in February – the previous month – was at the end of their year. It makes more sense of September, October, November and December being the seventh, eighth, ninth and tenth months respectively, but please, one is trying to make a point here."

"Of course, carry on."

"So, it's the end of the Egyptian year and we're in Egypt, so I thought a tradition of ours, regarding the extra leap day, might be applied here during Thoth's extra five days."

"Makes sense."

"And four of those days have gone, so this is the very last day of the ancient Egyptian calendar and the last of Thoth's intercalary days."

"Indeed."

"And we're in Egypt, and when in Rome and all that."

"Yes."

"So..." Earnestine lifted her skirts slightly and dropped to one knee. "Captain Caruthers, will you marry me?"

Time seemed to stand still as if Ra had paused his solar barque in the heavens to see what the fuss was about.

"Sorry? What? Crikey!" Caruthers blathered and spluttered, but, eventually, he managed, "By George."

Mrs Merryweather

It was not over yet, and Georgina knew how it was done.

Pippa was asleep in her cot.

It was now or never.

I must warn you. I will fulfil the obligation diligently and uncover the truth wherever that takes me, she had said.

He had said he understood.

Captain Caruthers, of all people, had stood on the deck in the shadows. He was there for no other reason. He waited until Mister Rake came around and then shot him along the passageway.

Mister Rake, mortally wounded, had staggered into the Library and bolted the door behind him. The shot was heard because it was fired *outside* the Library. In all the confusion, the Captain was able to move along the deck fore and thus pretend to come from his cabin. Everyone else approached along the sunny side or along the interior passageway.

And why? Because of that dreadful business in India.

The Captain in the Library with his revolver.

Shocking – but undeniable.

Why else would he be skulking in the shadows?

"Farouk," she said. "Get everyone together in the Smoking Room please, I have an announcement to make."

She would do it. It was her duty. She had been tasked with this investigation and she had promised to see it through no matter where the trail led.

And it led to the Captain, their friend.

She saw him now lifting Earnestine to her feet.

She'd seen her sister kneel down as if she'd dropped something and–

Of course!

Captain Caruthers had been waiting in the shadows to talk to Earnestine. That was a motive, which meant he'd been going to meet her.

And she had been waiting for him.

Two of them: white knight and white queen.

Kneel down – oh, of course. He knelt down.

Farouk came to tell her that the passengers were gathering in the Smoking Room. The Egyptian guide went over to the Captain and her sister, interrupting them, and then they too went indoors.

Georgina stared at the desert as she gathered her thoughts. When she was ready, she made her way to the Smoking Room.

She saw everyone gathered through the glass fixed in the top half of the door. It reminded her of a framed picture, a daguerreotype, even though the scene was partially obscured by the fine lettering that spelt 'Smoking Room'.

Georgina checked her dress, took a deep breath and became the focus of attention as she entered.

"Thank you all for attending," Georgina said. "We were all here at the start of this, when my sister, Miss Deering-Dolittle, said that one of you is a murderer. I was made the Investigating Officer. I have diligently sorted the facts from the fictions and, well, one of you is indeed a murderer."

She looked around the room, considering each of the suspects in turn.

1. **Colonel Fitzwilliam**, brandy glass in hand.
2. **Miss Deering-Dolittle**, standing tall and proud.
3. **Captain Caruthers** beside her.
4. **Doctor Timon**, his eyes large behind his glasses.
5. **Sir Archibald Reevers** looking thunderous.
6. **Mrs Albright**, flustered and heavily made-up.
7. **Monsieur Jacques**, amused.
8. The chair where **Pandit Singh Maçon** used to sit.
9. **Miss Charlotte**, thankfully dressed properly.

There were two other empty seats; one for herself and another that used to be Mister Rake's favourite.

"It was the Indian blighter," Colonel Fitzwilliam said, nodding over to the empty chair and the table with the chessboard.

"Colonel," Georgina said. "There were motives. The Indian business–"

"Hardly a motive."

"Colonel, please, it is still a motive for yourself and Captain Caruthers. Next was the robbery of the Captain's plans and equipment."

"That Singh Maçon."

"Colonel!"

"Beg your pardon."

"Finally, the robbery of Mister Djehuti's book."

"Research, Mrs Merryweather," Sir Archibald insisted.

"Be that as it may, Mister Rake stole something of value and that means that those who value money – Monsieur Jacques for example – would be tempted."

"Moi? I am maligned."

"You tried to sell me!" Charlotte accused.

"And there is the matter of the artefact itself, the knowledge," Georgina continued. "Sir Archibald and Mrs

Albright were avowed Egyptologists and would pay handsomely for such. And perhaps kill."

"Oh, oh... Archie, she cannot mean us," Mrs Albright said.

"I'm afraid she does, my dear," said Sir Archibald.

"And Doctor Timon as a Doctor might well be interested in the Philosopher's Stone."

"That, Mrs Merryweather, is a myth," Doctor Timon said.

"A myth that has a basis in fact, as my sisters and I discovered."

"We only have your word for that," Doctor Timon said, looking to the others for support. "Talk of gods and people living forever. Ridiculous in this age of modern medicine."

"It was a religious artefact," Colonel Fitzwilliam insisted, "so that thieving Pandit should be your chief suspect."

"Quite," Georgina said. "This brings us to opportunity. Everyone at this end of the ship could easily have reached the Library, so everyone had the chance."

"But it could not be done," said Monsieur Jacques.

"And that neatly brings us to the method. How was the trick done?"

"Oui."

"Let us look at the facts. Mister Rake was in a locked room that could only be opened from the inside. People heard a shot when no-one could have been there. There was a scorch mark upon the floor in the storeroom. Doctor Timon examined the body in full view of witnesses. I examined the body too in the cold store where all the bloodless chickens are stored. Everyone was assembled within ten minutes here in the Smoking Room. The door to the staircase opens onto the corridor to the Library."

"Scorch mark?" Charlotte asked.

"The lanterns on board are cheap and the tin at the base is thin. They have a tendency to scorch anything underneath them. Such blackening occurred on Sir Archibald's crate when a lantern was placed upon it. And such blackening is present in the side storeroom. Someone hid there before the murder."

"The murderer?" Caruthers asked.

Georgina smiled knowingly.

"Oh Gina," said Charlotte, "you do know how it was done."

"There's also the question of the gun," Georgina said. She held out her hand. "Captain?"

Once Captain Caruthers realised what she wanted, he handed over his Webley Mk 1.

"This is a heavy calibre gun. The sort used by army officers, like the Captain here, and the Colonel," Georgina explained before she returned it to the Captain, who put it safely back in his holster. "Whereas... Monsieur Jacques?"

"Pardon."

"Your firearm, s'il vous plait."

"Ah, oui."

She took his smaller weapon: "This is a smaller calibre, see..." She showed it around.

"It's a .32 Browning," Charlotte said when she saw it.

"Yes, although still quite deadly." Georgina handed it back to Monsieur Jacques. "Monsieur."

Monsieur Jacques placed the gun back inside his jacket.

"So, his might have been the quieter shot, but not the louder one," Sir Archibald said. "Does that mean we can rule Jacques out?"

"We can rule out the absent Pandit," Georgina continued. "He did not have a firearm or would have certainly used it when the ship was attacked. And when the murder occurred, he had the alibi of stealing the plans from Captain Caruthers. But there is the question of Mister Rake's own gun. A gun Captain Caruthers found and gave to Charlotte."

"Oh," said Charlotte, "I lost it when..."

"Quite, but I found it again."

"So, the murderer used Mister Rake's own gun after hiding in the storeroom?"

"The man hiding in the storeroom was Mister Rake himself. Everyone else was playing bridge or drinking or walking on deck, so he hid there to meet someone and sell the book."

"Sell the book he stole for me," said Sir Archibald. "The cad. He kept asking me for money."

"Yes, but instead, he was murdered, there in the storeroom."

"That was the loud gunshot?" Charlotte asked.

"No," Georgina replied. "That was the quieter shot some people heard. The storeroom has the same design of door and it was shut. The loud gunshot that came later from the library with the door open. This shot was to make a hole in the chaise and to attract everyone's attention."

"Impossible," said Doctor Timon. "I examined the body. He'd clearly been murdered in the Library."

"That's correct," said Colonel Fitzwilliam. "I'm afraid we all saw the blood."

"Doctor Timon, you examined *a body*."

"What are you implying?"

"You are the only person who went close to the body. You made sure of that. You insisted everyone go to the Smoking Room. You even gave Miss Deering-Dolittle smelling salts to keep her back. So, everyone else stood outside, they saw your actions, saw a body you covered with a cloth, and saw that you could not have shot him. But they did not see the body."

"This is absurd," said Doctor Timon, looking to the other men for support. "Mister Rake was shot. If you don't believe me, go down to the hold and look."

"Let her finish," Captain Caruthers said.

"Thank you, Captain," Georgina replied. "I did go down to the hold and examine the body. He had scorch marks on his body indicating that he was shot at close range, and yet the way everyone described how the body fell, suggested otherwise. No, the body in the Library was someone else pretending to be dead, using blood from the slaughtered animals in the kitchens. It was that person, who had bolted the door from the inside. Once the charade of the discovery had been staged, then that person collected the real body from the storeroom, placed it within the Library in the same pose, and stole around the ship to enter from another direction."

"It couldn't have been done," said Doctor Timon.

"Of course it could. No-one could see the door properly as Doctor Timon stood in the way, and the glass is only in the top half of the Smoking Room door. The murderer, your accomplice Doctor Timon, simply crawled out on his hands and knees."

"But who?" Sir Archibald asked.

"Someone who fits the description of Mister Rake, someone tall and thin or rather 'grand et mince'."

"Jacques!" Captain Caruthers exclaimed.

"Oui."

"Pourquoi," Monsieur Jacques exclaimed. "But why would I do such a thing?"

"Doctor Timon paid you, just as you worked with Pandit Singh Maçon to steal the Captain's equipment, and kidnap and sell my sister."

"I saved her from death."

Earnestine was appalled, "By giving her over for a fate worse than death!"

"You did it," Georgina said, "for francs."

"What if I did?" Monsieur Jacques said. He pulled his gun from his jacket, cocking it quickly. "Keep back!"

"And Timon?" Sir Archibald said.

"He did it because of you, Sir Archibald," Georgina said, ignoring the armed Frenchman. "You told him about your research into the Philosopher's Stone, and your correspondence with the god Thoth. Doctor Timon could not resist the temptation."

"To save lives," Doctor Timon said.

"It is academic now," Monsieur Jacques said. "You will all sit here, and we will disembark at the Suez terminal. Any foolishness and – *poof* – I will not be held responsible."

"Of course you are responsible," Georgina said. "Don't blame us, your intended victims. You are holding the gun, you would be pulling the trigger, you would be the one to commit murder – again."

"Not if you stay right where you are, Mademoiselle."

"It's Madame... Madam." Georgina stepped forward. "I am the Investigating Officer and I am taking you into custody."

"I think not."

He pointed the gun right at her forehead, almost at point-blank range.

Georgina flinched, but held her ground.

Miss Charlotte

Charlotte jumped forward to stand between the Frenchman and her sister.

Jacques moved his gun between them.

"I will shoot them both," he said. "Keep your hand from your holster, Captain."

Charlotte felt nudged to one side when Earnestine stood with them.

"You can't kill us all," Earnestine said.

Charlotte agreed, "Browning's only got seven rounds."

"She's right," Caruthers said.

The Colonel put his brandy down and eased himself onto his feet.

"Quite," added Sir Archibald.

"There are only seven of you," said Jacques as they crowded him to the wall of the Smoking Room.

"Give it up, Jacques," Doctor Timon said.

Jacques shrugged in an exaggerated way and then handed the weapon to Georgina.

Caruthers had his Webley out smartish and covered Jacques.

Doctor Timon sat in his chair, his head in his hands.

"Doctor Timon," Georgina said, "why?"

"Why not?" Doctor Timon said. "One death to save thousands. In India, the lower castes drop like flies. With the Philosopher's Stone, I could synthesise the essence of immortality. You risk your lives to save others, and you are considered brave because of your Derring-Do. I was simply doing Mister Rake a favour by making him a hero."

"But only posthumously," Georgina said. "Captain, if you'd be so kind."

"Yes, Ma'am," Caruthers said.

Captain Caruthers and Sir Archibald escorted Doctor Timon and the ghastly Jacques away at gunpoint.

"Oh my, oh my," Mrs Albright said. "I feel a head coming on."

"Calls for a drink to celebrate," the Colonel said. "You were jolly brave, Mrs Merryweather, and you, Lottie and Miss Deering-Dolittle."

"The Derring-Do Club forever," Charlotte said.

"You didn't need to," Georgina said. "I had everything in hand."

Charlotte opened her mouth to complain, but saw Georgina holding up a magazine, the short kind that went inside a Browning automatic.

Charlotte didn't mind. She knew she would have saved the day if Georgina hadn't already saved it. Or Earnestine would have. The Derring-Do Club, standing shoulder-to-shoulder, could take on anything.

Earnestine herself stepped over to face Sir Archibald, towering over the seated President of the Royal Expeditionary Society.

"Sir Archibald," she said, "I wish to break off our engagement."

Sir Archibald flustered, "What? Whatever for?"

"To be frank, one was perturbed to be abandoned in the desert."

"Well really, I hardly think, my dear..."

"It's all right, Archie," Mrs Albright said. "Here, come with me."

Mrs Albright took Sir Archibald's hand, glanced daggers at Earnestine and then, just as they slipped out of the Smoking Room, Charlotte saw the American's face crack all her foundation with a beaming smile.

"It'll be you next," Georgina said to Charlotte.

"Yes, once I'm married, you'll have no more excuses," Earnestine added.

"But– but–"

Charlotte was saved by the return of Captain Caruthers.

"It'll be the noose for them," Caruthers said.

"Where are they?" Georgina asked.

"Tied up in the hold with Rake, that fake mummy and that mummy of the High Priest," Caruthers said. "We'll hand them over to the Protectorate Authorities once we reach the Port of Suez."

Georgina nodded.

"You did well, Mrs Merryweather."

"I very nearly accused you, Captain."

Captain Caruthers smiled, and Georgina smiled too. As she turned away, she hummed to herself – always a sign that she was happy.

"And Pandit Singh Maçon?" Colonel Fitzwilliam demanded.

"I think we'll be meeting him again," Caruthers said. "We'll need to recover the 'tank' and the plans."

"India, yes," the Colonel agreed, knocking back his brandy. "We'll chase him, even with my war wound."

"That's the spirit, Fitz."

"Captain," Earnestine said. "I have broken off my engagement to Sir Archibald."

"There was something of an overlap," Caruthers said.

"Hardly, one waits to be asked."

"Ah, didn't you... proper form. Yes. In that case," Caruthers said. He hitched a trouser leg up slightly to drop to one knee. "Miss Deering-Dolittle... I... that is to say... will you..."

"Yes."

"Thank you."

"You were taking forever over it," Earnestine chided.

Congratulations were in order.

"Spiffing, Ness."

"All the best, Ness, Captain."

"About time, Caruthers."

They all went out onto deck to enjoy the cool evening air, just as the SS *Karnak* finally steamed out of the canal, into the wide-open expanse of the Red Sea. The port beckoned, where they'd transfer to a new ship for the voyage across the Indian Ocean.

Charlotte leant on the rail and opened her book ready to return to the racy adventure of Mavis – what an exciting, modern name despite what Georgina said about it being made up for the novel – in *The Sorrows of Satan* by Marie Corelli. She wanted to finish it before they reached Bombay.

"You'll need this," Georgina said, handing her a card.

It was Charlotte's bookmark, the tarot card a gypsy fortune-teller had given her back on Dartmoor.

She flipped it over: 'Death'.

Anyway, Mavis... and she was sure that Lucio character would turn out to be the Devil.

"Let's look at the desert," Georgina suggested.

"Why?"

"So we don't intrude on the Captain and our sister."

"Why?" – Charlotte craned her neck to look – "What are they doing?"

"Don't look."

The Captain and Earnestine stood together on the deck and, with the setting sun behind them, they hugged and... well, generally it was jolly sickening.

"What now?" Caruthers asked.

"Oh," Earnestine said, "something else for *The Sightseeings of Mrs Caruthers...* or *The Explorations of Mrs Caruthers?*"

Caruthers smoothed his chevron moustache in thought before he replied, "I think, as a husband's instruction trumps a mother's – hear me out – and I would much prefer *The Adventures of Captain and Mrs Caruthers.*"

The End

THE DERRING-DO CLUB

will return in

THE
SISTERHOOD
OF THE
DEATH-GODDESS

David Wake launched each instalment of the **Derring-Do Club** novels at a different convention: *ArmadaCon 25* (where he was a Guest of Honour), *Loncon 3*, *Mancunicon*. For this one, he chose *Ytterbium*.

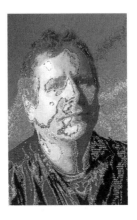

Thank you for buying and reading *The Derring-Do Club in Death on the Suez*. If you liked this novel, please take a few moments from your own adventures to write a review and help spread the word.

For more information, and to join the mailing list for news of forthcoming releases, see www.davidwake.com or www.derring-do.club.

Many thanks to: –

A. Abbott, Dawn Abigail, Helen Blenkinsop, Andy Conway, Tony Cooper, Linda Currin, T. K. Elliott, Jordan Mullett, Najum Qureshi and the West Midlands Egyptology Society.

Cover by Smuzz: www.smuzz.org.uk.

A ripping yarn of cliff-hangers, desperate chases, romance and deadly danger.

Earnestine, Georgina and Charlotte are trapped in the Eden College for Young Ladies suffering deportment, etiquette and Latin. So, when the British Empire is threatened by an army of zombies, the Deering-Dolittle sisters are eager to save the day. Unfortunately, they are under strict instructions not to have any adventures...

...but when did that ever stop them?

"Think 'Indiana Jones pace'. It's fast and dangerous and does not involve embroidery!"

★ ★ ★ ★ ★

"A brilliant, fast paced steampunk adventure, trains zombies and zeppelins, what more could you want?"

★ ★ ★ ★ ★

Putting their best foot forward,
without showing an ankle, since 1896

The first novel in the adventure series
available as an ebook and a paperback.

A ripping yarn of time-travel, rocket-packs, conspiracy and *sword fighting!*

The plucky Deering-Dolittle sisters, Earnestine, Georgina and Charlotte, are put to the test as mysterious Time Travellers appear in Victorian London to avert the destruction of the world…

…but just whose side should they be on?

"Loved it! […] Fast paced and exciting another great adventure for three Victorian Young Ladies."
★ ★ ★ ★ ★

"…if I had been wearing a hat, I would have taken it off to David Wake."
★ ★ ★ ★ ★

(THE DERRING-DO CLUB)

Putting their best foot forward, without showing an ankle, since 1896

The second novel in the adventure series available as an ebook and a paperback.

A ripping yarn of strange creatures, aerial dog-fights, espionage and *pirates!*

Strange lights hover over Dartmoor and alien beings abduct the unwary as the plucky Deering-Dolittle sisters, Earnestine, Georgina and Charlotte, race to discover the truth before the conquest begins...

...but betrayal is never far away.

"Well-written, fast-paced, and dangerously addictive - but with some extra thinking in there, too, should you choose to read it that way."
★ ★ ★ ★ ★

"As with previous adventures I really enjoyed the imaginative scene setting, building intrigue into unexpected twists and a spectacular ending."
★ ★ ★ ★ ★

THE DERRING-DO CLUB

Putting their best foot forward,
without showing an ankle, since 1896

The third novel in the adventure series available as an ebook and a paperback.

A tonic for the Xmas Spirit

Being Santa's daughter would be a dream come true for any child, but for Carol Christmas, the fairy tale is about to end. Evil forces threaten the festive season, and only Carol can save the day...

A grim fairy tale told as a children's book, but perhaps not just for children at all.

"This starts out as a delightfully childlike modern take on the Christmas myth - the kind of Pixar-esque story that can play to the kids and give the adults a knowing wink or two, but it gets dark. Very dark."
★ ★ ★ ★ ★

Available as an ebook, paperback and audiobook.

A bloke-lit tale of political intrigue and beer

CROSSING THE BRIDGE

DAVID WAKE

Guy Wilson lives in the past.
Every year, he and his friends re-enact rebellion.
Every year, they celebrate the Jacobite's retreat.
Every year, they have a few drinks and go home...
                                    ...except this year, they go too far.

An unstoppable boozing session meets an unbreakable wall of riot police in this satirical thriller. Guy struggles against corrupt politicians, murderous security forces and his own girlfriend in a desperate bid to stop a modern uprising.

And it's all his fault.

Will anyone survive to last orders?

"Witty, warm and well-written, "Crossing The Bridge" was so enjoyable that I didn't want to finish it."

★ ★ ★ ★ ★

"My sort of book. Couldn't put it down. Comedy, tension and an uncanny resemblance to the moral fibre of some of our elected representatives."

★ ★ ★ ★ ★

Available as an ebook and a paperback.

Do you fear technology? We have an App for that.

Your phone is your life. But what if it kept secrets from you? What if it accidentally framed you for murder? What if it was also the only thing that could save you?

In a world where phones are more intelligent than humans, but are still thrown away like yesterday's fashions, one particular piece of plastic lies helpless as its owner, Alice Wooster, is about to be murdered...

In this darkly comic near-future tale, a very smart phone tells its own story as events build to a climactic battle. Can it save all the virtual and augmented worlds? Can it save the real one? Can it order Alice some proper clothes?

Available as an ebook and a paperback.

Think *Black Mirror* with a Scandi-crime feel

Twenty years from now, everyone's thoughts are shared on social media: the Thinkersphere. Privacy is dead and buried. Pre-mediated crime is history. So who killed the woman in Chedding car park?

Detective Oliver Braddon is plunged into an investigation to track down the impossible: a murderer who can kill without thinking.

Hashtag is a gritty, dystopian neo-noir that poses uncomfortable questions about our obsession with social media and presents a mind-bending picture of what life might be like when our very thoughts are no longer our own.

Book One of the Thinkersphere series
available as an ebook and a paperback.

The dark sequel to *Hashtag*

Black Mirror meets Scandi-crime in a mind-bending dystopia where 'likes' matter more than lives.

Detective Oliver Braddon's investigation into an apparent suicide leads him to a powerful media mogul and a mission into the unknown. Is he the killer?

In this alarming vision of the near-future, everyone's thoughts are shared on social media. With privacy consigned to history, a new breed of celebrity influences billions.

But who controls who?

A gritty, neo-noir delving into a conflict between those connected and those with secrets to hide.

Book Two of the Thinkersphere series
available as an ebook and a paperback.

Printed in Poland
by Amazon Fulfillment
Poland Sp. z o.o., Wrocław